L.A. BLACK AND BLUES

I drove to her apartment and waited. Waiting is always hard. Waiting for Maggie is often harder. Forty minutes later the red Volvo appeared. I walked to it slowly and she got out and gave me two paper bags. One of them was groceries and the other weighed more than an elephant. "What's in here?"

"Quarters. I hit the jackpot on one of the airport slots." Then she looked at me with that look of hers I can't stand to look at. She shook her head and turned sideways and lifted her skirt to her thighs. The bruises started just above the knee and went all the way up. They were already the color of overripe avocados. She opened her jacket and showed me her blouse. It was torn at the collar and the front was splotched with blood. She looked at me. "The blood's theirs, not mine."

THE
OPEN SHADOW

BY THE AUTHOR OF
THE GONE MAN

BRAD SOLOMON

AVON
PUBLISHERS OF BARD, CAMELOT AND DISCUS BOOKS

AVON BOOKS
A division of
The Hearst Corporation
959 Eighth Avenue
New York, New York 10019

First Avon Printing, July, 1980

AVON TRADEMARK REG. U.S. PAT. OFF. AND IN
OTHER COUNTRIES, MARCA REGISTRADA, HECHO EN
U.S.A.

Printed in the U.S.A.

For my mother and father

PART ONE

1

I didn't like the looks of it at all. He was sitting behind a desk, slitting the tops of envelopes with a fancy letter opener.

I went to the desk and shoved out my hand. "Morning. I'm Lieutenant Fredericks. Homicide."

He put down the letter opener and shook my hand. "Paul Brade."

"Nice to meet you, Paul." I sat on the edge of the desk. "Haven't seen you around here before. What're you, a secretary?"

He shook his head and answered quickly. "I'm an operative. This's my first day. I used to be with the Carne Organization for six months."

"Carne?" I took another glance at the letter opener. It was carved bone. The carver had known his business. "Carne's not bad. Pays good money." I looked around the office and laughed. The walls were as bare as a bride on a wedding night. "Better money'n you can get here."

He answered quickly again. "I didn't like it at Carne. Too big."

I turned on the desk and my leg slid next to the letter opener but I didn't touch it. "That's the way those places usually are. They paying you all right here?" He nodded. I pointed a thumb at the door to the inner office and his eyes followed my thumb. "They both in there?"

"McGuane's here. Theiringer isn't in yet."

"Theiringer." I laughed. "What do you think of Fritz Theiringer? Like him?"

He shrugged. "Haven't met him yet."

"Theiringer's a royal pain in the ass." I got off the desk and walked across the floor toward the inner office. I had the letter opener in my right front jacket pocket.

3

2

I went into the office and closed the door behind me. Mc-Guane very carefully didn't look up. I went to the refrigerator and took out a Coke but said nothing.

"Look at these damn books! We've got a bill here for a pickup truck!"

I went to my desk. "I wanted to look at books, I'd be an accountant. I wanted to be yelled at I'd be married."

"I'm not yelling!"

"The level of volume you're currently using's what civilized people call yelling. I don't like it. I especially don't like it on a Tuesday when we didn't get a damn thing to do all day Monday.'"

McGuane's restless fingers punched the keys on the pocket calculator with all the mercy of a voodoo drummer at the height of the tourist season. "I don't remember renting any pickup truck."

I opened the Coke. "I suppose I should've suspected something. 'You look tired, Fritz, you ought to go home.' I *was* tired. I *went* home. Considering the way you operate, I definitely should've suspected something." I took a long drink. "How much'd the new desk cost out there?"

"I got it from a guy who's moving out on the fifth floor. He's going bankrupt, he was glad to get rid of it."

"How much's it costing us for the kid who's sitting behind the new desk?" I took the letter opener out of my pocket and felt its weight. "He's got hair down to his shoulders. I suppose that's costing us extra."

"He throws the hair in for free."

I put the letter opener next to my phone. They looked nice side by side. "Generous of him. He says he worked for Carne, you bother to check him out?"

4

"I checked him out, he's okay. Your name's on the bill for renting the pickup."

"The Snyder case. The kid says he left Carne 'cause Carne's too big. Bullshit. Who'd you check him out with?"

"You told me you were going to borrow Joe Bergen's station wagon for the Snyder case!"

I flipped through my calendar. It looked empty. "Joe had to drive to San Diego, I had to rent a truck for a couple hours. Who'd you talk to at Carne?"

"The hell it was a couple hours! Eleven goddamn hours! I billed Snyder two weeks ago! I didn't bill him for a goddamn truck! What'm I supposed to do now?"

"Bill him for a goddamn truck. Who'd you talk to at Carne?"

"What if he tells me to go to hell, he already paid his bill, he isn't going to pay another goddamn bill for a goddamn truck?"

I put down my Coke. "Next time we need a truck I'll drive up the coast, I'll park by the side of the road, I'll make it look like I got a flat. A truck driver stops to help me, I'll sap him and tie him up and take off with his truck. Won't cost us a penny."

"Good idea! Get caught while you're at it!"

"If I get caught, it'll cost you to bail me out."

"I'll let you do the time!"

"You would. Thanks."

"My pleasure!" The desk drawer jerked open, the calculator flew into it, the desk drawer slammed shut. "You ran this business, we'd be broke!"

"The way you run through desk drawers that desk'll be broke."

"We'd be running things out of a goddamn shoebox somewhere in Venice!"

"I was doing fine in Venice. I was alone."

"Maybe you ought to still be alone!" McGuane walked across the office and opened the safe and took out a Smith & Wesson .38. "I'm going to the firing range."

I leaned across my desk. "Someone's sure acting defensive this morning. Got something to be defensive about?"

"I'm not defensive! I'm pissed! A goddamn truck! Eleven goddamn—"

"A goddamn kid! Sitting behind a goddamn new desk in the goddamn front office doing goddamn nothing!" I can yell too once I've found something worth yelling about.

"Quiet! He'll hear you!"

I raised my voice. "Good! Let him! Stop waving the gun!"

Just then the kid stuck his head in the door and looked at McGuane. "Excuse me, you got a client out here."

3

"Good." I spoke quietly. Clients are something I don't like to scare off, at least not till I've had a chance to see them. "Close the door and come in here."

Paul looked at me but didn't close the door. Then he looked at McGuane, who was still holding the gun. As soon as he looked away I got the letter opener away from my phone and slid it into my desk drawer.

McGuane put the gun back in the safe. "Close the door." Paul closed the door. "What kind of client?"

"A woman. Mrs. Elizabeth Isenbart."

"What's she look like?" I said.

Paul said nothing. He looked at me.

"What's she look like?" McGuane said.

Paul bit his lower lip and stared at me. "Late thirties. Dark hair. Well dressed."

"She look like money?" McGuane said.

"Yeah. Could be."

"Sit with her a minute, then bring her in."

I went to the mirror to see what I looked like. Paul

6

was still looking at me. "You better stop looking at me and get back out there before Mrs. Isenbart runs away." Paul shook his head and went out. I waited for the door to close. "Isenbart sounds familiar."

"Not yelling any more?"

"I wasn't yelling. You were."

McGuane laughed. "Mrs. Isenbart had an appointment to see us a couple months ago. She never showed."

"How come?"

"I don't know. We'll ask her, maybe she'll tell us." I turned around and smiled. "I look okay?'

"I'll get a photographer up here fast before you lose it."

The door opened and Paul brought her in and I stepped forward and shook her hand. "Good morning, Mrs. Isenbart. I'm Fritz Thieringer. Nice to meet you."

Mrs. Isenbart's hand felt very unsure of itself.

McGuane didn't smile, didn't offer a hand, didn't even bother to come out from behind the desk. "Good morning, Mrs. Isenbart, I'm Maggie McGuane. Please sit down and make yourself comfortable."

4

There's a kind of woman who always wears the right clothes, always fits the current styles. There's another kind of woman who looks so flawless it hardly matters what she wears. Mrs. Elizabeth Isenbart was both kinds of woman. The combination was lethal. She sat on the sofa and crossed her legs. I had to lean against something solid pretty fast. Before I could ask anything, McGuane came out with, "Paul. See what Mrs. Isenbart wants."

Paul didn't move. Then he nodded and fixed a chair so he could face her. I hoped he knew what he was doing,

I don't like to lose them before we even know what they've come for.

"Mrs. Isenbart smiled a nervous smile and stared at her hands. She opened her pocketbook and reached in and came out with a cigarette case, popped it open and fumbled inside, got out a cigarette, and maneuvered it into her mouth. "It's my husband."

"What about him?"

"I think someone should keep an eye on him." She took the cigarette back out of her mouth, looked at it, tapped it against the table like she didn't have the faintest idea why she was doing it, put it back into her mouth, dug into her pocketbook again. She couldn't seem to find what she was looking for. It looked like it might be more than just an act.

Paul just watched her. I sat next to her with a lit match and managed to get her cigarette going without anyone getting burned. "How serious's it, Mrs. Isenbart?"

Her eyes drifted away.

"You said somone should keep an eye on your husband. That can be arranged. It helps if we know why." She tried shaking cigarette ash toward an ashtray but there was no ash yet. "You worried he's seeing someone?"

She turned with a start. "No. My husband wouldn't do that sort of thing."

"I didn't think he would. I had to ask. We had to get it out of the way."

Papers shuffled behind me on a desk. I turned and looked into Maggie's eyes. They were as sharp as twin daggers that'd just come off the whetstone. I moved against the far corner of the sofa and motioned toward Paul. He leaned forward to get her attention. "Mrs. Isenbart? Are you scared of something?"

That did it. Mrs. Isenbart dropped her cigarette on the floor and started crying.

Paul stamped out the cigarette before it could burn a hole in the rug. That gave me time to offer my handkerchief and a sympathetic look. She finished her cry and her hand toyed with the ashtray. Her hand left the ashtray, moved across the table and picked up one of

Maggie's film journals. She started leafing through it, then suddenly looked up. "He almost won an Academy Award, once."

I tapped a finger against Paul's legs where she couldn't see it. Paul looked at me blankly, then seemed to realize. "Who? Your husband?"

"Yes."

"Is he an actor?"

"He's a dress manufacturer." She thumbed through the magazine. *"The End of Pamela."*

Paul said nothing. I tapped him again. He said, "What?"

"That was the name of the film. *The End of Pamela.* Did any of you see it?" I took the magazine out of her hands. She turned her attention to the arm of the sofa. Her voice stayed thin. "It was years ago."

Paul leaned forward. "Was he an actor then?"

Her face darted at him. "Of course not! He designed the costumes! I just told you, he's a dress manufacturer! Aren't you listening to me?" Her eyes burned at him and her hand went inside her pocketbook again. When she got out the cigarette she let me light it for her and then she sucked it like she hadn't had one in days.

I left the sofa slowly and walked toward Maggie's desk. "There's people been in movies more'n thirty years, they never been nominated for an Oscar. Getting nominated's more difficult'n most people think." Maggie already had a glass out and filled. I took it to the sofa. "I remember *The End of Pamela.* Good picture. So were the costumes." I settled on the sofa and dropped my fingers over hers. Hers were colder than Boston in January. I put her hand around the glass.

"I don't like to drink this early in the day."

"It's just a little. You won't even taste it."

"No. It's too early." Then she swallowed it fast. She made a face. I put the empty glass on the table behind me. "Someone's watching him. A boy."

"All right, Mrs. Isenbart, that gives us a place to start." I took her hand again. "What else can you tell us?"

She put her other hand over mine and held on tightly but her eyes looked away and she said nothing.

"How old a boy?" Paul said. "Fourteen? Fifteen?"

"Older. About your age."

"I'm twenty-two."

"You don't look that old."

That shut Paul up.

"Younger'n twenty-two?" I said.

"Seventeen. Eighteen. I'm not sure."

I wonder if she knew how tightly she was holding my hand. "He's watching your husband. Your husband's actually seen him?"

"We've both seen him. He lets us see him."

"He said anything? To your husband? To you?"

She spoke tonelessly. "Last night. We were at Lawry's. He was there. When we went out, to the car, he was standing there, watching us. Max yelled at him to get away from the car. He wouldn't get away. Max asked him what he wanted." She looked at the floor. The words hardly got out of her mouth they were so soft. "He looked at Max and said, 'I've come to watch you die.' Then he walked away."

5

I said, "We'll have to know a few more things, Mrs. Isenbart. Your husband done anything about it?"

"What do you mean?"

"He gone to the police?"

"No."

"You gone?"

"No."

"Why not?"

10

"Max says the boy must be some sort of kook. That I shouldn't worry about it."

"Your husband's probably right. But we can look into it if you want. You got any idea who the boy is?"

"No."

"Your husband got any idea?"

"No."

"What's the boy look like?"

"You mean, how tall is he? Things like that?"

"Exactly."

"He isn't too tall."

"Is he short?"

"No, he isn't too short. I don't think he is."

I kept my eyes on her. "Paul. Stand up." Paul got to his feet. "Taller'n that?"

"I don't think so."

"Shorter?"

". . . No."

"About the same height?"

"Yes."

"Fine. Thinner or fatter?"

"About the same. Maybe a little thinner."

"Which one? Paul or the boy?"

"The boy."

"How about the hair?"

"Not as long."

"Color?"

"He's white."

"Hair color."

"Oh. Not as dark. Not as curly."

"Anything strange about him? Unusual? Any marks? Scars? A high voice? Anything like that?"

"I don't think so."

"How about—"

"A scar."

"Where?"

"On his face."

"Where on his face?"

"Over his eye."

"Which eye?"

"The left eye."

"Anything else? A mustache? Beard?"

"I don't think so."

"You're not sure?"

"He might've had a mustache. I don't think he did."

"Why didn't you come in when you had an appointment to see us a couple months ago?"

Her face twitched with surprise. "What?"

"You made an appointment, you didn't come in. Why not?"

Her eyes wandered aimlessly. "Oh. Yes. I should've called and canceled the appointment. I'm sorry."

"Why didn't you come in?"

She looked at me. "He stopped coming."

I rested my back against the arm of the sofa. "He was coming to see your husband a couple months ago and then he stopped coming. When'd he start again?"

"Last night. At the restaurant."

I rubbed a finger across my upper lip and kept watching her. Her face didn't change. "All right. Anything else we should know?"

She shook her head. Her face still didn't change. I looked sideways at Maggie. Maggie said, "We charge by the day, Mrs. Isenbart. Our rates—"

"Oh!" Mrs. Isenbart turned toward her. "You expect me to pay you. I'm sorry, I can't pay you. My husband's the one who pays our bills." She folded her arms in front of her and looked at the floor. I was already looking at it.

I got off the sofa and walked across the room. Maggie's face was as blank as an unused check. I leaned against her desk. "Mrs. Isenbart, this idea of coming to see us, did you discuss it with your husband?"

"Yes." Her eyes stayed down. I was afraid of this.

"What'd he say, Mrs. Isenbart?"

"He said I shouldn't come here." Then her face came up fast. "But don't worry, I'm sure if you go to see him, he'll hire you. You'll. . . ." Her eyes pleaded with me. "You'll just talk him into it, won't you? Aren't you trained to do that sort of thing?"

6

Paul came back into the office shaking his head. "She the kind you usually get?"

"I kind of liked her," I said.

"Of course you did," Maggie said. "She was wearing a skirt. Glad you're showing some interest in women closer to your own age. It's possible the boy's been watching too much TV."

I smiled at her. "Got something?"

"Channel Five's doing a Dashiell Hammett festival this week. One of the Thin Man movies's got an old man living in a big house in the middle of nowhere. A guy's coming to see him and that's what he says, that he's come to watch him die."

I considered it. "Ever see one called *The End of Pamela?*"

"Thought you said you saw it."

"Never heard of the damn thing before."

Maggie tapped a pen against her phone. "Cheap costume epic back in the early fifties. Not bad, but not Stewart Granger."

"Good enough for an Oscar nomination."

"That doesn't mean shit." She threw the pen down. "Okay, you can take it."

Her fingers drummed the desk noncommittally.

"Go ahead, Mag, it's okay. I'd just's soon get you out of the office. You're worse'n a mouse in a snake's cage."

"I know! Why haven't you stopped me!"

"Haven't been able to figure out how." I went to my desk. "Go ahead. Maybe, you smile a lot, the guy'll hire us."

13

The front door slammed open and Elizabeth Isenbart came in. She looked at the sofa, saw I wasn't there and found me at my desk. "A limp! I just remembered! He had a limp last night!"

"Right leg or left leg?"

Her eyes went wide. "God! I don't remember!" Her hand came up toward her face but didn't touch it. "Let me think!"

"Last night the first time he had it?"

Her eyes went wider. "He might've. . . . I don't know!"

I went forward and took her arm. "It's all right. We'll look into it."

"You will?"

"I'm going in a minute," Maggie said.

Mrs. Isenbart turned around. "You? You're going?" She turned to me. "I thought you were going."

"I'm just finishing up a case. It'll save time if Maggie talks to your husband first, so we can get started right away."

She dropped to the sofa but came off it just as fast and ran to Maggie's desk. "He won't listen to a woman. He doesn't like women. I mean, in business. I used to work for him, as soon as we got married he made me stop. He wouldn't allow it. Max hates women in business." She turned to me with a desperate smile. "Please, it's got to be a man. Won't you go? Please?"

I didn't look at Maggie and prayed she wouldn't throw anything into my back. "All right, I'll go."

Mrs. Isenbart's face lit up but then changed suddenly as she grabbed both my arms. "You have to promise me one thing, Mr. Thieringer."

"What?"

"The boy. You won't hurt him. He's so young. I wouldn't want to see him hurt. Don't let him do anything to Max, but don't hurt him. Please!"

"I'll do my best, Mrs. Isenbart."

Paul took her through the front door and down the hall.

Maggie picked up her pen and poked at the phone. "Damn." She raised the pen and brought it down and tapped the phone twice. She put the pen between her teeth. "Wonder if she's just naturally jealous, or if she's got a reason to be." She tapped the phone again. Then again. Then again much harder. "Take Paul with you."

"You hired him, Mag. Not me."

"Take him!"

I thought. "What if I lose him?"

"Try not to!" She started to hit the phone again but this time she stopped in time. "Come on, Fritz. Humor me."

"Humoring you's turning into a full-time occupation." I took two Cokes from the refrigerator, put on my hat, a wide-brimmed Panama, and looked into the mirror to get its angle right. I saw Maggie's reflection. She was nibbling the edge of her thumb. "You going to tell me, or you going to keep it a secret?"

"Keep what a secret?"

"The Thin Man movie. The old man in the house in the middle of nowhere."

She put her chin in her hand. "Yeah, the old man died."

7

"Which car's yours?"

"The Maverick. Over there."

"Never been in a Maverick. Open it up, let's see what kind of leg room they give you." Paul opened it up. I got in. It was like sitting in a sardine can. "Roomy enough. Let's see how it rides. Drive up to Sunset and down to the Strip."

"Maggie said I should make sure we get right down there."

"Up to Sunset, down to the Strip."

"Maggie said—"

"Up to Sunset, down to the Strip."

We went through Westwood, up past the university, right onto Sunset. He signaled his turns late, other than that he drove okay. The Maverick rode like every other Maverick I'd ever been in. Like it'd been made by people whose minds had been on something else. It'd probably ridden fine for its first six months but American cars aren't made to age well and it usually shows sooner than it should.

I like Sunset. It's a good road. It starts at Union Station and winds all the way west to the ocean. You can find everything there is, somewhere along it. Every economic class, every kind of food, every kind of girl, every kind of anything. Plenty of the things you'd rather not find. It's all there if you know where to look and sometimes you don't even have to look. A real good road.

"What'd you make of her husband?"

"Mrs. Isenbart's husband?"

"What're your feelings, from what she said?"

He answered fast, too fast. "He hasn't gone to the cops. That could mean something."

"Could mean lots of things. Could mean nothing. What about him not liking women in business?"

Paul shrugged. "Some guys're like that."

"Are they?"

He thought it over. Maybe it was a trick question. "You think it means something?"

"What kind of mileage you get with a Maverick?"

"You think it means something?"

"Don't you know what kind of mileage you get?" He turned and looked at me like that might get him an answer. "Please keep your eyes on the road when you're driving and I'm riding. You never know when a turn'll come up out of nowhere."

The Strip looked good, especially a new guy I'd never seen before. He was tall and trying to keep his balance on six-inch platform shoes. His arms were as stringy as strands of spaghetti. White clown makeup covered his face. A cardboard crown studded with rhinestones perched on top of his head. *Singin' in the Rain* came out of his mouth. I liked him so much I waved my Coke at him. He smiled and turned and spoiled the whole effect. His back carried an ad for a new rock group.

I'd begun to wish Paul would stop tapping the steering wheel every time we stopped at a light. "You this icthy when you worked for Carne?"

"I'm not itchy. I just want to get there."

He kept tapping the wheel. Maggie does that sometimes when she's nervous. It's not one of her more endearing features.

We ended up parked in front of an office building down at the end of Wilshire.

"Give me a ten-minute start. Come up like you got nothing to do with me. Tell 'em you're a messenger and use a name something like your own, so if they call you you'll know they're calling you and you won't stand around waiting to see who it is they're calling. Paulson. Tell 'em your name's Paulson and you got a message for a fabric salesman named Neuhaus. He's supposed to be stopping there today, if he hasn't been there yet you're supposed to wait for him. It's a private message, you can't give it to anyone except Neuhaus."

He rubbed his hand along his leg. "Okay. I'll be careful. Don't worry."

That's when I worry the most. When they tell me don't worry.

8

I went through oversized glass doors into a reception area. A counter faced with mirrors threw my face back at me. More mirrors covered the right wall. The left wall had shiny things that looked like someone'd stolen a thousand hubcaps and then hadn't known what to do with them. The ceiling was covered with reflective paper. The floor wore the kind of wax shine you never see anywhere except in commercials. The whole effect was like you'd stumbled straight into the beam of one of those klieg lights they once used for Hollywood openings and now use for political rallies.

A row of chairs to the side of the doors held two men. They both had faces tanned as dark as the leather on their sample cases and their faces showed almost as much life.

I took my life in my hands and walked toward the counter of mirrors. The girl looked up from a magazine and her eyes made a fast trip from my head to my toes and back to my head again. I gave her a smile and her magazine went down.

"Tell me you're not married."

"I'm not married," I said.

"Engaged?"

"People still getting engaged these days?"

"Good." She smiled. She was blond, too. I knew I had to watch myself. I'm a sucker for that type. I'm a sucker for most types. "Nice hat you got."

"It's a Panama. I found it in my stocking last Christmas."

"Must've been a big stocking."

"You should've seen the way it looked with the hat in it."

"You got plans for dinner tonight?"

I think I was still breathing. "This what women's lib's all about?"

"Sure." She ran fingers through her hair. "If you want to call it that. Dinner?"

"I might be working tonight."

Her eyes twinkled, as if it was necessary. "Better be careful. That was your first wrong answer. You were doing so well."

I was hoping she'd stop playing with her hair that way. I was supposed to be there on business. "Maybe I'll be lucky and I won't be working tomorrow night. Mr. Isenbart here?"

She made a face. "You're changing the subject."

"Same subject. I don't earn a living, I'll never get a night free to take you to dinner."

She studied my eyes like she thought she'd figure out what was really behind them. "Okay, Mr. Isenbart's here. He expecting you?"

"My name's Fredericks. I handle some insurance for him. I got to check some things quick so I can get out to West Covina."

"West Covina? Are there really people in West Covina."

"A couple. There's one we think burned down his own store."

She moved closer and her voice got softer like we were conspiring. "That's not good enough. He's busy with a buyer, and he's got those two waiting to see him. Better give me a better reason to get you in first."

"It's the forms he sent in, we can't make sense of 'em." I took out a small notebook and opened it to a page filled with numbers. The numbers meant nothing. You could spend all day looking at them, they'd still mean nothing. I showed them to her. "It affects his premium and his premium's already past due. We don't get it fixed, something happens around here, he wants his insurance, he won't get it. He'll get cards out of a computer. I been through it."

Her hand covered mine. "Those numbers really mean something?"

"They could mean trouble."

"That's what *I* mean, sometimes." Her fingers stroked under my shirt cuff and across my wrist as if they'd been there before. "This does look serious. I'll get Mr. Isenbart. Don't go away, Mr. Fredericks."

She went through an arch and then came back. He came out behind her and grabbed my arm and pulled me to the side and poked a finger into my chest. "You aren't my insurance guy. Joe Livingston's my insurance guy. I'm all paid up with insurance. I'm trying to run a business here." His finger kept driving. "You're trying to sell me something, I ain't interested. Understand?"

"I understand. You don't have to be so rough about it."

He shoved me aside with more force than seemed necessary and went to the men sitting by the doors. They already looked like soldiers in front of a drill sergeant. "I need crushed velvet. Dark brown, light brown. Three thousand yards each. What've you got?"

"Sure," one of them said. "Next Tuesday."

"I could be dead by Tuesday."

"Friday!" the other one said. "*This* Friday!"

"Friday I can live with. Where's your samples?"

"I got to go back to the office."

"I want to see samples by three. And you can't get me three thousand each by Friday, it's no damn good to me, understand?"

The man was off the chair, on his feet, out the door. Isenbart was past me, not bothering to look. I followed him through the arch. He turned. "Whatever the hell you want, you're wasting my time and your time. I don't give a damn about your time, my time's worth something. Get out of here."

"My name's Thieringer. I'm a private detective. Your wife says you need some help."

His eyes slid off me. "What I need's a new receptionist. One with some brains." His hand came up palm first, then went down waving me away. "I'm trying to run a goddamn business here. Give me a break." He went around a corner.

9

An underfed girl in a cream-colored dress turned slowly in the middle of the showroom. A man with a cigar sat in front of her and every time she moved he coughed smoke. A thin wispy man with wavy hair knelt in front of her and arranged the drape of the dress. Max Isenbart brought his hand up again. "Carl! What're you doing?"

Wavy hair looked up. "Mr. Grossman wanted to see the hem a little higher."

That changed everything. Isenbart sat next to the cigar. "I can give you fifteen hundred pieces on the other unit, Sol. Dark brown, light brown, half and half. Two weeks okay?"

The cigar sat behind his cloud of smoke and watched the hem of the dress going up the girl's leg. "Ten days."

"I can make it. Ten days."

The cigar coughed. "What else you got I can see her in? Something a little. . . ." His hands broke through the smoke in curved gestures.

"Ten days, Sol? Can we write it up?" The cigar's hands kept gesturing. Isenbart turned to the wavy hair. "Carl, show Mr. Grossman Seventeen-B."

Carl took his wavy hair and the model toward a door in the back wall. The cigar pulled himself out of the chair. "If it's really ten days, Max, you can write it up. Don't mind if I take a look back there, do you? Maybe something'll look good to me."

"Sure, Sol. Go ahead. Look all you want."

The cigar went through the door. As soon as he was gone, Isenbart brought his hand down on his leg in a flat slap. Then he stood up and turned around and saw me standing there. He turned away and went down a corridor. I went after him.

I chased him into an office. The top of the desk, the top of the filing cabinets, the top of everything was covered with drawings and material samples. The place was a goddamn mess. It was the only thing so far I liked about him.

He picked up the phone. "Get out of here or I'm calling the cops."

"Call 'em. I always enjoy a good talk with the cops. They always ask such interesting questions."

He stared at me, then turned away and talked into the phone. "Annie? Get me Bernie, quick." He hung up the phone but kept looking at it.

I stayed on my feet and waited for something to happen but when nothing did I said, "Your wife said—"

"Don't tell me what my wife said. I go home tonight, she'll tell me what she said. I don't have to hear it from you. My wife's got a mouth on her, you can't shut her up." He held out his hands palms up. "Give me a break! I'm trying to earn a buck here. Can I at least earn a buck?" The phone rang. He grabbed it. "Listen, Bernie, I . . . I said listen! I ain't got time for that! You'll have six thousand yards of crushed velvet by Friday! I got to have fifteen hundred pieces of Twenty-five-D by the end of next week! . . . I know! Fifteen hundred's the best I can do! . . . You think I don't know?" He hung up the phone and by the time it'd settled in its cradle he was out from behind his desk, out of the office, and down another corridor.

I followed him through the reception area and saw Paul at the counter talking to the girl. I didn't look at Paul, Paul didn't look at me. I followed Isenbart into the showroom. The cigar was back in his chair watching the model. What she was wearing wasn't much. The cigar wished it was less. Isenbart sat at his side like a supplicant next to a guru. They said something but I couldn't hear what it was.

Isenbart jumped up and walked the model across the room and talked to her quietly. The cigar took out a notebook and peered into it as if Isenbart's talk had nothing to do with him.

The wavy hair came over and smiled tentatively. He slipped a cigarette pack out of his pocket, shook it carelessly and when a cigarette showed he offered it to me. I shook my head. He took the cigarette for himself, lit it and stared at the burning tip. I watched the cigar, and Isenbart with the model. Wavy hair went away.

He came back with a dress displayed over his arm. "What do you think? I'm doing it in a lower neckline too. In camel. I think it's going to be big for us. You like it?"

Before I could answer, Isenbart came away from the model. "Carl. Come here." Wavy hair turned toward him. Isenbart looked at the cigar. "I think we're all set, Sol. Two thousand units?"

The cigar nodded. "Sure. If we're all set."

Isenbart touched wavy hair's arm. "Write it up, Carl." Isenbart walked the cigar across the room, through the arch and into the reception area. They stood by the glass doors. Isenbart wrote something on a piece of paper and put it into the cigar's pocket. Isenbart patted the cigar's shoulder once and then went down a corridor.

The cigar went through the glass doors and stood in the hall and took out the paper and looked at it carefully. His mouth spread in a smile full of teeth.

10

Isenbart dodged in and out of rooms and I dodged after him and finally he gave up and went into his office. He picked up the phone and dialed. I tried to catch some of my breath.

"Excuse me, Mr. Isenbart, we going to do much more running around?"

He covered the phone with one hand and smiled at me. "Good for you. Keeps you thin."

"I'm thin enough." He didn't look like he was going to ask me to sit so I sat anyway. "I don't mind the exercise, I'm just curious as to how many times you plan to go in the same circle. I'd just's soon try a new route, next time out."

He looked at me some more and finally sat down himself. "You and me both. See the way I got to keep going around here? Either everything happens or nothing happens." He sounded almost pleasant. Then he realized he was still holding the phone and slammed it down. The wavy hair came in with an armful of drawings, looking at me briefly. "Carl? What's the matter now?"

"You said we'd go over the new designs, Max."

Isenbart rubbed his forehead. "Not now."

"Won't take long. I just have to know—"

"Can you understand English? Not now!" He turned toward the window.

Carl held his ground. "Things can't keep going on this way, Max. You're putting off too many decisions. Something's got to change."

"I got too many things on my mind right now! Can't you. . . ." Isenbart paused and took a roll of Tums from his pocket, slipped one wafer into his mouth. He breathed in and out. "Maybe you're right. Let's see what you got." He spread the drawings flat on his desk and stood over them. "Yeah. Pretty good. Just wish to hell I had the money to do this stuff justice."

"These won't be expensive, Max. I got it worked out."

"I got news for you, Carl. To do 'em right's going to be a hell of a lot more expensive'n you got it worked out." He flipped through the rest of the designs. Carl took the cigarette out of his mouth and looked at its tip with a resigned face. "We were doing decent business, it'd be a different story. But we ain't doing decent business." Isenbart turned one of the drawings so I could see it. "Not bad, huh? He's thinking about going to New York. You know what? That's where we all ought to be going. New York. That's where the business is. Out here? Nothing."

24

He took Carl's arm and led him to the door. "I'll go over the drawings, maybe I can cut a few corners."

Isenbart started to close the door. Carl took one more look at me before the door shut. Isenbart went back to his desk and looked at the top drawing and shook his head. "Jesus Christ. What an incompetent. You believe these things? I want to sell anything around here, I got to design it myself." He collapsed into his chair. "He can't even do knockoffs right. Always got to change something. He takes Pauline Trigere, he drops the neckline, raises the hem, he thinks he's done something. He's changed the one goddamn thing that shouldn't be changed. Go into the dress business, it'll drive you nuts." His hand dragged wearily across his face. "I got buyers that're more interested in what's wearing the dresses than the dresses. I got a designer who doesn't know shit about design. I got a girl out front, she spends the whole day trying to pick up everything that comes in here wearing pants. She can't pick it up, Carl will. I got a factory, it never turns out a goddamn thing in time. Now I got you." He set his elbows on the desk and leaned forward. "First thing I got to do, I got to get rid of you. Then I got to get myself a decent designer. I can afford a decent designer about the same's I can afford a private detective. You think you can make any money out of me, you can think again."

He took a cigarette from a pack on the desk and lit it. He kept the match lit. He picked up the top drawing and touched the match to its corner. We watched the design turn to ash. He dropped what was left into the waste basket and looked at it. "Don't look half bad, now. Now I almost like it." That made him feel better. He laughed. His face relaxed. "All right, my wife came to see you. My wife's nuts. She's got two stories, one's about the IRS, the other's about some cockamamie boy. Which one'd she give you?"

"I haven't heard the one about the IRS. I'd like to hear it, if it's short."

His face didn't look so relaxed. "You married?"

"Not so I remember."

"Stay that way. Let me tell you about wives. The Los Angeles variety. Too much sun, too much swimming

25

pools, too much clubs, too much shrinks, too much. . . ."
He laughed. "I sent her to a shrink once. She almost
drove the poor bastard out of his mind. He told me he
wouldn't charge me if I made sure she didn't come to see
him any more." He laughed again.

I had to get him off that kick. "She told me you designed a movie and almost won the Academy Award."

It got me a bigger laugh. "I almost got nominated,
that's what I almost got." He stubbed out his cigarette and
stopped laughing. "Movies. You know this town? Everybody's got to be in the movies. You aren't in 'em, you
pretend you are. Or were. Who'll know if you're lying?
Who'll care?" He lit another cigarette.

I tried again and put a curve in it. "Our rates're five
hundred dollars a day." His mouth dropped open and he
said nothing. Exactly the effect I was after. "For that you
get a full-time staff of trained operatives with years of ex-
perience. We give you twenty-four-hour protection."

He sputtered a little. "You got a lot of nerve."

"I got to. This city's built on nerve."

"This city's built on nothing!" He took out a bottle
and a glass. One glass. I wasn't invited.

"Make the check out to McGuane and Thieringer. We
need a thousand dollars as a retainer to get us going."

"You ought to be a goddamn dress salesman. You
got the right approach." He lit another cigarette. That
gave him two that were lit.

"Let's get down to business, Mr. Isenbart. I've seen
what a hard guy you are. Let's get past that."

He leaned back in his chair and drank. "Hard guy.
Sure. You know what I just went through to make a sale
out there?"

"I don't know what you went through. I think I know
what you did."

His hand went into his pocket for his Tums. "I feel
sick to my stomach about what I did. I'm no better'n a
goddamn pimp. The things you got to sell, just to sell a
couple dresses. Why the hell didn't she just say no?"

"Maybe she was scared to say no."

"She figures she can use the money. Everybody can
use the money." He tapped a single finger against his

glass. "What kind of condition was my wife in? She do a lot of yelling?"

"Hardly any."

"You ought to hear her when she's been drinking. Bust your eardrums. She's a good woman, she's just a little—"

"I liked her."

He looked up. "Did you?"

"Yeah. Maybe, you give me a chance, I'll even like you."

"I should care what you like." He started to pour another drink but stopped. His hands flattened against the top of his desk.

11

I waited for someone to say something but nobody did, not even me. Finally the boy came halfway into the office, moving slowly and favoring his right leg. The first thing I didn't like was the scar. It was over his right eye, not his left. The second thing was his hands. He couldn't keep them still, like maybe he was on something. The third thing was Isenbart's hands. They were no longer on the desk. Then I heard a drawer slide open. As soon as I did I got to my feet and stood in front of the boy.

"You'll have to get out of here." The boy stepped sideways to get his eyes on Isenbart again. I stepped with him. "Look, I'm sorry, it took me a week to get over here. We're in the middle of business. You'll have to come back later."

Now his eyes saw me as if for the first time. He stayed still a moment, then stepped back. His hand went into a pocket. It jerked back out and something clicked and what he was holding turned into a switchblade pointed at my throat. I didn't move.

The blade moved. It wouldn't stay still, his hand shook so much.

I grabbed his wrist and twisted it. The knife didn't drop. He squirmed beneath me like a snake. I still held his wrist. His knee came forward. I turned sideways and it missed. He tried again and this time his shoe got me just below the knee. I twisted harder, bending his wrist, forcing him backwards. The knife dropped.

His mouth opened and yelped. I pulled him out the door, still holding his wrist. We went into the hall. He kept trying to rip free. He had twice the energy he should've had. He turned and landed an elbow in my stomach. I still had his wrist. He hurtled his whole body at me. We went sideways and crashed into a wall. Pain ran from my shoulder to my elbow.

He got away and went toward the office but I grabbed his wrist again and stopped him. His free hand went toward his waist but I swung him in a circle before he could reach what he was reaching for and moved behind him and grabbed his other wrist and held both his hands behind his back.

I pulled him toward the reception area. He wouldn't give up. His feet kicked at me one at a time. He got me below the knee again. People tried to get out of our way. I saw Carl's face, the girl behind the counter, Paul, someone I hadn't seen before, then I collided with the counter and went down to the floor and the boy jumped on top of me.

I pushed him aside and got him beneath me and grabbed his arms from behind again and got to my feet and pulled him up. His feet tried kicking me again.

I dragged him across the reception area and pushed my back into one of the glass doors and got it open and threw him out. He sailed all the way to the far wall.

He turned quickly and faced me but stayed where he was. Then he reached into a pocket and this time his hand came out with little colored things which could've been candy but weren't. He popped one quickly into his mouth, swallowed it down and put the rest back into his pocket. We stared at each other.

He turned suddenly and moved down the hall. He went to the elevator and pushed the button. Paul moved to my side. I spoke quietly.

"He's on something. He just took more of it. I took a knife off him. See where he goes. Don't let him see you. He gets in a car, get the license number. Don't get close. You lose him, you lose him. Don't take chances."

The boy stepped back from the elevator and looked up the hall at me. I stayed inside the reception area. I turned away from the glass doors and my eyes saw the face of the girl behind the counter. She was looking at me like I'd done something I ought to be proud of. I didn't feel proud. He hadn't looked like much. Just a scared little kid. But you never know.

12

Max Isenbart was kneeling on the floor in front of his desk. His head jerked up as I came in. Then he looked down.

"What'd you break?"

"Nothing. A glass. I knocked it off the desk." He wrapped the broken pieces in a scrap of material and put it all in a wastebasket. He took more material and patted the rug dry.

I calmly bent down and picked up the switchblade. I closed it and put it in my pocket.

His breathing was still heavy. He went to his desk and took a cigarette pack and shook it. Nothing came out. He shook it again, suddenly ripped it apart. Half a dozen cigarettes fell onto his desk. He grabbed one, jammed it into his mouth and lit it. "Someone's playing tricks on me. It's not serious."

I stayed standing. "Then you know who he is."

"No." He took out a new glass and poured more whiskey. He poured too quickly and the whiskey almost overran the top of the glass but he caught it in time. He drank some down, then sank deeper into his chair and closed up like a fist.

"Whoever he is, he's on some kind of pills."

"All right."

I kept it soft. "What I said before, far's our rates go——"

"He's some crazy kid! I'll take care of it myself! He's just trying to scare me!" He picked up the glass and drank quickly. "Nobody's going to get hurt. Leave me alone." His mouth gulped more of the whiskey. His hand slid the glass away. He got up from his desk and went out.

I waited a moment, he didn't come back. I walked around the side of the desk, sat down and opened drawers. In the bottom drawer on the right I found what he'd reached for. A .32 caliber Colt. I checked it, it was loaded. I left it where it was and closed the drawer gently.

I opened more drawers. I took two pieces of stationery that said *Lybart Petites* and folded them neatly and put them in an envelope that said *Lybart Petites* and put that in my pocket.

Five ball-point pens said *Lybart Petites*. I put two in my pocket.

Half a dozen cigarettes lay spilled across the desk. I put two in my pocket and went out.

13

I couldn't find Paul. He wasn't downstairs, he wasn't at the car. I walked three blocks in every direction and still didn't see him. I went back to Lybart Petites. Nothing. I went down in the elevator and checked the lobby again.

Just inside the front door there was an old man giving shoe shines. I gave him two dollars and described Paul to him. He hadn't seen him. I described the boy with the limp. He'd seen the boy with the limp. The boy had gone out of the building alone about fifteen minutes before.

I went through the lobby, through a door, upstairs. Just below the second floor landing I found Paul. His head rested against the corner of a step. His face was drained white. His eyes were shut. His left leg was bent under him, his right arm reached out toward the railing.

I knelt down and rubbed his arm softly. Nothing happened. I touched him again and he started to move. I tried to pull him into a sitting position and his left arm came up and took a swing at me. A soft swing. I pushed it aside.

He opened his eyes, blinked, saw me, turned away, and vomited.

I leaned him against the side of his car, got his keys out of his pocket, got him in on the passenger side and left him there. I found a drugstore in the next block. I bought a small bottle of aspirin and got a large paper cup of water and went back to the car.

Paul tried to sit up. I tilted him back and fed him two of the aspirins. I soaked a handkerchief with what was left of the water and draped it across his forehead.

He tried to sit forward. "I heard him coughing. Then I didn't hear him coughing."

I pushed him back against the seat. "We're not in any hurry. Give the aspirin time to work."

He tried to sit up again but I didn't let him.

"He was down at the elevator. Then he moved and I couldn't see him. I pushed the glass doors open and looked out, and he was gone. I went down the hall. The lights showed the elevator was already down at the lobby. It couldn't've got down there that fast. I opened the door to the stairs and I could hear him, below me." Paul touched his forehead with his fingers and rubbed gently, then took his hand away. "I started down, I was quiet, then I heard him stop. I waited till I heard him going down again. Then he started coughing. He sounded like he was about two floors below me. Then the coughing stopped and I waited, but I didn't hear anything. I leaned over the railing and looked down the stairwell. The crack wasn't big enough, I couldn't see anything.

"I went down another flight and looked over the railing, I still couldn't see him. I went down to the next landing—" He turned his face away. "I heard something behind me. A door." He breathed in slowly. "I started down again like I didn't know he was there. He told me to stop, or he'd blow my head off. He was right behind me. I turned a little. He had a gun. His hand was shaking so bad he couldn't keep it still. He made me turn around again and while I was turning he hit me." Paul's hand rubbed mechanically along the edge of the car window. "Wasn't much."

"What?"

"The gun. Wasn't much."

I stared through the windshield. "Just for the record, how much was it?"

He rubbed the back of his neck. "Twenty-two automatic."

I watched an old man trying to jaywalk across the middle of the street. Car horns screamed at him. He shook a cane in the air and continued on his way. "'A twenty-two automatic puts out a slug that weighs approximately

32

one-twelfth of an ounce. They put it in the right place, it's just about enough to take care of anyone. The OSS used twenty-two automatics with silencers during World War II. They're decent guns and they're the only production model handgun you can silence so the silencer does any good. The CIA's got 'em. The Mafia's got 'em. Maggie's got one, in the office. Very popular little weapons." The old man reached the far side of the street. Then he turned and came back into the street again, shaking his cane, daring someone to hit him. "Don't tell me a twenty-two automatic isn't much. The ground's full of people who found out different." I opened the car door.

Paul leaned across the seat. "Think we should call the cops? Because of the gun?"

I turned back and faced him. "What the hell, you think we're going to call the cops, we don't even know what the fuck's going on here? You got a hell of a lot to learn about cops! And clients too! We aren't calling the fucking cops! You got a hell of a lot to learn! You better learn fast!" I slammed the car door.

I stood there a moment, saying nothing. I finally looked at him again. He had his head down and I couldn't see his face.

I went across the street and into the building. I knew I should've seen that the kid had had a gun. And I hadn't seen it. Damn it.

14

I went into the showroom. Isenbart wasn't there. I tried another room and found Carl working at a drafting table. He looked up and smiled. "Didn't know you're still here. Want to see some things?" He put down his pencil and reached for rolls of paper. "I can show you some drawings." Then he put the drawings down and moved off his stool and crossed the room to a rack of dresses. "The model's in the other room. I can show you some really nice things, you got a few minutes."

"I wish I did. I don't. I'm trying to find your boss."

"You try his office?"

"The girl out front said he's not in there."

Carl shook his head and sat on the stool. "Hell. I know where he probably is."

The model walked in. She went past me, over to the rack of dresses. She was wearing a black lace bra, a black garter belt, black fishnet stockings, very black very high heels. Her panties weren't there. The way she was acting, she must've thought I wasn't there. She looked at the dresses. "You know what this business is, Carl? A load of crap. That's what is is."

Carl took out a cigarette and put it in his mouth. "You could've said no."

"Sure. Sure. Max says I'm supposed to wear Thirteen-C."

Carl went to the rack and took out a long dress. The girl put it on over her head, turned her back to Carl and waited for him to zip it. "Hell. I'll probably smell like cigar smoke for a week."

"You could've said no."

"You seen my bank account lately?"

Carl went back to his stool. "Not lately."

The girl faced the mirror, then turned her back to it and looked over her shoulder at herself. "I've seen my bank account lately. What there is of it."

Her lips tightened and she turned away from the mirror. She finally looked at me. Her face showed no expression at all, her eyes were as lifeless as a burned-out tenement, and if she really saw me she didn't show it. She went out the door.

Carl lit his cigarette and stared at the burning tip the same way I'd seen him do it before. "She could've said no."

"She couldn't afford to. Or she didn't think she could afford to. You said you knew where Isenbart probably is."

He still stared at his cigarette. "The roof. Spends half his life up there. It's getting terrible."

"Can I get up there? The roof?"

"Straight down, turn left, you'll see a door." He put the cigarette aside and bent down over his drafting table.

I went up to the roof. Isenbart was leaning against the wall, watching the city. He turned quickly when he heard my steps. Then he turned away and refused to look at me. I went over next to him and rested my elbows on the edge of the wall. "You and I got to talk some more. The boy's got a gun." He stiffened but said nothing and still wouldn't look at me. I leaned closer. "I got an operative sitting in a car downstairs. The boy almost busted his head open."

"I told you not to do anything." He kept his eyes on the city. His voice got harder. "I told you, I can handle it myself."

"Maybe you already tried.'" He looked at me suspiciously.

"Maybe the boy's been shaking you down on something. Maybe you gave him some money to go away, a couple months ago. Maybe he went away. Then maybe he decided you hadn't given him enough and he came back for the next installment."

Isenbart moved along the wall. "I don't know what you think's going on here, Mr. Thieringer, but you're wrong."

I moved along the wall after him. "I'm often wrong."

He kept looking away. "I told you, I can take care of this myself." He started talking more quickly. "It's my business. Don't push me. Just leave me alone." I reached toward him and turned him. "Hey! What're you doing!" I kept one hand on his shoulder as my other hand went into his outside pocket. "Hey!"

I came out of his pocket with his .32 Colt. I moved back a step. "It looked like a familiar bulge, Mr. Isenbart." I looked down at the gun. "Got a permit for it?"

I was lying on my back. My back hurt, so did my jaw. I shook my head to clear it. My jaw still hurt. I turned over and got to my knees and tried to focus my eyes. All I saw was the dirty roof, and my hat, lying on its side about a foot in front of me. And then I saw the gun a dozen feet away. A hand went down to the gun and picked it up. I looked up to see if I knew who owned the hand.

He put his gun carefully into his pocket. "I'm sorry. I didn't mean to. . . . Leave me alone, please, just. . . ." He started backing away. His face looked as worn as the sidewalk. "Someone wants to scare me, that's all. The boy's been paid to. . . . It's not serious, I can—" His back hit the wall and it stopped him. He looked at me like I wasn't even there. His words came mechanically without any emotion. "I told you not to push me. You pushed me. I. . . ."

He turned and opened the door and went through it as if in a daze. The door closed slowly behind him. It made a scraping sound like it didn't fit properly in its frame. Like it could've used an extra shove to get it shut right.

I waited for my head to clear, then got to my feet. I touched my jaw, which was stupid, it only made my jaw hurt more, and I should've known it'd make my jaw hurt more. I walked to the edge of the roof.

The city lay beneath me. Busy streets, with a dull haze of smog floating above them. It almost seemed like the haze was slowly pressing lower as I watched it. It wasn't pressing lower, it just seemed like it was.

15

I placed my left hand on the doorknob and twisted it and pushed the door open. I held Paul up with my right arm around his waist, but as we went in he reached for the front desk to steady himself and pulled a phone book off it. It slapped the floor like a falling body. Maggie appeared in the doorway to the inner office. She saw us and came forward quickly. Before I could say anything she had both of us turned so we were facing the wall.

Elizabeth Isenbart came out of the inner office. She saw Paul staggering and started forward.

With Maggie on one side and me on the other we got Paul past her. We took him into the inner office and put him on the sofa. Mrs. Isenbart came in and tried for another look. I took her arm and led her out to the front and sat her down on the sofa out there.

"We had to check that other job I told you about, after we saw your husband." I turned and shut the door to the inner office. "We ran into a little trouble. Nothing serious."

"Is he all right?"

"Got the wind knocked out of him. That's all."

"Are you sure?" She leaned toward me. "The way he looked! You should call a doctor!"

Then she sat back very still and put her hands at her sides.

"You feel okay, Mrs. Isenbart?" She said nothing. "You want something to drink?"

She folded her hands in her lap and looked straight ahead. "No. I'm all right." Her words came like whispers. She breathed in and out, first heavy, then light. Then she sat straight. "You said you saw Max. You arranged things?"

"I'm afraid not. I couldn't get anywhere with him."

Her eyebrows lifted slightly. She nodded automatically.

"Mrs. Isenbart? You hear what I said?"

She stood up. Sat down. "Yes. I heard you." Her fingers rubbed softly along the top of her dress, then tugged the edge tightly against her legs. "I don't know what to do. What am I going to do?"

I leaned against the corner of Paul's desk. "I can call the police for you."

Her head nodded softly. "Max doesn't want that. I can't do anything that Max doesn't want me to do." Then she looked at me with the kind of eyes you can't look away from.

I went to the sofa and sat next to her. "If your husband hires me, I'll do whatever I can do, Mrs. Isenbart. He doesn't hire me, I can't do anything."

She nodded again. I spoke distinctly, almost biting off each syllable. "I can't do anything, Mrs. Isenbart. Not if I haven't been hired."

16

Maggie closed the door behind her. "Nice work, Fritz! Nice fucking work! Paul says the boy hit him with a gun! Where the hell were you?"

"Talking with Isenbart."

"Very clever of you!"

"The boy was limping. He had a scar—"

"She told us he was limping and had a scar! What the hell happened with Paul?"

I put my hands in front of me on the desk and kept very still. "She told us the scar was over his left eye. It's over the right eye."

Maggie thought a moment. "She'd be looking at him. The scar's over his right eye, she'd see it on her left. She'd mix it up. You're paranoid."

"Maybe. I'd like to be sure the boy I saw and the boy she saw are the same boy. He's on something. Pills."

"Terrific." She sat on the corner of my desk. "What kind? Speeding him up or slowing him down?"

"Speeding him up. He had this." I took the knife from my pocket and slid it across the desk.

Maggie picked it up and clicked it open and studied its length. "Sweet. What else'd you rip off?"

I shrugged but she kept looking at me till I took out

the *Lybart* envelope with the stationery and the two ball-point pens.

"The kid could be eighteen, could be younger. About Paul's size. Just a kid."

She closed the knife and dropped it on my desk. "Don't tell me he's just a kid. Half the crimes in this country're being done by kids. Murder, rape, armed robbery, arson, the whole works. I was reading the paper yesterday, they had a story on a sixteen-year-old, he served his arithmetic teacher a cup of coffee laced with hydrochloric acid. Don't tell me about kids." She rapped a knuckle twice against the desk. "I don't much like what happened to Paul."

"I don't much like it myself. I told Paul to see if he got in a car, and if he did, to get the license plate. I told Paul I'd taken a knife off him so he better keep his distance."

"Did you tell Paul the kid had a gun?"

"I didn't know he had a gun."

"Brilliant!" She hit the desk again. "What's the mark on your jaw?"

"Nothing."

"Uh-huh." She came around the side of the desk. I turned my chair on its swivel but she swiveled me back and tilted my head and looked at the bruise. "Very nice."

"The kid. When I took the knife off him. Caught me off guard. I was concentrating on the knife."

"Got dirt on your hat, too."

"It fell off when he hit me." I got away from her and went to the refrigerator. "Paul tell you how he got caught? The kid started coughing—"

"I heard."

"Amateaur night."

Maggie walked next to me. "Amateur night was you getting caught on the jaw." She went to her desk.

I opened a Coke and took it to my desk. I sat in the chair and swiveled away and when I thought she wasn't paying attention I pulled up my right pants leg. The bruise still looked bad. It was just below the knee. The skin hadn't broken, there was no blood, but it looked bad and hurt bad. Next time I'd wear boots that went all the way to the waist.

The jaw still hurt too. I slipped the aspirin bottle out of my pocket and held it so she couldn't see it and opened it quietly and put two into my mouth and quickly drank Coke.

"What's that?"

"Candy."

"Looked like pills."

"They're selling a new kind of candy. Looks just like pills."

"What the hell was it?"

"Vitamin C."

"Sure."

She didn't say anything else. After a while I finally turned front in my chair and she was still looking at me.

"What're you looking at?"

"You." Her voice sounded smaller. "You all right?"

"I'm okay." Then I looked at my desk and kept quiet. But her voice had sounded nice that time.

17

"We had a man in while you were gone. He owns hard-ware stores and he needs security guards. Unfortunately we don't have security guards."

"I didn't think we did."

"I gave him a couple of places to go to. Some agency's going to make a mint off him."

"Not today, Mag. I been through enough for the morning. What was Mrs. Isenbart doing back here?"

"All I could get is what she gave us the first time. I think she didn't have anywhere else to go. Big George called. He needs work. I told him we'll give him a call if we get anything." She snapped her fingers. "Almost forgot! They had a story on the news about some guy in New York who had a stomachache. So he went to the doctor but the doctor couldn't figure out what it was. They cut him open and guess what they found."

She loves this kind of thing.

"Come on, Fritz. Guess."

"Judge Crater?"

"Metal! Coins! Subway tokens! Broken thermometers! Keys! He's been eating the stuff for years! Over five hundred pieces! Can you believe it?"

"Yeah. You'd ever spent time in New York, you'd understand."

Her fingers drummed the desk.

"What's the matter?"

"Nothing! . . . I'm edgy." She started nibbling her thumb.

"Come on, Mag. Patience."

"How long do you think it's going to take?"

I drew a face on my blotter. "I don't know. Patience."

It took another hour. The front door opened, a moment passed, our door opened. A messenger came in with an envelope. I opened my drawer and reached for the carved-bone letter opener but Maggie grabbed the envelope and ripped it open and her face brightened for the first time all morning. "A thousand dollars. Twice the usual. Not bad."

I looked at the check—$1,000, all right. "Something's wrong."

"What the hell's wrong?"

"I thought he'd call first." I held the check in two fingers and stared at it. "He sent us this much 'cause I told him we charge five hundred a day and he'd have to give us a two-day deposit as a retainer."

"No wonder you couldn't get us hired!"

"I told him we'd negotiate it down. Made no difference. The reason he wouldn't hire us's something else. He was scared to hire us. Wasn't the money." I brushed the check against my chin as if I expected it to fall apart. "But he was complaining about money."

"You just said he wasn't!"

"I said money wasn't the reason he didn't want to hire us." I looked at the check again. It was still in one piece. "He kept saying business's bad, he can't afford to turn out designs the way they ought to be turned out. Now he sends us the check without even calling to negotiate. Something's screwy."

She reached for the check. "Something's always screwy, with you! He sent us the check and my half of the business isn't sending it back!"

"No, we'll keep it. We'll worry about the final bill when we're finished." I put the check on her desk. "But something's screwy."

"Good! I like it that way!" She was already writing out a deposit slip for the bank. "Got any ideas about how to play it?"

I went to the window and looked down at the street. "They're both scared. Him and the kid. Isenbart's older. Tougher. He'll give us a bigger fight." I tapped a finger against my upper lip. "We better concentrate on trying to break the kid."

18

People started coming out of the building around five. None I cared about. Most of them looked happy. A primary difference between East Coast and West. Back East they run from their jobs on the edge of a scream. Out here it's different. People still look human at five, still have energy, they're ready to spend a couple hours searching for all kinds of hell to get into. A different type of danger completely.

People kept coming out. Carl with the wavy hair came out, the girl from behind the mirrored counter came out—

I ducked behind my steering wheel. If she saw me, I'd be stuck.

I was stuck.

She looked through the window on the passenger side. "Hiding from someone, Mr. Fredericks?"

"Your boss. I'm going to have to catch him off guard and see if I can talk him into—"

"The insurance thing?" She opened the door and got in beside me. "I'll bet it's got a lot to do with insurance." She dropped her hand cross my leg like it lived there. "Tell me about insurance, Mr. *Thieringer*."

Hell.

"Come on, tell me about insurance. You do have something to do with insurance, don't you?"

I tried to remove her hand. I did, but it was no good, it turned out she had two. Her second slid up my leg. "This isn't the time or place."

"Call me Annie."

"This isn't the time or place, Annie."

"I've got the time if you've got the place. Come to think of it, I've got the place too."

Across the street Max Isenbart came out of the building. He carried a package about half the size of a shoebox.

Her mouth nuzzled my ear. "What should I call you, Mr. Thieringer?" Isenbart walked into a parking lot down the street. Annie's leg slid over mine. "Come on, what should I call you?"

I kept an eye on the parking lot and pushed her back into the passenger seat.

"Hey! Come on! I'm just playing!" She pouted. Christ, did she have a wonderful pout. "You're terrible."

"I know. I always have been."

She put her hand where it'd been before and laughed lightly. "You going to tell me you're not interested?"

My face must've been the color of a pomegranate. "It'd be a waste of time, you already know different, but not tonight." Nothing had come out of the parking lot yet.

Annie scribbled something on a piece of paper and stuck it in my pocket. "Call me. We'll have fun." She gave me a squeeze in a place she shouldn't've given me a squeeze. "If you don't call me, I'll have to come looking for you. And I'll find you. I'm good at finding people." She let me go and got out of the car. "Give me a call."

I smiled at her. "I'll give you a call."

She smiled back and walked away. I groaned quite a bit.

A silver Monte Carlo pulled out of the parking lot. I started my car and followed him.

Down Wilshire. I kept half a block behind. At the first stop light I took out Annie's paper. *Annie—HO9-5642.* I turned it over and wrote down the license number of the silver Monte Carlo. I followed him all the way to Santa Monica. He parked in front of a bar. I pulled in and drove to the far end. He didn't seem to see me. He got out of his car and went into the bar.

19

He came out walking like a man who'd just spent an hour in a bar. He went in the wrong direction, realized his mistake, turned and started for his car, then saw me leaning against it. He came forward slowly. He grinned at me and fumbled his keys out of his pocket. He slid them along the side of his car door and all the way to the lock and past it. I took the keys from him and opened the door. He got in and leaned his head against the rest.

"Can you drive?"

". . . Sure!" He pushed his keys toward the ignition.

"Wait a minute, Mr. Isenbart. I got something to say. We forced you into this. Your wife and me."

He leaned back with his head against the rest again.

"She came down to the office, she started giving me. . . ." His mind seemed to wander. "My wife's a child. She gets scared of things. She doesn't understand. . . ." He turned and peered at me like he wished he could read my mind. "I'm paying you to do what I want you to do! You better do it!"

I leaned down so my face was level with his. "What do you want me to do?"

He thought it over. "I don't know who he is. I don't think he's dangerous. He's just trying to. . . ." His mind went somewhere else again. He stared into the distance. "Someone's trying to scare me. He thinks I'll crack. But I won't crack. You keep him away from me. The kid. Keep him so I don't see him. My wife doesn't see him. Nobody at work sees him." His eyes blinked at me. "My wife can't handle this kind of thing. Got me?"

"I'm listening."

He nodded and kept nodding. "Couple weeks. All I need." He turned the key in the ignition. "Keep it confidential. I'll go along with it. Couple weeks. Shouldn't take more'n. . . ."

I reached in and touched his arm. "You sure you can drive?"

". . . I can drive."

He inched his way slowly toward Beverly Hills. He pulled into the driveway of a corner house. I drove past and went down to the next corner and turned and came halfway back and parked. The house was laid out just right for me. I had a clear view, there was no good way for anyone to come at it without me seeing.

Max Isenbart went into the house. I reached under the passenger seat and took out my Pearlcorder-S. It's smaller than a checkbook and no thicker than a deck of cards. It weighs 12 ounces with batteries. It's so sensitive you can record a conversation without taking it out of your pocket. It takes microcassettes that go for 60 minutes each. It costs, but I knew a guy and he gave me a price. And it's so damn small you can stick it under the passenger seat and nobody'll see it so nobody'll break into your car to steal it.

I plugged in the earphone and put in a microcassette and listened to Charles Ives. I unwrapped a tuna fish sandwich and got a Coke out of the ice bucket in the back and had dinner.

When it got as dark as it was going to get I turned off the Pearlcorder and stuck it under the seat and got out of my car and went toward the house.

Well-watered grass. Well-trimmed bushes. Swimming pool. Back door. I tried the door gently. Locked. Lock seemed okay. I looked through the window. The kitchen was empty. Dark.

I continued around the house and found a large picture window on the side. I looked through it at the living room. High ceilings, white walls, modern paintings, polished floor, mirrored bar, small tables with mirrored legs. He sure liked mirrors.

Metal hung from the ceiling, some kind of mobile. It could do something bad to you if its pieces started moving and you didn't.

Isenbart sat with a glass in his hand and there was a TV against the far wall and it was on and he didn't seem to be watching. Mrs. Isenbart came in and said something. He didn't seem to hear. She spoke again, got no response and went to the bar.

Isenbart jumped out of his chair. He turned toward her. He sat back down.

She went to him and said something. He looked away.

She went to the bar.

He got out of his chair and went to the bar and grabbed her by the arms and pulled her away from the bar.

She went across the room. He went after her. He seemed to be yelling. She took it in silence.

I went to the front door and rang the bell.

After several moments a peephole opened in the door and an eye looked out. The eye went away and the door unlocked and opened.

"I checked the door in back, Mr. Isenbart. It's locked. But someone stands by the side of the house over by the trees, they can see right in through that picture window. They can see anything that's going on in the living room pretty good. You got curtains on that window?"

He rubbed the side of his face and spoke quietly. "Yeah."

"Good. Close 'em. Good night, Mr. Isenbart."

I turned and walked toward the street. I waited till I heard the door close behind me. When I did I turned and looked at the house and in a dark window to the side I saw a face. Elizabeth Isenbart.

"The front door opened suddenly. Max Isenbart came out and down the walk. "I'm a little jumpy, Mr. Thieringer. I mean, it's been a long day." He held out his hand. "I just want you to know, I'm glad you're here. I really am."

I shook his hand. It was wet and cold like fear is wet and cold. The front door was still open. Mrs. Isenbart stood in it watching us.

Mr. Isenbart let go of my hand, stepped back, took a quick look down the street, then looked the other way, then looked at me. He nodded once and turned and went back to the house. He and his wife stood a moment at the front door and then went inside. I watched the front door close.

20

The last light in the house went out at just after one. I turned off the Pearlcorder and started my car and drove to the nearest phone. I called Maggie. There was no answer. There was supposed to be an answer. I called the service. "This's Fritz. Maggie leave a message for me?"

"Just a sec." Silence. "Yeah. She said something came up. You're supposed to call Paul. She gave me Paul's number, it's—"

"Forget it."

I figured she was probably really home so I dialed her apartment again and let it ring. Still no answer. Damn her. I called a couple other places she might be. She wasn't. Or at least they said she wasn't. I tried her apartment again and got no answer again. It was taking too damn long. I had to get back to Isenbart's house. I dialed another number.

"Hello?"

"It's Fritz. Anything up with you tonight?"

"The usual. Cards."

"Winning or losing?"

"Last time I looked, I wasn't exactly winning."

"Beverly Hills. Watching. Can you handle it? Now?"

"Now? *Right* now? It's one-fifteen already."

"I can go for another couple hours if I got to. How you doing on sleep?"

"Well, I slept all afternoon, I was planning to spend tonight earning some bread at the card table, but it doesn't seem to be working out that—"

"Look, you can't do it, tell me. I got to get back there and—"

"I'll do it! Hell, I'll do it. How bad is it? Should I bring something with bullets in it?"

". . . Yeah."

21

Ring.

Ring

Ring.

I kept my eyes closed. Maybe it'd go away.

Ring!

Ring!

It wasn't going away. "Hello?"

"I just got in. Paul's here. Why didn't you call him to replace you last night?"

"I called *you*, like I said I would. You didn't seem to be home."

"I had to go somewhere. Did you call the service? I left a message on the service."

"I called the service. Christ, you woke me out of a dream just now, you know that? Nubile young women were—"

"Paul says he was home all last night but you didn't call him."

"He's right, I didn't call him. I called Big George."

"What did you call Big George for!"

"Cause you were sitting in your apartment not answering your phone when I called you."

"I wasn't home!"

"Like hell you weren't. You been doing too goddamn many things behind my back lately, kiddo. I don't goddamn like it."

"Wash your mouth out with soap. There're ladies present."

"That's a highly debatable statement, kiddo."

"Suck eggs."

"Same to you, kiddo."

She hung up the phone. She hates it when I call her kiddo. I turned over and tried to sleep. No good. I pulled the phone to the bed and dialed.

"Carne Organization. Good morning."

"Glad to hear it's good, I was starting to wonder. Rittenhouse, please."

"Yes, sir. One moment, please."

It took more than a moment. I heard funny metallic sounds, then, "Rittenhouse," in a low impressive voice.

"Thieringer," I said in an equally false way.

"Fritz!" came back at me in his normal voice. "Must be a year! Up early these days!"

"So're you."

"We keep banker's hours around here. We're very professional, ain't you heard? Heard a rumor you're still hangin' your shingle with that skirt."

"Wilwood Building, third floor."

"Westwood? Movin' up in the world."

"Not me. Her. All it took was one look at the Wilwood Building, next thing I knew she had the lease signed, sign painters painting the door, the door spelled out *Investigations*, under that it said *M. McGuane*, under that *F. Thieringer*. You notice which one of us got stuck with second billing."

"Driven you nuts yet?"

"She's trying. What's up with you?"

"Got a case out in Compton. Goin' to make me famous. They had a carnival out there over the weekend. Must've rigged their wheel of fortune or somethin'. Somebody got mad and stole their carousel. Middle of the night. Took the whole damn thing. Only thing they left behind's tire tracks. I been goin' through the files. First time in twenty years. Last time was back East, Albany, New York. May 13, 1956."

"Maybe this's their twentieth reunion. How confidential can we get?"

"Confidential's you want."

"Doesn't he have the phones bugged any more?"

"The old man thinks he does. I found a way to disconnect the thing before all my calls." Sure. The funny metallic sounds I'd heard before he'd answered. "Sometimes I leave it operatin'. That drives him nuts. He can't figure out why I'd leave it operatin' sometimes and not others. Figures the bug must be defective. Every couple weeks he tries puttin' in a new one, or a new phone. Costin' him a goddamn fortune."

"Ever hear of a guy named Paul Brade?"

"What's he done to make him famous?"

"Used to work for you."

"That won't make him famous. Any stories come out of here, they got only one name on 'em. The old man's. See the pictures on the Mendenhall trial? Mendenhall, his lawyer, the old man? Carne didn't have a fuckin' thing to do with it. Mine. All mine. Comes time for someone to take the credit, you see who's standin' front and center."

"Take the cash and let the credit go. What do you call him the old man for? You're older'n he is."

"Nobody's older'n he is. Nobody's been older since the day he was born. The doctor held him up, he was wearin' a three-piece suit, he was smokin' a cigar and he needed a shave."

"Skip the bitters. Can we get back to business?"

"Paul Brade. Got it memorized already. Used to work here how recent?"

"He says recent."

"What about him?"

"That's what I'd like to know. Whatever you can give me."

"May take a while. Got to find that carousel."

"You know where to find me."

"Same place I find me. Wherever there's trouble."

22

I walked down the street near Isenbart's office to the Volkswagen. Big George was sitting in the driver's seat and his feet were sitting in the passenger's seat. His knees were sticking in the air. His head was resting against the driver's window and his face looked asleep. I stood there looking at him for a moment and then his eyes opened and one eye winked at me and his mouth smiled. I opened the passenger door. He swung his legs up to the dash-board so the soles of his shoes stared through the front window. I squeezed in beside him.

"Why don't you get a car that fits you?"

"Can't afford one. Didn't expect you so early. You said noon."

"Some wise guy woke me up with a phone call around nine. Couldn't get back to sleep. Anything?"

"Nope. Nobody with a limp, nobody with a scar." His near eye opened again. "You brought food?"

"Oranges and candy bars. Take your pick."

His hand reached over and picked candy, both bars. His mouth took four bites and there was nothing left of either of them.

It was a normal Los Angeles day. The sun was out, the smog was fighting it. What it added up to was heat. Plenty of it. Somewhere in the middle of it people were going nuts. People in this town are always going nuts. Nobody's ever figured out how to stop it. Nobody ever will.

"Got any more candy?"

"You ate all I had. Have an orange."

"Fuck, you eat like a native. Know what I got to do?" He went on before I could ask. "Got to generate some money is what I got to do. Should've done like you, hooked up with someone. Makes it look more legitimate, you got a partner."

"Pick a name, any name, put it on your door, put it on your cards."

His feet moved off the front window and stretched across me till they braced against the door. "What if a client wants to meet him?"

"Tell the client your partner's out on a case. Better that way. Between you and me, having a partner ain't the sweetest thing in the world."

His laugh filled the car. Filled what space was left that his body wasn't taking up. "Get a divorce, Fritz. Come in with me. Levison and Thieringer."

"Everyone wants to give me second billing."

His face turned sideways. "What'd you think, I said I was getting out?"

"Business'll pick up. Paint your office a new color. Take a bigger ad in the yellow pages."

He grunted. "Can't afford the ad I got." He flopped a hand as big as a catcher's mit over the steering wheel. "Maybe I ought to lower my rates."

"Better to raise 'em. Seems to impress people. They think you must be good or you couldn't get away with it."

A sigh the size of a windstorm came out of his mouth. His near eye opened. "That him? Across the street? Brown jacket?"

"Yeah."

"Thought so. Still got eyes, huh? Not much of a limp." Another sigh. "Going to take him?"

"You can do it."

He tried not to answer too quickly. "I can, if you want me to."

What the hell. "I want you to. Want to give him the idea there's lots of us watching him."

He tried to move his legs over to his side of the car, at the same time trying to act like he didn't care which one of us took the boy. "All right, I'll handle it, that's what you want."

"He had a gun yesterday. Probably'll have it today. He's just a kid. I don't know what his motives are. Try not to hurt him."

He grabbed his right foot with both hands and pulled it past me. "Kids kill, too, case you haven't heard."

"Let him get all the way up to the fifth floor if you want, but don't let him get into the office." I leaned forward in my seat. "Hot day to be wearing a jacket."

"What?"

"His jacket's hanging a little lower on the left side."

Big George peered over the steering wheel. "Uh-huh. I can take the gun off him, if you'd like."

"Try not to. Don't want to spook him too early. But don't let him hurt you."

He growled out a laugh and shot me a look. "Don't take anything from my car while I'm gone, Fritz."

I said nothing. I kept watching the boy. Big George unwound from the Volkswagen and went out the door without tearing it off. He lumbered across the street like a worn-out grizzly who'd seen too many fights and slouched into the building ten paces behind the boy. I tried the glove compartment and it was unlocked but all it had was road maps and a flashlight with dead batteries and a broken crystal.

23

By the time the boy came out of the building I was sitting in my own car. The boy held his arm and moved quickly. He walked down the street and got into a beat-up green Mustang. The Mustang didn't move.

Big George came out of the building and stood there a moment letting himself be seen, then came over to me. He was moving quicker, his steps were almost bouncy, like he didn't have a care in the world.

"We went up together in the elevator. Soon's we reached the fifth floor, he started out. I grabbed him by the neck of the jacket and pulled him back. I faced him into the corner and hit the button for the second floor. We went down to the second floor. He started reaching for the gun. I had to slap his hands a little. I pushed the button for the fourth floor, we went to the fourth floor. Then I put him in the other corner and we went down to the lobby."

"I told you not to be too rough with him."

He looked at his hands. "I wasn't too rough."

"Maybe you didn't mean to be. He look high?"

"Like the birds."

"He's still around. That green Mustang down the block."

Big George turned his head. "Want me to go down and encourage him to move?"

"God, no. Leave him in one piece. Go back to the front of the building and stand there. Look down the street at him. He'll get the idea."

Big George nodded and turned toward the building but then turned back. "Fritz, I just wanted to say. . . ." He looked at his hands again, then mumbled, "Thanks."

He turned quickly and went to the building.

24

I dialed and it rang and it got answered.

"McGuane and Thieringer."

"Good afternoon, sunshine of my existence."

"Oh. You. Thought it might be someone interesting."

"Nope. Just me."

"I haven't got time to listen to any apologies regarding this morning's conversation. I'm trying to do some business here."

"Good. I'm on the boy. Up Laurel Canyon Boulevard, west on Kirkwood, all the way, last house. Cheap-looking place. You could probably rent the whole thing for a hundred a month. Ninety, you knew how to negotiate. Haven't got a look at the inside yet. Big enough. Two stories."

"Any trouble?"

"Not yet. We owe Big George for nine hours. Better mark it down.'"

"I'm not too happy about that."

"All right. Send Paul out here."

". . . You mean it?"

"I don't know. Yeah. Send him quickly before I get smart and change my mind. I'm parked a hundred yards down from the house. Tell him to park a hundred yards behind me and walk up. Tell him, he sees anyone else around, wait till he doesn't see anyone else around."

"Don't go away before he gets there."

Wouldn't think of it.

25

He parked where he was supposed to and he sat there longer than he needed to and then he finally came up the road so slowly a snail could've beaten him. I took my eyes off the rear-view mirror and looked at my book.

He got in beside me and waited to see if I was going to say anything. I didn't. I waited to see if he was going to say anything. He didn't. I liked that.

I looked up the street. "Last house on the right. There was a girl out back hanging laundry, little while ago. I couldn't get close enough to see if there's more'n the two of 'em."

He nodded. "What're we going to do?"

"Sit. The kid comes out, we're going to follow."

I started reading again. He settled quietly into the passenger's seat but after a minute he was tapping his foot. Another minute and he took out one of those six-inch pocket telescopes that cost about a buck.

"What's that for?"

"To watch the house."

"Is the house moving?" He looked at me quizzically. "Look, Paul, someone goes by, they see you sitting here with that, next thing you know we'll have cops all over us."

He put the telescope into his pocket. I started reading again. His foot started tapping again.

"Paul, you were working at Carne, they ever teach you to sit still?"

His foot stopped tapping. I took out the Pearlcorder and put on Neil Diamond. It usually works for me, I hoped it'd work for him. I reached behind me and opened the ice bucket and took out a Coke. He watched me reach back and saw my hats.

"Holy cow. How many hats you got back there?"

"As many as'll fit. Maggie said you had a customer in the office when I called. Was she telling the truth?"

"Small guy. Very nervous."

"They're all very nervous. They weren't very nervous, we'd be out of business." I gave him a Coke to get him occupied with something besides why we were there.

"He said he was going to be carrying a lot of money tonight, and he wanted someone to go along with him."

How much'd he mean by a lot?"

"He wouldn't say."

"That's a good sign. How long a job?"

"Couple hours, after dinner. He thought he'd be finished by ten or eleven."

"He wanted the guard armed?"

"He said it might be a good idea. Whatever Maggie thought was necessary."

"She'll probably take an arsenal."

A car drove past us. A yellow Chevette. It went all the way up to the last house and parked next to the Mustang. A boy got out. About nineteen or twenty. He looked to be at least four inches taller than the one I'd followed there. You wouldn't mistake one for the other. He walked across the road and up the steps and into the house.

"Where's he taking the money to?"

Paul kept his eyes on the house. "He didn't say."

"Maggie ask him?"

"Yeah. He said he couldn't tell her."

"She ask him if it was somewhere in town?"

"Yeah." Paul inched forward in the seat, watching the house. "He told her he wasn't sure yet."

"She ask him if he'd ever paid blackmail before?"

It sat there a minute, then Paul looked at me. "Yeah. He said it wasn't blackmail."

I looked at my book like I wasn't all that interested in the conversation any more. "But he sounded a little more nervous after she asked him."

That got him pretty bad. "What makes you so sure it's blackmail?"

I wasn't sure. Maggie hadn't been sure either. That's why she'd asked. "Any other visitors?"

He turned in the seat to face me. "One."

I kept my eyes on the book. "Well?"

"I don't know. Maggie took him into the office and closed the door."

"What'd he look like?"

His thumb rubbed the side of his leg. "He looked like he could use a meal."

I nodded slightly. Let's see if I could do it again. She took him into the office and closed the door and he needed a meal. If I got this one right he'd really think I was something. *Needed a meal. She closed the door.* I gave it a try. "Curly blond hair, about six feet, big shoulders, good looking?"

His hand clenched but not much. Enough to let me know I had him. I stayed quiet. He tried to wait me out but it got him nowhere. "Who is he?"

I turned a page. "Nobody. Just a guy we know."

A guy named Harry. Maggie came home one day, he wasn't there. He'd packed his clothes and left. No note, nothing. The next morning she got a telegram from Mexico telling her he'd filed for divorce. Two months later he finally got up enough guts to come to see her. He told her why he'd married her in the first place. He said he'd married her because he'd been scared and lonely and insecure and hadn't thought he could make it unless they were married. Now three years had passed and he found he was scared and lonely but he didn't feel insecure any more and he didn't think he could make it unless he was alone. So he left her. That's what he told her. That's what she says he told her. I don't know if it's what he really told her. You never do know about these things. Anyway, he's an actor and whenever he's out of work and out of funds he pays her a visit. She gives him money, he says goodbye. Some people don't know how to say goodbye. Some people know how to say it, but it never means anything.

The girl who'd been hanging laundry came out of the house. Paul turned front to watch her. "I wonder why they call it blackmail."

I pretended to look at my book but kept both eyes on the girl. "That's how it used to be done. They'd write you a letter and send it in a black envelope. The letter'd tell you what they had on you. And how much they expected you to pay, if you wanted 'em to keep it quiet. Sometimes there'd just be a black dot in the corner of the envelope, but when it started the whole envelope was black."

The girl came down the steps and crossed the road and got into the green Mustang. She pulled into the road and came past us.

I put down my book and leaned back. "I'm going to sleep. Our boy comes out of the house, wake me up. You get hungry, there's a couple oranges next to the ice bucket. There's a jar of peanut butter in the glove compartment."

"I'm not hungry."

"Grab food when you can get it, grab sleep when you can get it, grab anything when you can get it. There's going to be too many times you won't be able to grab anything." I adjusted the seat into a better angle for sleeping. "You take any peanut butter, don't make too much noise taking the top of the jar off. I sleep light."

It was quiet for a moment but only a moment.

"Think we ought to go up there and look around? I can go up there, you want me to."

"I don't want you to."

It stayed quiet.

26

When I woke up it was almost dark. Paul was reading my book. The green Mustang was back.

"I said anything to you about your hair yet?"

Paul looked up. "What about it?"

"There's too much of it. You got enough hair to put rugs on half the agents in Hollywood. You get in a fight, it's going to be in your eyes."

"I like it this way."

"Someone'll give it a yank and the next thing you know you'll be lying in a bed with your neck in a brace." I straightened my seat to its sitting position. "You're not proving anything, you know. A couple years ago, most of us learned it doesn't make us any older, or any younger, and it just takes longer to dry when you wash it."

He went back to the book. "I like it long."

I was glad I was finally getting a rise out of him on something. "Go get us something to eat."

"What?"

"Food. Nourishment. Go to a burger pit or some place." I ticked off the items on my fingers. "I want two cheeseburgers and some french fries. Find a fruit stand, pick up a couple apples and some bananas. Whatever looks edible. Pick up the cheeseburgers last so they'll still be warm by the time you get back here."

"Where'm I supposed to find that stuff around here?"

"Hurry up. I'm hungry."

He jiggled on the seat. "What if the boy takes off while I'm gone?"

"I'll tell him to wait till you get back."

He grimaced and put down my book and got out of my car and walked down to his car. I watched him in the rear-view mirror. As soon as he drove off I flipped my hat into the back and got out of the car and crossed into the woods.

I worked my way through the woods, tree by tree. The last tree took me within fifteen feet of the house. I walked forward slowly. I wasn't so much worried about them seeing me moving in the dark. It was all the dry twigs on the ground—anything snapped, it could sound like a gunshot out there.

I stood in shadows near a window. The living room showed a lot of bare floor. Oversized pillows. No chairs. Plants. Bookshelves made of boards and cinder blocks. Posters on the walls. Beads hanging over the windows.

The kind of stuff lots of kids go for at that age. Then they grow up and settle for pretty much the same things their parents settled for.

The three of them were in there, lying on the pillows. There was a portable TV on the floor, showing an old movie. Alan Ladd, Brian Donlevy, Veronica Lake. Next to the TV there was a large apothecary bottle. The oversized kind you often see filled with jelly beans or candy canes. This one didn't have jelly beans or candy canes. It had pills.

The girl crawled across the floor and took the top off the jar and reached in for a pill and popped it into her mouth.

I worked my way around the house. Dark rooms behind dark windows. I couldn't see in. I pressed my ear against the windows and listened carefully and heard nothing.

I went back to the first window. The three of them were still there.

I picked up a stick and threw it against a tree. It made a good amount of noise but none of them reacted. I waited a few minutes, then did the same thing again, trying to make it louder. Then I did it a third time. Still no reaction from inside the house.

27

"You owe me two forty-two for the cheeseburgers and the fruit."

"I'm a little short right now. Trust me on it?"

Paul nodded. We ate in silence. I finished first. I waited till he was finished. "Want to try the house?"

"Now?"

"Now." He opened the door. I grabbed his arm. "Not

so fast. Work your way along the trees. There'll probably be lots of dry twigs. Be careful where you walk. You hear any doors or windows open, freeze where you are. Then get next to a tree and stay there till it gets quiet again."

He bit his upper lip. "Okay. Let's go."

"You can handle it yourself. Just take it slow. See if there's any more in the house'n the three we know're in there. Don't spend too much time at it. Any windows you can't see in, forget about 'em."

He nodded and got out. He went slowly up the road, past the house next to us, then off the road and into the trees. When he disappeared in the darkness I gently edged open my car door and got out. I listened and heard something crack. A twig. Then I heard nothing.

A few minutes later I got a glimpse of him close to the house. For a second he passed through a shaft of light from an upstairs window, then I lost him.

I saw him again outside a downstairs window. He inched closer, looked inside, slid down to the ground, crossed under the window and kept going. He went around the house and I couldn't see him any more.

I heard something in the woods to my right. I got into the car and took out a flashlight and snapped it on and made it look like I was reading my book.

He got in beside me, breathing heavily. "The two guys were in the living room. The one we're following went out. I circled around the house, by the time I got to the kitchen the other guy was in there. He got a beer and went out. I saw him again, in a bedroom. The girl was in there, trying on dresses. The guy got something out of a desk and then he went out. I saw him and the other one in the living room again."

"All right." I closed my book and turned off the flashlight. "I better go see what the layout is myself, so we'll both know it."

I got up there fast enough, the girl was still in the bedroom, still trying on dresses. When she took off the dress she was wearing high heels, nothing else. She went into a dancer's pose, went through different positions, danced in front of a full-length mirror as if in a dream. Or a haze. She reached out for a partner—Nureyev, Baryshnikov—found him—danced with him—

She went to the desk and set up a folding mirror and started fooling with her hair. Wrapped it tight and pinned it in place. The apothecary jar sat beside her on the desk. Without looking at it she reached in and took out a pill and popped it into her mouth. It would be easier for her to see Nureyev now.

She went back to the full-length mirror and took off the heels and went through the ballet positions again. I'd liked it better with the heels. She went close to the mirror and cupped both breasts in her hands and rubbed her fingers across her nipples and rubbed her hands down her body and offered herself to the mirror.

The boy with the limp came in. He went to the desk and took a pill from the apothecary jar and swallowed it and took the jar and went out.

The girl unpinned her hair and shook it loose. She put on her shoes, put on her dress, turned off the light and went out.

I went around to another lit window. The kitchen. The boy with the limp was in there and so was the apothecary jar. The girl came in and opened the refrigerator and took out food and opened a cupboard and took out a mixing bowl and a pan.

I went through the woods and back to the car.

28

They came out of the house. The girl went to the Chevette, the boys lagged behind. The one with the limp picked up stones from the road and went through the motions of a baseball pitcher, throwing stones at a tree one at a time. He didn't hit the tree, his coordination looked off. The other boy tried and couldn't hit it either. The girl yelled at them. It got her nowhere. She opened the car door, slammed it shut, leaned against the car.

"Paul. Listen carefully. Get your car and follow 'em. They go anywhere near Isenbart's house, drive up next to them and honk your horn till they go away. They come back here in less'n an hour, honk your horn twice to warn me in case I'm still in the house. Twice, just twice. You do it more'n that, they might notice. Go."

Paul got out of the car and went down the road. It was worth the gamble. They were all high and the girl was going with them. None of that had to mean a thing, but they weren't in a hurry. That probably meant something.

The boys kept throwing stones at the tree. The girl yelled at them again and picked up a stone and threw it at the boys. When she threw another one they all got into the Chevette.

The Chevette started down the hill, not coming slow enough or straight enough. The beams of its headlights brushed down the road in a crazy zigzag. They slid through the darkness toward my car, across the windshield. I was already bent down under the dashboard. The lights slapped over me and away.

29

I tapped the front door lightly with my fingers and got no answer so I knocked several times with my fist. Nothing came to investigate. I slipped plastic gloves on my hands and opened my pocket knife and started to work on the lock. The lock was a joke.

The house was darker than the devil's conscience. I took out my pencil flashlight and went through the living room to the kitchen. The back door was latched. I un-latched it and pulled it open several inches and left it that way.

The kitchen table was covered with dinner dishes, three glasses, none of which matched, the apothecary jar. I took some pills from it and held them in my hand. They felt as light as dreams and just as deceptive. I put them in my pocket.

In the living room a corner of a magazine stuck out from under a pillow. I checked it for a subscription label. Jane Harvey. A postcard on the bookcase said "Dear Jane, We may come up to Los Angeles in July. Steve thinks he can get off after the fourth. I'll let you know when we're definite. Barbara."

I went to the bedroom the girl had been in and opened drawers. Nothing much.

I tried the bedroom next to it. A couple books, no names in them. I opened drawers in the desk. I found a picture of a boy and a girl, and the boy was the one with the limp. I found another picture of an older woman. I found some letters addressed to Gene Morrison. The letters told me nothing else. A couple bills. I searched the drawers of the dresser. No more knives, no guns.

Glossy faces in glossy pictures stared at me from the walls. I let my flashlight play against them. Stills from old movies. Cornel Wilde, Joel McCrea, Barbara Stan-wyck, others I didn't recognize.

From somewhere far away a car horn sounded twice.

I went down the hall and passed stairs to the second floor, no time to look up there, I went through to the kitchen and through the back door and closed it gently behind me and turned toward the woods.

From somewhere far away a car horn sounded again.

30

The Chevette was parked on a diagonal in the middle
of the road and right behind it was Paul's car. Right behind that was the girl. The two boys stood in front of
Paul's car and hammered the hood with their fists.

I moved through the woods as quickly as I could.
Morrison started rapping his fists against the driver's window. The other boy climbed on the hood and sat on it
and started bouncing up and down.

I started for the road. There was a house opposite
me and its front door opened. A woman came out. I
moved behind a tree.

The girl walked away from Paul's car and went
across the road toward the house. Paul had a chance to
back the car down the road, but he didn't do it.

The girl said something to the woman at the house.
The woman stepped back, went into the house, and closed
the door. The boy sitting on Paul's hood got to his feet
and climbed to the top of the car, stood on it and stamped
with his feet.

The girl came back to the car and said something
to the boy and to Morrison. Then she turned and went
toward the Chevette. The boy climbed down from the
roof and went to her. They seemed to argue.

Morrison walked away from the driver's window,
walked around the front of Paul's car and went to the
passenger side. All I could see of him was his back.

The girl yelled something at Morrison. Morrison
kept facing the passenger window and kept his back to
the others, his back to me.

The girl got into the Chevette and started it and
drove up the road. The boy turned to Morrison and

yelled something. Then he turned and ran after the Chevette.

The Chevette parked opposite the house. The girl got out and crossed the road and went up the steps and into the house. The boy reached the house and ran up the steps behind her.

I could see Paul's face behind his windshield. His face was still. His lips were drawn back away from his teeth. Both his hands were showing on top of the steering wheel. I moved closer to see more of Morrison than his back. Then I saw his right hand, and the gun in it. And I had nothing to stop him with.

31

Morrison hit the window on the passenger side with his gun. The window cracked. "Get out of there! Get out!" A moment passed, I heard a click, the car door opened. Paul got out. They faced each other across the top of the car. Morrison rested his right arm on the roof and pointed the gun at Paul's face.

I couldn't see Morrison's hand, if it was shaking like it had with the knife. I didn't have to see it. I could hear the gun butt tapping a nervous tattoo against the roof of Paul's car. I slipped behind a tree. "Morrison. Gene Morrison. I'm behind you. I have a gun." Silence. I peered around the edge of the tree. "I have a gun, Gene. Don't move."

Morrison didn't move. Neither did Paul.

"Paul. Get down."

Paul didn't move.

"Paul! Get down!"

Paul's face went away. Morrison was left aiming at nothing.

I couldn't stop to let Morrison think. "Take it easy,

Gene. I don't want to hurt you." He didn't move. "Listen to me carefully, Gene. Hold your right hand out and drop the gun." He still didn't move. "Hold out your right hand and drop the gun." His hand didn't move. His head turned, slowly, toward my voice. But then all he saw was the tree, and my right eye looking around its edge. "Do what I say, Gene! Drop the gun!" He looked at my eye and his right hand moved away from the roof. The gun moved slowly, in my direction. The gun kept moving. "Drop the gun in the road!"

The gun dropped to the dirt.

"Lie down in the road, Gene. Turn your face toward the car." He hesitated, then went down. He lay on his stomach. He looked toward the car.

I came out from behind the tree and walked to the gun and picked it up and put it in my pocket. "Get in the car, Paul. Turn on the motor."

I kept my eyes on Morrison. I heard Paul moving on the far side of the car and heard the car door open and close and heard the key in the ignition and the motor starting.

"All right, Gene. You can get up. I won't hurt you."

Morrison got up. Then he turned and saw my hands were empty. He came at me with both fists.

I turned him around and pushed him against the car. I leaned against him and pulled the door open. The seat was covered with broken glass. I pushed the seat forward and forced Morrison into the back and went in after him.

32

Morrison started yelling as soon as the car moved. The car went off the road and almost into a tree. Morrison dove forward. He tried to claw his way to the front door. I pulled him back. His mouth opened and he yelled again.

He went for my throat. I pushed him into the corner and held him there.

Paul pulled the car back to the road.

Morrison went limp. I let him loose. That was a mistake. He started all over again. He reached forward and wrapped an arm around Paul's neck and pulled. The car swerved out of its lane. We all flew backward. Then Paul hit the brakes and we all fell forward.

Paul started over the front seat with his fist back. I reached forward to stop him. Morrison lunged. I tried to stop him. Morrison's hand swung. So did Paul's. One of them got me in the face. I shoved Morrison into the corner.

Paul came halfway over the front seat again. "You goddamn son of a bitch! I'll tear your goddamn fucking head off!" He reached out. Morrison squirmed against the side of the car. "You stop moving and shut up! I'll tear your fucking head off! Understand?" Paul's face was red as a beet. Morrison nodded. Paul glared at him, then turned to me. "Your nose."

"What?"

"Your nose, Fritz. It's bleeding."

I put my hand to my nose. It came away with blood. I took out a handkerchief and leaned my head back. Paul turned in his seat and the car moved up the hill. Morrison stayed quiet.

Morrison huddled in the corner with both arms wrapped around himself like he was freezing. His eyes looked out of focus. Paul was hunched over the steering wheel, breathing like he'd just run the mile. I took away my handkerchief and looked at it. The bleeding had almost stopped. I turned to Morrison. "All right, Gene. We better talk."

"I don't want to talk!"

Paul turned and glared at him. Morrison turned his face to the window. Then he reached into a pocket. I pulled his hand out. Pills spilled out of it, onto the floor. He reached for them but I stopped him. He turned and tried to roll down the window. I took his arm.

"Don't touch me!"

"Don't touch the window."

"I'll touch it if I want to touch it!" He ripped away from me and his fingers slapped at the window like moths against a lampshade.

"He said don't touch it!" Paul said. "Stop it!"

Morrison stopped slapping the window. He tried to hide deeper in the corner. He squeezed his hands to his mouth. "I want to go home."

I took his gun out of my pocket. "Got a permit for this?" His fingers covered his mouth and his nose. "You don't have a permit, we'll have to take you to the cops."

He sneaked a look at Paul, then looked away. "I got a permit for it."

I put the gun back into my pocket. He reached down suddenly and before I could stop him he had a pill from the floor. He popped it into his mouth and swallowed it quickly. Then he laughed insanely. He went for the window again.

"Leave it alone!" Paul said.

Morrison jerked back, then opened his mouth and let out a yell. Paul reached for him.

"All right, Paul. Easy. Nobody's going to hear him."

Paul stared at me. Morrison kept yelling. Paul turned in his seat and faced front. I put my hands over my ears and waited for Morrison to get tired. They usually do, sooner or later.

I started again softly. "Want to tell me what you got the gun for?" He put his fingers over his face. "Okay. I got a message for you, Gene. He might be willing to pay, you give me a reasonable number. Maybe it's just you been asking too much, so far. What's your price?"

His fingers opened and his eyes looked through them. "A million dollars."

"That sounds reasonable."

His fingers stayed open. "Two million?"

"Sure you need that much?"

His fingers came down. His mouth grinned. "I'm just watching him. You can't stop me from watching him."

"Watch him. But then we got to watch you. There's

70

lots of us. We're working in shifts, night and day. Seven of us. We can keep it up a pretty long time."

His face hardened. "You don't scare me!"

"I didn't think we did."

"I'll get help! I got friends!"

"Your friends put you up to it?" He pressed his nose against the window and started to hum. "Sure you can count on your friends? Maybe they're taking you for a ride, Gene. What've they promised you?"

"You got seven men on me? My friends got twenty men on you! You better be careful!" He leaned forward and laughed in my face, then looked sideways to see if Paul was doing anything. Paul was just sitting there, shaking his head. Morrison started humming again, a thin tune, hardly any melody to it.

I opened my window and let the night drift in to cool us. "Back to where we came from, Paul. Better make it quick."

33

Paul stopped the car at the bottom of the road. I got out. Morrison came out swinging. I snapped my head out of his reach but it started my nose bleeding again. Morrison laughed. "You aren't so tough."

"Don't get overconfident. I just got a glass nose." I took out my wallet and dug out a card and handed it to him.

"What's this?"

I put my handkerchief against my nose. "That's my card." He took my card and dropped it in the road. "Go ahead. I've seen my card treated a hell of a lot worse." He spat at it and rubbed his shoe over it. "That's the only card you get, Gene. You don't keep it, you won't know where to pick up your gun."

His face changed. "It's mine! I want it back!"

"Give us a call, we'll discuss it. Call collect if you don't have the money. We'll pick up the charges."

He didn't know what to make of it. He stepped back. "Okay. Keep the gun. I got another one in the house." He took one more step back. I didn't move. He stuck his face out. "You letting me go?"

"Looks like it, doesn't it?"

He stepped sideways and kicked at the car. Paul jumped out on the other side.

"Paul—stay where you are."

Paul stayed. Morrison looked at him. At me. Then he laughed. Cut it short. Rubbed his hand across his chest. "You don't scare me. Either one of you."

"We're not trying to, are we?"

He rubbed his hand along the side of his face. He pointed a finger at Paul. "You stay where you are!" He came forward carefully, kept his eyes on Paul and picked up my card. He wiped it on his pants and started moving backwards. Finally he turned and started running. He disappeared into darkness. Then his steps stopped.

"Move away from the car, quick."

I went off on my side of the road and Paul went off on his. We did it just in time. A soft swishing sound came down the road. The rock hit the dirt about five feet in front of the car, bounced and hit the fender, rolled to a stop. Laughter came down the road at us. Then it was quiet.

I walked toward the car. Paul came around and knelt to inspect the damage. "He's crazy."

"It's the goddamn pills. And he wanted to see how far he could push us before we'd get mad."

Paul's hand found the dent next to the headlight. "Look at this."

"One of the fringe benefits of the occupation."

Paul looked up the road. "He's crazy."

"Don't be so quick to figure out how other people see the world. Sometimes you can't even be sure you understand how you see it yourself. He's got the card. He ever comes down from the clouds, maybe he'll be smart enough to talk to us about whatever it is he thinks he's doing. Or someone's paying him to do."

Paul shook his head. "He's probably going up to his house to get his other gun."

"I don't think he's got another one. I didn't see one. I'm not so sure he's got any friends either. I think it was just talk."

"He's crazy."

"Apparently you were never his age. I was, fortunately for him. We'll leave him alone and give him some time, then we'll try and crack him."

I started up the road. Paul mumbled something and I turned. "What'd you say?"

He hesitated, then, "You sure you know what you're doing?"

"No. I probably don't. One of the highlights of this business, you usually don't. Till we do, or think we do, we'll give him time and see if he comes down from those pills." I kept my eyes on Paul and something occurred to me. "I told you to honk twice. Just twice. What happened?"

He froze just like he had before when he was in the car and Morrison had the gun on him. "They were driving up the road too fast. I was worried you wouldn't hear me. They'd catch you in the house."

"Instead of catching me they caught you. Why didn't you take off?"

"I didn't get a chance." He moved sideways. "They stopped too quick and—"

I waved my hand. "Okay. You might as well go home. One of us'll be enough, the rest of the night." I started up the hill.

His voice came louder. "You should've—"

"I should've what?" I turned quickly and came back down to him. "Broken his head? Like you were ready to? That would've got us someplace?"

"I don't know—"

"I don't know either." I put my finger into his chest. "I don't know whose side we're on yet. I like to know that before I break heads. Whatever's going on with you, you better control it."

"He had a gun on me!"

"He didn't have it when you went after him, did he?"

I took away my finger and moved up the hill.

"Fritz. . . . You were behind that tree. . . . You didn't have a gun, did you?"

I stopped. "No. I don't like guns. They have a tendency to go off too often when they're not supposed to."

He said nothing and just stood still. Then he turned suddenly and got into his car and drove off. I watched him go. I wondered what the hell that'd been about.

I walked up the road into darkness. I waited, and listened, and heard nothing. I went slowly to my car and shined my flashlight at it. No damage. I got inside and took a Coke from the ice bucket and drank. I pulled the handkerchief away from my nose. The bleeding had stopped again. I still had the aspirin bottle from the day before. I took it out and washed down two pills with more Coke. At the same time I was wishing the damn aspirin would stop coming in so handy. For want of anything better to do, I took Morrison's gun from my pocket and opened it up to take out the bullets. The gun was empty.

34

A car approached on the road behind me. I clicked off the Pearlcorder, took out the earplug and adjusted my rear-view mirror. A red Volvo. It stopped. The motor turned off. The door opened and the driver got out and started walking toward my car. The walking was very stiff and slow.

She pulled open the door and got in and then shut the door too loudly. She took a deep breath. "What're you doing? Just sitting here?"

I watched her carefully. "I was reading a play before. Paul must've taken it when I wasn't looking."

She nodded weakly. "That reminds me, Paul said he can't find his carved-bone letter opener. Have you seen it around?"

"No." I kept my eyes on her.

"Uh-huh." She was breathing heavy. She leaned forward and rested her head in her hands. "Any action with the boy?"

"His name's Gene Morrison. I took his gun away from him." I tried to get a look at her eyes but she wasn't letting me. "It wasn't loaded. The gun. I talked to him a little."

"Uh-huh." She shook her head back and forth slightly. "I thought you wanted to rattle him some more before you talked to him."

"I did." I touched her leg lightly. "Things didn't work out that way."

"Uh-huh." She straightened her back and let her head fall back. Then her hands started to go up toward her throat but changed their mind halfway there and settled in her lap. "What'd you make of him? The boy."

"A small dog who likes to bite ankles." I raised my hand slowly till it was behind her neck. I rubbed her there gently. "He doesn't have the brains to check how thick the ankles are before he sinks his teeth into 'em. He's in the clouds. Pills." She sighed. I kept rubbing. "I think he's just a mixed-up kid. I don't think he knows what he's doing."

She suddenly came alive and turned toward me and laughed. "What's the matter, Fritz? Does he remind you of someone?"

I forced a smile and watched her eyes carefully. "They did a study of highly successful men, Mag. Found out most of 'em went through a delinquent period when they were boys."

She took her eyes off me. Her hands started for her

throat again but stopped. "Some of them never got through the delinquent period."

"Maybe." I swallowed hard. The muscles in her neck and shoulders were still tight as hell. "He thinks he's tougher'n he is. Wild."

She chuckled. It was hollow. "So he *does* remind you of you."

"I was never wild."

She patted my leg. "You were never tough either."

"I kept it within bounds. They never convicted me of anything."

"That's the law for you, Fritz."

She'd answered me quick so I still kept it going. "Actually, that part of it was worth it. Gave me a fine understanding of our legal system."

"And now you're repentant!"

"Hardly."

She hesitated as if confused. "But you're feeling compassion. For the boy. Gene Morrison."

"Just following instructions. Mrs. Isenbart said she didn't want us to hurt him."

She faced me and laughed aloud. "Since when do you follow instructions?"

"Since next year."

She stopped. She faced front. Her fingers went lightly to her throat. I still didn't say anything about it. She said, "How about Paul? Did he handle himself okay?"

I could've spent an hour on that one but I didn't. "Once Paul gets going, he's a real tiger."

She nodded. "I told you he'd be all right." She rotated her head slightly. I couldn't tell how bad it was, it was too dark and her eyes were off me again. "Got you a roast beef sandwich. In case you're hungry."

"Fine. Where is it?"

"It's. . . ." She looked at her lap. She sighed. "Must've left it in the car. I'll go back and get it."

I took her arm and stopped her. "I'll get it."

She nodded.

I walked back to her car. At first I thought she was wrong, there was no sandwich. Then I saw it. It was down on the floor next to the gas pedal. The way it'd been flattened she must've been putting her foot down on the sandwich, not the gas pedal. It was bad all right. I stayed there a moment and tried to calm down, then I picked up the sandwich and came back to my car.

I opened the foil and straightened out the sandwich. I offered it to her and she finally took half. She didn't bite into it.

"I was on a job tonight, Fritz." She paused. She stayed quiet. One hand came out and reached toward my glove compartment. Her fingers couldn't open it so I opened it for her. I took out a pint bottle of vodka.

She shook her head. "No. Where's your flashlight?"

I kept my voice even and showed no emotion. "It's in there."

"Shine it on me."

I braced myself and took out the flashlight and shined it on her. Her hand reached toward the collar of her blouse and pulled away the scarf. She turned to face me. Marks on her throat stared back at me.

35

It took her about two minutes and several deep breaths and then she got on with it.

"I got to Mr. Lewis's house a little before six. He came out with a big briefcase. We drove down to Pico and Robertson and parked on the street. A pay phone started ringing. He jumped out and answered it. We drove all the way down to Santa Monica and Lincoln. He pulled over to the curb and started looking around. I told him I saw a pay phone across the street. He made a U and we waited a couple minutes, then it started ringing.

"We headed for the beach. Another phone. It was already ringing by the time we got there. While Lewis was talking I got out of the car and put my hand over the mouthpiece and told him I wanted to know where we were going next. 'Malibu,' he whispered. I told him I wanted to know where in Malibu. He said he was supposed to go down to a bar, go into the parking lot, leave his car there, unlocked, and go into the bar. He was supposed to wait twenty minutes, come back out, and drive home.

"I took the phone away from him and said tell the man it's no deal, you'll be in the car, if he wants the money he's got to come for it. Lewis just looked at me. I had to pretend I was going to hang up the phone. Then Lewis said what I'd just told him to. Then Lewis whispered the guy wouldn't do it that way. Then I said to tell him either he does it that way or he gets no money. Then Lewis told him. It worked."

"It did? Sounds like the other guy was a schmuck."

"I thought so, too. I tried to pump Lewis about just what it was. He wouldn't tell me a damn thing. I let it go till we got to the bar. When we drove into the lot I said, 'Look, you hired me to protect you, but I have to know some things or I leave, right now. What's he got on you? What're we buying? Tell me fast or you're on your own.'

"Lewis didn't like it any more'n I did, but he talked. It was his daughter. She's sixteen. She was out on the beach and she met this man. He told her he was a professional photographer. He took some pictures. They ended up in a motel and he took some more pictures. About a week later Mr. Lewis received two of them. Then the man called and said the rest of the photos and the negatives'd cost five thousand dollars."

"Was tonight the first payoff?"

"I didn't get to hear any more of it. I heard someone moving in the sand. I told Lewis to keep quiet and look front. I heard a couple of shoes leave the sand and hit concrete and the steps came closer. He waited a minute, then he came over and stuck his hand in the window. He had a forty-four Magnum. If anyone came walking by, they'd see it and he'd panic and shoot.

"He said to Lewis, 'I told you to come alone.' I said, 'I'm Mrs. Lewis, before we give you the money I want to see the pictures.' He said he didn't give a fuck what I wanted and he turned the gun toward me. I told him if he shot the gun the parking lot was going to be full of people, and I still wanted to see the pictures.

"He told us to get out of the car and go over to the sand. I grabbed the briefcase away from Mr. Lewis and went over to the sand. Lewis came after me. The guy waited for us to get pretty far out. He had the gun down at his side. He sailed an envelope at us and laughed and told us the pictures were worth it and told me to throw the money over to him. I went over to the envelope and picked it up. The money, he said, and brought the gun up, waist level. I stepped in front of Mr. Lewis and gave him the envelope. He ripped it open and the negatives weren't there and then he got excited and started forward. By that time the guy had his gun aimed right at us. It was a good twenty-five feet, it was dark, I didn't know if he could shoot or not, and I knew we didn't have the negatives, so I was stuck.

"The guy said, 'This time you get the pictures, next time you get the negatives.' He sounded a little nervous and I figured we better get out of there. I swung the brief-case back to throw it. Lewis tried to stop me but he couldn't. I threw the thing as far as I could. It was dark enough, I heard it land but I couldn't see where. I told the man to call us tomorrow and we'd get the money for the negatives and I started pulling Lewis over to the car. Lewis didn't want to go. The guy was twice Lewis's size and he had a gun and Lewis wanted to go after him.

"I got Lewis into the car and drove around the back of the parking lot to the far side of the bar where the guy couldn't see us. Lewis was yelling at me. He was getting hysterical. I pushed him out of the car and told him to stay right there for ten minutes, then go into the bar and call a taxi and go home and he'd hear from me. He looked like he didn't understand a goddamn thing I was saying. I had to say it again. Then I drove out from behind the bar and over to the exit.

"I had to wait to make the turn. That gave me a couple seconds. I twisted the rear-view mirror and I could see across the parking lot and the guy was still there, in the sand. He was watching the car but it was pretty far, I didn't think he could see I was alone. I started toward town. I drove about half a minute, I found a place to make a U and I came back. I drove past the bar on the opposite side and pulled off the road.

"I finally saw him. Just a shadow, going back and forth, searching for the briefcase. Took him almost five minutes. As soon as he found it he went across up to a restaurant, went into the parking lot and got into a red convertible. I followed him to a beach house about ten miles farther up. I parked up the road and walked back. I went around to a window, he was alone in there, in the living room. He was stacking the money on the table. The forty-four was on the table next to the briefcase. When he went into another room I checked the window. It wasn't locked. He came back with a beer and started counting the money. I slid to the ground and sat there.

"About forty-five minutes later the light went out. Another light went on, in the back. I went back there, he was in the bedroom, getting into pajamas. He turned off the light and I went back to the living room window and waited about twenty minutes. Then I scratched on the window a little. He must've been asleep. I opened the window and went in.

"I put the money and the forty-four in the briefcase and I went through the house looking for the negatives but I couldn't find them. He had a darkroom but they weren't in there. So I had to wake him up.

"I went down the hall and stood outside the bedroom. He was snoring. I reached around through the doorway and found the wall switch and turned the lights on. He jumped up and blinked his eyes and then he saw me. I had the twenty-two automatic with a silencer. It didn't matter, he started for me anyway. He had a very fancy headboard on the bed with wooden knobs all along the edges. I shot once and I splintered a whole bunch of the knobs about a foot and a half from his head. The shot didn't make much noise, it could've been a hiccup, but it stopped him. He stayed there on the bed and made a sort of a wheezing sound and then he was quiet."

"Then his eyes started moving toward his nightstand.

I told him his gun wasn't there, he'd left it in the living room with the money. He just stared at me. I told him he better tell me where the negatives were, right away. He stared at me some more and then he said they were in the second drawer of the dresser. I kept my eyes on him and moved over to the dresser and pulled out the drawer and let it drop to the floor. I waited a moment and then I looked down fast and there was a lot in there. Negatives. It had to be more'n just Lewis's daughter. I checked another drawer. There was the same thing. Full of negatives.

"Then something happened. He threw a shoe at me or something. I don't know what it was, but by the time I got the gun on him again he had me. He knocked the gun out of my hand and got his hands on my throat and dragged me across the room. I was reaching around and I felt a doorknob and I pulled on it but it turned out to be the wrong door. It was the closet. He pushed me back through his clothes and I hit the wall and I couldn't move with all these clothes around me and he still had one hand on my throat and then he was laughing and then I felt his other hand between my legs. I just couldn't move. There was no room. He was right up against me and I was starting to feel dizzy and I tried kicking him and then he pushed my head back and banged it against the wall. I must've been out for a second cause the next thing I knew he was pushing at me and both his hands were around my neck and I couldn't get loose. It was just crazy. He was choking me to death and lunging at me at the same time and then his mouth was right against my cheek and I realized he was kissing me. His ear was right next to my mouth. I got it in my teeth and I bit him as hard as I could. He screamed like I'd killed him. He broke away and he was yelling his head off. I hit him with my fist right in the neck. He stumbled back a step and I got past him and when he finally turned around I had the gun again and he came at me anyway but I shoved it right in his face and that stopped him.

"I kept the gun on him. I got some handcuffs from my pocketbook and threw them at him and made him put them on. I made him take all the negatives out of the drawers and then we put them in the wastebasket and started burning them. It took half an hour, maybe more. I took him down to the darkroom. I made him tear the whole place apart. I made him wreck everything. He had a Nikon and two Minoltas. I made him smash the Minoltas against the wall. I put the Nikon in the briefcase with the money. Then I took him outside with me and opened the trunk of the car and told him to get inside.

"I drove up into the hills. I found this cliff that looks down at the ocean. Nothing around there. No houses, no nothing. I got him out of the trunk and walked him over to the edge. I told him I didn't like blackmail. I told him the next time he started thinking about taking pictures of naked girls he better think about that. And he better remember I knew who he was and where to find him. Then I stuck the gun in his face again and ripped the pajamas off him. I left him there."

36

I sat very quietly and stared through the windshield at the darkness outside. Maggie was leaning against the door on the passenger side and crying. I kept silent. Finally she stopped and wiped her face with her handkerchief and then she saw the pint of vodka I'd taken out of the glove compartment before. She twisted off the cap and gulped some down.

I found I still had my half of the roast beef sandwich in my hand. I found I hadn't eaten any of it. I put it in my lap and left it there.

Maggie recapped the bottle. She held it tightly in her hand. She inhaled deeply. "Well. If I was him, I think I'd have second thoughts next time, huh?" She twisted the cap on the bottle back and forth. "Hell. He'll try it again. But maybe it'll be a while at least, after tonight." She opened the glove compartment and pushed the bottle inside it and closed the glove compartment softly. "Well. I did what I could. I guess." She sat very still and looked straight ahead. "Harry came by the office today. He didn't look too good."

"Yeah?"

"Yeah. Said he hasn't been getting too much work lately. It's getting to him. He looked pretty down so I gave him a little money. Didn't give him much, just a few dollars. He said he'll try to get it back to me at the end of the month."

She looked at me to see if I was going to say anything. I didn't. I just kept my hands clenched tightly and nodded in the darkness. She saw my half of the sandwich in my lap. "Aren't you going to eat that?"

"You can have it."

She took it and bit into it and chewed it but kept talking. "He made his decision. He walked out. Why can't he leave me alone? People're hardly ever fair to each other, Fritz. You know that?" She took another bite. "Harry can't help what he does. Most of us can't." She finished the sandwich and looked at her watch. "Still early. Might as well stay a little longer." She folded her hands in her lap and sat quietly.

"You want to talk any more?"

"I don't think so, Fritz. Let's just be quiet."

"You can go to sleep if you want."

"I don't want to go to sleep. I'm going home in a little while. I'll just keep you company a little longer." She laughed and put her hand on my knee. "Cheer up, Fritz. Things aren't so bad. What's the matter? No music tonight?"

I turned on the Pearlcorder and adjusted the volume. Edith Piaf started singing her heart out like she always does. The strongest voice of sorrow I've ever heard. Strong and unbeatable and worth every penny that was ever made. *Non, je ne regrette rein.* No, I regret nothing. You also had a good sense of humor, Edith.

37

Ring.

 Ring.

  Ring!

  Ring!

"Hello?"

"When I left you last night I told you to put Paul on Morrison this morning. I just got in. Paul's here. Who's on Morrison?"

"Christ. Will you stop waking me up every morning? You know I didn't get to sleep till a couple hours ago."

"Who's on Morrison!"

"Big George. Been on him since seven o'clock."

"Are we going to spend all our profits subsidizing George Levison? Why didn't you put Paul on it?"

"I don't know what Morrison's up to yet. Let me handle it my way."

"You're costing us too much money doing this your way!"

I hung up the phone and put some force behind it when I did. But she'd already fixed me. I couldn't get back to sleep. I picked up the phone and dialed.

We live in an age of science and technology. The trick is to know how to use it. Lots of computer systems can be contacted by using the phone lines. If you know the right numbers you can dial right into the systems and pull information out of the memory banks before they've got a chance to sneeze. The electronic security measures are supposed to be highly developed but they aren't and Shelley knows that they aren't.

"Hello?"

"Morning, Shelley. It's Fritz."

"Sing to me like the robins of June."

"You're in a good mood."

"I'm going through this month's receipts. Your check's here, I'm happy to note. What's on your mind?"

"Lascivious thoughts."

"Like to help you, Fritz, but I can't over the phone."

"Can you trace a gun permit for me? Morrison. Gene Morrison."

"Local?"

"Yeah. He says he's got a permit. I'd like to know if he really does, and if he does, I'd like to know when he got it."

"Anything else?"

"All for now."

"Love and kisses. Talk to you later."

I hung up the phone. As soon as I did, it started ringing.

"Hello?"

"Don't tell me I'm waking you up again! I just tried you and your line was busy! You're still up!"

"What is it now?"

"Paul just told me what happened last night with Morrison! Why you had to take the gun away from him!"

I looked at the wall. "That was a damn stupid thing for Paul to tell you."

"Yes, it was. You told me he did okay last night."

Damn stupid thing. "So now you know why I put Big George on Morrison today."

"You should have told me what happened! You didn't have to cover for Paul!" The line went quiet. "I'm going to have to talk to him about some things."

"Tell him to get his hair cut, while you're at it."

"I've got to go to a screening. I'll be back here by twelve-forty-five."

"I'll be in around one, if you'll let me get some sleep."

She hung up the phone. So did I. I took it off the hook real quick before she could find something else she thought we had to talk about.

38

As I walked through the door Paul put his finger to his lips and pointed at the inner office. The door was open. I stayed where I was and listened. All I heard was Maggie's typing, but then,

"What is that you're typing?"

"Movie review. *Missouri Breaks*. New Arthur Penn movie. Brando and Nicholson. Opens tomorrow."

"You write movie reviews?"

"Got started in college. Used to write a regular column for the *Free Press*. Film and theater."

The typing continued. I leaned closer to Paul. "How long she been in there?"

"About five minutes. Maggie told me to stay out here so she could pump her. She said if you came in, I should keep you out here."

I went to the chair by the door and sat. The typing continued.

A few minutes later the typing stopped and steps came across the floor toward the door. Maggie came out of the office with an envelope. She put it on Paul's desk, turned around, saw me, shrugged, went back inside.

"If you're hungry, I have some apples and cheddar cheese. Fritz has gallons of Coke in the refrigerator. Just don't tell him I gave any to you."

"No, thank you. I'm not in your way here, am I?"

"It's a slow day. I like the company."

"I had to get out of the house. There was no place I could go to. I was going to go down to Max's office, but he doesn't like it. I go down there too often. Do you like it, being in business with Mr. Thieringer?"

"I try not to think about it that much. Fritz's got his

points, I guess." And what are those, I wondered. "He's got very little sense of humor and his manners aren't too good and he's a bit tight when it comes to money and his temper's a little shorter than it out to be on occasion, but other than that he's got his points."

Maggie's a real doll.

"The world you've grown up in, it's different than mine was."

The voice almost sounded wistful. Maybe we'd get something.

"You're not that old, Mrs. Isenbart."

"I'm thirty-eight."

"There's just a dozen years between us, that's all."

"You must've thought I was a fool, the way I came in here the other day. The way I acted."

"You were worried. You showed very good sense coming here."

"Max is very scared. He doesn't want anyone to know it, but he is. He was. . . ." Come on, keep it coming. "He locked himself in his study last night. So I wouldn't see him. But I could hear him. He was crying. He was. . . . I don't know what to do. I've done everything I can think of, he won't let me do anything. He never lets me do anything. I want to help him."

I heard a desk drawer open. Two glasses clinked against each other, a bottle was opened, liquid poured, a chair slid along the floor, steps came across the floor. Maggie always looks forward to the chance to offer booze. Especially when she can arrange to join in the drinking.

"Have you made any progress? About why the boy is watching Max?"

"You'd have to ask Fritz. It's his case."

"I can't think of anything it could be. And Max won't even talk about it."

It went quiet and stayed quiet.

"Is it difficult being in business for yourself?"

"Sometimes it is, sometimes it isn't."

"I've always wondered what it must be like. I used to work. For Max, before we got married. I enjoyed it. It made me feel like I was worth something. Do you know what I mean? When you don't do anything, when you don't have anything to do, it makes you feel like you're not worth much." It was coming faster now, a steady stream of it. "I used to be a dress model. I still do exercises, at the club. It's good for you. It gives you something to do." The sound of a bottle meeting the edge of a glass. "Max didn't want me to work any more, when we got married. He didn't like it. I suppose if it'd been like things are now, maybe I'd be the kind of woman who'd tell him it wasn't his choice. That if I wanted to have a career, it was my right to have a career. When I was twenty I could be whatever I wanted to be but now. . . . I never believed in myself. I wanted someone to take care of me. And I got married and Max took care of me. I don't think that's what I really wanted. Now I feel like I've been held back. You see what happens these days, with models? They do these magazine things. Commercials. TV. Movies. And they can't act. Most of them can't. They have looks. All they need is looks. And I had that. But I was young and I didn't know what to do. I needed someone to take care of me so I got married. I mean, I loved Max. I still love him. But I feel . . . held back. I should've become something. And I didn't. I won't. It's too late." A bottle touched the edge of a glass again. "That's all you need today. To be young and beautiful. They send you to all parts of the world and they take your picture. It wasn't like that, not back then. Or maybe it was. For some girls. It wasn't for me. I was scared. Scared to be something."

It went quiet again. That seemed to be all she had in her.

I took a piece of paper and folded it into an airplane and sailed it toward the far wall. It went past the open door and hit the wall and dropped. I threw another plane with the same result. Then I heard sounds from inside the office and a moment later Maggie came out and looked at me. I took another piece of paper and wrote—"Ask her if she thinks her husband is having any financial problems with the company. I'd like to know if it's phony or not." Maggie nodded and went back inside.

39

She stared at me. "I'm mad at you. You were going to call me and you didn't. Bet you don't even remember my name."

It came to me just in time. "Annie. You gave it to me."

The stare relaxed slightly. "Gave you my number too. Two days ago." She cocked her head to one side and studied my face. "Something happen to your nose?"

"I think I walked into a door or something."

"Better call me or you'll walk into another one." She turned around on her stool and opened a magazine and started flipping its pages so fast she tore one. It was a cute little maneuver and I liked the way she did it but I didn't have any time right then so I started down the hall.

"I mean it, Fritz. You better call me."

I turned around sharply. First she'd known Thieringer, now she knew Fritz. I didn't think I liked that. She kept her back to me.

I went down the corridor to Isenbart's office. His door was closed. I tried it and it was locked.

"Who's there?" came abruptly from inside the office.

"Thieringer."

". . . Wait a minute."

A minute passed and then the door unlocked and opened. He let me in, closed the door behind me, and went to his desk. He took a package off his desk and put it on the shelf under the window. It looked very much like the package he'd been carrying the other day when I'd followed him home. It was about half the size of a shoebox and wrapped in brown paper.

"Haven't seen you around."

"You haven't seen the kid around, either. We been watching him."

He dug into a filing cabinet. "For the money you're getting you better be."

"You said you wanted us to keep you protected for a couple weeks. That's what we're doing. You want us to do more'n that, we can do more'n that."

He kept his back to me. "What's that supposed to mean?"

"We can find out who he is, if you want."

"I don't give a damn who he is. Just keep him away from me. He doesn't even bother me. It's my wife, she gets nervous."

Someone tried to open the other door to the office. Isenbart jumped slightly less than a yard, then went to the door and unlocked it and opened it. He had a lot of doors locked today. I wondered why.

Carl stepped in with a drawing. Isenbart looked at it. Carl looked at me.

"What's this?"

"The Bill Blass knockoff."

Isenbart studied the drawing. "It is? What'd you do to it? You changed something. Didn't this come across here a little fuller?"

"Yeah." Carl took out a cigarette and lit it. "I think it looks better that way. I can change it back if you want."

Isenbart grunted and slid the drawing onto his desk. Carl stared at the burning tip of his cigarette, then past it at me. "You're becoming a steady visitor. You were going to come back so I could show you the line."

"Haven't had time yet."

"Whenever you got time, I'll be happy to show it to you."

Isenbart tapped his desk. "Carl, we're in the middle of something, okay?"

"Sorry. Didn't know I was in the way." He threw me one last look and went out.

Isenbart went to the door and closed it and turned

back to me. "Annie doesn't get you, he will. Want me to fix you up with him?"

"No, thanks. Our ages're off."

"Carl likes 'em older too. Carl likes 'em anyway they come. Goddamn fag. Him and Annie, it's a hungry generation. Everybody in this place's on the goddamn make." He went to his desk and picked up the design. Then he threw it aside. "Christ. This's all we do here. Steal designs. Bill Blass, Beane, Parnis. They design, we steal. Only way to make a goddamn buck in this business. You design anything of your own, they stay away in droves."

"Business's bad?"

"It can always be better." He slipped into his chair and tilted it back and looked at the ceiling.

I leaned forward. "Your wife says business's bad."

His head tipped slightly and turned as little as possible. "That what my wife says?"

"She says you're worried you might have to sell the company."

His face stayed still. Then he turned it and filled it with a smile. "Don't listen to my wife. She never gets anything straight." But the smile didn't last and he stared at his desk. "I got my life's blood in this company. *I* get sold before this company gets sold." He found a dying cigarette in his hand and stubbed it out. He shook another cigarette from a pack on his desk. He tapped it on the desk. "They got oil companies that're buying up guys like me. Who the hell can fight an oil company? I want to peddle a couple dresses, you think I got a chance?" He stuffed the unlit cigarette into his mouth and slumped back in his chair. "Maybe that'd solve everything. Just sell the damn thing. Today's market, you know what they'd offer? Beans. Not even beans. Twenty-five cents on the dollar. They want to force you out. They want to crowd you and come in and take it for peanuts."

He took matches from his pocket, struck one and lit his cigarette. I nudged an ashtray across the desk toward him. "The oil companies?"

"Sure. Oil companies, conglomerates, other guys in the business, they want to get rid of the competition. They come in and tell you they want to buy, they try to force you up against the wall so you got to sell, they think they got you, they give you an offer, the offer's shit." He rubbed the tip of his cigarette against the edge of the ashtray. "I can understand it, it comes from a goddamn oil company. But you get a guy in the business, he knows your operation, he wants like hell to get rid of you, he could at least make you a decent offer. Sure. He makes you an offer, you could live maybe six months on what he offers."

He wiped a hand across his mouth and his tired eyes looked at me. Then they looked down. "All the same. All looking out for themselves. They think they got you on the run, they stick it to you. Even guys I knew from the old days. All end up the same. They don't care. They figure they got you down, it's time to give it to you." He leaned forward and stared at the ashtray. He snorted through his nose. "I was in business here, two years. A guy I used to know, he came out from the East. He needed a job, I gave him a job. Worked for me a year, went off some place else. One of the biggest guys out here, right now. Everything clicked for him. Nothing went for me, *everything* went for him. The golden touch, he's got it." His eye flickered toward the far wall. "He'd like to buy me. The bastard. I take just enough of his market, he'd like to buy me." He turned back to me. "Know what he'd like to do it for? Peanuts. He figures I'm on the ropes, that's what he offers me. Peanuts. He can go to hell. Anyone thinks they're getting my company for peanuts, they better start thinking some more."

He stubbed the cigarette out in the ashtray and brushed flakes of ash across his blotter. "And you. Five hundred dollars a day to watch some fucking kid." He blew air through clenched teeth. "You ought to be watching the goddamn Queen of England for five hundred a day."

I nodded like I saw his point. "All right. I told you I was willing to negotiate the price down if you couldn't afford it. I'm still open to the possibility."

He laughed bitterly. "I bet. Sure. Offer me a bargain. Four hundred and eighty a day instead of five hundred, huh? Everybody wants to offer me a goddamn bargain. Hell, you're all the same. All of you."

He swung away from his desk and got out of his chair and went out of the office. I went to the door and watched him. I watched him go all the way down the corridor, through the back room, and away.

He'd left the package on the shelf under the window.

If I took it, he'd probably know who took it. He had it wrapped too well. Scotch taped and tied with string. If I tried to take it apart, I wouldn't be able to get it back together the same way and it was wrapped so well someone might come in while I was still fooling with it. I stood there another moment and looked at the package like I thought it might stand up and unwrap itself. Things usually don't, but sometimes I watch anyway, in case they do.

I finally turned and walked across the office and got all the way to the door. Then I came back and walked to the desk and went around behind it. I opened the bottom drawer on the right to see if the Colt was in there. It wasn't.

40

I drove back to the office and parked in the underground garage and as I was walking to the elevator the red Volvo sped past me. It slid into a space and screeched its brakes and slammed to a stop. Maggie jumped out.

"We're not timing you, you know. You don't have to break any speed records pulling in here."

She danced toward me. "I like going fast! There's a freedom to it!" She snapped her fingers at me like her fist was a machine gun spitting bullets. "Keeps you alert! Keeps your skills sharp!"

"Don't cut yourself, you might be a bleeder."

She spread her arms wide and circled toward me like a glider coming in for a landing. "I've been out in Chatsworth. Saw an old woman who might want a detective."

"Sound interesting?"

"Mrs. Apcar wouldn't tell me what it was. First she wanted to know what month I was born, what day, what year, all that kind of stuff. Then she wanted to know if I've got any siblings, where my parents came from. Now she wants to sleep on it."

"Hope she wakes up in a good mood. Mrs. Apcar got money?"

"Looks like she's got lots!" The elevator door opened. Maggie took my hands and we twirled in together. "Anything from Isenbart?"

"Could be he's under pressure to sell the company."

Her eyes started to sparkle. "Any connection to Morrison?"

"Don't know. Don't even know if I got it right. Have your talk with Paul? Tell him to cut his hair?"

"I'm not his mother." We waltzed a tight circle. "He says you had a bloody nose last night."

"He must've been seeing things."

Her smile came closer. "He thinks you're soft."

"I *am* soft. Want to feel?"

The elevator door opened and she stepped away. "No. Time to be businesslike." She walked down the hall and into the office with a face as straight as a plumb line.

I waited for her to go into the inner office and then I draped myself over Paul's desk. "You took my book of plays by Pirandello. You did not ask me if you could take it."

He tried to act surprised. "Sorry. I started reading it and I put it in my pocket and I forgot it was there."

"Return it!" I leaned closer. "Which play you start reading?"

"*It Is So If You Think It's So.*"

94

"Figure out which character's telling the truth yet?"

"Not yet."

It'd take him forever to figure that one out. Pirandello knew what he was doing. "I take very unkindly to people who take my books and do not return 'em. Return it."

I swung into the office in time to grab the phone on my desk as it rang the first time. "Thieringer and McGuane."

"Thought it was McGuane and Thieringer."

"Only when she gets to the phone before I do. What's the story with Morrison?"

"He went to the goddamn library. I never knew libraries had girls with legs like that. I'm going to have to go back there some time. He went to a movie bookstore up on Hollywood. Lots of nice legs there too."

"Good-size bookstore? Larry Edmond's place?"

"Yeah. You been following us?"

"Famous place. Like Schwab's used to be. Actors who want to be discovered hang around there trying to look semi-successful."

"He's at his house now. So're the others. I'd like to get relieved."

"Any sign of another gun?"

"Not on him. He's been wearing jeans and a shirt all day. I would've seen it."

"Half an hour?"

"See you at Morrison's house."

I hung up. "Big George's had it. I'll go relieve him."

Maggie went to the table by the sofa and straightened the magazines. "Morrison doesn't have a gun today?"

"Big George says he doesn't. I didn't think he had another one."

She looked at me sharply. "You pretty sure of that?"

"Pretty sure."

Maggie stepped to the door. "Paul, I have to go down to the Mark Taper tonight, they're doing a new play and I'm supposed to review it and Fritz wants to come with me. Big George just called in, he's watching

Morrison's house and we got to replace him right away. If Morrison goes anywhere near Isenbart, stop him, but if he doesn't, stay away from him. Don't take any chances in case he's got another gun."

"Okay."

I heard quick movement in the front office. The front door opened and closed and once it was closed Maggie turned to face me.

"Nice work, Mag."

"Thank you."

"You see your hole, you slip right in there like a high-priced halfback. What's the name of the play we're seeing at the Mark Taper?"

"*Ashes*. You'll love it."

"Sure I will. I love comedies."

41

Isenbart came out of his office at 5:30 carrying the package, the one wrapped in brown paper. He got his car out of the lot and drove to Santa Monica. Same bar. He came out half an hour later and drove home. I was sitting there, a block and a half away from his house, around 9:30, watching the house, munching my way through a sub sandwich with the works, listening to Miles Davis do *Sketches of Spain* on my Pearlcorder, when the red Volvo came flying down the street and made a quick turn in a driveway and parked behind me.

She got out of her car and came over to mine. She sat sideways on the passenger seat and crossed one leg over the other and showed me the smile I always see when she wants something. She turned off the Pearlcorder.

"You got a call after you left. Deveraux."

"Deveraux?"

"No cases named Deveraux? A secretary called and asked for Fritz Thieringer. Left the name Deveraux."

I kept the sub sandwich out of her reach. "Leave a number?"

"No." She moved slightly and her skirt drew halfway up her thigh. It's tough to go up against a woman who's got good legs and knows it.

"What do you want, Mag? You can't have the sandwich. I'm hungry."

She slapped her hands together. "I think I can get a terrific deal on some car phones! We have to be realistic! Now that there's three of us—"

"Forget it. Too expensive."

"I just said I can get us a *deal!*"

"I just said forget it!" I could feel indigestion coming already.

"I suppose you think we ought to have CBs."

So that's what she really wanted. The car phones were just a ploy so I'd say yes to CBs. "No CBs. I'm not putting one of those things in this car. I don't want this car ripped off any more. They see you got something like that, they'll crack the door to get at it, once they got the door cracked they figure the hell with it, they take the whole car. Forget it!" I glared at her and sunk my teeth into the sandwich.

She tried to stare me down. When it didn't work she said, "You're a relic, do you know that? We could make a lot more money if—"

"Let's start serving subpoenas."

She let her teeth show. "I'll look into it!"

"You probably already have."

"I'm going to look into security work too."

Why can't they ever leave you alone till you've at least had your dinner? "That's why you hired Paul in the first place. You figured you'd farm him out as a guard. That works, you'll hire a couple more kids, pretty soon we'll be a goddamn corporation the size of Burns. You're hopelessly upwardly mobile."

She cocked an eyebrow. "I've been doing some research. By 1960, Burns was billing twenty-nine million.

By 1975, they were up to a hundred and eighty-one million. Know why? They have twenty-nine thousand guards. That's where ninety percent of their profits come from—security. Do you want to hear about Pinkerton's?"

"There once was a girl from Nantucket. She told all her boyfriends to—"

"We already have Paul. We can get a few more—"

"I love the way you count your chickens before the hen's even said good evening to the rooster. We don't even know if Paul's going to work out. We may find out pretty soon. Morrison's coming down the street."

She turned around. "What?"

"The green Mustang."

She looked through the windshield. The Mustang was three blocks away and coming fast. "I don't see Paul."

"Neither do I." I opened my car door so I could get out fast if I had to.

"Wait a minute, Fritz. There he is."

Paul's Maverick turned into the street two blocks behind Morrison. Morrison came toward us and turned the corner at Isenbart's house and parked. Paul stopped one house before Isenbart's and parked. Nobody got out of either car.

Then Morrison got out of the Mustang and looked across his car at the house but didn't move. He didn't seem to see Paul's car. He didn't move for almost a minute. Then he closed his car door but still didn't move. Paul hadn't gotten out of his car yet. I pushed my car door open slightly and put my left foot on the street and tried to keep still.

Morrison limped around the back of his car and went slowly across the sidewalk toward Isenbart's house. Paul opened his car door and got halfway out. Morrison turned at the noise and saw Paul and jumped back a step. They stared at each other.

Morrison turned slightly and now I could see it, his jacket. It wasn't hanging evenly. It wasn't hanging evenly in the same way it hadn't hung evenly the day before. I turned in my seat and moved my right foot across and started to get out. "He's got another gun, Mag."

Her words came thinly. "You said he didn't."

"I was wrong. He does."

But I stayed as I was, halfway out of my car. Paul stayed as he was, halfway out of his car. Morrison stayed at the edge of Isenbart's front lawn. I waited for Morrison's hand to move toward his jacket pocket but it didn't.

Maggie opened her pocketbook and reached inside and took out a Smith & Wesson .38. She put it in her lap and sat quietly.

Paul took a step forward. Morrison's hand went into his jacket and came out with a gun but he left the gun pointing at the ground.

I didn't move. Maggie didn't move. Paul didn't move.

Morrison turned suddenly and got into his car and started the motor. It took a second before any of us could react. Then Paul dove into his car and started the motor. Morrison drove off, Paul drove off.

"Better stay here and keep an eye on Isenbart, Mag. I don't like it, it's not fitting right."

42

Paul stayed two car lengths behind Morrison and I stayed ten car lengths behind Paul. We hit the freeways. Morrison got off the freeway in Burbank. Paul followed him, I followed Paul. Morrison drove aimlessly, then parked in front of a drugstore and got out of his car and went in. Paul parked in the same block, about five cars back. I turned right and circled back a block and parked.

Several minutes passed. Morrison came out of the drugstore and stopped on the sidewalk and looked up the street at Paul. Then he turned and looked in the other direction, turned and looked back at Paul, turned and got into his car.

We hit the freeways again. We got off in Glendale. Morrison drove slowly, then pulled into a restaurant. It didn't look like much of a place, no bigger than a hamburger stand and probably just as hopeless. Morrison parked on one side of the lot and Paul parked on the other side and I drove into a closed gas station across the street and parked in what little shadows it had.

Morrison got out of his car and turned and looked at Paul and turned and went into the restaurant.

Minutes passed. People went into the restaurant. People came out. Morrison didn't come out.

More minutes passed. Twenty of them. Still no Morrison. Paul got out of his car and walked back and forth across the parking lot and went toward the restaurant and looked through the glass doors. Suddenly he went inside.

A few minutes passed, Paul didn't come out. Then Morrison came out. He came through the glass doors and turned quickly and looked inside. He kept his eyes on the restaurant and started limping backwards toward where he'd parked his car.

I took off my hat and flipped it in the back and got out of my car and crossed the street quickly and went into the parking lot. He didn't see me coming. I came up behind him and grabbed an arm and swung him in a half-circle and then let him loose. He shied away like a spooked horse. Then he stopped and stared at his gun in my hand and watched me put it into my pocket.

He put both hands up defensively. "Please, don't hurt me."

I stayed where I was. "I'm not going to hurt you." I turned and looked quickly toward the restaurant and saw nothing and faced Morrison again. "I hope this's your last gun, Gene. I don't like the idea of you carrying guns."

He started backpedaling toward his car. "Don't touch me."

"You sound lucid tonight. You off the pills?"

He pointed a finger. "Stay away from me! I didn't do anything to him!"

I didn't like the look in his eye. "I didn't say you did, Gene. Take it easy." I turned toward the restaurant again.

I heard steps behind me and I turned and watched Morrison run to his car. He got in and struggled with the keys. The car backed out of its space and turned quickly and Morrison drove forward, his eyes on me. I stepped back between two parked cars. He didn't try to hit me. He drove past and over to the exit and directly into the street without stopping. His head turned and his eyes looked at me momentarily and then he was gone. I turned quickly and went into the restaurant.

43

I looked in the men's room. Nothing. The kitchen. Nothing. The ladies' room. Nothing. I went into the kitchen again. Cooks and waiters stared at me as I went past them and out the back door.

The alley was dark. There were people in it. Two men. Big. One of the men was swinging Paul by the arm. Paul bounced off a wall. The other man hit him in the stomach. Paul doubled over.

I reached into my pocket past the aspirin bottle and closed my fingers on a sixteen-ounce sap. I stepped forward. The man nearest me turned around in time to meet my sap across the front of his face. As he went down my knee went into his chest. He went over on his back.

The other man had Paul by the hair now. He swung him in a circle. As I went forward he swung Paul toward me and let him go. Paul stumbled and rolled at my feet and I stepped over him and kept going forward.

The man stepped back reaching inside his jacket. I swung the sap at him and he groaned. I hit him again and grabbed his tie with my free hand and swung him against the wall. As he came off it I brought the sap up into the chin and he grunted and went down. I reached inside his jacket and found a gun in a shoulder holster and removed it and threw it in a corner.

I heard noise behind me and turned and saw Paul trying to get up. Behind him the first man was also trying to get up. I pushed Paul aside and went to the man and kicked his hand out from under him. He went down. My sap went down. It connected with the back of his head. It connected again and again. The man stayed down. I knelt beside him and reached inside his jacket. No shoulder holster. The gun was in his belt. I took it and threw it into shadows.

A hand at my shoulder turned me around and a fist went into my stomach. I fell against the wall. He swung again and I blocked with my free hand and swung the sap toward his face but missed. He kept swinging and kept finding my stomach.

I kicked him hard below his knee and he groaned and his hands went down. I brought the sap across his shoulder and he groaned again. I took the front of his jacket and pulled him off balance and as he went down I swung at his head. He lay on his back on the ground and groaned. His hand reached up to me. His arm tried to wrap itself around my leg. I kicked the arm loose and swung the sap again. That did it.

I went to Paul and got him standing and pulled him down the alley and around the corner to the front of the restaurant. I took him inside, his arm over my shoulder. Nobody even bothered to look at us, they were too busy struggling with their food. I put Paul in a booth with his back to the front doors and sat opposite him. "Give me your keys." He didn't react. "Your car keys! Quick!"

He raised his head slightly. "How many of them. . . ."

"Two! Give me your car keys, damn it!" His hand went slowly and uncertainly into a pocket and came out with his keys. "I'll be back in five minutes. Either one of those guys comes in here, yell your head off."

I went out to the parking lot and got into Paul's car and drove it out to the street and went five blocks straight down and made a left and another left and came five blocks back and parked on a side street in shadows.

44

I stood next to the car and looked at the restaurant. Nobody came out of the alley behind it. I crossed the street quickly and went into the restaurant. I sat opposite Paul and faced the front doors. Paul leaned against the back of the booth with his eyes closed. I took the aspirin bottle from my pocket and spilled the contents out on the table in front of him. He popped aspirin into his mouth and drank water. I cupped my hand in front of me, gathered the aspirins together and put them back in the bottle. I put the bottle in my pocket. I did all of this without taking my eyes off the front doors.

"There they are. In the parking lot. I can see 'em through the front window. Don't turn around."

His mouth made funny sounds. "How many . . . two of 'em? . . . You took something . . . they had—"

"Guns. I took the guns off 'em."

His hands went limply to the back of his neck. "You move . . . pretty fast. . . ."

I laughed quietly. "Sure. Except when they knock me down first." He started to turn around. "Don't turn around!"

He stopped as he was. "What if they come in here?"

"This's the last place they'd look. I moved your car. They won't see it. Sit still, they'll figure we're gone."

I watched the two of them stumbling in the parking

lot. They looked big enough and mean enough. Thank God they hadn't been quick enough. They climbed into a Buick. I'd seen it before, it'd pulled into the lot a little after we'd gotten there. Now it took almost a full minute before it got out of the lot.

When it was gone I leaned back in the booth and looked at Paul. "How you feel?"

He had his head down low. "Like my neck's almost broken."

"One of 'em had you by the hair. He was swinging you against the wall like you were something on the end of a rope. Remember?"

He didn't nod and didn't answer. Then, "I got one of 'em. In the stomach. When they grabbed me."

"Congratulations."

He looked up suddenly. "Morrison! He got away!"

Paul tried to get up. I pushed him back down. "Maggie's parked outside Isenbart's house. Morrison goes back there, she'll stop him."

His eyes gaped at me. His hand slammed the table. The sugar container tipped. People turned to look. "Thanks for trusting me! Thanks a hell of a lot! Damn it!"

He squeezed against the corner of the booth and stared at the table.

45

A waitress brought menus. We ordered. The waitress went away. She came back with food. Paul had a steak sandwich and coffee. The steak looked like something you could wear on your feet for a ten-day hike. Paul ate it anyway. I had french fries and a large Coke. I doused the fries with plenty of mustard. The mustard wasn't bad.

I spoke softly. "Morrison went into that drugstore

in Burbank. He could've made a call and told someone he was being followed. He drove out here and stayed in the restaurant till you came in looking for him. You knew his car was out in the lot. You could've waited for him to come out. Why didn't you?"

Paul looked at me bitterly. "I looked through the front doors and I couldn't see him. I figured, what if he did make a call from the drugstore, or from here, and someone was going to meet him? He could've been leaving the car out front to fool me and someone was going to meet him in the back and they were going to take off."

I nibbled a french fry. "All right. You came in. Where'd you look?"

"All over. He wasn't in the men's room and he wasn't in the kitchen. I went out to the alley and those guys grabbed me."

"Was Morrison in the alley?"

"I don't know. I didn't get to see much." He went back to his steak.

"Next time you look, look in the ladies' room too." He looked up, mouth open. "All I know, he came out a couple minutes after you went in. I took the gun off him."

Paul's eyes burned at me. "Last night you said you didn't think he had another gun."

I rubbed a thumb along the edge of my empty plate. "I was wrong. Sometimes I'm wrong."

The waitress brought the check. I looked it over and it added up right and I gave it to Paul. "Most of this's yours. You might's well take it."

He looked at me briefly, then dug into his pocket and took out his wallet. His face winced and he tried rubbing his neck again.

"Neck still hurt?" His face wrinkled up. "Fine old custom, mugging. Goes all the way back to the 1860s. They used to rob drunks. They liked to do it with a garrotte. As the drunk was being strangled he'd make very painful faces, like you're making. Like maybe he was a comedian mugging for an audience. Of course he wasn't."

"That's where *mugging* comes from?" His face changed to a smile. "That like *blackmail?*"

"Blackmail?"

He leaned forward. "Remember what you told me? *Blackmail?* The black envelopes?" He looked at me evenly and then his smile got broader. "I asked Maggie about that. She said blackmail goes back to the middle ages. She said there were black knights, knights dressed in black armor. They rode around the countryside, selling their services. Every time they found a town that was holding a tournament they'd enter it, but since they were professionals, they always won. What they'd usually win was the horses that belonged to the losers. Since these black knights were always traveling, they didn't have any use for extra horses. They'd sell the horses back to the losers. That's how blackmail started. You had to buy something back that'd belonged to you, and you were buying it from a knight in black mail. Black armor. Didn't have anything to do with black envelopes." He folded his arms across his chest and stared at me.

I looked him in the eye. "That's what Maggie told you? That's very interesting." My mouth started to smile a bit. "And you believed her?"

He smiled back. "That's right."

"She also told you we were going to the Mark Taper tonight to see a play."

His smile went first. Then his stare. Then his arms unfolded and hung at his sides.

I watched him get into his car and then I followed him for a mile to make sure he could drive a straight line. When I was sure he could I left him and drove home. I pulled up in front of my house and turned off the engine and sat quietly. Gene Morrison had told me he had another gun. I hadn't believed him. He'd told me he had friends. I hadn't believed him. I thought about it some more and then I reached into my pocket and took out his gun and flipped it open and saw exactly what I was afraid I was going to see. It was loaded. He'd been on pills the other night. Maybe he'd taken the gun and hadn't even thought about loading it. But tonight maybe he hadn't been on pills and maybe he hadn't forgotten.

Maybe.

PART TWO

46

I finally got a morning when I wasn't woken up by the phone. What I got instead was a cat lying on my chest and purring in my ear. I wondered how the hell he'd gotten in. I tried to push him off. Big mistake. As soon as I moved he knew I was awake. There's no dealing with a cat who knows you're awake.

I stumbled into the kitchen with the cat attacking my feet and I took out a dish and filled it with cat food. I knew the cat so I added tomato sauce and garlic powder. That'd get him off my back. I started to open the back door and found it was already open. About an inch.

I put the dish on the back steps and the cat started to devour it and a voice came at me from the next door. "Fritz! Morning!"

"Morning, Joe." I leaned against the doorway. "Been teaching your cat to open my door and come in to mooch a free meal?"

"He's a smart cat!" Joe picked up a pebble and threw it high and far. "Working today?"

"Not till later. You want to come over, let me get a shower and something to eat first."

I started out of the kitchen but something stopped me. A very faint smell of coffee. Fresh-brewed coffee.

I didn't like it. I hadn't made fresh-brewed coffee for three days.

I did sit-ups and push-ups, I showered and shaved, I dressed and went back to the kitchen. Joe was sitting at the table. I grunted at him. "This mean you haven't had breakfast?" He mumbled something I couldn't make out. "What was that?"

He looked out the window. "Had some juice. Trying to lose some weight."

I threw a package of English muffins at him. "Cut 'em and toast 'em. I'll make the eggs. You want coffee, you got to make it yourself."

He fumbled with the muffins. "No, thanks. I don't want coffee."

That meant I'd have to make the coffee for him too. When it comes to food Joe's an eater, not a maker. I put up water and took out eggs, cracked six into a bowl and dabbed in sour cream and mixed it up. I added black pepper and chili powder and onions and green pepper and a few squirts of hot sauce. That's as inventive as I felt. I looked to see how Joe was doing with the muffins. He was doing okay. Toasting muffins he can handle.

Aside from the fact that Joe's a cop and I'm not, we have a lot in common. We both came out of the East and neither of us plans to go back. Admitting you like L.A., the city that isn't one, is as good as admitting you're certifiable. I can see the insanity in Joe's eyes every time I look, so I try not to look too often. I shudder to think what he sees when he looks into my eyes.

Whatever's wrong with us, neither of us has the inclination or the money to solve it with psychiatry so we turned to a much safer kind of therapy. We made over my extra bedroom into a workshop. We put shelves along one wall and filled them with paint and paint thinner and wood stain and turpentine and rags and brushes. Another wall holds lumber. We've got a six-foot-high doubledoored tool chest that holds everything we need to rip a house apart and put it back together so nobody'd know the difference. We've got a Homecraft nine-inch table saw that I picked up from a guy I know for $125 total. Joe said it was such a damn good price the saw had to be hot. I told him I was sure it wasn't, and he looked at me a long time but didn't say anything else, and neither of us have ever brought up the subject since then.

I heated up the skillet and scrambled the eggs and set them out on two plates along with the muffins and put a jar of guava jelly down beside them. I poured a cup of coffee for him and another for me and put a Coke beside mine.

He got his teeth into a muffin and talked between chews. "My wife's making a goddamn mint. Last night I tell her I don't go on till four today, we could go to the beach. She says fine, she'll take the day off. I get up this morning around eight, she's in the living room reading the papers. She's smiling. I didn't like it already." He stuffed eggs into his mouth. "She says some TV stars're getting divorced, it's there in the papers. She knows their house. They just moved in last month right after they got married. She figures it's true, they're getting divorced, they'll want to sell the house. Next thing I know, she's outside, she's in the fucking car, she's burning rubber all the way to fucking Bel Air. You know what she can make, a deal like that?" He waved his fork at me. "Her commission'll be more'n you and me'll make all year."

I sipped coffee. "Speak for yourself. I'm having a very hot year."

"I know the kind of hot years you have, Fritz. She'll make more on this house'n you'll see in five years of your hot years."

"She want a new partner?"

He put a fist under his chin. "I'm thinking about it myself. They got me partnered with Lynch again."

I put down my cup. "I thought Lynch got transferred."

"They sent him back. Nobody else could stand him." He stared at his eggs. "Think they'd do anything to me, I lost him in a dark alley and came back without him?"

"Give you a medal."

"Can't trust him." Joe shook his head back and forth. "Never there when you need him. Even when he's there he's not there."

I took another forkful of eggs, which I probably wouldn't be able to taste now. "You can't do anything about it?"

"The people upstairs say I got to take him, so I got to take him. You don't fuck around with the people upstairs. I think the department's got this system worked out, you got an I.Q. around thirty, they move you upstairs. You're smart enough to spell your name right, twice in a row, they keep you where you are." His teeth ripped an English muffin in half and chewed it methodically. "It's got me scared, Fritz. You can't count on a guy like the lyncher. One of these nights one of us's going to be suddenly dead. I got a feeling it ain't going to be him."

The phone rang once. Joe took the receiver off the wall and handed it to me. "Hello?"

"You're awake?" The voice sounded disappointed.

I laughed into the phone. "That's right, Mag. Tough luck. Joe's cat beat you to it. He snuck in through the back door and started purring into my ear. His purr's softer'n yours."

"Should've locked your back door."

"Thought I had. What's up?"

"Morrison tried Isenbart's house again around midnight. I scared him off. He went home. Big George is on him now. I'm at the office with Paul. You know Paul didn't have a gun with him last night?"

Hell, yes, I knew.

"Fritz? You there?"

"Yeah. I knew."

"Since *you* didn't talk to Paul about it, I guess *I'm* going to have to. Oh, remember Mrs. Apcar? The lady in Chatsworth? I called Shelley yesterday and asked her to check Mrs. Apcar's worth. Shelley just called. She says Mrs. Apcar's bank account is up in the several millions category."

"Those people never like to pay. Shelley have anything for me?"

"She can't find any gun permit listed for Gene Morrison."

"He's got no permit, he's just got guns. I took the one he had last night away from him. It was loaded. Anything else?"

"After I talk to Paul I'm going home to get some sleep."

"Want some help?"

"I can manage by myself, thank you."

"Okay. Hey, Mag. . . ." God, I hated to ask her

this. "This story about blackmail, what you told Paul, knights in black armor. . . ."

"What about it?"

"Is it true?"

"Sure it's true."

"I mean, is it *really* true?"

"Sure it's really true. Do you think I lie?"

She hung up fast before I could answer.

47

Joe put the phone back on the hook and laughed. "Partners. Hell. Least you got to choose yours."

I finished my coffee and started on the Coke. "Choose ain't exactly the word I'd use."

"What word'd you use?"

"I think they call it karma."

Something scratched the screen door. Joe opened the door and his cat came in. Joe smiled at it. "Hello pussy pussy pussy pussy. Come to say hello pussy pussy pussy pussy?" The cat gave him a look and strutted past him and jumped into my lap and turned over on its side. Joe grunted. "Fucking loyal cat, ain't he?"

I stroked his back. He arched and shook his fur on my pants. "He remembers who fed him."

Joe leaned across the table and poked his face at the cat and smiled sweetly. "Why don't you ever sit in *my* lap, you furry little bastard?" The cat stretched its front paws out and purred in my lap. Joe gave him the finger and looked at his empty plate. "That all the eggs?"

"The plates're clean, Joe. That must be all of them."

"Any more English muffins?"

"We ate all you toasted. I got more if you want to toast some more."

113

He looked up innocently. "You feel like toasting some?"

"No."

He grunted. "All right, I'll skip it." He poured himself what was left of the coffee and started dipping his spoon into the jar of guava jelly and licking it clean in that way only a close friend or a perfect stranger would ever try. "Maybe I won't go in today. Haven't reported sick for a while. Maybe today I can't face the lyncher." He threw the spoon down. "How's it going with you? Anything interesting?"

"Shadowing a kid. Looks screwed up. Eighteen years old. Spends most of his time on pills."

"Too many of 'em doing that."

Joe put his coffee cup on the table and slid it two inches away the way he always does when he's finished eating. "Fucking kids. They get caught up with pill pushing, they're too damn young to know what they're doing. But what they're doing's got to be stopped. I got to stop it." He shook his head sadly. "Fuck."

Neither of us said anything for quite a while, and then I said, "Those kids you talk about, Joe. I used to be one of 'em."

"I know. Once in a while I grab one of 'em and that's what I think. I could be grabbing you. And if it was you, would I be sealing your fate, catching you before you got old enough to work your way out of it by yourself."

I stared out through the screen door. "Sometimes I wonder if I ever have worked my way out of it."

48

Joe and I spent some hours in my workroom and around 1:30 we were lugging a bookcase out to Joe's station wagon when Paul's Maverick came down the road and stopped in front of my house. What got out of the Maverick didn't look much like Paul. The hair didn't hang down to his shoulders any more. I was glad he'd learned something in that dark alley the night before.

He walked over holding a brown paper bag. Joe gave him a short look and walked into the house. I looked at the paper bag. "How you feeling today?"

"Okay." He looked around like he was looking for something but I didn't think he was looking for something."Maggie said you'd fix up the car for me."

I scratched my ear. "You caught me in the middle of something. Wait out here, it'll take me a couple minutes."

He nodded and walked back to his car. Damn Maggie. I went across the grass and into my house and found Joe standing at the side of the front window watching him.

I tapped Joe on the shoulder. "What're you doing?"

"Watching."

"You're more paranoid'n I am."

He grunted. "I'm still alive, too. Who's the kid?"

"He's working for me."

Joe's head swiveled around. "Working for *you?*"

"Maggie hired him."

He looked through the window. "Doesn't look like much."

"He's okay."

Joe shot me the same short look he'd given Paul a minute before. Joe and I can never hide anything from each other. He grunted and went into the workroom and as soon as he was gone I went to the phone and dialed the Carne Organization. I asked for Rittenhouse but Rittenhouse wasn't there, probably out chasing his carousel. I hung up the phone and looked out the window at Paul and I had bad feelings and didn't know what to do about them.

I went outside and leaned against his car. "I haven't asked you why you wanted to be in this business. Maybe you don't know. I don't know if *I* know. There's something about it that grabs you, I guess. Sometimes you know you ought to get out, and pretty soon you start to figure it's too late for you to get out. But you're still starting, and maybe it's not too late for—"

"Maggie said if you gave me any trouble I'm supposed to give you this." He brought a sealed envelope out of his pocket and handed it to me.

I ripped the envelope open and took out a single piece of neatly typed paper. *F. Don't give him any speeches. Just do it. M.*

I crumpled the paper in my hand and went into the house and got my tools. Well, I was never much for speeches anyway.

I lay half-inside his car with my back against the floor, and facing the driver's seat I slashed through the leather beneath the seat with my mat knife. I cut three sides of a rectangle and flapped it open. I reached inside the brown paper bag and took out the Smith & Wesson and its holster. I pushed the gun and holster through the flap and set them snugly between the springs and adjusted the angle. Then I sat in the seat and reached under and through the flap and let the gun slide easily into my hand.

I reset the gun in its holster and left it. I cut a rectangle of Masonite measured one quarter of an inch less in length and width than the rectangle of leather. I spread Elmer's glue across one side of the Masonite and pressed it slowly against the back of the leather. I held it there till it started to set. Then I put a piece of quarter-inch plywood on the other side of the leather to act as a temporary brace and attached miniature clamps to hold it all together till it dried.

Paul and I went into the house and back to the kitchen. He sat at the table like a limp dishrag and looked at the back yard. I put up water for coffee and while it was heating Joe came in.

"I'm going to take the book case over to Charlie's."

I nodded. "Tell him it costs ten bucks more'n the last one. Tell him the price of lumber's gone up again."

Joe gave me one of his looks. "The price of lumber hasn't gone up for three months, Fritz."

I shrugged. "Sorry. Just an idea."

He crooked a finger at me and I followed him out to the living room. "What's wrong with your employee? He looks like he's going to faint."

"I'm making coffee. It'll pick him up."

He laughed. "Lots of luck." He stretched out his arms. "Well, guess I'll go to work after all. I don't go in, the lyncher won't even be able to get the car out of the garage by himself."

I studied his face. "You all right?"

"Sure. I was worse last night." He laughed again. "I was rotten last night. Almost came over to talk to you."

I started back toward the kitchen. "Wouldn't've done you any good. I didn't get home till almost one."

"Fritz." I turned. I didn't like the sound of my name. Not the way he'd said it. His eyes were cold. "Not till one?" I nodded. He rubbed the side of his face. "I looked over here last night, when I got home. That was around eleven. There was a light on in your kitchen. Looked like someone was moving around in there."

We stared at each other but neither of us said anything.

49

Paul pushed the screen door open and stepped out. Then he came back in. He returned to the table and sat and drummed fingers on the edge. He sipped more coffee and stared at the cup. I didn't like any of it. He took out a pack of cigarettes and slipped one out and tapped it against the table. He offered the pack to me but I shook my head. He lit the cigarette and took a long drag and then looked at the burning tip.

He kept looking at it. He looked at me, then looked at the burning tip. I looked at the tip, then looked at him. "Well? What is it?"

His eyes slid over to mine. "That other morning, at Lybart. I was sitting there with those salesmen when Morrison came in."

I nodded slightly. "What're you remembering?"

He looked back at the tip. "Morrison didn't go down the hall right away. He looked around the reception area, at the salesmen and me, and he looked around some more. . . ."

I tried not to say anything too fast. "All right. What else?"

"There was a thin guy with some dresses over his arm. He was talking to the receptionist. He turned around and looked at Morrison. He took out a cigarette and he lit it and he looked at the tip." Paul looked at the tip. "And then he looked at Morrison."

I let it sit there a moment. "Like he knew him?"

"I'm not sure. But he kept watching Morrison and then Morrison turned around and I think he looked at him. And then Morrison went down the hall."

I yawned slightly. "They say anything to each other?"

"I don't think so. I just remember the look. It struck me. But then I forgot about it."

I got a Coke from the refrigerator and needed another moment so I poured it into a glass. Then I said, "The guy with the cigarette's the designer. Carl. He's gay. He tries to pick me up every time I'm over there. He was looking at Morrison, he was looking at me, he was probably looking at you when you weren't watching. He's on the make."

Paul looked up. "You don't think it's anything?"

"I doubt it."

The phone rang. I picked it up. "Hello?"

"Fritz? Good, you're there. Didn't get any answer at the office." His voice sounded rushed. "I'm down at Griffith Park, they're shooting a film. Morrison and his roommates, they're working as extras. Been here all day. Couple hundred people here. I talked to a guy on the crew, he says they're going to be here till six. Maybe later. I just called my service, I got something. Sounds lucrative. But I got to see the guy right away. It's the first call I've had in a week, Fritz."

I checked my watch—2:20. "Can you last another forty-five minutes?"

"Hell, Fritz, that'll be fine. You know, I'd stick with it, but the first call in a week. You know how it is."

I knew exactly how it is. "I took another gun off Morrison last night. You think he's got a new one today?"

"Down here? They got all the extras stripped to pants and shirts. He had a gun, I'd've seen it."

"Okay, George. Forty-five minutes."

I hung up the phone. Paul was looking at me with a hungry face. "Was that Big George? He needs someone to relieve him?"

119

50

Ring.

    Ring.

    Ring.

    ". . . Hello?"

    "What's the matter, I wake you up?"

    ". . . Yeah!"

    "Good! About time I got even! Got to make this fast, Mag. Morrison and his roommates're doing extra work on a movie in Griffith Park. Big George called me to get relieved. Paul was here when the call came in and he wanted to go. After what happened last night I figured, I didn't send him up there, he'd figure we don't trust him worth shit."

    "Which you don't."

    "You got to get to Griffith Park before he does."

    "Come on, Fritz! If Paul sees me there, he's going to know we don't have confidence in him!"

    "I got it figured out. You get there first, you get Big George out of there, Paul shows up, you tell him Big George left a message on the service, he must've left it before he got me at home. You got the message, you went out to relieve him. You didn't know Big George'd gotten through to me. That way you can stick with Paul and he won't know it's fixed."

    "I'm not going! Let Paul handle it himself! We have—"

    "You get out there and cover it so he doesn't know he's being covered or *I'm* going out there and he'll *know!*" I gave her a moment to sulk in quiet. "Which way you want it?"

120

"All right, all right, I'll go!"

"Better give me a call around four-thirty to bring me up to date. I'm going to try to get some sleep. I got things to do tonight."

51

The alarm went off. I punched it quiet and got up and looked in the full-length mirror. My pants were fine but everything else needed a change. I washed my hair and dried it with a towel and combed it with my fingers. I combed it straight front with a slight part in the center.

I had two full beards in my dresser. I took the one that looked like it could use a good trim. I didn't want to look too manicured.

A pipe would be good. I went through the rack and chose a straightforward briar and stuck it in my mouth and checked to see what the mirror thought of that. Pipe. Beard. Good.

The phone rang. "Hello?"

"It's me, Fritz. I'm still at Griffith Park. Maggie's here, too."

"She is? How come?"

"She got a message on the service that Big George needed relief. She got here before I did."

"Sounds like the Fourth of July. What's going on there?"

"They got people running all over the park. Lots of fireworks and smoke. They're shooting some kind of protest scene."

"They get too much smoke out there, make sure Morrison doesn't disappear in it. Big George said his roommates're there, too. Can you see all three of 'em?"

"They're right down the hill from me. They're running across the park. Here, Maggie's coming."

Paul went away and all I heard was chanting and yelling and noise and then: "It's a mob scene. They're fooling with smoke pots now. They set off a car a couple minutes ago. Then the director started yelling it was the wrong car. The movie business. They've got private guards all over the place."

I stopped looking at myself in the mirror. "Private guards? No cops?"

"There's plenty of cops, Fritz. Private guards too. I checked it out. Guy I know from UCLA is on the crew. He told me this flick's being shot by an outfit called Red Wind Productions."

"You say it like it means something."

"It does. Red Wind's made up of two producers. Ted Silverman is what we laughingly call the artistic one. He's had a string of losers for about ten years. The money man is Nicholas Capanegro."

The name rang like a struck bell. "Any relation to Tony Cap?"

"Tony Cap is his father."

The bell got struck again. "That's all we need. After those two goons grabbed Paul last night, I don't want to hear names like Tony Capanegro passed around."

"Could be just a coincidence. One of the private guards is roaming the park with a camera so they'll have a record of who's here. I've been avoiding him but I think he got Paul."

Wonderful. "Paul says there's smoke. Don't let Morrison sneak off in it. And if you have to get near him, try to play it gentle. Maybe tomorrow I'll be able to get close enough to him to see if he's being used or not."

"You think you know something?"

I laughed. "Not even my own name."

I stared at the mirror. I still looked too much like me. It was the eyes that were doing it. I put in blue contact lenses and it was better. I put on my navy pea coat and turned up the collar and it was better still.

I went into the kitchen and locked the back door and went out the front and locked the front door and went to my car. I rummaged through the back and came up with a Greek fisherman's hat. That would do it just fine. I walked across the yard and rang the bell next door and after a moment it opened.

I graveled my voice. "I'm lookin' for Joe Bergen." She gave me a funny look. "He's not here."

I put a hand on the door frame. "You his wife? I gotta see him about somethin'. It's important."

Her eyes turned doubtful. "Give me your name, I'll tell him you. . . ." Her head cocked to one side. "Is that you?"

I smiled broadly. "How do I look?"

She sighed and shook her head with relief. "Like the kind of guys Joe writes reports on." She straightened. "You talk to him today?"

"Yeah."

"He looked terrible last night. He wouldn't tell me what it was."

"He's got Lynch back as a partner."

She stepped back without meaning to. Her hands came up. "How can they do that?"

"They can do anything they want to do. Joe's a careful man, he'll be all right."

She shook her head again. "Damn it."

I knew what she felt because I felt the same way. "I got a favor to ask. Could we trade cars? I want to be completely incognito tonight."

She gave me a look but then went away and came back with her car keys. She gave me hers, I gave her mine. "Thanks a lot, Dorothy." I walked across the lawn.

She came out through the door. "One thing, Fritz! It's three-quarters full! I want it three-quarters full when it comes back! Last time the tank was almost empty! I didn't like that!"

52

I parked on the street near Lybart Petites. When Annie came out she walked past me and didn't even give me a look. When Carl came out he got into a Kharmann Ghia and drove off. I followed him across the city to a small white house two blocks below Sunset. He got out of his car and went inside. I drove past and turned at the corner and parked.

Forty minutes later he came out. What went in wearing blue denim pants and a red striped shirt was now wearing black leather pants, a green crepe shirt open halfway to the belt and a thin black scarf. He walked past his car and went toward Sunset. I got out of my car and went after him.

He turned left on Sunset and walked west for five blocks and went into a bar. The neon on the front said *Slimjims*. I went into a joint across the street and sat near the window and ordered a taco-burger and a chili-dog and french fries and a Coke.

Time passed. It got darker. He didn't come out. I finished my third Coke and paid the check and went next door and browsed in a bookstore. He still didn't come out.

I walked across the street and went in.

Some were dancing and some were at tables and some were at the bar and all were men. Hot music and talk. Leather and suede. Musk and sweat. Smiles and laughs. Pickups and rejections. Noise.

He was standing at the bar, watching the dancers. He seemed to be alone. I walked along the bar and brushed him as I passed and as our bodies touched lightly I glanced at him. He glanced back and then away. I continued down the bar.

I stationed myself at the corner and ordered a rum and Coke. I waited another minute and then looked across the bar and caught him looking back at me. He looked away quickly.

I held my glass in both hands and stared at it like I was sad and I could see him in the mirror behind the bar. He'd turned away from the dancers now and he kept stealing glances at me. Then I felt a hand at my elbow. I turned to see what was there. From the belt up he was silk. His face was as smooth as a pearl and his smile was as wide as Wilshire Boulevard.

"Haven't seen you in here before. You alone?"

I nodded.

"It's a nice place. Nice and friendly." He nestled closer and his hand covered mine before I could move. "It's your first visit, maybe I could buy you a drink." His fingers reached under the sleeve of my pea coat and found my wrist. "We could have a little drink together, a little talk."

My eyes turned down. "I'm real down tonight. Wouldn't be much company. Gotta be by myself."

His fingers stayed on my wrist. "Just starting out?" He inched closer. "Loosen up. We all got to start sometime. We all been through it. Got to let yourself go with it."

I put my hand over his and kept my voice soft. "You don't understand. I just broke up with someone. I'm not ready yet."

His eyes searched mine. "You sure?"

"Gotta get him outa my system first."

He nodded and patted my arm. "I know how things are. I been through it, too. Maybe another time."

I nodded and he nodded and he cruised away. I watched him go and as soon as he'd latched on to someone else I put the rum and Coke to my lips and looked down the bar. Carl was looking at me.

I stayed looking at him over the rim of my glass and he looked away but then looked back. Our eyes locked and stayed locked.

I put down my glass and played nervously with my pipe. He started down the bar toward me. I moved back a step to give him room. He slid into the space and neither of us spoke and he sipped at his drink and it was three-quarter's gone. I called the bartender over and asked him to fill it and Carl nodded at me quietly and accepted the drink. Then he took out a cigarette and lit it and looked at it and then stopped looking at it and looked at me.

"Thanks for comin' over. I kinda wanted to talk to someone."

He nodded and drank and said nothing.

"I kept lookin' at you 'cause you remind me of someone." I touched his arm tentatively. "You don't mind, do you?"

"No. I don't mind."

I lowered my head and spoke softly. "I broke off with someone last week. This's the first night I got up enough nerve to go anywhere." I made a weak attempt at relighting my pipe. I failed at it and dropped it on the floor and bent down to get it and came up slowly and weakly.

He helped me up. "You all right?"

"I don't feel good. I gotta get outa here." I took a step and let my legs go rubbery and turned back to the bar.

He still held my arm. "You want to sit down?"

"Lemme stand here a minute." I held on to the edge of the bar with both hands. "Shouldn't've come here tonight. Ain't had much to eat today. I. . . ." I took another step from the bar and then started to sink. He pulled me back up. "It's bad in here. Too many people. Gotta get outa here. Ain't had nothin' to eat. . . ."

"Can you walk if I help you?"

I put my arm over his shoulder. "Is it hot in here?"

He nodded quickly. "You want to go outside?"

"Yeah."

He guided me along the bar and around the edge of the dancers and toward the front door. He supported me with one hand and opened the door with the other but before we could get out a hand took my other arm and spun me around.

Angry eyes looked out of a pearl-smooth face. "You were after someone else, you could've said so! You didn't like my type, you could've been honest about it! You didn't have to lie about it for Christ's sake!"

Carl pulled me toward the door but Pearl Face still had my other arm. Carl swung around. "He's not feeling well. Let him go."

Pearl Face hissed at him. "Don't tell me he's not feeling well, you bitch!" Pearl Face's fingers bit through my coat sleeve like steel tongs. "Listen to me, you bitch—"

"Let him go!" Carl slapped his hand off my arm. "Don't touch him!"

The slap was so sudden and quick it took all three of us by surprise. Pearl Face looked like he could break Carl apart with two fingers but Carl didn't back off. "He's got to get outside! He needs fresh air!"

Pearl Face smiled. "Well, I didn't know you could talk, bitch. I thought all you ever did was come in here and watch."

Carl started to say something but didn't. He pulled me outside and the door closed behind us. Carl glowered at the door. "That. . . . He's always in there. He never lets anyone alone. He thinks it's his own private preserve." His bravado was so thin you could've peeled it off his face with a tweezers. His whole body shook with terror.

I started to move away from the bar. "Lemme walk a couple steps. Maybe I'll feel better." I turned so I was headed toward his house. "Felt hot in there. Gotta walk a little."

He came up beside me. "You need something to eat? There's a place across the street."

I was already in the middle of indigestion from the place across the street. "Wanna walk a little first." I kept going up the street. I turned once to see if Pearl Face was coming after us.

"You want to stop someplace? Get something to eat?"

"All those people. Too closed in." I started walking

more steadily. Come on, Carl. Sure I want to eat. Ask me.

He walked by my side, touching me lightly to keep me steady. "I live near here." I nodded and looked at him and kept nodding and kept walking. "Just a couple blocks. We could go there." I nodded and kept walking.

53

Carl stopped in the middle of a block. "There's a shortcut we can take. Down here."

He went along the side wall of a grocery and turned into an alleyway and as he turned I stopped briefly again and looked behind us. I didn't get enough of a look to tell me who was back there. It could've been anyone. Pearl Face, Morrison, anyone. I put a hand inside the pocket of my pea coat and closed it on my sap.

I followed Carl through the alley and somewhere behind us I heard steps. Carl didn't seem to hear them. Or he was damn good at pretending not to hear them. We went through the alley with no problem and went down the street toward his house.

"How far's it?"

Carl raised his arm and pointed. "Second white house on the left. You'll be able to sit down and relax."

"Wait a minute." I stopped and pushed both hands into pockets. "My pills."

"What?"

"I got pills I gotta take. Must've left 'em in my car." I acted like I was nervous and turned abruptly and walked away.

He came after me. "Where're you going?"

I kept moving. "My car's inna next street over. I gotta get my pills."

"I'll go with you."

I turned and faced him but kept moving backwards and waved an arm up to stop him. "Just be a minute. Meet you at your house."

He hesitated and while he did I turned around and went into the alley.

The alley was empty.

I flattened against the wall in the middle of a large shadow and kept my eyes on the far end and waited. When nothing came in I started moving forward, sticking close to the wall like a fly on flypaper. Halfway down there was a patch of brightness. Lights on the roof of the grocery were making the street gleam like a movie screen. It was too much brightness to walk through so I moved sideways to the opposite wall and put my back against it and got ready to move forward again and then I heard breathing coming from a doorway ten feet further down.

My hand came out of my pocket holding my sap.

The breathing came quicker, nervous breathing, frightened breathing. I moved forward slowly. There was just enough light to show me the toe of a shoe.

I moved quietly to the opposite wall and flattened against it and faced the doorway. From this angle I could see more of him. I could even see his right hand and the gun in it.

There was no time to think about what I was going to do. That was just as well 'cause I'd have to go ahead and do it without thinking and that way I might have a chance. I raised my right hand up past my shoulder and next to my right ear and was ready to throw the sap at him as soon as he moved the gun. I cleared my mind of everything else and took one more step forward and saw him in profile.

I lowered the sap. "Come out of there."

He didn't do anything. I spoke softly again. "Come on, out of there."

It got very quiet and then he slowly moved forward and came out of the shadows. The gun hung from his right hand and pointed to the ground.

54

"Fritz?"

I put the sap in my pocket and found my voice again. "Yeah, it's me."

He stepped closer. "I didn't recognize you. The beard—"

"You're still holding the gun. Please put it away."

He stopped and looked at the gun in his hand, then put the gun in his belt and closed his jacket on it.

I looked toward where I'd come from to make sure Carl wasn't there. "How long you been on him?"

"Since he left work."

"You see me following him?"

"I saw a Mercedes following him. I didn't know it was you. It wasn't your car."

I faced him again. "I didn't see you at all. Not till after I came out of that bar with him. Even then I didn't get a good enough look to tell it was you. You did a good job of following." He didn't nod. He didn't think it was much of a compliment, I guess. "What'd you tell Maggie so she'd let you go off alone on this thing?"

He shrugged. "I just told her there was something I had to do. She said it was okay, she'd stay on Morrison." He came up next to me. "You said you didn't think the designer had anything to do with Morrison."

I met his eyes without blinking. "I still don't think he does. After you left, I decided I better check it out, case I'm wrong." He stayed still a moment and then nodded slightly. I rubbed my neck like I was thinking it over. "I made the contact, I better stick with him."

"Want me to stick around?"

I rubbed my neck some more and then shook my head. "Just complicate things."

We stood there a moment and then he finally turned and started to walk away. His whole body seemed to sag like he'd just put on fifty years. Damn it, I wished I knew how to handle it better. "Your instinct was good, Paul. So was your initiative. But next time tell us about it before you do it, okay?"

It made no difference. He nodded and kept going. I stood silently and watched him disappear into the darkness at the far end of the valley.

I hoped next time he wouldn't let himself get caught in a dark alley with nothing but a gun in his hand.

I hoped next time I wouldn't let myself get caught with nothing but a sap.

55

A rya rug with a golden sunburst covered a good deal of the living room floor. Its colors were repeated throughout the room. Brown leather dominated the furniture. Crystal vases full of flowers were everywhere. The paintings were what gets called tasteful without being daring. The tables were wood and well made. Dark-stained shutters covered the windows. I looked at it all admiringly. "Nice place. Nice feel to it. Good eye for color, good eye for design too. Oughta be inna business."

His hand played with the arm of the sofa as he stood behind it. "I'm a designer. Clothes. Women's clothes." He nudged an ashtray till it was centered on an end table. "Want something to drink?"

I rubbed my hands together. "Sounds good. Where's the bar?"

"In the kitchen."

"Where's the kitchen?"

He smiled slightly and went through a door. I went

after him. He was a good deal more nervous now that we were alone.

He poured gin and a sprinkle of vermouth into a pitcher and stirred, then opened the refrigerator and took out ice. While he was doing it there was scratching against the far side of the screen door. I looked toward the door but all I saw was darkness. Then the scratching started again.

Carl put down the ice and opened the door and a German shepherd leaped in. It saw me and stopped on a dime and faced me and froze in place and didn't make a sound. Carl opened a can of dog food and dumped it in a dish and put the dish on the floor but the shepherd kept looking at me.

Carl patted his head. "Come on, Caesar. Food." The dog moved out from under the patting hand and came forward a step. I'd seen the look before, sometimes in animals, sometimes in men. It always meant the same thing.

I stayed as still as possible. "Is he friendly?"

"Sure." Carl patted the dog's side but the shepherd shook him off and kept coming forward as if in slow motion. When its lips curled back over its teeth my hand went softly into the pocket with the sap.

Carl reached for the dog's collar but the dog kept coming and his nose started twitching and twitched more as he got closer to me. A low growl started at the back of his throat.

Carl snapped at the dog. "Caesar! Don't do that!" Caesar kept growling. "Caesar!" Carl slapped the dog behind the ears. The slap produced a bigger growl and Caesar showed more teeth. My feet moved backwards toward the door.

Carl grabbed the dog's collar and gave it a yank and Caesar's growl turned into a squeal. Carl yanked again and the dog's paws flew backwards over the linoleum. Carl pulled him to the screen door and kicked the door open and forced the dog outside. Carl closed the door. I went to it and locked it. The dog was standing on the back steps and it stared at me with its eyes shining.

Carl returned to the refrigerator. "Maybe he smells

something on you he doesn't like. Dogs're funny when they think they smell something."

The one thing I hadn't changed before I'd left home. My pants. And that's where Joe's cat had been sitting.

"Take off your coat. Stay awhile."

I moved across the kitchen out of the dog's sight and took off my pea coat and dropped it on a chair. Carl stirred the martinis and poured two glasses of precisely the same height and gave one to me. We clicked glasses and drank.

He went into the living room and put on Bette Midler and came back and poured refills on the martinis. He started to put dinner together.

He was shy now. The martinis and the record and starting to make dinner were excuses so he wouldn't have to make the first move. He took out chicken livers and spread them on a plate and seasoned them carefully.

I opened the refrigerator and took out what I wanted and cut tomatoes and cucumbers and green peppers into a salad. We worked side by side putting the meal together but no words passed between us. As I started tossing the salad I heard something behind me and I turned and noticed two small fiery eyes in the shadows on the other side of the screen door.

I put the salad on the table and sat in the one chair where the dog couldn't see me.

56

Carl's arms sprawled across the table circling his plate and his hands closed on a glass of half-drunk martini. I put my hand on his arm. "You said you're inna dress business?" One eye flickered at me and he nodded and then his head dipped again. "That a good business?" His hands left the glass and pushed his plate away and his elbows rested on the table and his forehead rested in his hands. "I hear you gotta be good, make it inna dress business. Hear it's pretty competitive."

He took the glass again and drank what was in it. "Tough business. Eleven manufacturers folded last year. Bankrupt. Kaput."

I refilled his glass. He leaned back and the chair started to tip but he caught himself and leaned his elbows on the table again. "Got to be up-to-date. Keep up with things." He punctuated his words with his right fist hitting the table. "You don't keep up, you're out just like that!" He tried to snap his fingers. "Dirty business."

I crossed my forearms on the table and put my head against them. "What makes it dirty?"

"Everyone steals." He laughed. "From everyone else. Big round robin. You design something, first thing you know, it's coming out of some other company. You got to be ahead of the competition or you don't have a chance, and the competition's putting out the same stuff you're putting out."

I kept my head down but sighted my eye along the surface of the table and watched his hand close on his glass and pick it up. I heard him swallow.

"You got to have two men in the dress business. A designer and a salesman. That's what you got to have. Or you're kaput." The hand with the glass came back to the table. I turned my head and looked up at him. He nodded at me. "We got a designer. We ain't got a salesman."

"How do you sell things?"

He shrugged. "We don't." He looked at me intently. "You aren't drinking. Why aren't you drinking?"

I slid my arm along the table and gathered in my glass and dragged it back across the table and pulled it to my lips.

He tapped the table with his fingers. "My boss used to design. Him and a girl, and me, I designed a little. Then the girl left and Max and me designed. But nobody was selling. And Max can't design. He's rotten." He

134

laughed. "He can't sell either." His mouth smiled sadly. "How the hell we going to make any money?"

His head circled up slowly and he stared at the corner of the ceiling and his head kept circling till he was looking at me and then he got up and stumbled out of the kitchen. As soon as he was gone I sat up and poured what was in my glass into his glass, then dropped my head to the table again.

He came back in with a portfolio and sat next to me and pushed my plate aside and threw his arm over my shoulder and opened the portfolio on the table in front of me. I looked at it but I had to blink my eyes before the drawings would stay still on the page. I wasn't as drunk as he was, but I was more drunk than I thought I was at the time.

He laid his hand against a drawing. "Anybody ought to be able to sell the kind of stuff I design. Anybody. Look." He turned a page. His voice whined. "We could be big. Very big. He doesn't give a damn. I don't know what's wrong with him." He turned more pages and stopped on something with reds and oranges in it, but the lines were blurry or my eyes were blurry or something was blurry, I couldn't make it out. He looked at it lovingly. "Did this stuff in college. Trade Technical, down on West Washington. No problems in college. Don't have to sell anything in college."

He shook his head wearily. "I got a whole collection planned. Sell each part separately. The customer can buy one piece at a time and group 'em one way or another way, different combinations. Different colors. Different fabrics." His face started to brighten and he took his glass again. "Wool jersey and poplin. Poplin and suede. And colors—green and pumpkin, camel and burgundy. . . ." His free hand started to wave. Then it stopped abruptly. "We could knock 'em on their asses if Max gave a damn."

He looked at his glass and found it was empty. He walked the few steps to the counter and leaned on it with his back against the wall and poured from the martini pitcher into his glass. He swung his eyes toward me in a deep glazed look and held out the pitcher. I nodded like I was expected to and pushed my glass across the table in his direction. He looked at my glass and I looked at him and neither of us moved.

"I'm not going to end up like Max. He doesn't like the way his life turned out. He feels cheated." He stepped forward and set the pitcher on the table. He set his hands on the table and leaned over it toward me. "I'm going to make it! I am! You got to think that way! You got to have persistence! You got to. . . ." He pulled out a chair and slumped into it and then his hand came across the table toward the portfolio but stopped halfway there. "Nothing's selling. Not the way it should." He looked into my eyes. "You think my stuff's any good?"

"Your drawings're fine. Beautiful."

He clawed at my arms. "No! Tell me the truth! You really think they're any good? I don't know! They're not selling! Why aren't they selling? Maybe it's not Max! Maybe it's me!"

He let go of my arms and looked at the floor. He rose slowly and took his glass from the counter and went down the hall. When minutes passed and he didn't come back I got out of my chair. Everything was off balance. I held on to the chair and shook my head and when it didn't fall off I went into the living room. He wasn't there. I went down a hall and found a light in a workroom and when I went in and looked around I found him in there too. Beside him a dress dummy wore something made of chiffon, and there was a sewing machine, and a drawing table, and material samples, and drawings, and a stool. I stumbled to the stool and sat. The stool didn't move. I put a hand on the drawing table so I wouldn't move, either.

Carl moved. He moved sideways straight into the wall, then slid down it and sat on the floor. "Fifteen, twenty years ago, Max was starting, it was different. Today you get your name known. Bill Blass, Ralph Lauren, Calvin Klein. Customers're willing to pay. Max doesn't understand that. He's killing himself."

I leaned across the drawing table. "Whaddaya mean, he's killing himself?"

"He won't change!" Carl crawled along the floor and put his hands on my knees and looked up at my face. "Why won't he change?"

"I don't know." Something could be starting to pay off if I could just stay sober enough to hear it. "Why won't he change?"

"I don't know!" His look turned inward. His face started to harden. "It's a tough business. You got to change. The only way." His head started to nod. "Yeah. There was a guy, started out like me. Working for Max. He got out. Maybe that's what you got to do. Can't let Max drag you down. Got to go to New York or something. Get away from Max. He did. He made it. Big as they come now. He made it, I can. Got to get away from Max. Poor Max."

Something was clicking somewhere. Like a fire trying to catch. I shook his shoulders. "How'd Sam make it?"

He looked toward the wall, then slowly looked at me. "Sam?"

I nodded solemnly and gave it to him again. "Sam. The guy who used to work for your boss. The guy who made it big."

He looked at me like I was crazy. "His name wasn't Sam."

I spoke quickly. "You just said it was Sam."

"I did?" His eyes opened wide. "David. David Greene. I said Sam?" He put his hand to his forehead. "I must be. . . ."

His words trailed off as his head turned toward the door. He stayed still a moment and then his hands went away from me and he crawled across the floor toward the wall and looked at the door.

I sat still and listened. I could hear it too. Something far away. The front of the house. It sounded like a door opening.

Carl spread his back against the wall and his mouth opened slightly. I heard someone coming in the front door and then I heard a growling dog, running through the house, coming closer.

57

I reached for the pocket of my pea coat to grab my sap but I didn't have my sap and I didn't have my pea coat. They were both in the kitchen. The shepherd burst into the room with its mouth open as wide as a bear trap. I kept the drawing table between us and stayed ready to push it over on top of him if I had to. He stayed on the far side of it, snapping his teeth.

The dog turned and ran quickly to the other side of the drawing table. I pushed the stool in his way and his head darted out as if to bite the stool but it was just a trick. He turned suddenly and circled in the other direction. By the time he got there I had the stool moved to that side. He jumped up and down and kept barking at me.

"Caesar."

The barking stopped.

"Caesar. Come here."

It was hardly more than a whisper, but a whisper was enough. The dog turned around and walked to the door and sat. What he sat next to didn't look happy. The man was my age and tired. He stayed in the doorway and patted the dog's head. "Carl? What's going on here? Who's he?"

Carl remained on the floor. "Nobody. We just met. Tonight."

The man nodded slowly and looked at me. "My dog doesn't seem to like you. You understand what I mean?" I understood it like it was written in flashing neon on the side of a building in five-foot letters. The man made no effort to get the dog out of the doorway. He looked sadly at Carl. "You been drinking?"

Carl smiled. "A little."

I could've done without his smile.

The man nodded and spoke softly. "It's late, Carl. Your friend outght to be somewhere else." He sighed and looked at me. "Got somewhere else to go to?"

I nodded. "Sure. Could you get the dog outa the doorway?"

He sighed again. He stepped into the hall and the dog went with him. I moved slowly across the room. Carl looked up at me and his hand reached out but I stepped past it.

I walked out of the room and down the hall and the man walked after me and so did the dog. I went into the kitchen and got my hat and my pea coat but as I turned to go out he stood in my way and looked at the kitchen table. Carl appeared behind his shoulder.

He didn't look at Carl. "You had dinner."

Carl said, "Yeah, but—"

The man waved a hand. He looked at me for a long moment and then stepped aside and signaled toward the front door. I went past him and past the dog and past Carl and through the living room. And they all came with me. It was a dandy parade.

Carl stepped out of line and spoiled it. "So you weren't here! So I had someone over! So what! It's none of your business!"

I felt like hitting him.

"You get that dog in that kitchen! Right now!" Carl stuck his nose in the man's face. "Take Caesar into the kitchen!"

The man didn't move. His voice came soft again. "I'm tired, Carl. I've had a long day."

It didn't get any better. Carl glared at him. "You get Caesar out of here! Right now!"

I moved closer to the front door and put my hand on the knob.

The man yawned and covered his mouth with his hand. Then he turned. "Caesar. Come here."

The dog turned abruptly and followed the man into the kitchen and the door closed silently behind them.

Carl held out his hand proudly. I felt sick to my

stomach but I shook his hand anyway. I looked past him and the kitchen door remained closed.

"I'll drop by *Slimjims* tomorrow around six-thirty." At least he said it quietly. "We could go someplace for dinner or something."

"I'll see if I can make it." I took my hand back and went out the door.

58

I crossed the street and moved behind a tree and turned to see if anyone was watching. I listened for sounds of a man or a dog moving in darkness but I heard nothing. I walked down the street and turned the corner and went to the car. I took out my keys and put them into the lock but before I could get the door open I heard them. Both of them. They came out of the shadows on the other side of the street. The dog sat on the sidewalk and the man came toward me. He figured he was big enough, he didn't need the dog. He walked toward me in a slow deliberate pace and stopped three feet away.

"We better talk some more."

I nodded. He had the tired eyes of a man who was in no mood for talk. I had my right hand behind my back holding my sap. "All right. Go ahead. Talk."

He moved sideways a step. "I don't think you should come around here any more."

I nodded again. "All right. I won't."

He yawned and moved sideways the other way. "We understand each other?"

"We understand each other." I knew I'd have to knock him down damn fast and get inside the car and get the car door locked because once the dog reached me I'd be finished.

He moved sideways again. "Then we got it straight?"
"Yeah, we got it straight." I nodded for him again.
He stopped moving and swung.

He was good. He put both his fists into my stomach
and sent me to my knees before I could use the sap at
all. He came to the ground with me. He gripped my
head with one arm and started to tighten. I could feel
the pressure around my head like a tight metal band. I
tried to swing my right hand up with the sap but it was
no use, I didn't have the sap any more.

He was like an ox. I couldn't break his grip. Those
spots were coming out a quarter of an inch in front of
my eyes. I hammered at his arm with my fists. I tried
grabbing his fingers to bend them backwards. It was no
use. His arm only got tighter, the spots only got bigger,
the spots melted together. My right hand swept the grass
searching for the sap.

It was dark. I was lying on my back. On grass. I
tried to turn over. I couldn't turn over. I heard footsteps.
I turned my head. The ox was gone. So was the dog.
Two people. A man. A woman. On the sidewalk. Coming toward me. Twenty feet away. They saw me. They
stopped. I rolled to my side. I reached my arm out.

I was still on the grass. A tapping sound. Coming
closer. High heels. I turned. Faced her. Reached out my
hand. A girl. A young girl. "Help me . . . please . . . help
me. . . ." The high heels left the sidewalk. They went
across grass. Away from me. Into the street. They kept
going. I came up on an elbow. "Please. . . . I need help
. . . please. . . ." She looked at me over her shoulder.
Her eyes. Frightened eyes. She kept walking.

Something touched me. A hand. On my chest. I
opened my eyes. A gaunt face looked down at me.
"Help me . . . please. . . . I need help. . . ." He pushed
me back to the ground. He searched my coat. Other
hands went through my back pockets. "No. . . . Don't do
that . . . please. . . ." My shirt ripped open. Hands

141

searched for a money belt. I reached out and grabbed a shirtfront and pulled him to me. "Don't do that!" Something hit me. Something hit me again. I lay still. I let the hands work their way through the rest of my pockets. I opened my eyes. I saw both of them now. One of them was on the sidewalk, crouched down like an ape, looking at something. I would've given anything for the strength to crawl over there and—

It was no use.

59

I was flat on my stomach and my beard was half off and my hat was gone and my coat was on the grass beside me. How nice. They'd left me my coat, and my shoes, and my life.

I got to my feet and stumbled toward the car. I was surprised it was still there. I reached for the door and then I felt sick again and I dropped to the grass. My hand touched something hard and I picked it up and looked at it. The sap.

Where the hell were you when I needed you?

My other hand touched something else. The car keys. I'd dropped them when the ox hit me. Just as well. If I'd had them in my pocket they'd be stolen now and so would the car.

I felt awful.

My wallet was gone and my ring and my watch— no, they'd left the watch. Too cheap a make, no doubt. I looked toward the sidewalk where the ape had been crouching and there was my wallet. I crawled toward it. They'd taken the money and credit cards but left the wallet. I picked the licenses and business cards off the grass and put them in my wallet so my wallet wouldn't feel as empty as I did. I tried to get to my feet but couldn't so I crawled along the grass to the car and leaned against it and folded my hands in my lap and found I was holding the sap again.

The sap. Terrific. Anybody else came along, I was ready for them. I'd sap their goddamn heads off. Hear me out there? I'll sap your goddamn. . . .

Like hell I would.

I lifted my head and tilted my wrist and looked at my watch and saw the reason they'd left the watch. Its face was smashed flatter than a stepped-on grape.

60

Ring.

Riinngg.

Riiinnnggg.

"What!"

"Fritz? I've been on Morrison all night. I need someone to relieve me."

What time was it? Morning? Next week? Next month?

"Fritz?"

"All right. Where are you?"

"You sound awful. Better go back to sleep. I'll call Paul."

"I'm all right." Oh, boy. "I'll be up there!" Oh, boy. "Where are you?" Silence. "Where are you!"

"Morrison's house. Are you all right?"

"I'll be up there! What time's it?"

"Almost seven."

"I'll be up there." I hung up the phone fast.

I tried to stand. I barely made it. Every bone felt like

it needed a vacation. God, I felt terrible. My head was throbbing. Crazy rhythms. Christ.

I went into the bathroom and popped aspirin and dropped to the floor and lay on my back and watched the ceiling and waited for the aspirin to do some good. Someone else would have to do my exercises today. No sit-ups, no push-ups, no hundred-yard dashes today. Blinking my eyes was going to be tricky enough today. I felt ready for the boneyard.

61

I parked my car and turned off the motor and pushed the door open and got out and tried to walk evenly. I pulled open the door on the passenger side of the Volvo and slid in.

"What happened to you?" She tried to take off my sunglasses but I pushed her hands away. "It's that bad, huh? I knew, the way you sounded, I should've called Paul. What happened?"

"Got into some problems last night. I'm okay."

"You get a chance to hit him back?"

"He was doing enough hitting for the both of us."

She muttered under her breath. "Was it worth it?"

I closed my eyes. "I don't know. I didn't get anything on Morrison but I may've picked up something else. The other day Isenbart told me he used to have a guy working for him and the guy left him and the guy's pretty big now. Isenbart said the guy wanted to buy him out. Isenbart ran out before I could get the name out of him but I think I got it now. David Greene."

"Do you have any idea what your voice sounds like?"

"I'd rather not know." I leaned my head back. "How'd Paul do last night?"

"What?"

"Paul. Remember Paul? He works for us? You were watching Morrison together? He handle himself okay?"

She stared straight ahead. "Sure. Paul was fine."

"Glad to hear that." I let a moment go by and then I looked at her. "Fucking liar. He turned up five steps behind me last night just when I didn't want him there."

She turned sharply, then turned away. A moment passed. Her knuckles rapped the steering wheel. "He told me he had to go see his girl. That lying. . . ." She dropped it and laughed. "He's learning, isn't he?"

I rubbed my forehead. "Let's hope so."

She touched my shoulder. "You look terrible, Fritz. Let me get Paul up here."

I shook my head slowly. "I haven't seen Morrison in over twenty-five hours. If he's any closer to breaking, I want to be there. Go home and get some sleep and when you get up maybe you could find out who the hell David Greene is and where we can find him."

She sat quietly. "Greene's big, huh? Some of the really big ones are owned by other people."

"What?"

"The kind of other people who filter their money through the companies to make it look kosher. They even pick up a little extra extorting money from the illegal Mexicans they have working in their factories. It usually adds up to a big investment."

I waved my hand at her. "You got Mafia on the brain, you must've seen too many thugs hanging around that movie set yesterday."

"I saw enough."

I pushed the door open and swung off the seat but her hand grabbed my shoulder and pulled me back. "Come on, Mag. Don't get rough this early in the morning."

Her voice came like a knife. "You're in no shape, Fritz."

"Let me borrow your watch."

"What?"

It'd thrown her. "My watch met an untimely end last night. Someone stepped on it. Unfortunately it was still on my wrist at the moment of impact."

She muttered under her breath. "You're not going to go home, are you?"

"I can't, Mag. I got to see what kind of shape Morrison's in today."

She gave me her watch. "I'll check into the office around three. Better give me a call so I'll know you're still alive." I tried to get out of her car again. "Fritz, will you please take care of yourself?"

"I promise I'll take care of all the important parts."

I went back to my car. As soon as she left I took a Coke from the ice bucket and opened the aspirin bottle and swallowed two pills. I wished I knew a way to stop the aspirin bit from becoming an integral part of my repertoire.

62

A door slammed and woke me up. Gene Morrison and both his roommates came out of the house and jumped into the Chevette. They barreled down the road and I went after them. At the first stop light I took two more aspirin.

Griffith Park.

I set myself up on the hillside in the shade of a tree. It was a losing battle. The sun kept finding me. I pulled down the brim of my L.L. Bean cap till it met the top of my shades and that cut the glare. I pulled the ice bucket closer and took out a fresh Coke and gripped its sides with both hands to cool myself from the heat and tried to fool myself into thinking I didn't feel as rotten as I felt.

Below me two hundred extras stood in a food line.

Production technicians engaged in discussions. Others ran wires across the grass. Gene Morrison stood in the middle of it holding a paper cup and looking up the hill at me. I toasted him with my Coke can and stayed where I was.

Cops circulated around the edges of the set and private guards circulated behind them. The private guards looked like the front line of the L.A. Rams.

Assistant directors yelled. Everybody moved. Extras ran across grass and more extras ran after them and too many people shouted too many orders and the whole thing was a mess.

One of the private guards wandered up the hill toward me. "Got permission to be up here?"

I looked up from under the brim of my hat. "Didn't know I needed it." He circled behind me. "I'm in the way, up here?"

He stood directly behind me. "What're you doing?"

"Just looking. Movies fascinate me." I could just about feel his eyes burning holes in the back of my neck.

Below us a dozen extras ran across the field and a series of smoke pots went off behind them. The L.A. Ram stepped beside me to watch the action and let his jacket flap open just enough for me to see the gun in his belt. When he was sure I'd seen it he buttoned his jacket.

I pulled the top off my ice bucket as slowly as I could and he watched every move without moving his head. I took out another Coke can and flipped it to him. He caught it with his left hand but kept his right hand close to his gun. He held the Coke a moment and then pulled off the tab. For a moment I thought he was going to chew the tab but he didn't.

I looked down the hill. "Movie business must be expensive."

"Must be." He sat on the grass beside me. "Who marked up your face, behind the shades?"

"I didn't get his name."

"Too bad. Hard to collect insurance on it, you don't get the guy's name."

"It'd been a friend of yours, I doubt I'd even be around to make a claim."

He liked the sound of that. He watched the field below. "Least with you I don't have to waste my time being subtle."

So that's what he was being. Subtle. He clicked his Coke can against mine and we drank. Below us the extras regrouped for another run across the grass and then a car exploded. A man in a baseball cap yelled, "Not yet! Jesus Christ, not yet!"

The Ram laughed. "Least today they blew up the right car. Stupid business." He balanced the Coke can on his knee. "I saw some of the script. Won't make a dime, you ask me. People today, they want skin. The thing to do, you get yourself a couple college chicks, give 'em twenty-five bucks for the day, go to some apartment, and shoot the whole thing in a couple hours. That's where the money is. No overhead."

"All you need's plenty of vitamin E."

He smiled. He was getting to like me. "Vitamins're cheap. I got a friend, he's doin' that stuff. Wants me to come in with him."

"You going to do it?"

"Can't." He snorted. "It's all those Sundays my mother dragged me to mass."

"Morality's a terrible thing, isn't it?"

He gave me a long look but I didn't disintegrate from it. Then he laughed and shook his head. Apparently it wasn't worth a reach for his gun. "Okay. You can stay up here and watch." He got rid of his smile. "Just make sure you *stay* up here. Thanks for the Coke."

He walked along the ridge of the hill toward a small group of spectators. He had a job to do. He had to act subtle with them.

Below me a tall blonde ran the length of the field and Gene Morrison and fifty others ran after her. The man in the baseball cap yelled instructions at them through a loudspeaker. The extras divided into two groups and converged on the blonde. A whistle blew and the baseball cap started yelling again and threw his loudspeaker at the grass. The crowd broke apart. Morrison came out from the middle of it with his eyes on me.

Technicians moved into the field and the extras moved off it and Morrison walked the length of it and joined the girl he lived with. When he finally sneaked another look up the hill I held up my Coke can and toasted him again.

63

The phone rang and got picked up. "McGuane and Thieringer."

"You mean Thieringer and McGuane. Maggie there yet?"

"No."

"She said she'd be there around three."

"She had to go out to Chatsworth to see that woman. Apcar. She said to tell you she traced David Greene. He runs a company called Amy Thomas. You got a call from someone named Shelley. She said she found Morrison's gun permit."

"Good! What else'd Shelley say about it?"

"That's it."

"That's it?"

"Yeah. Why?"

"Shit. I'll call you back later. I'm in Griffith Park."

I hung up but before I could dial Shelley I looked toward my ice bucket to make sure nobody'd swiped it and Morrison was there. I hung up the phone and walked over but when I got close he started to move back, so I stopped. "Afternoon, Gene. Want to talk?"

He stuffed his hands in his pockets and looked along the hill. His eyes seemed to hold for a moment on the L.A. Ram.

"Gene? Looking for someone?"

His eyes snapped back at me. His feet shuffled back

and forth. But he didn't look high. Maybe we were getting there.

I folded my arms on my chest. "I'm not going to do anything, Gene. You're safe company. I been thinking things over. It's occurred to me, maybe you're in over your head. Think it's possible? Want to talk about it?"

He put a hand up to stop me as if I'd moved forward, which I hadn't. "You got proof you're really a detective?"

I took out my wallet and dug out my license. That and my driver's license and social security card and a couple business cards and a ten dollar bill I'd stashed in my cookie jar were the extent of what my wallet was holding. I sailed the license through the air. It landed on the grass and he picked it up and looked at it like maybe there was a chip he could find if he looked hard enough.

"I don't want to hurt you, Gene. I wanted to hurt you, I could've done it a couple nights ago."

He put the license on the grass and left it there and backed away from it. He looked around and saw the nearest sightseers were twenty feet away and he considered that and then shook his head. "Too many people here. We finish shooting this scene, they said they're going to let us go. We'll drive home. You follow us. We get to my place, I'll get my car and I'll drive someplace. You follow me."

I nodded. "Fine. No guns, right?"

He jumped. "Look! I want to talk, damn it! You want to talk or not?"

"Quiet." I looked around to see if anyone had turned to watch us. The Ram was almost fifty feet away. I couldn't tell if he was looking at us or not. "We'll do it your way, Gene. Nice and easy."

"All right."

Below us an assistant director started yelling. Morrison took a hard look at me and then went down the hill and joined the other extras.

64

Another phone rang and got picked up. "Hello?"

"Shelley. It's Fritz."

"What's up, honeybunch? Sing to me like Neil Sedaka."

"Listen, how come it took you so long to locate the gun permit on Morrison?"

"You told me he's local. The permit wasn't local. Being conscientious, I checked out of town, and that's where I found it."

"Where?"

"Sausalito."

"I wanted to know *when* he got it."

"Oh. Sorry. Wait a minute." She went away. I watched the action down the hill. "We aim to please. I'm doing a land office business here. Going to have to put on some extra. . . . Here it is. Gene Morrison. April. April twenty-fifth."

"April twenty-fifth, this year?"

"This year."

I added it up quickly. "About six weeks ago."

"Wait, I got a calendar here. Yeah. Six weeks this Friday."

"I still could be right."

"What?"

"I love you, Shell. Thanks a lot." I hung up and dialed.

"McGuane and Thieringer."

"Maggie there yet?"

"Fritz, I. . . . Maggie's here. Wait a minute."

He went away quickly. His voice had sounded

funny. Maggie came on. "We've got problems, Fritz. I just—"

"I have to tell you what I got, Mag, and I have to tell you fast. Mrs. Isenbart told us the boy was coming to see her husband two months ago, then he stopped. Then he started again the other day and he had a limp and a scar over his eye. Six weeks ago Morrison was up in Sausalito taking out a gun permit. Let's say two months ago, or whenever before that it started, Morrison came to see Isenbart and Isenbart was scared. Isenbart sent some thugs to get rid of Morrison but the thugs fucked it up and Morrison got away, out of town. He figured he needed a gun for protection cause they roughed him up pretty bad. The limp and the scar. Morrison got the gun, two guns, and came back down here and started to see Isenbart again. Isenbart didn't want to hire us. I told you it had nothing to do with money.

"Morrison knew he'd been followed before so he was expecting to be followed again. That's why he was ready for Paul that first day on the stairs. The other night at that restaurant Paul thought he'd lost him so he went in after him and when he went out to the back alley two guys jumped him. We thought the guys were working with Morrison but maybe they were working for Isenbart and grabbed Paul by mistake. Isenbart's been trying to get rid of Morrison all along but his wife got us into it and we've been in his way.

"Morrison's starting to break. He wants to meet me alone. I'm supposed to follow him home, then he's going somewhere else so we can talk. You better get over to Morrison's house right now so you can back me up. By the way, I might have the whole damn thing wrong."

I waited for her to answer. She didn't. "Mag?"

"Isenbart was here, Fritz. He terminated our services."

65

I stood there with the phone in my hand, just looking at it. Finally I said, "What happened?"

"I just got back to the office. Isenbart was here, complaining to Paul about the rates. He said you told him we could charge him less and he couldn't afford us anyway and Paul didn't know how to handle him and somewhere in the middle of it Paul let it slip we know who the boy is. Paul said his name.

"Soon's Isenbart heard the name Morrison, he went white. When I came in he was acting like he could use a straitjacket. He asked me if we're sure the boy's name is Morrison. I told him I didn't know, it was your case. Isenbart started going around in circles and he wanted to know if we knew where the boy was from. I said we didn't know and then he said we had to stop this, we had to stop it fast.

"He looked at me like he'd forgotten where he was for a minute. Then he said we should forget the whole thing, he'd send us a check, and he took off. I went out the door after him and he started yelling at me that we're fired and then he opened the door to the stairs and ran down."

That's all she said. I stared at the phone. "It's too late, Mag. We've got to stick with it. I got to break Morrison. I got to see what it adds up to."

"You really think he's ready to crack?"

"I'll make him crack. Get out to Morrison's house right now and—"

That's all I said. The noise was sudden and frightening. I turned and saw smoke billowing up from the bottom of the hill.

"Fritz—"

"Explosion. I'll call you back."

I hung up the phone and ran across the hill. Below me there was nothing but smoke and confusion. People were yelling. Screaming. Running. Half of them were running away from it, half of them running toward it. I went down the hill. The smoke almost blinded me. I picked my way through it. Suddenly a man turned and it was the L.A. Ram. He put his hand toward me but I pushed it aside and kept going. Men were already at work with fire extinguishers. I could hardly see a thing. I heard crying all around me. Smoke cleared in front of me. I saw a young girl lying on the grass. Her legs were covered with blood. Her head was thrown back. Her mouth was open. No sound came out. The next one I saw was a man and the side of his face was gone.

66

I walked evenly into the office and went to the refrigerator and took out a Coke. I opened it and drank. I sat at my desk and opened the right bottom drawer and took out a pint of vodka. I poured vodka into the Coke can and gave it some time to settle and then I drank it. I noticed my hand was in my pocket. I took my hand out and found I was holding the bottle of aspirin and for no reason at all I threw the bottle at the wall. It hit and bounced back and lay still on the floor.

I drank more Coke and poured in more vodka and drank more of that and then put the can on my desk. I got out of my chair and picked up the aspirin bottle and threw it back down as hard as I could. It still didn't break so I smashed it with my shoe and then it broke.

Paul came in. Maggie waved him out. I went to my desk and sat in my chair and turned to face the wall.

After a few more drinks the sight of a smashed aspirin bottle in the middle of the floor started getting to me. I went out to the front and got the broom and came back and folded a piece of paper double and swept the pieces onto it and buried the whole thing in my wastebasket.

Maggie spoke softly. "The radio said four dead."

"Six. By the time I left the hospital, the count was six dead, eleven injured. The radio give the names?"

"Yeah."

"I saw him. He was all smashed up. It happened so quick, I doubt he even knew it was happening." I put the pint bottle of vodka in my coat pocket, took a fresh pint from my desk and put it in my other coat pocket.

"What're you going to do, Fritz?"

"I don't know."

67

I got halfway to Lybart Petites before I realized it was already well past six o'clock. I stopped at the nearest burger pit and picked up two hamburgers but only got through two bites of the first one. I drank some more vodka and picked up a newspaper and the late edition already had the whole damn thing. Not a word in the story I didn't already know and I read it anyway. Why did I read it? I don't know. I don't know why I looked at the pictures, either, but I did. Then I drove up to Beverly Hills.

His car wasn't there. I sat and waited and drank

more vodka and an hour passed. I went up to the house and rang the bell and nobody came quick enough so I started rapping on the door with my fist.

"Mr. Thieringer! What happened to you? Your face looks terrible!"

"I got roughed up a little last night. Where's your husband?"

"I don't know. What's the matter?"

"He been home since work?"

"Yes, but he had to go out." Her hand flew up. "What's the matter? Is it the boy? Is Max in danger?"

"It's not the boy. The boy's gone. You know where your husband's gone?"

Her lip started to tremble. "No. What's the matter?"

"Nothing's the matter. I just wanted to see him." I turned and stumbled toward the street.

"Mr. Thieringer! Are you? . . ."

I waved a hand at her and kept going.

"Should I tell Max you want to see him? When he comes home?"

"No. Don't bother."

68

Nowhere to go. Nowhere to go.

The streets were empty but they weren't dark enough. Los Angeles streets never get dark enough. Part of it's for safety, part's paranoia. People aren't sure what they've got here but whatever it is they're damn sure they want to keep it. They're afraid if they ever let too many of the lights go out, whatever they've got here might get taken away from them. It might even creep away under its own power. Sometimes I think it's already done that and none of us has noticed. Los Angeles.

Nowhere to go.

Santa Monica. That bar.
I drove to the bar in Santa Monica and there it was, the silver Monte Carlo, parked at one side of the lot.

69

I worked my way slowly through the bar. I put my hand on a chair to steady myself and I missed the chair and leaned on a shoulder by mistake. It got me a sharp look. I muttered something that was supposed to be an apology and kept going forward.

He looked up and saw me, and looked down.

I slapped my newspaper on the table in front of him. He looked up, ashen faced, blurry eyed, and picked up his glass and emptied it. I sat down across from him and a waiter came over. Isenbart ordered a refill, I ordered straight vodka. The waiter went away. Then the waiter came back, and pretty soon he was coming and going with great regularity.

Isenbart rubbed his hands in his eyes in slow circular motions. I watched him very carefully. He took his hands away and his eyes looked at me with no emotion at all.

"You know what the dress business's like out here? Same's New York. I should've stayed." He closed his mouth and tightened his lips. "Couldn't. Had to come out here. Get things. Do things. All I got, I got nothing." His fingers brushed the table. "You fight every inch of the way. Everybody you deal with's out for themselves. None of it's worth it."

The waiter brought us another round without being asked. Isenbart smiled at him. Then he looked at his hands. "That's your partner I saw today? That woman?"

"Yeah."'

He laughed. "This life, you're alone! No partners!" He glanced at his drink like it must belong to someone else. "You need something done, take care of it yourself."

"That what you did today? Take care of it yourself?"

His head nodded down once and his eyelids closed and when they stayed closed I reached forward but before I could touch him he looked up and grabbed my arm. "I know what things're like! I needed help! Anybody help me? Nobody! Goddamn nobody!" He stared at my face, then realized he had his hand on my arm and took it away. He found his glass and emptied it again. The waiter was at his elbow before the empty glass hit the table. Isenbart drank from the new glass and then tried to get out of the booth but his body sagged suddenly and he couldn't make it. He dropped all the way back into the booth and sat sideways with his back against the wall. "They got you by the balls, everywhere you turn. So you deal with 'em. You pay 'em off. This business, you're a fucking pimp! Everybody's got his hand out! Once they got you they never let you go!"

He laughed. He tipped his head back and looked at the ceiling. "City of the angels, city of the goddamn. . . ." His eyes came down slowly. "Only angels out here, they got their fingers at your throat, squeezing you dry. They squeeze till there's nothing left." His mouth grinned. "Then they keep on squeezing. Don't they?"

The waiter came again with another round. Isenbart was too far gone to notice. He shook his head. "I saw it all. TV." But then he suddenly picked up the paper and stared at the pictures. "You get buried fast in Hollywood. Hollywood. Everybody's got to get into the movies, huh?" He threw the paper down. "Ever deal with those guys? In films?" He sat forward and shook his fists at me. "I could've been something out here! I could've made it! I tried to give 'em what they wanted! How the hell can you give those guys what they want when they don't *know* what they want? Guys sit in their offices, they got Academy Awards on their shelves, they got certificates on their walls, they're supposed to know something! So you ask 'em what they want! They don't *know* what they want!" He emptied his glass and looked away. "The hell with it. It's over." He laughed again. "I paid 'em off. I had to get money? I got money. Couldn't get it from banks? I got it where I had to get it. I did what I had to do. Myself. All I had, just myself. Long's I kept going, maybe I had a chance. But I didn't have a chance. Should've disappeared. Should've got the hell out of here so nobody could find me. But I couldn't. Had to stay here. Hollywood. Hollywood. Movies."

Just as it looked like he was finally finished he faced me again with eyes of stone. "I'm never going to make it." It wasn't nervous this time, or frightened, or angry. It wasn't much of anything. Just a simple unemotional statement of fact. "That's the worst thing of all, Thieringer. Admitting to yourself that you aren't going to make it. That you haven't got a chance."

Then he laughed. A very quiet laugh with very little intensity. He grinned at his glass. "You're young, you got dreams, you come out West, you're ready to beat the world." He picked the glass off the table and moved it back and forth watching it all the time. "Twenty-five years later, you're sitting in a cheap bar in a cheap town, you're trying to figure out what the hell went wrong." He put the glass down, then looked at me and smiled. "Better to stay in New York."

He kept looking at me. Then he reached for the glass and knocked it over. Scotch spilled across the table. I saw it coming in plenty of time but it didn't matter, my reflexes were too slow. It spilled over the edge and into my lap. I watched it spill and listened to another of his empty laughs.

I mopped my pants with a napkin, then leaned across the table at him.

70

"You thought you knew who he was and what he wanted. Maybe you tried to pay him off. Maybe that didn't work. Anyway, you tried to scare him off, and you thought you had, but he came back. And when he came back you knew you'd have to kill him. But your wife got us into it and you couldn't get us out. So then you tried to kill him the other night. You sent two goons to grab him, but they ended up in a dark alley behind a restaurant and they grabbed the wrong kid.

"You set it up again for today. You knew when it was going to happen and you arranged to be in our office when it happened, but something went wrong again. You found out who he really was. Gene Morrison. Whoever the hell Gene Morrison was, he wasn't who you thought he was. He was something different, and it scared the hell out of you. Suddenly you didn't want it to happen any more. You ran out of our office, and maybe you even tried to stop it, but you were too late. It was done."

He chewed his bottom lip. He picked up the fallen glass and unconsciously put it to his lips as if it still held something.

"What'm I going to do?" He tipped the glass as if he were drinking. "What's left for me to do?"

I kept going. "I don't know if it can be proved, but if it can, I'm going to prove it. If you did it, you're going to fall for it." I kept pushing the words through the haze in my head. "Whatever reason you had, I'm going to know it! You understand?"

He smiled at me and shrugged. He put the glass down. His hand gripped the edge of the table and he pushed himself out of the booth. He reached into a pocket and pulled out a wallet and flipped through a roll of bills and tried to count them. "Aww, the hell with it. It's just money. What the hell's money? What the hell difference does it make?"

He threw the whole roll of bills across the table. They landed on spilled Scotch and stuck where they landed.

He started for the door. I staggered out of the booth and went after him. "I'm on you, Isenbart. Whatever it is, I'm going to know it."

He smiled again. "Leave me alone. You're going to know nothing."

People looked up as we stumbled past their tables.

"I'm going to know who you are! I'm going to know who Gene Morrison was! I'm going to know everything!"

"Not tonight." He smiled at me again. "I've had too much tonight. I can't take it. Leave me alone." He brought his hands up slowly, palms facing me, then turned them inward. "All right?"

He reached suddenly for the door and pulled it open. I reached for it and pushed it shut. He turned to face me. His hand went inside his coat and came out with his .32-caliber Colt.

For a moment I froze. Then I stepped back. One step. I already knew there was no time and no place to step back to. The gun pointed at my eyes. I kept moving backwards, uselessly. The gun lowered and aimed at my chest. Behind it the smile was gone and his face was wet with sweat. Behind me chairs moved as people tried to get out of the line of fire. None of it made any difference any more. I had seen a boy killed, and I knew I should've been good enough to stop it, and now I was too drunk, and I was going to be dead, and none of it made any difference.

A woman screamed behind me. It was a wild, nasty sound. I turned to look at her. When I turned back, Isenbart was gone.

I counted to ten. I counted to ten again. I pulled the door open. There was no one in front of me. I stepped forward and heard an engine starting. I saw the silver Monte Carlo backing out of its space and something insane made me go toward it.

Isenbart turned and saw me. "Don't come after me! I'll kill you! I mean it!"

It finally struck home. Something seemed to snap. I clenched my teeth and jumped back against the entranceway where he wouldn't be able to see me. I heard him gun the motor and a second later I saw the car whip past. He looked at me once and kept going, went through the front entrance and straight into Santa Monica Boulevard. Tires screeched as drivers jammed on their brakes. The silver Monte Carlo honked at them and raced off.

The front door opened and hit me in the side. It felt like a biting snake and I jumped away from it in an involuntary movement.

I stopped and turned and looked behind me and saw the waiter standing in the open doorway. "Wow. Was that a real gun?"

I looked back at the street. The taillights of the speeding Monte Carlo were farther away.

A hand took my arm. "What should we do? Should we call the cops? Did you get his license number?"

I stepped away, just enough to get free of his hand. "I didn't get his license number. It was too fast."

71

I parked on the dirt road in my usual spot. The house up above me was dark. The green Mustang was parked across from it but the Chevette wasn't there. I got out of my car and shut the door. It wouldn't shut right. I kicked at it and it clicked. I went up the road and stood in front of the house and looked at its dark windows. I went up the steps and knocked on the door. No answer. I knocked again with my fist. No answer. I tried to open the door but it was locked. I took out my knife and tried to force the lock but I was clumsy and the knife fell from my hands. I heard it hit the steps but it bounced off them and fell over the edge into dark grass. I needed my flashlight to search for it but I found I didn't have my flashlight, I'd left it in the car. The hell with it. I turned to the door and pushed at it and it wouldn't open, so I kicked it and kicked it again and there was a cracking sound and the door swung open.

I stumbled through the dark living room and down the hall and into Morrison's room and switched on the light and started opening drawers. All I saw were all the things I'd seen the other night. The same picture of him and the girl, the same picture of the woman, the same letters, the same bills, the same glossy pictures on the walls.

I switched off the light and went down the hall and climbed the stairs to the second floor.

I switched on a light. A small room. With more glossy pictures on the walls. Hundred of movie stills in nice straight lines from floor to ceiling. No recent movies, only from the fifties. No big movies, just the kind of things you used to see on the bottom half of double bills. Cardboard boxes sat against the wall and one of them was open and I looked inside. Xerox copies of newspaper articles and the top one was a movie review. *The End of Pamela.*

My husband almost won an Academy Award once. *The End of Pamela.*

A girl screamed below me.

72

I snapped off the light.

I could hear them downstairs, two of them, they were talking to each other. I couldn't make it out.

I sneaked into the hall and I could hear them better. They sounded like they were still outside the front door. The house was still dark so I started down the stairs and I was almost at the bottom when the step beneath me seemed to snap like a breaking pencil and the girl screamed again.

A voice yelled, "I got a gun! You come out here! I got a gun!"

It went silent again and I shook my head. Things started to come to me very quickly. I hadn't gone into the kitchen tonight. I hadn't given myself a way to get out.

A light snapped on in the living room. I dodged back into shadows. I couldn't be sure if they'd seen me or not. I stayed where I was.

Whispers. "Let me go." Don't go in. Be careful. "Let me go." A shoe touched floor. One of them was in the living room. Twenty feet away.

I saw a panel box on the wall opposite me and I

reached for it and opened it. I turned off the switches. The house went dark again. The girl screamed.

I went through a door and into a room and struggled with a window. It stuck. Then I heard footsteps coming cautiously through the house. I put all my strength into it. The window went up. I went through it and out and landed feet first on the ground. Twigs snapped beneath me like tiny explosions and I stepped forward and my foot slid out from under me and I went straight down.

I got back up and started running in a crouch. It was too dark to see, branches brushed my face. I kept running. I heard someone behind me running along the edge of the house.

Then the girl's voice. "No! Let him go! I'll call the police!"

I fell once more and got up and kept going. I stopped for a moment and listened and it sounded like he'd stopped running after me. Then I heard something bounce off a tree about five feet away. He'd thrown a rock.

I went deeper into the woods. He shouted at me. Things flew through the air. Rocks. Sticks. I ran and then stopped, circled a few feet, moved behind a tree. More rocks and stones flew into the woods but not so near me any more.

I looked and finally made him out in the dark. He was standing near the house now and the girl was about ten feet behind him. He had one arm in a cast. He reached down with his other hand and picked up a stone and threw it into the woods and then stood still and listened. The stone hit something almost thirty feet away from me. He picked up another stone and threw it and it came closer but it was just a wild shot. I didn't move.

He threw a few more stones. Finally they went around to the front of the house. A moment passed and I saw a small light inside the house. A match, or a cigarette lighter, maybe a candle. They'd be going for the phone to call the police.

I went deeper into the woods and then circled and came out near my car. Other houses had lights on but the people were staying inside. Please stay inside. Please don't get involved.

I started the engine and turned the car slowly and went down the hill at a nice even pace.

Damn you, Fritz, what were you down to now? Frightening kids?

73

The phone rang and I picked it up but before I could say anything I heard, "Where have you been?"

"Out. Just got home."

"That much I know. I've been trying to get you all night. You didn't do anything stupid, did you?"

I flopped into a chair. "I sure's hell didn't do anything smart. What about you?"

"Tried to get drunk."

"Any luck?"

"Not much. My tolerance's getting too high. I rode the freeways for an hour and a half. Ended up in a movie. Truffaut. *Shoot the Piano Player*. Couldn't watch it. Came home." Her voice sounded like I felt. "How about you? Settled down at all?"

"Solid. Solid's the rock of Gibraltar." I stuck my finger into the phone cord and twirled it around. "Unfortunately I got a feeling the damn rock's sitting on top of the San Andreas fault." I could almost hear her nodding.

"How much have you had tonight?"

"A little."

"I wish you'd remember you can't drink like I can."

"Who can?"

"What else did you do? Besides get drunk?"

I rubbed a tired finger across my lip. "None of your business."

Her voice sharpened. "What did you do?"

"Nothing."

"Damn it!" She paused. "How bad was it?"

Bad enough. "I'm home, Mag. I'm ready to crawl into bed, just me and a bottle of. . . ." I looked at the empty pint bottle of vodka in front of me. "Just me."

"Want me to come down there?"

"No."

"You sure?"

"I'm all right."

"Better not come in tomorrow till you've slept it off and cooled down."

I pushed the neck of the pint bottle softly, kept pushing till it fell. "I'm going to have to get him, Mag. I don't know how yet, but I'm going to have to—"

"Sleep on it. We'll talk it out tomorrow." She sighed into the phone. "You sure you're all right by yourself?"

"I'm easy, Mag. Easy." I picked up the bottle and set it on the table. "I'm nice and easy." I knocked the bottle over again.

"Where'd you go tonight, Fritz?"

"I don't know. Where'd I go?"

"I think you went out and did stupid things you're ashamed to tell me about."

I said nothing. I hung up the phone. I picked up the bottle and knocked it over again.

74

"The coffee hot?"

Paul nodded. I went across the office and poured my-self a cup of it. I could've used a gallon. I collapsed in a chair and gulped some down and looked at the closed door. "Maggie in there?"

"She just got back. She was in Chatsworth all morn-ing. The Apcar case."

"How come she's got the door closed?"

"Some guy's in there with her."

I put my hand on the doorknob and started to twist it.

"Mrs. Isenbart called you, Fritz."

I left the door closed. "What'd she want?"

"She wanted you to call her. Been calling here all morning."

Laughter came from behind the closed door. Mag-gie's laugh and another laugh. Unfortunately I recognized the other laugh. I went to Paul's desk and tried the phone. Mrs. Isenbart's line was busy. I swallowed more coffee and refilled my cup and tried the line again. Still busy. I pulled myself straight so I'd look a little taller and went into the office.

What was sitting on the corner of Maggie's desk and holding her hand could've passed for the cover of *Gentle-man's Quarterly,* if you counted nothing but his clothes. His suit was pressed, his shoes were shined, his teeth were capped, his eyes were as shifty as O.J. Simpson coming through the line. His name was Hilinsky. He liked it when you called him Lieutenant Hilinsky, but I'd never given a damn what he liked.

He came over to pump my hand. I got my desk between us and didn't give him the chance.

He smiled anyway. "Long time no see, Freddie."

Another ten years might be long enough. Probably not.

"Looks like you got your face marked up a little, Freddie."

I shrugged. "Looks better'n it did yesterday."

He nodded seriously. "Too bad I didn't stop by yesterday." Then he smiled and spread his arms open like he wanted to hug me. "Come on, Freddie. Let's bury the hatchet. Make me feel at home. Offer me some coffee."

"You like some coffee?"

"Sure."

"Cream and sugar?"

"Just sugar."

"I'll get you a cup." I sat behind my desk and put my feet up.

Hilinsky came closer and gave me his famous I've-got-a-badge-and-you-don't-and-I-won't-forget-it-and-*you*-better-*not*-forget-it grin. He had it down pat but I'd seen it too many times on too many faces to care about it any longer.

"What's the matter with him, Maggie? Freddie's a very mean-spirited guy this morning. He doesn't want to make up with me."

Maggie smiled at me. "Pete was just telling me he almost got transferred out to Downey."

"Downey's gain is our loss," I said.

Hilinsky stayed smiling. "You look so nice, sitting there, Freddie. Feet up on the desk that way." He nodded his head. "Someone came along and tipped your feet up a little, you'd be flat on your ass." He rubbed a hand along the desk till it slid against my foot.

I stayed still. "How come they wanted to send you all the way to Downey? They catch you running numbers? Or prostitutes?"

169

His expression didn't change. He knew his game. "Didn't catch me doing anything."

"Maybe next time they'll get luckier."

His hand patted my foot. There aren't many bad cops, but there are always enough. And enough of them never get burned.

Maggie held up a familiar-looking piece of white cardboard. "Pete says someone was carrying our card."

I pushed my hat down to cover my eyes. "Lots of people carry our card. I carry a couple myself, occasionally."

Hilinsky tapped my foot with a knuckle. "This one was being carried by a boy who wasn't breathing."

I raised the hat brim and looked up, surprised.

"Young kid. Named Morrison."

I thought a moment. "Morrison?"

"That's right, Freddie. Mean anything to you?"

I turned my head. "Mag?"

"Not one of mine."

I nodded and dragged the desk calendar toward me. I flipped back a couple pages and pretended to read. "G. Morrison?"

"What do you know, Maggie? Freddie seems to've hit it right on the nose."

I nodded. "We got a call from a G. Morrison. Couple days ago."

He knuckled my ankle. "Well?"

I looked up. "He said he wanted to come in and talk. He never came."

"I see." Hilinsky reached for my calendar. I didn't give it to him.

"How'd he get dead?"

Hilinsky's hand stayed in midair. "That Griffith Park thing. Yesterday afternoon. You hear about it?"

"Saw it in the papers."

"Didn't know you read the papers."

"I look at the pictures, same's you do."

Hilinsky put his hand back on my ankle. "Morrison lived with a couple kids. House off Laurel Canyon Boulevard. Kids he lived with, they called the cops last night, said someone broke into their house." He stared at me. "You?"

I stared back and shook my head. I hoped to hell they hadn't found my knife in the grass near those steps.

Hilinsky moved off the desk and straightened. Then he put his oversized shoe with its steel toe on my desk and took a pencil and scraped dried dirt off his shoe. He built a tiny pile of dirt on my desk and left it there. "So Morrison called you, but he didn't see you, and you didn't see him. He must've wanted something. But you don't know what he wanted. I got it straight?"

I tapped my lower lip. "Straight's the crow flies."

He spread the pile of dirt with the pencil so it was flatter and covered more of my desk. "Way I heard it, the crow never flies straight, Freddie. Keeps going off course."

"I'll check my encyclopedia, maybe you're right."

"I'm always right." He looked up. "This Morrison case, you ain't interested?"

"Not unless there's some money in it."

He nodded. "I read the report on the break-in, up at his house. Doesn't look like money." He slid his shoe off my desk, leaving the dirt and a maximum number of scratches behind. He turned to Maggie. "See you around, Maggie. We'll have to get together for dinner or something." He started out. "Bye-bye, Freddie. Don't get caught with your thing hanging out. You might lose it."

"Nobody'd want it. It's used."

He laughed. "I doubt that." And he went.

75

I stayed looking at the door. "How can a classy broad like you stand to let something like that hold your hand?"

"I've had all my shots. Got a hangover?"

"Part of one."

"Drinking'll kill you. Leave it to the pros. I wish you'd stop acting so antagonistic with him."

"It's my nature." I looked at her. "Better'n holding his hand."

"You catch more flies with honey, Fritz."

"Flies're quick breeders. Sometimes you catch 'em real easy. Then you can't get rid of 'em."

"He's not that bad." She put her chin in her hand and looked at me. "Know what your problem is?"

"What?"

"You wouldn't mind him so much if he didn't touch me so much." I turned away. "Don't pout, Fritz." I put the calendar back on my desk and looked at the dirt and the scratches. "What'd you make of it?"

"Not enough to hang my hat on."

"He's got to know you're lying. He doesn't seem to care."

I brushed the dirt off the desk and into the wastebasket. The scratches I'd live with. "He cares. He cares, all right. He doesn't want to tell us anything about it, and for some reason I probably won't like, he wants to make sure we aren't going to tell *him* anything." I looked over at her and she was holding up an 8 x 10 glossy of a monstrously fat woman and a monstrously fat cat. "What's that?"

"Mrs. Apcar and cat."

"Which one's Mrs. Apcar?"

"The bigger one.

I peered at the picture. "Which ones the bigger one?"

"The one without the tail."

"Which one's the one without the—"

"Can it." She smiled at the picture. "Mrs. Apcar had fifty copies of these made up for me. The cat's missing. Mrs. Apcar wants him back. Mrs. Apcar instructed me to show the pictures around and see if anybody's seen him."

"Anybody's seen him, they ought to remember. He's the size of a horse."

Maggie frowned. "Don't make fun of Tulip. Mrs. Apcar suspects he was stolen by catnappers."

"A likely story."

"I liked it. She gave me a thousand-dollar retainer to make sure I liked it."

"Expensive cat." I picked up the phone and dialed. "What're you doing about it?"

"Showing the pictures around to see if anybody's seen him."

"Clever approach. Anybody seen him?"

She looked at me mysteriously. "If they have, they aren't admitting it."

"They been paid to keep mum."

Maggie nodded. "No doubt."

"You get all the interesting cases." The phone rang once and someone picked it up.

"Hello?"

"Hello, Mrs. Isenbart. Fritz Thieringer. I got a message—"

"Did you see Max last night?"

I answered evenly. "No, I didn't. Why?"

"He didn't come home!"

I sat still. "He didn't?"

"No! I called his office! He's not there! They say he hasn't been in today!"

I checked my watch—2:15. I still sat still. "He ever been out all night before?"

"No! Never! He hasn't even called me! Is there any chance. . . . You said the boy—"

"There's no way the boy could've hurt your husband last night, Mrs. Isenbart. You said you tried his office. When's the last time you tried there?"

"Just now! Just before you called!"

"He shows up or you hear from him, you call my office and leave a message for me. I'll see if I can find him."

I hung up the phone and sat quietly for almost half a second.

76

The silver Monte Carlo was parked in the lot next to Lybart Petites.

I went up to the fifth floor and through the glass doors and saw my reflection in the mirrors and didn't like the way I looked. Annie looked up at me and started to say something but I just nodded at her and must've looked funny or something because she didn't say anything. I went down the hall to Isenbart's office and tried to hear a phone slam down. A face looked up at me, a desperate, scared, confused face. It was Carl's face.

He stared at me and his confusion got bigger. Like maybe he could almost put me together with that man in the pea coat and the beard two nights before. I had to talk fast so he wouldn't have time to think. "Your boss here?"

"No, he's not here. He's—"

"I was supposed to meet him here at three o'clock. Where is he?"

"You mean. . . ." He leaned forward across the desk. "Did you talk to him? Today?"

"We made the appointment a couple days ago. Don't you know where he is?"

174

He couldn't take his eyes off me. He sensed something, but he wasn't sure what. I didn't have the beard, didn't have the same voice, didn't have the same color eyes—

But he sensed something.

I came around the side of the desk and stood next to him so he couldn't see me straight on. "What're you doing? Going over the books?"

Carl looked down at ledger sheets spread on the desk. "There've been calls coming in all morning. I don't know where Max is. I'm trying to. . . ." His fingers traveled senselessly down columns of figures. "There's something wrong here."

"What?"

"Calls're coming in for shipments and things. I had to check the books. But . . . something's wrong. Nothing adds up right. These numbers. . . ."

I turned the books sideways and looked at them. "He hasn't been here all day?"

"No."

"His car's downstairs. In the lot."

"What?"

"His car's in the lot. He must've been here and. . . ."

I didn't like the feeling. I'd felt it plenty of times before. It was that hollow feeling, the one that starts in the toes and goes all the way up and doesn't leave you till it's ready to. I moved away from the desk and took slow steady steps toward the door.

"You said his car's downstairs?"

I didn't answer. I went out of the office and down the hall. Carl's steps came after me. We went through the back rooms together but I reached the stairs first. I went up. Carl was still right behind me. I got to the top and pushed open the door and stepped onto the roof.

Isenbart was there, sitting on the roof. He had his back against the wall at the edge of the roof. He was dressed the same as he'd been dressed the night before. His feet were out straight. The soles of his shoes faced us. His arms were bent at the elbows and his hands held the Colt .32. The barrel of the gun disappeared inside his mouth and above his mouth there was nothing left of his face.

Carl started to moan like a sick animal. I got him turned away from it quick, grabbed him at the waist and guided him down the stairs. I put him in a chair and pushed his head down between his knees but he didn't throw up. He just kept shaking and crying. He brought his face up and it was as white as bleached bone. I pushed his head down again and held it there and steps came toward me.

"What's the matter?" A high voice. I'd heard it once before. "He all right?"

"Bring me a cup of coffee. Hot and black. Quick."

The model went away. She came back with coffee and I made Carl drink it slowly. When he stopped moaning I turned toward the model and made her sit and I knelt in front of her and held her hands.

"Listen to me carefully. This's bad. It's very bad." She nodded. "It's Mr. Isenbart. He's dead. He's on the roof. He's shot himself." Her face stayed blank. "You understand what I just said?" But I didn't repeat it. I didn't want to repeat it. She hesitated, finally nodded again, several times. "All right. You all right?" She nodded once. "Sit there."

I let her go and picked up the phone and dialed the police. When I heard a voice I put the phone to the model's ear. "Tell 'em what I just told you. He's on the roof. He's dead. Tell 'em."

She nodded and sat still. Then finally she started talking into the phone in a very quiet voice, but her words were the right ones. I turned back to Carl. He was quiet now and he was holding the cup of coffee in his hands like it was something special. Something so special the whole world depended on him not letting it go.

I turned away from him. I went out to the front and went through the glass doors and went down the stairs and went out of the building.

77

Maggie came into the workroom and stood next to me. "You all right?"

"I don't know."

"You want to talk about it?"

"No." I continued nailing pieces of wood together.

She went over to the side and sat on the bench and watched me work and after a while she said, "You eat yet?"

"No."

"You going to?"

"Yeah."

"I brought a steak and some stuff. Won't take long."

"I got to finish building this bookcase."

"Want some help?"

"No."

I put down the hammer as carefully as if it were made of spun sugar. I turned and looked at her, but I had nothing to say. I picked up the hammer and started nailing again.

I put my tools away and she swept the floor. I dusted myself and took off my overalls and she went out. I went into the living room and I could hear her in the kitchen. I put on some Harry Chapin but it was no help, I couldn't get into it, so I turned it back off. I looked out the front window. It was dark out there. Dark everywhere I looked. Too dark. And not dark enough.

I went into the kitchen and she had salad stuff out. I picked up a knife and she put a hand on my shoulder. "Why don't you just sit down and relax, Fritz?"

"I'm better off if I'm doing something."

She nodded and left me alone. I chopped onions and green pepper and celery and carrots and mixed it in with the lettuce and crumbled blue cheese over it and covered it all with oil and vinegar and then stared at the damn thing like it might tell me something.

We ate. Then she washed the dishes. I stared out the back door.

We went for a walk down to the beach and saw kids sitting at a bonfire roasting marshmallows. We went closer and one of them looked up. He looked just enough like Gene Morrison. We walked away.

We lay on the sand and my eyes searched the stars and her hand rubbed my cheek. "I had a dream about you, Fritz. You know that vase I've got? The red one from Morocco?"

I nodded my head slightly.

"I had a dream it fell off the bookshelf, and you were there and you saw it. You picked up all the pieces, and you had your glue with you, and you glued them all together again. But something was wrong. Either there were too many pieces, and they were all too small, or the glue was bad or something, 'cause it wouldn't stay together."

I nodded. "I don't much care for your dreams, Mag."

"And you kept at it anyway. You put more glue on it and stuck it together again, and it wouldn't stay together, and you wouldn't stop. And I kept telling you to stop, and you still wouldn't stop." She sat up and looked down at me. "Finally, when you weren't looking, I took the whole thing and threw it out. Then I went into the kitchen to get something to drink." She waited for me to look at her. "When I came back you were sitting at the table and you had the whole thing in front of you again and you were trying to glue the pieces together again. I tried talking you out of it. I couldn't."

I nodded in the hopes it'd stop me from saying anything but it didn't work. "Your dream have an ending?"

She looked across the sand. "I think so. Sure. It ended with you driving yourself crazy."

We didn't say anything for a while. Then I said, "That red vase. Yeah. It's a good-looking vase, Mag."

She shook her head slowly. Then she slid closer and I put my arm around her and held her tight. In the distance I could hear the seductive call of the sea. And above us the stars. None of it helped.

I came up on an elbow and watched the Pacific pour in on top of the sand. It came in softly. So softly. You'd almost like to go to sleep in front of it, just to see if there'd be anything left of you when you woke up.

PART THREE

78

Maggie disappeared for several days. She went into the wilds of Chatsworth to search for Tulip. I got some short jobs. A thin man with a fat wallet came in and said he owned a liquor store that was losing money it shouldn't've been losing. I spent an afternoon on it and went back that night. I turned up a clerk who was working his way through college with the help of the cash register and a friend who kept coming in pretending he was a customer. I put an end to it easily enough and got home in time for the beginning of the late movie on Channel 11. Laurel and Hardy. *Swiss Miss*. Lots of good laughs. I could use all they gave me.

Next morning at the office Big George called. He needed work. I had nothing to give him. The mail brought me two of my stolen credit cards. A desperate-looking middle-class mother came in and showed me a picture of Tracy—a runaway daughter the cops couldn't locate. It took me to Inglewood, then out to Hollywood, but the closest I could get was a full day behind her. Around two o'clock I found myself back in Westwood and I stopped by the office and Paul wasn't there.

I stopped by the office again around five. He still wasn't there.

I spent the night trying to trace Tracy and had no luck. At midnight I called Maggie's apartment and she was there but she wouldn't tell me where Paul was.

"I hope to hell you didn't send him on anything that might involve trouble, or guns, or trouble *and* guns."

"I didn't send him anywhere on anything."

"Where the hell did you send him?"

"Nowhere. Let me go to sleep. I been looking for that goddamn cat all day and I'm bushed."

The next morning Paul was still missing, Maggie was in Chatsworth, I was sitting at my desk staring at another credit card which had arrived in the mail. And whatever the hell it was that was eating its way through me, it felt like it'd gotten as high as my chest.

I took Tracy's picture back out to Hollywood and picked up a couple of new leads and at 11:00 that night I busted into a broken-down house in East Los Angeles. I didn't find Tracy. What I found was a dozen kids who showed the results of too much booze and too many pills. Not one of the kids looked to be over sixteen. Their faces were as empty as dead men's dreams.

I pressed Tracy's picture up against their faces and when one boy shook his head and the shake looked affirmative I put him in my car and drove him to the nearest pit and started filling him with coffee. Thirty minutes of burger-pit coffee got him talking what might be called English.

"Yeah, she was there, at the house."

"When was she there at the house?"

"Night. Last night."

"When last night?"

He opened a packet of sugar and spilled it on the table and tried to draw a face in it.

I took his hand with a slight squeeze. "When last night?"

"All night. Last night. Today. This morning. This afternoon. Then she split."

"She split? Where was she going when she split?"

His eyes clouded over. I brushed his nose with the edge of a ten dollar bill. "She said she was going home."

I left him there and went to a pay phone and dialed. The mother answered. "Yes! She's here! She got home in time for dinner!"

By the time I got home it was after three. I turned on the TV. No Laurel and Hardy. I looked through the bookshelves and tried reading a play by Dürrenmatt but only got through the first act.

79

The next morning Paul was sitting at his desk.

I nodded at him and went into my office and got a Coke and waited a minute and then came back and sat on the sofa in the front. "You still haven't returned my plays. Pirandello."

He looked up. "Sorry. I started reading another one."

I nodded and drank and stretched out my legs. "I tell you I take very unkindly to guys who borrow my books and don't return 'em?"

"You told me. I'll return it."

I yawned like I didn't have a care in the world and let another minute crawl by. "Get any time to read, during the job?"

He laughed. "Not much. Gruber wouldn't shut up."

I let another minute sneak past. "Gruber likes to talk, huh?"

He shook his head. "All the way to Albuquerque. Kept telling me insurance stories." I nodded and looked at my watch and closed my eyes. "Wouldn't let me drive, either. Real bummer. He kept asking me, was I covered for this, was I covered for that."

I nodded and yawned again. "Things turn out okay? Once you got to Albuquerque?"

"Wasn't much." Then he went quiet. I didn't push him at all. Sometimes they'll push themselves if you give them a minute. "He drove up to this house, far side of town, told me to keep my eyes open. He went up the walk and knocked on the door, this fat blonde came out. Had her hair up in curlers, looked half asleep. Gruber gave her the money. She looked in the envelope, she shook her head and went back inside." I kept my eyes closed and nodded. "Gruber came back to the car, he says, 'Christ, I'm glad that's over.' He drove out to a Howard Johnson's and treated me to dinner."

"Big spender."

"He kept giving me more insurance stories, all the way back. We got in around midnight."

"Yeah." I sat up and held my Coke can in both hands and looked at it. "Gruber say if he's going to want you again?"

"He said that should take care of it."

I took a sip of Coke. "Didn't have to use the gun at all."

"Nope."

All right. So he'd had it with him. All right. I stepped toward my office.

"You find that girl? Tracy?"

"She's home."

"You found her pretty quick."

"Guess I did." What the hell. I went through the door.

"Oh, Fritz, there was a call for you, someone named Deveraux. His secretary called. Wouldn't leave a number."

I stood just inside the doorway. Deveraux. Maggie had told me Deveraux's secretary had called once before. That night we were sitting in my car, outside Max Isenbart's house.

"And you got a long distance call from someone named Parking."

"Parking?" I said over my shoulder, "What's his last name? Garage?"

"Parking's his last name. Called for you or Maggie."

"*He* leave a number?"

"Nope. Said he'll call back."

I stayed by the doorway. "Everybody's paranoid, nobody wants to leave a number. Long distance from where?"

"San Francisco. I looked through the mail, not much. Check from someone named Snyder."

San Francisco. I stood by the doorway for another minute, or it might've been an hour, all of a sudden I wasn't keeping track. Then I went back into the front and got the check from Snyder. I folded it neatly into the shape of a rosebud and stuck it in front of Maggie's phone. Then I closed the door and sat behind my desk and drank Coke and stared at the walls.

San Francisco is right across the bridge from Sausalito.

And Deveraux's secretary had called while we were working on the Isenbart case.

San Francisco. Sausalito. Deveraux.

Deveraux. Sausalito. San Francisco.

This business was going to drive me nuts.

Going to?

80

"I found Mrs. Apcar's goddamn cat!"

She went to her desk and pulled open a drawer and took out gin. "I've been up all night, but I got the bastard!" She filled a glass and tipped her head back and threw gin down her throat. She dropped into her chair and laughed. "I'm bushed! Look at this!" She flipped a rectangle of paper at my desk. A check. Two thousand dollars.

"Nice. She missing any more cats?"

"Cost per pound, she got herself a bargain!" Maggie laughed again. "Want to know how I did it?"

"Dressed up in a mouse suit and ran all over Chatsworth squeaking your lungs out."

"Nope!"

"Put down a path of opened cans of cat food, up and down the streets of—"

"Nope!" Maggie put her left elbow on her desk and her right hand on the back of her chair and faced me smiling. "I found out Mrs. Apcar's deep dark secret."

"Everyone's got one. What's hers?"

"A room, in the back of the house. Door's closed. Curtains're drawn." She patted her chest. "I found out what she's got in there."

"I'm afraid to ask."

"*Mr.* Apcar."

"Dead or alive?"

Without standing up, Maggie rolled her swivel chair across the floor toward me. "He's got file cabinets and phones in there, regular office."

"He *do* anything back there?"

"He makes money."

"Prints it himself?"

"Stock exchange. On the phone, all day long, calling brokers, making deals, says he rakes in a couple thou a week. Buying, selling, buying, selling. Never leaves the room."

"Can he handle my portfolio?"

"Sure. List all your holdings on half a postcard and mail it to him." She winked at me. "I told him his wife's hired me to find the cat, and he says no wonder the damn cat's gone, she never lets it out of the house." Maggie tapped a finger against the side of her head. "Aha! I see the lay of the land! What I'm looking for is the horn-iest cat in the valley!" She squinted her eyes at me. "I checked out every house in a five-block radius. Marked down which ones had cats, especially female cats. As soon as the sun went down, I started my stakeout. At eleven o'clock, I heard a moaning sound down the next street. I get there fast and see a cat coming out the front door. She goes around the corner and I go after her.

"The cat goes down to an empty lot. Too dark I can't see her, so I listen. Pretty soon I hear her. She's not alone. I whip out my flashlight and turn it on and there he is. Tulip. He had a regular harem in there. I chased him all around that lot for ten minutes. He may be fat, but he can move pretty quick.

"I drove over to a McDonald's and got some fish

sandwiches and went back to the lot and crumbled them up and spread them on the ground. Pretty soon I'm knee-deep in cats. Every cat on the West Coast, except Tulip. Tulip might be on the chubby side, but he's got brains. But even Tulip succumbed to McDonald's fish sandwiches. While he's in mid-gobble I threw a burlap bag over him and dragged him back to the car. He must weigh seventy-five pounds and he wasn't too happy in the bag. I'm going to have to fumigate the car.

"Ten minutes later I'm knocking on Mrs. Apcar's door and trying to stop this burlap bag from dragging me down the street. Mrs. Apcar opens up. I threw him inside, he ripped the bag open and went flying out. He took one look at Mrs. Apcar and ran into the living room and made a dive for under the sofa. Couldn't make it. Sofa's too low for him. Mrs. Apcar says. 'The poor thing, nobody's been feeding him, he looks like he's lost ten pounds.' She wrote me the check and the last thing I saw was Tulip on top of the piano trying to leap at the curtains while she's trying to feed him a chocolate bonbon."

Maggie shook her head and sagged in her chair. She pushed her feet against the floor and rolled herself backwards to the desk and when she got there she noticed the rosebud in front of her phone. "What's this?"

"Open it up."

"It going to bite?" She opened it. "Snyder! He's paying for the truck!" She turned to me. Then her face changed. "What's wrong with you? Trouble with that missing girl?"

"I found the missing girl."

She studied my face. "Fritz? What's wrong?"

"You know damn well what's wrong. Close the door."

"What're you—" She stopped suddenly. She looked away. "Oh, no."

"Close the door," I said softly.

She went to the door and slammed it closed.

81

I sat quietly in my chair and spoke evenly. "A guy came in here the other day, Mag. I wasn't here. You were here. Guy named Gruber, insurance salesman. Had to drive to Albuquerque with some money. I don't think he said how much, but he said he didn't want to make the trip alone."

Maggie turned to face the far wall.

"Probably could've been anything, Mag. I don't think you knew what it could be. I think, without knowing what it could be, you sent Paul to Albuquerque with a gun. Fortunately it didn't pan out to anything. I don't think you knew that when you sent him." I stared at the back of her chair. "Either you *did* know the case wasn't going anywhere, or you were a little bit careless. Which was it?"

She kept her back to me. "The case didn't sound like much."

"In other words, you *didn't* know. Not for sure. Which means you were a little bit careless."

She swiveled to face her desk. "I told him to call me when he got back. He called me last night. Told me he had no problems."

"He was lucky. This time he was lucky."

She drummed her fingers on the desk. "He came to us because he wanted to see some action! He's not going to stay here if we stick him at the front desk and don't give him a thing to do!"

I didn't answer at first. I gave her a moment and then when I did answer I spoke softly. "There's something giving him problems. I don't want to take any chances till I know what it is." I paused. And watched her. "Or maybe you already know."

"I know what I see. He's all right."

"Why'd he leave Carne?"

She faced me with teeth showing. "Because he didn't like it there! I would've left, too! So would you! Listen to me, Fritz! You've had three days to get over what happened and you haven't gotten over it yet! Get over it!"

I didn't move. "Don't change the subject. I don't want—"

"I'm not changing anything! Let it go, Fritz! You can't change things once they're done! Let the damn thing go!"

I didn't move. "I don't want you sending Paul—"

"There's plenty you don't want! Most of it you're not going to get!" She turned away and refilled her glass.

I looked down at my blank green blotter. "Maybe it's time to cut some things, Mag."

"Yes! Maybe it is!"

The phone rang. It rang again and I picked it up. "Hello."

"I have a long distance call for Mr. McGuane or Mr. Thieringer."

I exhaled deeply. "Wait a minute, I'll have to see if Mr. McGuane's in." I put my hand over the phone. "Is Mr. McGuane in?"

"Go to hell."

I returned to the phone. "Mr. McGuane's out to lunch. This's Mr. Thieringer."

"One moment, please."

The line was quiet and Maggie faced the far wall again.

"Hello? Is this Mr. Thieringer?"

"Yeah."

"This's Ross Parking. I want to see you and your partner. Tomorrow morning. Nine o'clock."

"Let me check my calendar, Mr. Parking." I threw a pencil at Maggie. It hit her chair and she whipped around meanly. I motioned for her to get on the other phone. I spoke loudly so Parking wouldn't hear the click as she picked up the receiver. "Tomorrow at nine's okay, Mr. Parking. What's this in regard to?"

"We'll discuss that tomorrow, Mr. Thieringer. We'll be there at nine. Goodbye."

I spoke quickly. "Okay, if that's how you want it. Where you calling from? Your Sausalito office?"

Silence, then, "Sausalito?"

I gave *him* some silence. I could almost hear him thinking.

"Our office's in San Francisco."

"My mistake, Mr. Parking, thought you were located in Sausalito."

He thought some more. "No." More thinking. "The only thing we have over in Sausalito's the original Pirate. We're based in the city." He took some more time to think. "How'd you know what company I'm with?"

"We'll discuss that tomorrow, Mr. Parking. We'll be here at nine. Goodbye." I hung up before he could speak again.

Maggie looked at me. "What was that?"

I smiled and brushed dust off my phone with my fingertips. "He said we'll be there at nine. There's more'n one of him. You ever hear of anything in Sausalito called the Pirate?"

82

Long empty night. I ate half a sandwich and drank a Coke and listened to Beethoven and went through the pockets of a suit checking for loose change. I found two ball-point pens that said *Lybart Petites* and a *Lybart* envelope with two sheets of stationery in it. In another pocket I found a slip of paper with Isenbart's license plate number. I put it on the night table and stared at it.

I picked up the phone and dialed Maggie but nobody was home.

I stared at the slip of paper some more and turned it over and it said *Annie—HO9-5642*. I stared at that for a while and then I stared at the phone and then I picked up the phone and dialed HO9-564. . . .

Then I stopped. No, I wasn't that far gone. Anyway, I didn't think I was ready for anything that thought she had to come on with lights flashing and sirens screaming like a fire engine on a busy street. I waited a few minutes and tried Maggie again but nobody was still home. Or nobody was answering.

I went for a short drive and spent an hour at it and ended up slurping a useless drink at a place in Hollywood. I put in another call to Maggie and there was still no answer so I finally drove home and got there around 1:30. I went straight to the bedroom and flopped on the bed but couldn't fall asleep so twenty minutes later I went to the kitchen for something to chew on and smelled something I would've rather not smelled. It was the smell of coffee that'd been recently brewed. I looked quickly toward the back door and it was open a few inches. I'd thought I could stop locking it. I'd been wrong.

83

Paul was already at his desk looking at a magazine. I went into the back and Maggie was at her desk. She looked up. "Paul returned your book. Your Pirandello."

I froze. I knew she had me. I saw the book sitting in the middle of her blotter. I nodded noncommittally and took a Coke from the refrigerator and opened it and started drinking and after a proper amount of time I took a chance and went to her desk and reached for the book but I was right, she had me.

"Hands off."

"What?"

"I said hands off, Fritz! The book's not yours! It's mine! I looked through it! It's got my notes in it from when I designed *Six Characters* at UCLA! I thought I'd lost it!"

I returned her stare without cracking. "I was going to give it back to you."

"When? In your will?"

I said nothing and went to my desk and sat. When she thought I wasn't looking she put the book in her desk but I managed to see which drawer she put it in.

She went out but came back fast with coffee. "God, I was depressed last night."

I smiled at her. "Should've gone down to Pico Boulevard, Mag. They're doing Stewart Granger this week."

"I went. *Scaramouche* and *Prisoner of Zenda*. Saw both of 'em."

"Should've called me. Might've come and treated you. Might've popped for popcorn."

Her mouth grinned sourly. "That'll be the day. You still owe me for your half of the dinner at the Loft three weeks ago."

She was sure acting foul. Hell, the Pirandello was a paperback, it only cost about a dollar and a half. "I paid you back on that one."

"The hell you did." She opened her pocketbook and took out her small spiral notebook. "You owe me seven forty-three plus half the tip. Call it eight seventy-five."

"I paid you back."

"I still have it marked down. If you had paid me back, it wouldn't be."

I looked at my watch. "It's past nine. Where the hell are they?"

She leaned across her desk. "I didn't know it was past nine. Know why I didn't know it was past nine? 'Cause someone borrowed my watch and they haven't returned it yet!"

Oh. Yeah.

Then we heard the sound of the front door opening and closing. Then we heard noises. Maggie turned to her typewriter and stuffed paper into it and started typing. I opened a folder and pretended it had something inside it and pretended the something inside it was worth reading.

Paul brought them in. The man was in his mid-twenties. He was dressed in a three-piece, expensively cut, Gucci's on his feet, gold around his wrists, one of those natural-looking haircuts that set you back $50, they still call it natural. She was in her mid-forties. She had a smileless mouth and eyes made to look at you as long as they needed to without blinking. She had a face that'd seen too many of the things a face doesn't want to see. She was dressed in black. It was the third time I'd seen her. The first two times had been in a picture in a drawer in Gene Morrison's desk.

84

The man looked at me, and then at Paul, and then at me. "Wait outside, Paul. Close the door."

Paul nodded and went out but left the door open a crack. Good for him. I looked at the man and the woman. Neither of them noticed. The man looked at the sofa like he was appraising it for a fire sale and doubted it'd bring much. He stood aside and the woman sat at one end of it. The man slid a gold-ringed hand inside his jacket and came out with nothing more lethal than a gilt cigarette case. He popped it open and snapped out a cigarette and set the cigarette into a short stubby holder and put it in his mouth and lit it. Then he gave the lit cigarette to the woman. He walked to Maggie's desk and took an unasked-for ashtray and carried it to the sofa and set it on the end table. So far the woman hadn't looked at him once. He turned and gave me a smile as thin as a politician's promise. "Mr. Thieringer." He smiled at Maggie. "Miss McGuane." His head nodded toward the door behind him. "There's three of you. I ran a check on you yesterday, I was told there's only two of you."

I stared seriously. "Better run another check."

The woman tapped her cigarette into the ashtray. Very strong stiff taps. I was glad I wasn't the ashtray.

The man took a gold-plated pen and a checkbook from his pocket and, still standing, wrote out a check and put it in front of me. The writing was smooth and rounded and slanted and curved and probably had won him penmanship awards in school. The signature said Ross Parking. The amount said ten thousand dollars. Big amount. Too big. I left it where it was.

Parking talked. "According to my sources, you two're fairly reputable."

I put my elbows on my desk and smiled. "Good. You've got sources, we don't have to waste time giving you references. Let's get on with it."

"Very simple, Mr. Thieringer. I want to know everything you know about Gene Morrison."

"Gene Morrison." I made a face. "I don't know anything about him."

His mouth tightened. "Take another look at the check."

I took another look at the check.

He smiled. "You can't tell me anything, I'll have to tear the check up."

I nodded. "I'll tear it for you."

But before I could do it Maggie came over as I figured she would and took the check and looked at it and saw the amount and tried to control her face and looked at me and held the check out of my reach and finally looked at Parking. "We got a call from someone named G. Morrison last week. He wanted to see us, but he never came in. A few days later a cop came by and told us the full name was Gene Morrison and Gene Morrison was dead in that explosion in Griffith Park. According to the cop, Gene Morrison had our card on him when he died."

Parking's face remained unchanged and his right thumb and forefinger ran along the edge of his lapel. "What else?"

Maggie gave him a moment. "Nothing else." She sat on the corner of my desk.

Parking kept rubbing his lapel. "That isn't worth ten thousand dollars."

He waited for us to say something but he was too new at the game and didn't know how long to wait. He paced across the floor. "All right, let's say it happened that way. Just for argument's sake, why do you think someone named Gene Morrison would possibly want to see you?"

Maggie shrugged. "I suppose he needed professional help."

Parking turned sharply and pointed a finger. "I want to know everything you know about Gene Morrison. I'm willing to pay. But I'm not willing to waste time."

We watched him pointing his finger for a moment and then Maggie handed me the check. "Might's well start tearing, Fritz. This isn't going anywhere."

The woman said, "One moment."

Parking turned and went to her and we couldn't see her and then he stepped aside and when he did we saw cold eyes of steel peering at us.

"Miss McGuane, Mr. Thieringer, for your information, I can afford to sit here all day and tell Ross to write checks." She tapped her cigarette into the ashtray twice, very exact movements. "Can you afford to sit here all day and tear them up?"

I sighed. "Sometimes I spend entire days doing all sorts of things I can't afford to do."

"That's a foolish answer, Mr. Thieringer."

"I know, it was the best one I had. What do you want? Maybe we'd like to earn your money."

"What's your opinion about the explosion in Griffith Park?"

I put a thumb against my teeth and considered it. "I read about it. You usually can't go too far on what the papers decide to tell you."

She puffed her cigarette easily, then moved it an inch away from her mouth. "I've talked to the police. I'm not satisfied with the way they're handling it."

"How're they handling it?"

"A good deal differently than I'm used to seeing things handled."

I nodded. "Money didn't get you anywhere with them either, huh?"

The cigarette didn't waver. "I've had to pay off lots of people to get where I am, Mr. Thieringer. I've had the rates on my liquor licenses jumped too many times in too many years. I'm not planning to trust anyone who's supposed to be on the public payroll."

Maggie straightened a pad of paper on my desk and started doodling on it absentmindedly. I said, "Might get us somewhere if you told us who you are and why you're talking to the cops."

"I'm Virginia Morrison. Gene was my son."

I got out of my chair and went across the floor to take their eyes off Maggie. "Far's the cops go, I never had much reason to trust 'em myself. If you think they're botching it, you could be right. The system's got its faults."

She still puffed evenly and talked the same way. "I think you had something to do with my son. I want to know if you did. If you're honest with me it can mean some money for you. If you're not honest I can make it very bad for you, which I will do if I have to." She breathed out a long stream of smoke. "Simple enough?" I nodded. "Did my son hire you or not?"

"No." I walked close to her. "Right now I think I wish he had. Tell us about the explosion. You get anything from the cops?"

She tried to look through me. "The police advised me to sue the producers of the movie."

I nodded sharply and looked at her intently. "What else?"

She studied me. "At first all they'd tell me was that they thought there had been negligence. I paid some money to some people. I found out the district attorney's office believes there's possible grounds for prosecution. But not for negligence. They think the explosion may have been set on purpose."

I raised my eyebrows but not much. Maggie said, "Set on purpose by whom?" I turned and saw her drop the pad of paper nonchalantly on my desk.

Virginia Morrison looked at her. "The producers. Red Wind Productions."

Maggie walked to the other side of the room. "They think the production company tried to ruin its own picture?"

Maggie went to the far wall and Mrs. Morrison's eyes and Ross Parking's eyes went with her. I went to my desk and looked down quickly and saw what Maggie had written on the pad. *Pirate. The Hungry Pirate? Restaurants. Northern California.* I looked up, Mrs. Morrison and Parking were still watching Maggie.

"The district attorney's office believes they may have been doctoring their books to avoid taxes. They were on the verge of bankruptcy and they couldn't afford to finish the picture. They couldn't afford to close it down, because they'd signed contracts and couldn't get out of them. They may have done it for the insurance."

Maggie sat on the far edge of the sofa. "Are your sources reliable on this?"

"I had to pay a lot of money for that information. That hardly means the information's reliable." Mrs. Morrison turned toward me suddenly. "You never met my son?"

She did it good but I was better. "He never came in to see us."

She nodded and considered it. "As I said, I've dealt with police before."

"Yeah, so've we. Some you can trust, some you can't. It's never a sure thing."

"Regarding this explosion, perhaps you could look into it for me, if I wanted you to."

Parking stepped toward her and bent toward her ear. She signaled him away with a stiff left hand. "I want the two of you and the boy out front, the whole office. I want you on this and nothing else, full time. I imagine that will cost something. Will a thousand dollars a day cover it?"

Parking tried again. "Virginia, let me get some people we know. We can't trust—"

"Ross."

It stopped him. He stepped aside.

Maggie said. "A thousand dollars a day'll be fine, Mrs. Morrison. Should we use the check for ten thousand as an advance, or do you want it back?"

Mrs. Morrison looked at me. "Keep the ten thousand as a bonus, paid now in anticipation of your success. You see, I expect results. I also expect that if I'm buying you, you're going to stay bought. I hope we have that straight."

85

I took paper and pen and started writing. When they throw a thousand a day at you they expect you to be businesslike. "How old was your son?"

"Eighteen."

"Where was he living down here?"

"Ross will write down his address and phone number for you. He was living with some people. A boy and a girl."

"You talked to them?"

"Ross talked to them. He came down here earlier in the week, to get Gene's effects. He says the boy and girl were both there when it happened. Griffith Park. The boy was injured."

"Your son been living in Los Angeles long?"

"About a year, I think."

"Why'd he come down here?"

"He wanted to be an actor, I guess. He wanted to see if he could get into the movies. People who want to get into the movies are fools."

I looked up. "Some of 'em end up rich."

"They only end up rich fools, Mr. Thieringer."

I nodded in agreement. For a thousand a day I don't argue over the small stuff. "What else can you tell us?"

"Very little. I haven't been in close contact with Gene since he moved down here."

I started writing again. "What were his interests, before he moved down here?"

"Normal interests. Nothing unusual."

"But he was very interested in the movies?"

"Yes."

"One of those kids who was always buying movie magazines and stills from movies and stuff like that?"

"No, he wasn't like that."

I kept writing. "He have any college?"

"No."

"Just high school?"

"Gene didn't finish high school. He left during his senior year."

"Eighteen-year-olds can be sort of wild. He have any problems? Drinking? Grass? Pills? Anything?"

"No. Gene was a good boy. I never had any problems with him." She stubbed out her cigarette and handed the holder to Parking.

"Wait a minute, Mrs. Morrison. He have any sources of income you know about? Down here?"

"What?"

"A job or anything?"

"He was working in movies. Extra work. Whatever it was. He must've had some money from that."

"That'd give him something. You probably sent him some money occasionally?"

"Occasionally. Anything else?"

"That'll give us a start. We come up with anything, where do we find you?"

"The Beverly Hilton."

She gathered up her pocketbook and Parking and went out. As soon as she was gone Maggie came to my desk and took the check and went to her desk and started writing a deposit slip for the bank.

"It's nice, isn't it, Mag? When they want to impress us with how much money they got?"

She kept writing. "Too bad they don't do it more often."

86

I rang the bell once and waited and rang it again and
waited and then the door opened. I tried not to react. She
looked like something that'd been left behind by a windstorm.

"Mrs. Isenbart? You all right?"

She stared at me. "Oh. It's you." She rested her hand
on the door. "I'm just tired. Very tired." She turned and
wandered into the living room. I closed the front door
behind me and went after her. She looked at me again.
Her face looked so damn thin. "Least I haven't been
drinking. I haven't wanted to. I haven't wanted to do
much of anything." She sat and folded her hands in her
lap and looked at them. "I've stopped smoking. I've been
smoking since I was fifteen years old. I always tried to
stop, I tried twenty, thirty times. I never could stop.
Now I stopped, just like that." She laughed weakly. "I've
given up all my vices, Mr. Thieringer."

I sat across from her. "You had anything to eat today?"

She looked up and then her eyes moved slowly toward the far wall. "No. I don't think so. I wasn't hungry."

I watched her stare into space. "Could I have some
coffee or something?"

Her eyes came back and found me. "What? Oh. I'm
sorry. I should've offered you something."

She got to her feet and went to the kitchen. I followed after her and sat her down at the table. I opened
the refrigerator and saw what was there. I dropped bacon
into a skillet and put up water and put bread into the
toaster and mixed eggs in a bowl. When the bacon was

ready I put it on a plate and poured the eggs into the skillet and scrambled them lightly. I put the eggs on the plate next to the bacon and buttered the toast and put that on the plate and put the plate in front of her. I made two cups of tea and put plenty of sugar in hers and sat next to her and finally she ate.

When she was finished I washed the dish and the skillet and put them in the drainer and made her another cup of tea with sugar and watched her sip it slowly.

"I've never paid the bills. I've never had to balance the checkbook. I wasn't even sure how much money we had in the bank." She set the cup carefully into its saucer. "Max's lawyer went over it with me." She stroked the handle of the cup with her forefinger. "You get used to your husband taking care of things. You don't know what to do. Where to begin." She laughed that sad little laugh again. "Nothing seems to make sense."

"Have people been coming over? Relatives? Friends?"

She put her hands in her lap. "My friends were Max's friends. People he knew through the business. They weren't my friends." She glanced at the window. "I never went out much, except with Max. I've never known many people." Her face drained of color again. "I've got to do something! I don't know what to do!"

I put my hand on her hand. It was as rigid as a board.

She pulled it away. "I'm all right. It comes and goes. I'm just trying to think things out. Things don't seem to make sense." She put her hand on the teacup and stared at it. "I thought I knew him. I'm beginning to think I didn't know him at all."

Before I could speak she turned her face around and there was anger in her eyes. "That boy! You told me that boy—"

"The boy was gone at least half a day before it happened, Mrs. Isenbart. He couldn't've had anything to do with it."

"How can you be sure he was gone! Maybe he came back!"

I swallowed tightly. "He didn't come back. I'm sure of it."

I'd known this was going to be the toughest part. And it was. And it was tougher than I'd thought it would be, and I just had to sit there with it.

She got out of her chair and took the cup and saucer to the sink. She washed both and dried them with a dishcloth, then took the things I washed and dried them. She put them all away and folded the dishcloth neatly. Then she unfolded it and hung it over the edge of the sink to dry. Then she turned to me. "What're you doing here?"

"I wanted to make sure you're all right, Mrs. Isenbart."

"I'm all right."

I put a hand on the table and tapped my fingers lightly. "You said you saw your husband's lawyer. You all right for money?"

"Yes! I'm all right for money!"

Things had turned hard awfully quickly. Too hard. I got up and started for the door. "All right, that's all I wanted to know."

It caught her by surprise. She followed me into the living room. I searched around the room and found my hat on a table and picked it up. I spoke casually. "What's going to happen with the company?"

"There's a boy down there, Max's designer, he's trying to hold it together." She sounded slightly easier. "It's just temporary, till they see if anyone wants to buy it."

I nodded and started for the front door. "Yeah, I figured you'd sell it. Probably the best thing to do." I opened the door and went halfway out before I faced her. "No luck so far?"

She shook her head. "Max's lawyer, he talked to the designer, maybe he could buy a share of it or something, and keep it going. But they looked at the books, they said it's no use."

"No offers to buy it at all, huh?"

She looked at the floor. "I don't know what to do. I've got to do something." She looked up. "We'll have to declare bankruptcy."

I stayed in the doorway. Now that it looked like I was going to go she wasn't so worried about me any more. "Companies declare bankruptcy all the time. There's nothing wrong with it."

She looked past me, out toward the street. "It was Max's dream, his own company. He worked for years to build it up. He spent all those years."

"If there's no money to run it and nobody wants to buy it, you don't have any choice."

She nodded and said nothing. Her thoughts were somewhere else.

I took two steps away and then turned back. "I got a friend, he's an accountant. Maybe if he took a look at the books he might—"

"No!" Her eyes came alive again. "No. Max's lawyer, he's seen the books. It wouldn't do any good."

I held her look. "He's a good lawyer, Max's lawyer? You trust him?"

That set her back. She stepped into the house but didn't close the door. "I'd never seen him before. I don't *know* if I can trust him. I don't know if I can trust anybody."

"You never do, Mrs. Isenbart. Unless you try." I very carefully didn't move toward her. "Sometimes you got to try."

Her face brightened. "Maybe Max was going to do something! Maybe it was all right! I just don't know!"

"Max was a smart man."

"Come inside."

I went inside. She closed the door and turned away and went down a hall and up some stairs to the attic. It was full of dust and old furniture and cardboard boxes and clothes wrapped in plastic and memories of yesterdays and suitcases. She went to the suitcases. She faced me for a second with a desperate look. "I can't take it any more! I've got to tell someone!" She started opening the suitcases. Her hands clawed desperately at the catches as if she were dying in the desert and scratching the sand for water. She got three of the suitcases open and then suddenly moved away and went to the far wall of the attic. Her eyes still looked senselessly at the line of open suitcases. Inside the suitcases were small packages, each of them about half the size of a shoebox, each of them wrapped in brown paper. Some of them had been ripped open and I started opening more of them and they all contained the same thing. Money.

87

I went into the office quickly. "Paul, come here, I got a job for you." He left his desk and followed me to the back. Maggie was already there, sitting at her desk and tapping it with her fingers. I looked back at Paul. "I want you to go home and put on a suit. Something that'll make you look like you might be an accountant. Go down to Lybart and see that designer, Carl. Mrs. Isenbart called him, he's expecting you."

Paul put up a hand. "I was there. That day with you. They'll recognize me."

I smiled. "Your hair's shorter now." I opened my desk drawer and took out a pair of glasses with nonprescription lenses and gave them to him. "Wear these. Grab a hat from my car and wear it with the brim low. Get in and out fast. Just keep telling 'em you're an accountant. People usually see what they think they're supposed to see. Bring me the books, better go back at least three years. Don't worry about it, just do it."

Paul nodded and went.

Maggie leaned forward. "Well? David Greene made an offer yet?"

"No offers at all. Mrs. Isenbart says the place's ready to go bankrupt. She's a nervous wreck. She found money stashed in suitcases in the attic. I got tired of counting. I'd say there's half a million, probably more. Mrs. Isenbart's scared. She figures, they declare bankruptcy, there'll be people from the government all over the books and God knows what they might turn up. They find Isenbart had all that money in the house, it could lead anywhere. She doesn't know what to do."

Maggie closed her right hand in a fist and tapped her desk with her knuckles several times lightly. Then she stopped. "Let's say Morrison really had him scared. Isenbart started stealing from his own company so he could go on a long trip. Permanently."

"Maybe. I want to see how long ago he started taking the money. How'd you do on your end?"

Maggie swiveled to face me. "I went down to the union. The man who worked the explosives is named Frank Jarvis. I went to his apartment. No answer at the door. I went around back, he's got a balcony four flights up. Thought I might be able to get to it from the roof but the manager's wife saw me and wanted to know who I was looking for. I told her Jarvis, she said Jarvis hadn't been around for a couple days."

I stopped her. "How much was a couple?"

"She wasn't sure. Could've been pretty close to the day of the explosion. I told her I was from his union. I'd grabbed some pamphlets while I was there and I had 'em on my clipboard. I told her Jarvis was supposed to send me some information on time scheduling and he hadn't and if I didn't get it fast he'd get penalized. She went back to her apartment and got her keys and we went up. The place was empty. She stayed there watching me so I didn't get too much of a look but everything was pretty neat."

"Like someone'd been through the place before you, and they cleaned it up before they left?"

"Maybe Jarvis's neat. There's decks of playing cards all over the place. The manager's wife said he gambled a lot. Lots of liquor bottles too."

I smiled. "Starting to sound like your place."

"I throw the bottles away when they're empty. Smelled like the place'd been given a recent paint job. She opened the windows to air the place out, while she was opening I checked the bedroom. No signs he left quickly. I asked her about the paint smell, had he moved

207

in recently? She said he'd been there four, five years. Said Jarvis'd had some workmen in to fix things up, few days ago."

I raised a finger. "Before he left, or after he left?"

"She wasn't too clear on that. To tell you the truth, she was a little diddly. I think I was keeping her from her soap operas. Anyway, I couldn't see a thing that looked new or fixed or painted but she did say the workmen weren't the usual company that takes care of the apartments. Some private company Jarvis brought in. I didn't get to see if the refrigerator had anything spoiling in it. Went through his bookshelves but all he had was girlie magazines and books on explosives. I told her I really needed those time sheets or we'd have to dock him a full day's pay, did she have any idea where I could reach him? She shook her head and then she remembered she'd gotten a money order from him two days ago to pay this month's rent. She said he usually wasn't able to pay his rent on time but this time he had. I suggested maybe she still had the envelope the money order came in. That was a barrel of laughs. We went through her wastebaskets and turned up zilch. I got her to show me where they dump the garbage, and the thing was pretty full, like it hadn't been picked up for days. I conducted a very admirable search."

Maggie slid an envelope across my desk. Half of it was grease and the upper left-hand corner said *Capri Motor Inn, 1560 Timberline Road, Las Vegas, Nevada.* The postmark said *Las Vegas, June 6.* Three days ago.

Maggie smiled. "I've got a ticket on a flight up to Big Casino at two o'clock."

"Stay away from the goddamn tables."

"They have slot machines in the airport." She took the envelope. "I'll call down here around six if I can. If I miss you I'll leave a message on the service." She put the envelope in her pocketbook, went to the safe, took out a gun and shoved it in her pocketbook and kicked the safe door closed and stepped toward the door.

"Don't bet too heavy at the slots, Mag. She's only paying us a thousand a day and we got three mouths to feed, thanks to you."

88

I opened the office closet to see what I had in the way of a costume. I could go expensive or cheap. The problem with expensive was I probably couldn't go expensive enough. Especially since I wasn't sure what it was I'd be going to face. So I'd go cheap, dirt cheap. I'd try to look like something that might've been kicked off a cattle car and taken all the fleas with it.

A pair of jeans that were old and well worn and oil-spotted. Scuffed-up cowboy boots. A light-blue cowboy shirt, the one I'd picked up in Dallas. The torn suede jacket Maggie kept telling me to throw away. I took the jacket out to the hall, dropped it on the floor and kicked it around in the dust. I shook it once or twice to let the looser dust fly off and took it back into the office.

Next step. The trick was to look like a bum, but that screwy kind of bum who just might turn out to be a hell of a lot more than a bum. I opened my desk drawer and took out the Indian-head belt buckle with the diamond eye. It was a beaut. Someone had given it to me as a bribe a couple years before. I hadn't stayed bribed but I'd kept the buckle.

What else?

I opened another drawer and took out a cigar box. Four cigars left. Don't laugh, that added up to $80 worth of tobacco. They came from a rich client who'd liked me for reasons I never bothered to ask him about. I put two cigars in my shirt pocket so they were showing.

I checked in the phone book for the address of Amy Thomas and then locked up the office and went down to the car. I sifted through my hats and took out the black Stetson.

89

I walked confidently through massive wooden doors and found myself in jungle. Not the plastic kind. Real live foliage. I worked my way through it and found a girl who couldn't believe what she was seeing. I leaned across the counter at her. "Fredericks. T. J. Fredericks. Just flew in."

"Sir?"

"Tell Mr. Greene that T. J. Fredericks's here."

I waved my hand at her and she did nothing. I took out a cigar and waved that at her and lit it and when she smelled it she understood there could be money involved.

But she still did nothing. "Did you call for an appointment, Mr. Fredericks?"

She was one of those, all right. "Just flew in. Didn't have time to call for any appointments. Don't think I would've called if I'd *had* the time. Tell him I'm here and it could be worth some money to him. He's not interested, I got plenty of other places to go to."

Pencil-thin models walked by wearing the kind of stuff Elizabeth Taylor would have to sell off her diamonds to afford. I strolled after them like I was used to strolling wherever I felt like strolling. A man came to stop me. He was wearing a suit I couldn't buy even if I took out a second mortgage. I looked at him once and hooked my thumbs in my belt so the diamond eye on the Indian buckle winked at him and gave him a whiff of my ex-client's cigar and floated past him.

I heard commotion behind me and soon the girl from the front tried to take my arm. "Mr. Fredericks? Would you mind waiting out front, please?"

"I'm a man who minds waiting anywhere." I took

the cigar out of my mouth and looked at it with disgust. "Twenty dollars, they don't even know how to make 'em any more." I went into the nearest office and a man looked up from his desk. I went to him and found a wastebasket behind his desk and flipped the cigar into it and walked out.

The girl met me. "Wouldn't you like some coffee? Out front?"

"Could use some Chivas. Got some Chivas?"

The man in the suit gave it a try. "Mr. Greene's tied up right now. Would you—"

"Untie him. I haven't got all day."

"Would you mind stepping into my office for a moment?"

I frowned. "Got any Chivas in your office?"

He hesitated. "I can get some."

"Get it. Where's your office?"

He led me to his office and left me on a leather couch and went out. He came back with a bottle of Chivas and poured two glasses and left an inch clear at the top of the glasses. I reached across his desk for the bottle and filled my glass higher and then bent down to the desk and put my lips against the rim of the glass and sucked in.

"What business're you in, Mr. Fredericks?"

I cocked an eyebrow. "Only two kinds of businesses in this world. Buying and selling. I'm in both." I stretched my legs across his couch and he started to gasp when he saw the crud all over my boot and my boot all over his leather.

"You from Los Angeles, Mr. Fredericks?"

"From all over. Usually spend June and January in Houston, keeping an eye on things. Other'n that it's up for grabs. I didn't come here to talk to you. Came to talk to Greene." I lay back on the couch with the glass on my chest and closed my eyes.

After a while I heard the phone ring. I heard it get picked up and then put down. "Mr. Fredericks? Can you come with me, please?"

He went out the door stiffly and I wandered after him. I took the bottle of Chivas and the glass with me.

90

David Greene was reading a memo or pretending to read one. He looked up briefly with little interest and let his eyes scan me for a second before they passed on to the man who'd brought me in. His head nodded and the man turned and left. Greene ignored me and went back to his memo and I ignored him and settled into the most comfortable looking chair. I held the bottle of Chivas in one hand and the glass in the other and a few minutes stumbled by. Greene looked up.

"You wanted to see me about something, Mr. Fredericks?"

"You take too much time reading memos for my taste. Can't get much work done reading memos."

He slid the memo across the desk. "Thank you for the advice. What do you want?"

I nodded and sat forward and turned serious. "I'm not a man to fool around. How much you want for what you got here? The company. The whole thing."

He didn't blink. He rubbed a thumb along the edge of his ear and smiled faintly. "You want to buy Amy Thomas?"

I shrugged. "I always figured I ought to get something going for myself in L.A. My accountant tells me I got to diversify. What the hell, this looks profitable."

He nodded softly. "It is. I don't think I'm interested in selling it."

"Didn't say you were." I balanced the bottle of Chivas on my knee like it belonged there. "Said I was interested in buying it. Tell me what your number is, I'll tell you what I'm ready to offer. We'll see if you're interested. Understand, I want to keep you on to run things.

Set up your own contract. Ten years, fifteen, whatever you want." I leaned back. "I got a report on your books. I know you know what you're doing."

He studied his thumbnail. "Sometimes I do. Just who are you?"

"I'm from Houston. Your lawyers're any good, you'll know everything you need to know about me by twelve noon tomorrow. Always better to have your own people check these things. Then you know it's genuine. That's the way I did it. I could've come in here last week and asked to see your books. Had my lawyers do it. That's what they're paid for, might's well earn their keep. Didn't even know anyone was looking, did you?" He shook his head evenly. "Most of what I got's oil and I'm looking to diversify. Let your lawyers tell you the rest. Meanwhile, let's talk price."

He shook his head slightly again and put his right elbow on his desk and his chin in his right hand and looked at me with weary eyes. "There's companies all over this town, Mr. Fredericks. How'd I come up with the four-leaf clover?"

"You didn't." I let him consider that for a moment. "I was planning to pick up another company, but when I heard you were interested in it, too, I figured what the hell, easiest thing's to pick up both of you."

His mouth smiled neatly. "What company's that? Or do my lawyers have to check that one out too?"

He was starting to play with me. That meant he felt more comfortable and sure of himself. Which was how I wanted him. "You know what I'm talking about. Lybart Petites. I heard you made Isenbart an offer before he died. You think you're going to outbid me, you're wrong. I'll buy up both of you."

"No, you won't." He picked up the memo again. "But you can have Lybart. I'm not interested in it."

"Bulls ain't interested in heifers, either."

He looked at the memo. "The damn company already killed one guy. You want to be the second, I'm not going to stop you."

I sat up quickly. "What do you mean, killed?"

He turned. "Max Isenbart. He's dead."

I nodded vigorously. "I know he's dead. He's dead and they got to sell the company. What do you mean, killed?"

He put down the memo and his eyes narrowed. "I see. So you thought you'd pick it up cheap, while they had to sell. All right, Mr. Fredericks. I know your kind. Go ahead. Be my guest. Buy up Lybart. Nice company. Its boss committed suicide." I let his words smack me in the face. I sat back with my mouth slightly open. His eyes flashed at me. "You didn't know, Mr. Fredericks? Maybe you ought to get yourself some new lawyers to look into things for you."

I slammed down my glass. "Suicide! They didn't tell me that! Those stupid sons of bitches!"

He loved it. He snapped words at me. "Buy the company. You want to lose your shirt, I'm not going to stop you."

I let him glare at me some more but then I changed expression and poured myself a fresh glass of Chivas. "Bullshit. Way I heard it, you and Isenbart had a talk, couple weeks ago, about the chances of you buying him out. You're figuring to put me off so you can run in and eat it up yourself, but it's no good, I don't bluff."

Greene pushed his chair back. "We talked. Once. I talk to a lot of people." He got out of his chair. He was very big when he got out of his chair. "I've wasted some time talking to you." He gestured toward the door. "I don't care who you are or where you come from, Mr. Fredericks. You're not out of here in five seconds, I'm calling someone to get you out. I don't think I like you."

I laughed. "I don't think *I* like guys who got to call other guys to get people out of their office."

He came across the rug and took the glass out of my hand and while I was trying to figure my next move he almost took my arm out of its socket. He pulled me out of the chair and the bottle of Chivas started to tip but I grabbed it before it could hit the floor. Then he was walking me down the hall and he had a good grip and I wished it were on someone else's arm.

"You talked about Lybart with him. What're you going to tell me, he *asked* you to buy it?"

"This way, Mr. Fredericks."

"I'm coming! You don't have to squeeze the arm so hard! That it? He asked you to buy it? You didn't like the deal?"

"Hell, I made him an offer for old time's sake, that's all." He pulled me around a corner.

"Why'd you make him an offer if you weren't interested?"

" 'Cause he was a stupid bastard but I used to work for him once." He punctuated his sentences by shaking me. "Maybe I felt sorry for him. Then he got mad 'cause I wouldn't offer him more." He pushed me against a wall. "Max Isenbart was a casualty of this business from the day he started. I'm not surprised he killed himself. I'm just surprised he didn't do it years ago."

I smiled at him. "Okay, don't squeeze the arm so much. Isenbart wasn't any good at business?"

"He stunk!" Greene squeezed tighter. "He didn't have the balls for it! He had a goddamn persecution complex! I hated working for that bastard!" He swung me down the hall. "He couldn't figure out why he never made it big. He never made it big 'cause he wasn't cut out to make it big. Some people aren't. He wasn't. I am. Joanie, open the door."

The girl came out from behind the counter and ran to the massive wooden doors and pulled one open. Greene brought me around to face him and he looked mean.

"You don't have to squeeze that hard, Mr. Greene." His grip was like a tourniquet.

"You're right. I don't." He was liking it too much. "It hurts?"

"Yeah!"

He slammed me against the open wooden door. "Isn't that too bad."

I breathed quickly. "You didn't like Isenbart much."

"Not much. I don't know what you're fishing for but whatever it is I don't like that, either. I know when someone's fucking around with me. I don't like to be fucked around with. I don't think you got any oil in Houston and I think you're going to get the hell out of here."

215

He put both his hands on my arm and yanked it like he wanted to rip it off and didn't give a damn if it hurt or not and wanted me to know he didn't give a damn. He dragged me through the open door. I planted my foot against the closed door and grabbed his left arm just below the shoulder and yanked him back. I swung him around and slammed him against the wall and we found ourselves facing each other again. His eyes were wide with surprise.

"Yeah, Mr. Greene. I can do it, too, if I got to. You want to let go together? Might be easier that way."

He stood still and took a long breath. Then he nodded and took his hands off my arm. I took my hand off his. He rubbed his arm where I'd had it. "Who the hell *are* you?"

"I'm T. J. Fredericks from Houston. I got all the oil I told you I had. Nobody throws me out of offices. How long ago was that talk you had with Isenbart?"

He didn't answer so I stepped closer.

"I'm not sure. A while ago. If someone told you it was a couple weeks ago, they're wrong. It's longer ago'n that."

I barked at him. "How much longer? Months?"

He nodded. "Two months, three months, something like that."

"Thank you."

I turned and went out and tried to shake the stupid anger off. My arm hurt like hell. I tried to act like it didn't.

91

The office was unlocked and Paul wasn't in the front. I went to the back and found a man standing by the window. He was wearing a light-blue suit with faint white pinstripes running through it and a matching vest. He was as slim as a reed and old enough to be my father. "Your phone rang. I answered it."

"Thanks. You take the message?"

"Someone named Deveraux. Wouldn't leave a number."

"Deveraux never does." I sat on the sofa and watched him. "Wasn't the office locked?"

He looked at me as innocently as a cat who knows he's done something wrong. "It was. I didn't feel like standin' out in the hall." He smiled and sat at Maggie's desk and looked inside a drawer.

"Having fun?"

"Tryin' to."

I dragged myself off the sofa and went to my desk. "You been through my desk yet?"

"Your desk look like somebody's been through it?"

I opened two drawers and checked. "No."

"Then I guess I been through it." He rolled the chair back and leaned down and peeked under the bottom side of Maggie's center drawer. "You two kids don't leave much around that'd interest a guy."

"We can't afford to. We never know when a guy might pay us a visit. You the one who's been breaking into my kitchen at night?"

"Not that I recall." He straightened in the chair and rubbed a hand against his back. He smiled at me. "Who's dressin' you these days?"

"Fredericks of Houston. You want to talk about clothes, when'd Carne start putting you into government issue?"

His right eye threw me a wink. "Nice, huh? Three hundred dollars. A Carne operative dresses, speaks and behaves like a gentleman at all times and in all places. There're no exceptions to this rule." His fingers caressed the front of his jacket. "Want one like it? I'll get you a job there."

"I'd give anything for a suit that fits like it's supposed to. What's it come with, besides the vest?"

"Matching blackjack, shoulder holster and truss."

"The truss'd be useful."

He opened his jacket and the shoulder holster was steel-blue. I'll be damned, it *did* match. I put the bottle of Chivas on the desk in front of him. His eyes lit up. "Very impressive. Grateful client?"

"Not exactly. Help yourself."

"I hate to slurp out of the bottle in public."

"Try the bottom left drawer."

He opened the drawer and took out a glass.

I went to the closet and stripped off T. J. Fredericks and put on Fritz Thieringer. "Bring any news?"

"Just here for my health and the Chivas." He opened another drawer and smiled into it. "Paul Brade. Lasted at Carne for five months, two weeks, two days. Consensus is, the guy's very uneven. Might say, spooky."

"You sure's hell might!" He looked at me. "Christ! Either he freezes up like ice or he goes goddamn apeshit! One or the other! No fucking control!" I shut up and sat down. "He's working for us now."

"I know. I went through the desk in the front too."

I looked at him. "Why'd he get sacked?"

He shrugged. "Just wasn't reliable enough. Very edgy around guns—"

For some reason, that did it. "They're driving me goddamn crazy! I got a kid who's scared of guns! I got a woman who can't take a goddamn trip to Vegas without taking a goddamn gun with her! I'm going out of my goddamn mind around here!" He started laughing his

218

goddamn head off. "What the hell's so funny?" As if I didn't know."

"Brade's the one who's got no fuckin' control?"

That was enough. I pulled my chair up to my desk and sat there squarely. "Someone just got a little rough with me and then I got a little rough with him and I shouldn't've had to."

"Ahh." He opened another drawer. "So next time don't get rough if you can't take it." He pulled a bra out of the drawer and held it in front of him and inspected it. "She could be bigger."

"She's big enough."

"Right, you never did go for the top-heavy ones." He folded the bra neatly and replaced it in the drawer. "Brade used to be a cop, before he got to us. Didn't last long there either. Second day on the job he was on a grocery store holdup, he and his partner were the first ones there. It got messy. Brade shot someone. Dead. Accordin' to the records the shootin' team gave him a clean bill of health, but since it was only his second day out, a clean bill of health wasn't good enough. They kept a pretty good watch on him, and since they're usually not too delicate about these things, he must've known he was bein' watched. Went sour real fast. Didn't want to pull a gun under any circumstances, he could avoid it. I don't know if it was 'cause he was bein' watched, or 'cause he couldn't take havin' killed a guy. Anyway, he was out within two months."

I sat silently a moment. "So that's it. I thought he was just scared. It's a hell of a lot more 'n that. Hell." I looked over at Maggie's desk. "Goddamn bitch. I bet she knows. If she does, she knows damn well she doesn't want me to know." I wiped my hand across my mouth. "How'd he get into Carne? You guys usually trace these things pretty good before you hire."

"He wasn't hired as a field operative. He was doin' office work. Four months went by, the old man spread the word to send him out. You know the old man, he'll throw you in the water and sit on the shore and watch to see if you swim or drown and no matter which one you do he'll just sit there and eat his lunch." He poured himself another half-glass of Chivas and capped the bottle. "Brade started goin' out, reports started comin' in, he wasn't up to it, he got canned."

The front door opened. Without saying another word he closed the drawer he was looking into and slid out of the chair and stood at the window and did all of it without making a sound.

Paul came in carrying the books. He stopped pretty quick.

I leaned back in my chair. "Those the books?" Paul hesitated, then nodded. "Let's see 'em. Any problems?"

"No." He brought the books to my desk. "I got everything far's four years back."

I opened the cover of the top account book and glanced at it. Paul didn't move. I looked up. "Bill, this's Paul Brade. He's working for us. Paul, this's Bill Rittenhouse."

Rittenhouse took out a cigar and lit it. "About time you expanded the agency, Fritz. Pretty soon you'll be so big they'll have to list you in Fortune's Five Hundred."

Paul stared at him. "I used to see you around, Mr. Rittenhouse." Bill raised his eyebrows. "At Carne. I used to work at Carne."

Bill flipped his dead match at my wastebasket. "You were at Carne? When?"

"Half a year. Till the end of April."

Bill laughed. "Hasn't changed much since April." He blew smoke in my direction. "How you like the smell, Fritz? Grabbed half a dozen out of the old man's humidor when he wasn't lookin'." He shook his wrist away from his cuff so his watch showed. One of those jeweled chronometer-type things with all the gadgets on it for telling when you've been underwater too long. "Time to meet a rich client for cocktails. You hear anythin' on that guy we was talkin' about, let me know, Fritz." He started out.

"Sure, Bill. How much you pay me for it?"

He turned and sneered at me and then looked at Paul. "You work for a fuckin' mercenary. Good luck." He started out again.

"You find that carousel you were looking for?"

He turned again. He took a long puff on his cigar. "What're you askin' about the carousel for? You been talkin' to someone?"

"No." I rubbed a finger against my upper lip. "Didn't find it, huh?"

"I found it." He wrinkled his face. "After I found the fuckin' thing I lost it again."

I covered my mouth with my hand and tried not to laugh. It took a moment. "Nice work, Bill. You charge the client extra for losing it?"

He took the cigar out of his mouth and looked at it. "I'd rather not discuss it, you don't mind. I already discussed it with the old man. The old man's got the compassion of a fuckin' crocodile."

I nodded. "That's what it costs when you want to wear a three-hundred-dollar suit."

He stared at me. Then he shrugged. Then he put the cigar back in his mouth and went out. Paul watched him.

92

I told Paul it was late, he could split for the day. He hung around a few minutes, then went. I opened the windows, a Coke and Lybart's books.

Ninety minutes and four Cokes later I was more confused than ever. Yes, there was money missing, but exactly how much Isenbart had taken and how he'd taken it and even how much he'd taken at a single time, I wasn't sure. Because it wasn't just a case of him taking money out. There was also money coming in. How much was coming in, where it was coming from, *why* it was coming in, I didn't know. Whatever Max Isenbart had been doing with the books, he'd been an expert at it.

6:30. No calls. No call from Deveraux, no call from Maggie. Maggie'd said she'd call around 6:00.

7:00. I closed up the account books and locked up the office for whatever good it might do and put the account books in my car and drove to Beverly Hills. I spread the books across Elizabeth Isenbart's kitchen table and went up to the attic and brought down the suitcases and we started counting. It took quite a while to count up to six hundred thousand, seven hundred fifty dollars.

8:35. I pulled up in front of my house and walked all the way around to the back and discovered the back door still was locked. I started to open it and the phone inside the kitchen started ringing. It was the service.

"Got a message for you, Fritz. Maggie called in at seven-fifteen, from Las Vegas. She said she didn't find Jarvis but somebody found her and it was big trouble. She said she's coming home quick."

93

I drove to her apartment and waited. Waiting is always hard. Waiting for Maggie is often harder. Forty minutes later the red Volvo appeared. I walked to it slowly and she got out and gave me two paper bags. One of them was groceries and the other weighed more than an elephant. "What's in here?"

"Quarters. I hit the jackpot on one of the airport slots." Then she looked at me with that look of hers I can't stand to look at. She shook her head and turned sideways and lifted her skirt to her thighs. The bruises started just above the knee and went all the way up. They were already the color of overripe avocados. She opened her jacket and showed me her blouse. It was torn at the collar and the front was splotched with blood. She looked at me. "The blood's theirs, not mine."

She walked off fast, limping slightly. She went through the gates and up the stairs and into her apartment and straight to the kitchen. She tore open a small box. She rifled through it like she was going to rip it to pieces, then suddenly turned. "Don't just stand there! Take the groceries out! Put the chicken on a plate!" She pulled a card out of the box and threw the box down and read the card breathlessly. *"Poulet sauté Marechal Joffre.* Chicken in whiskey and cream sauce. Chicken stock. . . ." She leaned against the counter and tightened her mouth and spoke without emotion. "Chicken stock, white wine, butter, flour, heavy cream, mushrooms, hell! I haven't got mushrooms!" She stopped herself. "Chicken, salt, pepper, whiskey." She put the card on the counter. "Set the oven for three-fifty." She went out.

I lit the oven and went through the recipe card and did what it said to do. When the oven was at 350° I stuck the chicken inside. Maggie hadn't come back.

I found her in the bathroom. She was in the shower. "Mag? You all right?"

"I'm all right! I'm all right! I'll tell you what happened when I'm ready to tell you what happened! Leave me alone!"

I went back to the kitchen and sponged off the table and put up some rice and dusted some shelves and waited for her.

She didn't come, so I went back to the bathroom. She was still in the shower. I leaned against the sink and watched her silhouette through the glass door. Suddenly her hand flew up and went against the wall. The water muffled the sound but now I could see she was shaking.

"Mag—"

"What're you doing out there! Watching me like a peeping Tom? Leave me alone!"

I said nothing. I went out and down the hall and into the kitchen. All right, Mag, I'll leave you alone. Take all the time you want, I'll leave you alone. Sometimes people have to be left alone. Sometimes I forget that's the way it is.

94

I stared out the window and heard her behind me putting food on plates. I heard her go to the refrigerator and take things out and then she came over to me and offered me a Coke with ice. "I'm sorry I yelled at you before. It wasn't anything to do with you." She put the Coke into my hand. "Come on, Fritz. Let's eat, okay?"

She gave me her smile. She's got a killer smile.

We sat and ate and I must've been getting used to it, it hardly bothered me at all.

"Jarvis checked out of the motel days ago. I smiled a lot and the manager was very helpful. He let me see the records. Jarvis checked in the day after the explosion. But"—her eyes looked at me over a chicken leg—"the only time anybody saw him was when he checked in and out. I talked to the day maid and the night maid, both of them said Jarvis's room hadn't needed cleaning, all three days he was there. I looked at the card Jarvis signed when he checked in. The handwriting in his signature was exactly the same as the handwriting in his home address. The signature doesn't usually match the handwriting that well."

"You think it wasn't Jarvis?"

She put down the chicken leg and crossed her hands under her chin. "What if Jarvis wanted to skip and he figured he'd be followed? He's a gambler, probably gets up to Vegas often and knows people up there. He calls someone, tells him to check into a motel in his name, and sends down a money order to pay his rent. Anyone looking for him, they'll look for him in Vegas."

"All right. Maybe. What else?"

She looked at her plate and then looked away and took a deep breath. "All right. I was tailed, when I left the motel. Blue Buick. I couldn't lose it, we were in the middle of nowhere. As soon as the road looked empty it pulled up next to me and the guy in the passenger seat flashed something at me that looked like a badge. He signaled me off the road. I had a VW, I couldn't outrun a Buick, so I pulled off. Besides, it looked like it might be the real thing. I pulled off, they parked right next to me, half in the road."

"Cops park behind you."

She nodded. "I kept the motor running. The passenger got out, the driver stayed in the car. The passenger told me to show him some identification. I asked to see the badge again. He repeated his request. I had my pocketbook on the seat next to me but before I could get the gun out he had his out. He told me to turn off the engine and get out. I guess I was doing it too slow for him, because he jerked the door opened and pulled me out. He kept his gun down at his side and asked me what my name was. I gave him a name and he asked what I was doing in Vegas. I told him I was visiting relatives. He asked me how come I spent all that time talking to the manager at the motel. I told him my relatives were supposed to be staying there, but it turned out they weren't. All this time the driver's still in the car, watching the road to make sure nobody stops.

"The passenger took my arm like I was a piece of meat and started shaking me and pointed the gun at me and told me he wanted to hear a differenet story. I told him I didn't have a different story. He slapped me and pushed me aside and opened the door and reached in for my pocketbook. The driver was still watching the road. When the passenger got halfway into my car I slammed the door on him. Caught him at the waist. When he tried to get out I slammed it again. He lost the gun on the ground and I kicked it under the car.

"He tried to get out again and I got him with my

knee. He started groaning and holding himself but before I could get all the way into my car the driver was there and he pulled me out. I kicked him hard right below the knee and then I kicked his other knee and that stopped him. I got back in the car but then the first one got his arm around my waist and I couldn't reach my pocketbook. I grabbed onto the steering wheel to stop him from pulling me out. The keys were still in the ignition but before I could reach 'em the driver was climbing over the first guy and he had his hands around my neck.

"Then a funny thing happened. They were both trying to pull me out of the VW and I was holding on to the steering wheel and my head is turned so I'm looking out at the road and there were all these cars going by. And I could actually see the people in the cars. They were watching us, what was going on, and none of them were stopping.

"A hand was over my mouth and I bit it and then I got loose for a second and got the key turned in the ignition and the motor started. One of them pulled my forehead back so I couldn't see but I just grabbed for the shift. It was an automatic transmission, thank God, and I got my foot on the accelerator and the car started moving. I gave it the gas and it started to go like a bat out of hell. I couldn't see where I was going. Then all of a sudden they weren't holding on to me any more and I was barreling down the side of the road. I must've been doing close to sixty. I got the car back onto the road and pushed it up to seventy and kept going." Her hand grabbed her glass and she took a long drink of gin. "I don't know who they were, but they were big."

95

I finished washing the dishes and went into the bedroom. Maggie was quiet now. She was sitting in a chair holding her glass in both hands. Her eyes were closed. I turned to go out.

"I'm awake. Did you find out why David Greene wanted to buy Lybart and now he doesn't?"

I sat on the edge of the bed. "He says he never did want to buy it."

She looked at her empty glass. "What's that mean?"

"If Greene wasn't lying to me, and I wasn't lying to myself, Isenbart came to him a couple months ago and wanted to sell. Greene turned him down. Greene says he doesn't give a damn about Lybart and never did. But he got awfully mad when we started to talk about Max Isenbart, and he put a very strong grip on my arm."

"Good for him." Maggie tapped the side of her chair with one finger. "If Isenbart wanted to sell, he could've needed money for something. To pay off Morrison."

"Isenbart had six hundred thousand, seven hundred fifty dollars in his attic. You'd think that'd be enough to pay off anybody. Unless Morrison, or whoever was behind Morrison, wasn't interested in money."

Maggie smiled. "Maybe I was right. Maybe Isenbart was planning to take a long trip."

"But not as long as the one he took."

"Very few people want to take that one. Find anything in the books?"

I lay on my back and stared at the ceiling. "They make it look like the company's on the skids, all right. I don't know how Isenbart was taking the money out. I also don't know where he was bringing money in from, but he was bringing it in from some place."

Fingers snapped. "Maybe I was right again! Red Wind Productions! Capanegro! A laundering operation, feeding money through Lybart, dirty money to clean. People buy into companies like Lybart just so they can do that."

"But Isenbart was the one who was taking the money out."

"People wouldn't like that."

"No, they wouldn't." I sat up. "I'm going to have to go see those kids tomorrow. Morrison's roommates." I got to my feet.

"Put on some music before you leave, okay? Not too loud. Berlioz."

I went to the living room and sifted through her records. I slipped the *Symphonie Fantastique* out of its jacket and onto the stereo.

What did Isenbart *need* the money for? To get away from Morrison? To get away from someone else? And who the hell were the two guys in the Buick in Vegas?

The record dropped to the turntable. I watch the tone arm swing across and down and the needle found its groove. I adjusted the volume so Berlioz came softly out of the speakers on the bookshelf and my eyes wandered along the shelf from the one speaker to the other and passed by Maggie's books. Maggie's film books.

96

I took down the fattest one and flipped to the index. *The End of Pamela*, page 259. Page 259 showed me a picture the size of a postage stamp and it was a picture I'd seen before, on Gene Morrison's wall. I looked at the film's credits. *Pamela* was made in 1954. None of the names in the credits meant anything to me till I reached Costume Design. I recognized Max Isenbart. I didn't recognize Joseph Lydon.

Max Isenbart and Joseph Lydon.

Isenbart and Lydon.

Lydon and Isenbart. Lybart.

I turned to the index again. I looked under Isenbart. I found he'd made another film, *The Evil Edge*, and there was a picture from it and I'd seen that picture on Morrison's wall, too. The movie was made in 1957, three years after *Pamela*, and the costumes were designed by just Max Isenbart.

I turned to the index and looked under Lydon and found two more films besides *Pamela*. *The Silent Sister*, made in 1954, and *The Quarry*, made in 1955. Lydon had designed both films by himself. There were stills from both films. Morrison had had both of them.

97

Maggie was lying on the bed now and her eyes were closed. I looked at her. Time to go, Fritz. Time to go.

But I stood there and suddenly her eyes blinked open and her head jerked up and her hand went toward the drawer of the night table.

"It's all right, Mag. It's just me."

Her hand stopped. "Oh. I must've fallen asleep."

Her head dropped back to the pillow.

Time to go. Time to go.

I sat on the edge of the bed and put my hand against her cheek and left it there. She didn't move. I brushed the hair softly away from her eyes and she looked at me. I rubbed the side of her face gently and my other hand found her hand. I moved closer to her. She turned her face away. I bent closer.

"No, Fritz. Please."

I drew back but only slightly. "Could I maybe just hold you for a minute?"

"No! I don't want to be that close to anyone ever again! I've been through it and I had it thrown right back in my face!"

Her whole body was rigid. I took my hand away. Then neither of us moved.

I closed my fingers into tight hard fists with all the pressure I had so I could feel my fingernails digging into my palms. I sat through a long moment of that and then exhaled softly and relaxed and got off the bed. She had her face against the pillow now.

"I'm sorry, Fritz. It's got nothing to do with you." Her words were barely there.

"I know." I looked vaguely around the room. Then I laughed. "It was a hell of a lot better before we got to know each other."

"When we didn't know each other it didn't matter what we did. There wasn't anything at stake."

I looked at her again. "There wasn't?"

"No." She took a big breath and then spoke firmly. "It was anonymous." Her eyes closed. She rolled over and got her back to me. Then she spoke softly. "I'm not ready to get involved again. I'm not going to stake my feelings on someone and have them walk away from me again. Not again." Her head buried itself in the pillow. But then suddenly she sat up and crossed her legs on the bed and stared at the wall opposite. She wiped her eyes quickly and took a big gulp of air and then spoke. "I can't go through it again. You think someone means it when they tell you they love you, you don't think they're going to walk out on you. But they do, Fritz, they do."

I was in the doorway. I was rubbing my hand up and down the frame. "That's the chance you got to take."

"I don't have to take it." From the corner of my eye I could see her head moving. Up and down in strong slow nods. "I took it once. I don't have to take it again. I won't let myself be left again. I've been ripped open for the last time."

I stared at the door frame. "There're no last times, Mag. Not till you're dead."

Her voice rose suddenly. "Then consider me dead!"

I paused, then tried a laugh. "I can't. You make too much noise for a dead person."

It didn't work. Her voice was a monotone again. "People let you down. The only thing you can count on is that they're going to let you down."

I turned finally and looked at her. "It's not that we let each other down. It's that we fail. We're all fallible, Mag. We have our weaknesses and our blind spots. We fail each other. We can't help it, it's part of our nature. The great joke of the world, we never want to fail each other, and we always do fail, in some way. We can't let a stupid thing like that stop us."

She saw me looking at her and rolled on her side with her back to me again. "Just leave me alone. I can't stand you when you're like this."

"I know. But I'm like this. I'm built this way." I took two steps toward the bed. Her shoulder twitched and I stopped. I shook my head. "The other joke, Mag, is that we always expect people to give us more'n they can give us."

"He said he'd love me forever. Two years isn't forever, is it? It's long enough to rip you to shreds, but it isn't forever."

I looked at her another moment and then I got smart. "All right. I'm going." I turned toward the door.

Her voice got loud again. "Can't you at least get mad at me? I know I'm being rotten but I can't help it. Get mad at me!"

I turned around. She was looking at me. I opened my hands and shrugged. "I can't. I already got mad a couple times this afternoon. I used up my quota for the day."

That didn't work either. The next thing I saw was her back. The next thing I heard was "I hate you!"

I nodded. I stuffed my hands in my pockets and leaned against the door frame and neither of us had much left to say. It was pretty quiet. Then too quiet. I stood straight again. "Aww hell, I'm going home to take a hot shower. I'd take a cold one, but cold ones turn me on. I'm funny that way."

She still didn't laugh. I was striking out on all fronts. I went down the hall and into the living room and picked up the film book. I turned it over in my hands. It felt awfully solid. Permanent. Maggie didn't want anything permanent. Nobody seemed to, anymore. We're no longer interested in permanence, just change. Any kind of change. Max Isenbart wanted change. He couldn't make it in New York, he came out here to give it a try. Gene Morrison left San Francisco and came down here. Carl didn't like it here, he wanted to go to New York. I'd been in New York, I'd come west. New York was where Isenbart thought he should've gone back to. Maybe it's the advantage of modern transportation. Things don't work out for you here, you go there. And you hope.

I looked down the hall toward the bedroom. Hell. When Fritz Thieringer gets himself stuck in the middle of a dark night he sure knows how to dig himself into a hole. Enough digging, Fritz. Leave it. I just hoped she was asleep.

I took the film book into the kitchen and propped it against the toaster. I went out and down the stairs and out to my car and took a nice long drive. Los Angeles is made for nice long drives, but it didn't help enough. I still felt emptier than a poor man's wallet.

98

I started to open my front door and I saw a light some-where in the back. I thought I knew exactly where in the back so I stepped away and closed the front door quietly and walked softly around the side of the house. I took the sap from my pocket and let it hang loosely at my side and went through the shadows, listening for anything. I came around the corner and saw the back door was open. I moved toward it. Coffee was in the air.

The phone started ringing inside the kitchen. It scared the hell out of me but I stayed where I was and didn't make a sound. Then I moved slowly even with the door and looked inside. And we looked at each other for a very long moment.

The phone stopped ringing. She laughed nervously. "Didn't think you ever came home." I put the sap in my pocket. She looked at her coffee cup. "I guess I owe you some money for the coffee. I got nervous waiting. So I made coffee. But I always washed everything up and dried it." I stayed in the doorway. Her eyes looked at me weakly. "You never called me. You said you would."

I stayed at the bottom of the steps. "You come on too strong. You don't give anyone a chance to think about it."

She laughed nervously. "I've always been that way. I ought to stop. It doesn't seem to get me very far." She laughed again. "The funniest thing, it's all a front. I'm not like that at all." She wrapped her arms around herself. "This's a crazy city. It does things to you. Drives you crazy, makes you do things, want things." She looked down. "Makes you want to be with someone. Sometimes, just anyone." She shook her head quickly. "No. I don't mean that. Not just anyone. But someone. You just can't stand to be alone, some nights. L.A.'s so big." She brought her head up. "Don't you ever get lonely?"

The phone started ringing again.

She stared at the phone. "You better answer it. It keeps ringing, every couple minutes."

I came into the kitchen and picked up the phone. "Hello?"

"You took your time getting home. I went into the kitchen and I saw where you left the book. Took me ten minutes to figure out what it was there for, then I couldn't remember the name of the movie Isenbart designed, but I found his name in the index and I traced it that way."

I spoke carefully. "What'd you trace?"

"Joseph Lydon, huh? Lybart?"

I leaned against the wall and watched Annie stare at the coffee cup. "I suppose so. Got any ideas?"

"I looked through the credits, there was an assistant director on the film named Howard Sloane. He's a screenwriter now and I know him. I'll talk to him."

"Fine."

"Something the matter? You sound funny."

"I'm okay."

"Fritz? Are we still okay?"

"Sure. You take things too seriously. Go to sleep."

"You sure? I'll see you tomorrow?"

"You can bet on it."

"Okay. Thanks. Good night."

"Good night."

She hung up and so did I. I sat at the table. Annie looked at me just the right way to give me that helpless feeling I knew too well. She smiled emptily at the phone. "Will it ring any more?"

"I don't think so."

Her fingers traced a circle on the table. "I've been thinking, maybe I could try not coming on so strong."

I watched her finger circle. "Worth a try."

99

Sometimes the nights turn out to be not so bad after all, but the mornings are usually the same. They dare you to do better than you did yesterday, and you know you better do it.

I stood neatly in my conservative suit and my conservative glasses and my conservative pipe and knocked on the door. When the girl opened up I lifted my Indian madras sport hat a quarter of an inch. "Morning. Mr. Parking called you yesterday? To tell you I'd be stopping by?"

She didn't react. "Mr. Parking?"

"Mrs. Morrison's associate? I handle Mrs. Morrison's accounts down here." I relit my pipe. "Parking said he'd call you so you'd know I was coming. To check the house, see if Parking missed anything that belonged to Gene."

It hit her. "Oh, yeah, Parking. No, he didn't call."

I nodded. "Figures. Better call him, San Francisco. You don't want me going through your house unless you're sure I am who I say I am." I turned sideways and looked down the road. Let her call. I was covered. Mrs. Morrison had said they were staying at the Beverly Hilton. Parking wouldn't be in San Francisco. Let her call. "Parking said he'd call you yesterday. He always forgets what he says he's going to do."

"Well, we were out most of the afternoon." She looked me over. I looked straight as a banker on auditing day. "It's all right. You can come in."

She showed me into the living room. The boy was lying on the floor reading a magazine. His arm was still in a cast. He gave me a look that said he wasn't impressed by bankers. "Who's he?"

"He works for Gene's mother. He wants to see if there's still any of Gene's stuff here."

The boy got up and slouched across the room to a table which held the apothecary jar. He took two pills from it. The girl made a sound with her tongue and teeth. "Please. Jim. I don't have time for this today."

Jim popped both pills into his mouth and swallowed and went out.

The girl put her hands on her waist. "His arm got busted up in the explosion. He can't get any work. He won't be able to till the cast comes off." She gritted her teeth. "Excuse me, I'll be right back."

She went where Jim had gone. I looked around the living room. The apothecary jar. All those damn pills. I went over to it and reached inside and took out a handful. They felt like nothing. I heard steps behind me and I dropped the pills into my coat pocket.

She took me down the hall. Gene's room was clean. Nothing left behind except a few magazines and a notebook that had never had a chance to be used. I thumbed through the notebook. "Looks like Parking got everything that was here. I see you got a second floor. Anything up there?"

She turned in the doorway. "We didn't even think about looking up there. Jim and I never go up there."

"Could I take a look?"

She led me up the stairs.

"Mrs. Morrison said she didn't have much contact with Gene while he was down here. Just to send him some money, every once in a while."

The girl turned. "She sent him money?"

I kept my face straight. "Sure. Didn't you know?"

She laughed. "I didn't even think his parents knew he was down here. Money?" She laughed. "He sure kept it to himself. He kept a lot of things to himself."

I leaned against the railing and fidgeted with my pipe. "Yeah, the last time they saw him was when he came up to Sausalito, couple months ago."

She nodded. "So that's where he went."

"You didn't know?"

"He just split. Like one day, he was gone." She scratched her head. "Wouldn't tell us where he'd been, when he came back. Big secret. With Gene, everything was a big secret."

"He went up to recuperate. When he broke his foot."

She glanced down the stairs. "That's why I'm having trouble with Jim. He's pissed off about having the cast 'cause he remembers how Gene hated it."

"What happened to Gene's foot? Accident?"

She held up her hands palms up and made a face. "Who knows? Another one of Gene's secrets. You had to learn not to ask him about things he didn't want to be asked about." She turned and went into a room. The room looked pretty much the same as it had that night I'd been up there. The night after the explosion. She looked at the walls. "I forgot he had all these pictures up here. He was always collecting 'em." She walked along the wall, going from picture to picture. "Said there was something about their style he liked. The artistic approach they showed. Said he was going to write a film script, something to do with all these movies. He wouldn't say what his idea was, because if anyone else got the idea they might write it first. I know a couple other guys who want to be writers. They always tell you they got a great idea but they got to keep it to themselves. All of 'em have great ideas."

I knelt beside the cardboard boxes and opened the top one. "Least they're not as bad as those who got an idea and they won't shut up about it."

"I know one of them too." She looked over my shoulder. "He's always *going* to write the screenplay, which he never seems to do, but he's always *talking* about it. I heard the damn plot so many times I think *I* could write it."

I read the top Xerox. "He's got an old review here. *The End of Pamela.*" I stared at the Xerox. "Wonder whatever happened to these people. Directed by William Hollings. Ever hear of him?"

"No." She walked away. "Probably working in TV. They're all working in TV."

"Written by Jay Gramerson. Ever hear of him?"

"The business's full of names you never heard of." She ran her fingertips against the pictures on the wall. "That's the scary part. You're out here, trying to make it, I wonder if you ever know."

"Know what?"

She faced me. "If you've made it. There's actresses who make a couple of films, you think they've made it. Then they just disappear. You look through the Academy Directory, they're in there, but they aren't working. Scary business. Scary town." She walked past me to the window and looked through it.

I read her more names. "Producer, Thomas Coyle. Costumes designed by Max Isenbart. Ever hear of them?" She shook her head. "Big picture, two costume designers. Max Isenbart and Joseph Lydon. Ever hear of Lydon?"

"Probably working in TV now." She pressed her nose against the window. "Or selling used cars. I'm always reading about people who used to be in the business and now they're selling used cars. Whole country ends up selling used cars. Especially in L.A." Then she banged her fist against the window frame and set her jaw against whatever was outside. "I'll tell you one thing, I don't give a damn what it takes, I'm going to make it in this business. I'm not going to end up selling used cars."

I put the Xerox back in the box. "Must be tough, trying to break in."

"It's not tough. It's impossible. Just got to hang in there."

"Think Gene would've hung in?"

It floated for a second and then she turned. "What?"

"Think Gene would've made it? In acting?"

"Gene wasn't an actor."

I checked my pipe to see if it needed to be relit. "My mistake. He was on that film with you. I thought he was an actor."

"He needed the money." She went across the floor and looked at the pictures again. "Jim and I get a few days of extra work here and there. There's no auditions for extra work. They just call names from a list. Gene needed some money, so we got him on the list. That's why I was surprised when you said he got money from home. He must not've got much, he always needed some."

100

It took both my hands to hold the cardboard boxes so I bent over and got the elevator button pushed with my nose. The door opened and I went in and then someone yelled from behind me. I stuck my foot in the door so the door couldn't close.

He was wearing a blue velvet tuxedo and a rose shirt with ruffles. His tie was still tied but it was two inches off center. He spun across the lobby and into the elevator like a top that was all set to fall over. "Thanks. Don't think I'm up to handling the stairs right now."

I waited for him to push a button. He didn't. "What floor you want?"

He looked at the ceiling and wrinkled his brow. "Joanne Woodward."

"What?"

"Three Faces of Eve."

I wiggled a finger free and tipped the button for three. The elevator rose. He started to tip. The side wall stopped him. His eyes were half open and his mouth was half shut as he picked up a wrist to look at it. If he'd ever had a watch there, he didn't have it now. "What time is it?"

"Around eleven."

He giggled. *"The Horn Blows at Midnight."*

"It's eleven in the morning."

He cocked his head to one side. "What'm I doing up at eleven in the morning?"

239

"Maybe you didn't get to bed." The door opened and he didn't move. I couldn't get past him. "We're here. Joanne Woodward."

He went out and I followed. I stopped at the door to the office. He gyrated past, stopped, stumbled back and looked at the painted letters on the door and smiled. Just my luck.

I had my hands full of cardboard box and he had his head full of fog so I kicked the door twice in the hope someone would answer but nobody did. I got two fingers around the doorknob and twisted it and kicked the door open. He went in first.

Maggie appeared at the inner door and he saluted her. "Maggie! I got your message but I'm afraid I'm in the middle of a Ray Milland."

He started to tip again. Maggie caught him and looked at me. "He's in the middle of a *Lost Weekend*."

"You're telling me."

She hooked an arm around him and led him into the office. I dropped the cardboard boxes on Paul's desk and by the time I'd straightened my back she was standing by the coffeepot. "If that's your screenwriter, I can see he's going to be a lot of help."

"What's in the boxes?"

"Newspaper clippings. Morrison collected 'em. I talked to the girl, threw both names at her, Lydon and Isenbart. She didn't blink."

The sound of falling furniture came from the other office. Maggie filled a coffee cup quickly. "I better see if I can sober him up before he demolishes something."

"Skip the coffee and give him Eddie Condon's hangover cure."

She turned in the doorway. "Which one's that?"

"First step, you take the juice of two quarts of whiskey."

101

Paul came in full of energy and smiles. "I found the letters of incorporation. Isenbart and Lydon set up the company together. October 20, 1954."

"Lydon didn't get much of a chance to enjoy the fruits of the partnership." I pushed the top cardboard box aside. "Joseph Lydon's dead. He was mugged outside a bar in West Hollywood on May 12, 1955. Someone took his money and used a shotgun on him. Gene Morrison had Xeroxes of every report in every L.A. paper. He also had Xeroxes of every review of every movie either one of 'em designed."

Maggie came out tucking her blouse into her skirt. "Lord, the things I do to break a case." She filled a cup with coffee. "Come on, he's ready."

I watched her tuck. "Looks like he's not the only one who's ready."

I took both boxes into the office and put them on the floor next to my desk. Maggie went to the sofa and pulled the velvet-tuxedoed screenwriter into a sitting position and sat next to him and then he laid down with his head in her lap. He purred like a kitten. She purred back. "Time to talk, Howard."

"*Talk of the Town*. Cary Grant and Jean Arthur." He reached for her breast.

She stopped his hand. "We have company now, Howard."

"Company?" His head turned and an eye opened and saw me.

I smiled at him. "Thought you said he's ready. Thought you meant ready to talk."

She bent toward his ear. "Howard!" His eyes

popped wide open like exploding fireworks. "You were an assistant director on a film, Howard. *The End of Pamela.* Two guys designed the costumes. Remember?"

He massaged his ear. "That's from my early years. I blocked out my early years. Couldn't survive if I didn't do that."

"Max Isenbart and Joseph Lydon!" I said.

"On the Town!" Howard said.

"What?" I said.

"New York?" Maggie said.

"Sure!" Howard said. "Came from New York! Still looked white. Garment salesmen. Couldn't find their way across the city without a map."

Maggie smiled at me. "Told you he was ready." She stroked his neck. "How'd they get the job designing the costumes if they were garment salesmen?"

"They came cheap. *I* came cheap. We *all* came cheap." The corners of his mouth turned down. "Back then I came very cheap." He sat up and rubbed his hands together. "What a film that was. *Pamela.* Had to do it on a shoestring. That's why it worked. Guy named Tom Coyle produced it. Didn't have much money so he had to put every cent up there on the screen. Made money, lots of money. Coyle got a studio contract out of it." He flopped back against the sofa. "That was the end of Coyle. They stuck him in a big office and he got scared to take any more chances. Started turning out formula stuff. Lasted two years at the studio. I used to see him around. Always drunk, living on pills, ended up taking *The Big Sleep.*" He nodded slowly. "I could write a book about the guys who ended up taking *The Big Sleep* out here. Hell, Coyle had talent. Then he started making money and it ruined him."

Maggie put a hand on his shoulder. "What about the garment salesmen?"

He rubbed his chin. "I made contacts off of *Pamela.* Sold my first script. Bought my first Mercedes. Christ, I loved that car. Did okay on *Pamela,* too. Coyle couldn't pay us peanuts so he had to give us all percentages. He didn't think it'd ever come to anything, but it did. Bought me my first Jaguar." His mouth smiled broadly. "That was a good car, too."

I leaned across my desk. "Maybe Max Isenbart and Joseph Lydon made money on *Pamela*. Maybe they took their percentage and opened a company. Dress manufacturing."

He looked at me. "Yeah, they were always talking about starting some kind of company like that."

"Both of 'em?" He didn't react. "Were *both* of 'em interested in starting the company?"

He nodded. "One of 'em was a little lean, one was a little fat. I used to call 'em Laurel and Hardy."

"The fat one'd be Lydon. He designed a couple more films, by himself."

He thought it over. "Never ran into him again."

"The thin one designed another film, too. Just one."

Howard shook his head. "Laurel. Poor Laurel. He couldn't design his way out of a paper bag."

I came around the front of my desk. "Were they friends, the two of 'em? Good friends?"

"Sure. I told you, like Laurel and Hardy."

Just then Paul opened the door and stuck his face at us. "Mrs. Morrison's here."

102

Maggie and I wheeled Howard Sloane out of the office, each holding an arm. Virginia Morrison and Ross Parking were sitting on the front couch. I swiveled Howard to face them and made introductions. Howard recognized the smell of money and bowed deep at the waist. Maggie and I had to stop him or he would've fallen in her lap. Mrs. Morrison gave him her coldest stare. We dragged him away and down the hall.

"What're the introductions for?" Maggie said.

"Just seeing if anybody knows anybody. Howard? You ever see her before?"

Howard didn't answer. He put his fingertips against the mirror next to the elevator and tilted his head back and admired his image. The elevator arrived. We propped him inside it and I pushed the button for the lobby. He examined his bare wrist. "What time is it, Maggie?"

"Almost *High Noon*."

His face turned sour. "Noon. Got to go have a shootout with a producer up on Gloria Swanson."

Maggie turned to me. "Over on Sunset Boulevard."

"Story conference. Those story conferences drive me nuts. Those guys think they know how to write. They can't write." He stared at the floor. "They know how to write checks." He looked up and smiled. "And I know how to cash 'em. What the hell. Farewell, my lovelies." The door closed on his smiling face.

We went down the hall. "Stall Mrs. Morrison in the front about thirty seconds, Mag."

We went into the office and Maggie stalled. I went into the back and gave Gene Morrison's cardboard boxes enough of a kick to hide them behind my desk. Maggie came in. Mrs. Morrison looked disgusted. Parking trailed behind her, keeping the proper distance.

Mrs. Morrison set herself up in the middle of the couch. Parking supplied her with a lit cigarette and ashtray and sat beside her and crossed his hands in his lap and stayed quiet like the well-trained pet he was paid to be.

"You've had twenty-six hours. What have you found out?"

I sat up straight and tried to look officious. "Sometimes these things take more'n twenty-six hours. We don't give out daily reports. We tend to work better when we're left to our own schedules."

"I'm very impressed by your methods. I enjoy finding all three of you sitting around your office at twelve noon wasting time on drunken fools like that specimen you just showed me. That's definitely worth a thousand dollars a day." She blew smoke in our direction. "Have you talked to the man who was in charge of the explosives on that movie?"

I nodded slightly. "We're working on it."

"I don't want you to *work* on it. I want you to *do* it! I want you to do it damn quick!"

Now I understood the thousand dollars a day. It wasn't to impress us, it was to give her the right to yell at us.

She glared at me. "The man who set the explosives is named Frank Jarvis. He has an apartment in Hollywood. Ross'll give you the address." She sucked smoke. "I did some investigating myself."

Maggie started tapping her desk nervously but before she could say anything I said, "We've been to his apartment, Mrs. Morrison. He's not there. He's gone."

That didn't stop her. "I *know* he's gone! I'm surprised *you* know he's gone! I would think, if you knew he was gone"—her eyes traveled from me to Maggie and back again—"at least one of you would be out *looking* for him!"

Maggie's fingers drummed her desk. She looked at me. "I don't know about you, Fritz. I've had it." She got out of her chair and walked across the room. "We've been looking for Jarvis, and we plan to look for him some more. We'll do it when we want and how we want. If you don't like the way we do it, there are other places you can spend a thousand dollars a day. I'll be happy to give you a list of them."

Mrs. Morrison smiled thinly. "I've decided to spend my money here."

"Then get this straight!" Maggie put both hands on her waist and stood straight. She was really carried away with herself. "I don't like people telling me how to do my job. I don't care who they are, I don't care how much they're paying, if they don't like what I'm doing they can go elsewhere. If they don't want to do that, they can just be patient and wait for me to do what I'm going to do. One thing they can't do is come into my office and tell me what to do. I don't accept that." She had a bad case of anger, all right. All I could do was watch.

Mrs. Morrison watched too. She relaxed against the

back of the sofa and smiled. "I don't give much of a damn what you accept, Miss McGuane. You've had damn sufficient time to come up with something." She tilted her head up and flicked ashes on the rug and I didn't like how coolly she did it. "I've done a little more investigating. Would you like to hear about it?"

Maggie spat it out. "I'd be delighted!"

I was still hoping it was an even match, but it wasn't.

"You've got an undergraduate degree in English, Miss McGuane, and a graduate degree in theater arts. You got both degrees on college loans from the government and you haven't paid the government back yet. You're also paying off a car loan and both of you are paying off the loan you took out two years ago to get this business started." She paused to puff smoke.

"It gets expensive to open a first-class operation," Maggie said. "Mostly licenses and guns." But Maggie was only wasting time with that, the lady was a pro and the way to take her was to take her fast. Maggie wasn't doing it. "Especially guns. They're very expensive these days, because so many people want them. You have to—"

"You used to have a husband. You lost him."

Mrs. Morrison paused again. I think Maggie still had a good chance to jump in there, during that pause, but the pause came and went and Maggie said nothing and then Mrs. Morrison said, "The divorce didn't do you any good financially because you didn't ask for alimony. If you had asked, it wouldn't've made any difference. He's a third-rate actor and he doesn't even get enough work to support himself."

Maggie took a half-step backwards and rubbed the back of her neck and I knew she was done for and I tried my best to stop it. "This'll get us nowhere, Mrs. Morrison. If you—"

"You can shut up, Mr. Thieringer. I'll get around to you soon enough." Her eyes sparked back toward Maggie. "Whenever your ex-husband gets hungry he comes to you with his hand out for money and apparently for some stupid reason you give it to him. I hope you don't give him much because I know how much this agency grossed last year and it wasn't enough to feed two of you, much less a runaway husband and that boy you have sitting out front. Unless you hired the boy so you could deal with all the extra business you're doing this year, of which there isn't any. Or maybe you two have got money coming in under the table. If you do, I might look into that." She handed the cigarette holder to Parking to give her a refill. "Or I might tell some people I know in authority to look into it, unless you start living up to my expectations. Which means doing what I want you to do and doing it when I want you to do it, without any backtalk."

We all sat quietly while Parking lit the new cigarette for her. She took it stiffly. "As for your debts, I can very easily pay you enough to get you out of them. If you have other clients who can pay that well, by all means go to them." She leaned forward sweetly with one hand palm up. "Otherwise sit down, shut up, and listen to whatever the hell I'm in the mood to say to you."

She waited for an answer. Maggie turned slowly and looked at me and nodded. "Well, I tried."

"Better sit down, Mag."

Maggie stood still. More cold words came from behind her. "Ready for the rundown on you, Mr. Thieringer?"

"God, no, I've heard it all before, it bores the pants off me."

Maggie went to her desk and revealed Mrs. Morrison's alert face again. "Where should I start? Boston? New York? Chicago?"

"Chicago? Hell, I only spent one night in Chicago."

Her face brightened. "But you spent it in jail."

I returned her smile. "I hated to turn down the offer of a free bed."

Her mouth tightened. "You received the offer so frequently."

"I was young. I got put behind bars a couple times. As I got older, I decided to put other people there. It's ancient history, Mrs. Morrison, it won't get you anywhere. Your son have any other reason to come down here besides wanting to get into the movies?"

It didn't touch her, at least not visibly. "I can't think

of any. If you find there was something, I'd like to know what it was."

"Your main office's in San Francisco. You live in the city or out in Sausalito?"

She hesitated a moment and half-looked at Parking but then looked back. "Sausalito. Why?"

"Your son visited you up there when his foot was broken a couple months ago. He tell you how he broke his foot?"

That definitely did something to her. I leaned forward. "He did stay with you in Sausalito, didn't he?"

She searched beside her for the ashtray. "He didn't tell me how he broke his foot."

I kept going. "Was he making any progress down here?"

She looked up. "What do you mean, progress?"

I spoke quickly. "The movies. Meeting people. Getting auditions."

She nodded. "He told me he was seeing people. I didn't ask about it thoroughly."

I looked at my calendar as if there was something there. "Where did you say you're staying? The Beverly Hilton?"

"I have to fly north, at two-thirty. You can reach me at my office there. Ross will give you the phone number."

Ross didn't move. She looked at him. He came forward quickly with a card. I waved him off. "If we call and you're not there, you want us to give the message to Mr. Parking?"

She sat quietly. "If you come up with something, you talk directly to me."

I opened a drawer and searched inside it. "See my man in the front, Mrs. Morrison. Give him your home address, home phone, business address and business phone." I kept looking into the drawer. She finally stood. "Give him your social security number too. We need it for our records, in case someone tells the federal government to check us out and we have to prove everything's above the table." I looked up. "Which for some peculiar reason it happens to be, currently."

She walked stiffly to the door but then stopped and

turned back. She looked more human now. "I may be a little hard to put up with sometimes. I've found I have to be that way, to get anywhere. But if you do a thorough job for me, I'll compensate you very well for putting up with my bad manners. Whatever there is to know, I want to know it." Her voice could be soft when she wanted it to be. But then something must've gone through her mind because it showed in her eyes. Her words came sharply again. "I'm paying you a ridiculous amount of money. Whatever there is to know, I want to be the *only* one who knows it. Don't make any mistakes about that." The softness was gone, her face was as blank as a slab of metal. "I understand money, and what it can do. If you understand it, we'll get along. We'd better be leaving."

She turned abruptly and stepped out. Parking remained on the sofa.

"You're quiet today, Mr. Parking."

"I like to listen sometimes." His mouth curled at its edges. "She means it, you know. You screw up, she can take care of you."

I tapped my chin lightly and stared back at him. "We'll have to make sure you get a front-row seat."

He stood up and straightened his jacket and buttoned it. "Don't worry about me. I've already got my ticket." He grinned like a man with a secret and went out.

What I like most about this business is you meet such friendly people.

103

Maggie waited for the front door to close. "You shook her, Fritz. She didn't know he'd been up in Sausalito."

I opened my hands. "What the hell got you going at her like that?"

She looked at her desk. "Talking about how we

weren't doing anything to find Jarvis. Christ, my leg bothered me all last night. I had to take something so I could sleep, and you know how I hate to take pills."

I looked at the ashtray on the sofa. "She's a woman who believes in the golden rule. Whoever's got the gold can make the rules."

"She shouldn't've brought up Harry! I would've demolished her if she hadn't brought up Harry!" She turned to me. "Have you been talking to her behind my back? No trick to take her, Mrs. Morrison. Just hit her with Harry, she'll fold like a house of cards. Knockout!"

"Cool it, Mag."

"I'm trying to." She hit her desk. "Do you have a secret formula?" She picked up the phone and dialed. Into the phone. "Roger? Maggie. I need a movie or something to take my mind off things, anything you want reviewed?" She listened. "Fine, I'll cover it." She slammed down the phone. "A horror movie. That's all I need. Do you have something to do?"

I nodded. "Got to see how Mrs. Isenbart's doing today. Paul! Bring me Mrs. Morrison's social security number."

Paul brought me the number. I called Shelley and gave her the name and number and told her to get me a work record to go with it. I hung up the phone and Paul was looking at me. "You don't trust anybody, do you?"

I laughed. "Hardly. I'm like a loan officer in a bank. Besides, she was lying through her teeth."

"Would it matter if she wasn't?" He looked grim. "You don't trust anybody, do you?"

I felt like hell. He'd figured out what Rittenhouse had been doing there the day before. I turned to Maggie. "She's awfully eager to have us on the case, Mag. She doesn't want some other agency, she wants us."

"She likes us. Probably your virility. How much lying was she doing?"

"Either her son was lying to her or she's lying to us. He wasn't an actor—he was doing extra work for the money. And yesterday she told us she sent him money, and I don't think she did. She's too damn suspicious that Gene didn't die the way it looks like he died. I want to know her work record to see if she's ever spent any time in L.A." Paul was still staring at me. "Occasionally I trust myself, Paul, if it's an even-numbered day and the wind's blowing in the right direction."

He spoke evenly. "I don't know if I could live that way."

I laughed. "Think I can live that way? Drives me crazy. I trust Maggie."

"What?" Maggie said.

"Sure. Mag, you're a different story. I always trust you." She put a hand over her mouth. I spread my arms wide. "Hell, I always trust you, Mag!" Her eyes started to wrinkle at the corners. I had her already. "I'll make you a bet I trust you almost as much as you trust me!" Her cheeks started to puff out like balloons. I looked at Paul. "Get the idea?" I smiled back at Maggie. She was really cracking. "Tell him how much you trust me, Mag! Come on! Don't keep it a secret! Tell him!"

She couldn't keep it in any more. The laugh came out as naturally as tomorrow's weather. It was a good throaty laugh, open and full. She's not a giggler or a chuckler or a nodder or a smiler, she's an honest-to-God laugher. It's the best thing about her. I love to hear her laugh. Nothing can bother me when I hear her laugh. It blocks everything else out. It pulls me right into it like she's a magnet and I'm metal. Her laugh's better than sunshine on a cold day. She laughed, and I laughed, and Paul watched us, and it kept going, and it felt damn good, and it kept getting bigger and better, and when the two men wearing uniforms came into the office even that wasn't enough to stop it.

104

Hilinsky sat in his favorite chair and kept humming his favorite tune. It was the song of a door on rusty hinges. You had to ignore it as long as you could and hope it'd drive him nuts before it drove you nuts. I stretched out my legs and dropped the brim of my hat to hide my eyes and pretended to nod off. The hummimg continued.

"Pete?" Maggie said. I knew she'd break before I did. "You going to keep us here all day?"

I tipped my head and sneaked a look. He had his feet on the windowsill and was looking out. "Thought we had it straight, Mag. The Griffith Park thing had nothing to do with you."

"Who says it does?"

He clasped his hands behind his head. "You were up in Vegas asking questions about Frank Jarvis just for the hell of it?" He swiveled his head and slid his eyes at her. "I expect that kind of shit from Freddie. Thought you and me had an understanding."

Maggie stayed quiet. I feigned sleep. What the hell, *I* wasn't the one who'd been in Vegas. Let's see her get out of it.

"When you came to see us, we didn't have any interest. Now it's different. That boy who had our card, his mother found out about it and came to see us. She must've liked us. She hired us to see if the explosion was really an accident." She was good when she made her voice soft.

"Tell her to go ahead and sue. She might have a case. Negligence." Hilinsky picked up a pencil and rubbed a finger along its length. "Anything else you want to tell me? Jarvis?"

"Jarvis wasn't in Vegas."

"I know. He took off." He lined up the pencil parallel with the edge of his blotter. "He'll turn up. He doesn't, we'll turn him up. Meanwhile, I got a message for you." He picked up the pencil and threw it at me. It hit my knee. "Freddie? You listening?" I nodded. "Leave it alone. I don't want anyone in my way on this."

"If that's how you want it," Maggie said.

"That's how I want it."

"We like to have it the way you want it," I said. I picked up the pencil and put it in my pocket. "But what if Jarvis never went to Vegas?"

Hilinsky stayed impassive. "Jarvis's a heavy gambler."

Maggie leaned forward. "Winner or loser?"

"You know many winners?"

Maggie laughed. "Not many."

Hilinsky glanced at a clipboard. "Jarvis was at that motel, the Capri. Got out before we caught up with him."

I gave it another try for the hell of it. "It was a blind trail, the Capri. We know that, you know that, why're you pretending he was there?"

Hilinsky shoved the clipboard aside and leaned low over his desk and rubbed a hand across his mouth and looked at me like I was his dinner.

A door opened behind me and a skinny antiseptic-looking young man in wire-rimmed glasses and shirt-sleeves came in. "You got anything for me yet?"

Hilinsky sat up as quickly as an ant crawls from here to London. "Not yet."

"I told you to have it for me by two o'clock."

Hilinsky looked at his watch and nodded sincerely. "Sorry. Hasn't come in yet."

"Sorry doesn't do much for me." The young man started forward. "Sorry doesn't do *shit* for me!"

Hilinsky nodded sincerely at that. "I'll do something about it."

"You better do it quick."

Hilinsky nodded. The young man went out. Hilinsky's eyes watched him all the way to the door and waited for the door to slam closed and gave the young man who'd slammed the door time to get down a hall and out of the building. Then Hilinsky laughed. He looked at us and talked quickly. "You're wrong about Vegas. We talked to Jarvis's landlady, Jarvis's a card player, he's always going to Vegas. Stay away from the Griffith Park thing." He looked calmly at Maggie. "I mean it, Maggie."

I sat up. "Someone bought you off on this one?" Hilinsky's hand came down on his desk. I'd wanted to go, till then. Now I spoke slowly. "What're your rates these days?"

"Don't give me trouble, you asshole! You take—"

What stopped him was the door opening again and the young man coming in again. As soon as he entered Hilinsky froze, then smiled.

The young man didn't smile. "Who're these people?"

Hilinsky's mouth closed slowly. The man stepped forward. Hilinsky watched him like he was a fly on the wall. "This's McGuane, that's Thieringer. I wanted to talk to 'em."

The man looked at Hilinsky, then at us, then at his watch. He shook his head and looked at Hilinsky again. "I'm working up in Maroni's office. Bring 'em up to me in ten minutes." He tried to stare Hilinsky down but it was a waste of time. He turned and went out.

Hilinsky went to the door and closed it. He walked to his desk and started to sit but changed his mind and stayed standing. He rubbed the side of his face. "I'm going to be up there, too. Either of you say anything, I'm going to be right there listening. You keep your minds on that." He smiled and faced the window and stayed there and we all waited for ten minutes to go by.

105

Hilinsky pushed the door open and went in first. The young man sat at a desk looking through a folder and didn't bother to look up. "Sit down, both of you." He tapped a pen against his teeth and kept scanning the folder. Hilinsky motioned toward two chairs facing the desk. Maggie sat, so did I, Hilinsky moved silently to the side.

An uneaten sandwich sat among papers at the corner of the desk. The young man's hand went toward it and then stopped. "You two want something to drink? Coffee?"

"Coffee'd be fine," Maggie said. "Black."

"Mr. Thieringer?"

"I'll take a Coke if you got one."

"One black coffee and one Coke." He looked at Hilinsky. "Got it?"

Hilinsky sighed and went out. The young man watched him leave and went back to the folder. "Margaret Anne McGuane. Everything seems in order." He put down the folder and opened another one. "Frederick D. Thieringer." He read. "Got yourself into some bad scrapes when you were young."

"Most of us do. You grow up, you haven't killed anyone, they aren't supposed to hold it against you anymore."

He glanced at me. "Quite a delinquent. Got on some pretty thin ice a couple times."

"I was always light on my skates."

He nodded. "Still in practice?"

"I can do figure eights if there's a call for it."

"I'm surprised you got a license."

"So'm I. What scares me most is wondering who the hell else they're giving 'em to."

Hilinsky came in with the coffee and Coke and while

he was giving them to us Maggie gave me a look. Hilinsky returned to the side wall and the young man watched him. "Something else, Lieutenant?"

Hilinsky waved some fingers. "No, Mr. Steeg. I'm just—"

"Close the door on your way out."

I kept my eyes on Steeg. Steeg kept his eyes on Hilinsky.

I finally heard Hilinsky's steps cross the floor behind me. I didn't hear any growl. I heard the door swing softly. Steeg returned to my folder.

I waited a moment and then got out of my chair and went to the door.

"What're you doing?"

I pushed the door all the way shut. It clicked. I turned around.

"Oh. I see. Thank you." He waited for me to sit. "Miss McGuane, Mr. Thieringer, just what're you two doing down here?"

Maggie shrugged. "We don't know, he sent for us."

Steeg sharpened his look. "He give you any problems?"

Maggie sat still. "What kind of problems?"

"Christ." Steeg reached for his sandwich and took it this time but didn't bite into it. He leaned back in his chair and looked at Maggie. "McGuane. You were the one in Vegas yesterday looking for Jarvis. We couldn't pick up a thing on him. You have any luck?"

"Very little."

Steeg stared at her a moment. "Christ." He put down the uneaten sandwich and his mouth took the slowest turn into a smile I've ever seen. "Jarvis never went to Vegas. Someone wants it to look like he did. You don't know that, you ought to find yourselves a new line of work."

Maggie met his smile with her own. Hers was better. "Where'd Jarvis go?"

Steeg's hand traveled across his desk till it found the phone. He stroked it gently. "Maybe out of the country."

Maggie pushed it a step further. "Which direction?"

Steeg shrugged. "Maybe Mexico. Maybe I don't know yet. Maybe I got some people working on it."

Maggie sat back. "Maybe Lieutenant Hilinsky?"

"Oh, yeah, the good lieutenant thinks he's working on it."

Maggie sat forward and put her coffee cup on the edge of the desk. "You don't trust the good lieutenant?"

"I trust him to get coffee and Cokes."

It went quiet. It stayed that way so I said, "What's this got to do with us?" Maggie waved her hand at me. It was below the front of the desk and Steeg couldn't see it. I stayed quiet.

Steeg looked at Maggie. "I just gave you where I think Jarvis is, now it's your turn to give. How you're tied in to the Griffith Park thing."

Maggie leaned into one of her coyer poses. "A mother of one of the kids who got killed in the explosion hired us to see if there was anything funny about it. She heard somebody thought the explosion might've been set on purpose. Maybe the producers wanted to collect insurance."

It caught him as he was ready to bite into his sandwich and he put the sandwich down. "Your client's got connections. Or money. Or both." He looked at his empty hand. "Fuck. Everybody's got connections." He looked up. "Got an angle on it?"

"Not yet. Haven't had time yet."

"Sure." He leaned forward. "You got something, I'd like to hear about it. I got very good ears." Maggie shrugged. Steeg leaned back. He stared at the wall. "Connections. Fuck." He thought it over awhile and then looked at Maggie. "You know how to keep your mouth shut?"

"If there's a reason."

Steeg looked at me. "What about your partner?"

"You don't hear him talking, do you?"

He looked at the wall again. He put his chin in his hand. "I can afford to give you some stuff without it giving me any problems. Stuff I can't give you, I won't give you. Don't feel you got to go talking about what I do give you. Clear?"

"What're we giving you in return?" I said.

He looked at me. "We'll worry about that later. Right now I'm just an assistant D.A. who's cultivating you for future possibilities. You don't see it that way, it'll cost you hard, eventually."

"Feel free to cultivate," Maggie said.

Steeg looked at me. I said nothing.

"Come on, Fritz, lighten up."

I nodded, very slightly.

Steeg turned his chair to face us. "You know Tony Capanegro?"

"Not intimately."

"You know about Red Wind Productions. His son owns half of it. I been going over their books. I think they started shooting this movie and they realized they were stuck. Another week or two, they wouldn't've met their payroll. Capanegro's son, Nick, he never worried about that kind of stuff before 'cause he could always get his father to slip some money into the company and bail him out, but Tony Cap's got problems of his own. The IRS's running their yearly audit on him and this time they got the state and city looking, too. I was working on it, before this thing happened. Tony Cap's got no clean way to move his money around right now.

"The son, Nick, he figured if he had to shut down the film he'd get hit with problems 'cause of all the contracts they got signed. He couldn't pay. Looks like he's also been fooling with numbers. The kind of stuff he could get put away for if Red Wind had to declare bankruptcy. He knew it'd come down extra hard on him 'cause of whose son he is. An explosion, that'd bring him negligence suits, but he's got insurance to cover negligence suits."

Steeg crossed his hands and stared at them. "What I'm talking about's just a theory. I can't prove it. You know how it works, just 'cause we know who a guy is and what he might be doing, or might've done, turning up enough hard evidence to put him away's sometimes a little impossible. We lost some of our best weapons, thanks to Nixon and Hoover and what they had the guys under 'em doing. Eighty percent of the information we used to get on the mob came from bugging and wiretapping. It's a different story now, we got a whole new set of rules.

We're goddamn crippled." He smiled sadly. "Used to be able to look at tax returns, that's another thing Nixon screwed up for us. That guy did a lot of harm to this country in ways people haven't even given a thought to yet. We got to cover a lot more ground these days if we want to get results." He looked up. "And the mob's got a lot more lawyers'n we do."

Maggie nodded. "In your theory about the explosion, how come people got killed?"

"I don't think that was part of the plan. Just enough to shut things down. But this guy Jarvis, he was a bad drinker and I think he screwed it. That's why he took off. He's not just hiding from us, he's hiding from Capanegro."

Maggie tapped the desk. "What if it was done behind Jarvis's back? But maybe Jarvis knew something, and they had to get rid of him?"

"I considered it. We got over to Jarvis's apartment next day and he was already gone. There was money in the apartment. Lots. I think he got paid ahead of time, but when it happened like it did he was scared and he took off without the money."

Maggie's finger drew a line across the desk. "The money could've been planted in his apartment. To make it look like a payoff."

Steeg swung away from his desk and stared at a corner. "Yeah, I considered that too."

Maggie looked at me briefly and then back at Steeg. "If it was a straight payoff, can you be sure it came from Capanegro and not someone else?"

Steeg sat still for a moment and then slowly turned. "Someone else? You got a reason to think that?"

"I'm just thinking out loud. It's a possibility."

Steeg considered it. "So far, everything I got leads to Capanegro. I got Red Wind's books in here. Got the son all tied up in knots. There's anything to get him on, I'll get him." He straightened. "It's something else, I'll get that too."

He considered it some more and I decided to clear my throat. He looked at me and I looked back. "You're telling us everything except one thing."

"What's that?"

"The reason you're telling us any of it."

His eyes stayed still a moment and then he stood and went out to the front and talked to the secretary out there. The secretary left her desk and Steeg watched her leave. Maggie leaned closer to me and whispered, "What're you so friendly for?"

"Sometimes you can trust a guy. It's stupid to trust a guy just 'cause he happens to hold a particular job."

"Sure. It's also stupid *not* to trust him just because he holds a particular job."

I sat back. "I know. Haven't got that part worked out yet."

"You never will." She looked over her shoulder. "We have to feed him something or he's not going to feed us."

Steeg came back leaving the door open and sat against the front of his desk and kept his eyes on the open door so he could see if the secretary or anyone else came into the front office. He spoke very softly. "Hilinsky doesn't like you, Thieringer. Maybe I like the way he doesn't like you. This's my first case down here, this precinct, and I can see some things and some of 'em I don't like. I'm not getting the action I ought to be getting. I can work around it but it's causing me a lot of small dumb shit I can live without. There's always guys around who ought to get kicked out but till they get caught with their pants down they don't get kicked. Maybe, I play this right, I'll catch him. Maybe not just him."

"If you think that interests us, you're wrong," I said. "There's too many bent cops around for us to lose sleep over just one."

He kept his eyes on the door. "Don't give me that shit. I know how you feel about him. I'll give you another reason. This's going to be a good case, and the people who're behind me on it're going to end up a lot better'n the people who aren't. Hilinsky's already made his choice. The wrong one. You two're smart, you'll make the right one. You pick up something, give me a call. I like to see my friends come out on top. Those who get in my way. . . ." He turned suddenly and went behind his desk. I heard steps coming in behind me.

"I took it down to him, Mr. Steeg. He says he'll check it."

"Thanks, Helen." The steps walked away. Steeg leaned across his desk. "I walk into the grand jury, I like a good solid case in my folder. You can make it solid, you do it. One thing I want right now is Jarvis. I'll have a good memory for any help that comes my way." He put his voice even lower. "Watch yourselves with Hilinsky. I'm in a position to handle him. You aren't." He moved some files and put them on top of his uneaten sandwich without realizing he'd done it. "Get out of here." He buried his face in another folder.

Maggie and I went out and down a hall and then I laughed. "He'll handle Hilinsky. First he's going to have to find a sledgehammer, then he's going to have to find someone to swing it for him. They ain't making assistant D.A.s like they used to."

Maggie laughed too but there was no humor in her laugh. "Easy, big shot. If he wants to go after you, he won't need a sledgehammer."

I stopped laughing. "That much I know."

She put an elbow into my ribs. "There's one thing you ought to like about him. He's more paranoid than you are."

106

We went back to the office and asked Paul if there was any news.

"Plenty. Shelley called, Virginia Morrison is the president of a chain of restaurants called The Hungry Pirate, Inc. Back in 1968, when she became president, there was just one restaurant. It was called Pirate's Cove, up in Sausalito. She first started working there in 1957, and back then she only drew fifty dollars a week. My guess's she was a waitress and collected a fifty-dollar paycheck and the rest in tips." I nodded. He went on. "Between 1957 and 1955 there's no record of employment at all, but before 1955 there's plenty, and they're all in L.A." I snapped my fingers and it felt so good I snapped them again. Paul smiled. "Want to know where she was working till June 1955? Lybart Petites."

I went into my office and opened a cardboard box and took out a Xerox of an article of Joseph Lydon's death. "Lydon was shot in May 1955. And Virginia Morrison left in June."

Paul's voice came through the open door. "When she started to work at Pirate's Cove she listed her name as Virginia Morrison. Before that her name was Virginia Moore."

I dropped the Xerox. "When Isenbart heard the name Gene Morrison he wasn't sure if it meant anything or not. He knew the name Moore, he didn't know the name Morrison." I came through to the front. "I'm on my way."

Maggie threw me a quizzical look. "Do you have any idea where?"

"To see how Elizabeth Isenbart's doing."

Paul's hand reached toward me. "You had another call. Deveraux. Wouldn't leave a—"

"The hell with Deveraux. I'm rolling."

107

The mirrors on the front of the counter looked as solid as ever. They threw my face back at me and my face looked eager. Maybe too eager. I had to do something about that. Above my reflection I saw Annie's face, and that one looked eager too. What the hell had I gotten myself into now.

I searched her eyes. Whatever this thing turned out to be, I hoped she wouldn't be part of it.

And if she was part of it, I hoped I'd know in time.

Before either of us could speak a buzzer went off in front of her. She picked up a phone and listened and started writing madly. It continued for almost a minute. She covered the phone with her hand. "Madhouse. An absolute madhouse." She listened again and put the phone down and picked up another one and dialed. "I called you at your office to say hello and see if you're free tonight. You free tonight?"

"Don't know yet."

She talked into the phone and I went down the hall and then I stopped and turned and came back and looked at her. "You called my office?" She looked up and nodded and kept talking into the phone. "Your last name Deveraux?" She nodded and kept talking.

Son of a bitch.

108

Mrs. Isenbart was also talking into a phone. "You'll have the entire order by the middle of next week, Mr. Burns. We never received a cancelation, so the order is still in effect. . . . That's right. Fine. Goodbye."

She hung up and started to say something and the phone rang. She smiled helplessly and answered it. "Hello? . . . They'll have the check by the end of the day, Bernie. I'll send it to them by messenger. . . . No, I'll handle it, you keep your mind on what you're doing down there."

She hung up and started to say something and the door opened. Carl came in with material samples.

"I have to know if you want to go with—"

Mrs. Isenbart nodded. "Which one do you suggest?"

Carl stopped. "What?"

"Which one do you think would be the best choice?"

He looked at her. "Burgundy." He held up a sample.

"Go ahead and make it up."

He stared at her. "Don't you want to see the drawing first?"

She shook her head. "I've got to take care of something for Bernie. I'll come back there, we'll make a decision on everything else before—" she looked at her watch—"four-thirty."

Carl stood still a moment and looked at me and then went out shaking his head.

Mrs. Isenbart sighed. "I haven't had a chance to stop since I came in. I don't know where I'm going, I'm just going. I went to the bank first like you told me and put twenty-five thousand in the Lybart account. I came over here and the first thing I knew I was answering the phone and telling people what to do." She shrugged. "So far it's working."

"Fine." I sat across from her. "I need to look at some more files so I'll know what he was doing with the money so we can make sure everything's working out right. If I don't, you might have problems accounting for what you're doing."

Her eyes showed no doubt. "I ought to pay you, Mr. Thieringer. For helping me to—"

"Money's not necessary, Mrs. Isenbart. I'm glad to help."

We worked around each other for the rest of the afternoon. She ran between the files and the phone and the rest of the office but I stuck with the files. Lybart Petites had been born in October of 1954 and business was bad. In February of 1955 a lump sum of $35,000 came in, but not from sales. That could've been more of their percentage on the profits from *The End of Pamela.*

In May of 1955 Joseph Lydon died and that's where I started looking carefully.

The first thing I caught was a small thing, a listing of a check made out to cash for $100 in August. I would've passed right over it except I'd just seen the same exact listing two weeks before in July. As I kept going forward I found more listings. Checks—made out to cash—$100—every second Monday. Not much as these things go, just $200 a month.

In November the checks jumped to every Monday, and that made it $400 a month.

In February the checks stopped.

That didn't necessarily mean they'd really stopped. Isenbart had probably learned how to hide them by then. Maybe the checks had gotten so large he had no choice but to hide them.

109

People can be the strongest things in the world. Also the weakest. It doesn't work out neat, so they're one way or the other. They're both. You never know which side is going to turn up at a particular moment, they keep surprising you. So I'd have to push Mrs. Isenbart hard, but not too hard, 'cause right now she looked strong but somewhere underneath it she was fragile as hell. I didn't know for sure what was underneath that.

She collapsed in the chair. "I don't know how I did it. I don't think I ever put in a day like this in my whole life. I didn't think I had it in me."

"Maybe you lost something. Maybe you found it again."

She didn't answer. She didn't even hear me. She looked at her watch. "It's seven? Already?"

"There used to be a bottle and a couple glasses in the bottom drawer on the left side. They might still be there."

She looked at me, then opened the drawer. She took out bottle and glasses and poured. When her glass was empty I filled it again. I needed her a little bit smashed. Dulled. Anesthetized. Enough to take whatever I was going to give her.

Her eyes wandered across the office. "Max spent twenty years building this company into something. He put his heart and soul into it." She nodded several times. "Whatever it takes to keep this company going, I'm going to do it."

Maybe she was tough now. Maybe that was how I wanted her. I filled her glass. "I found some more problems in the books, Mrs. Isenbart. They go back pretty far." She nodded absentmindedly. I leaned forward. "You make any mistakes, you're going to have government people all over here, you'll have to answer questions. Not just about the money he hid in the house, about everything back to the beginning of the company." She nodded and drank. I spoke clearly. "If your husband was hiding something, I won't be able to stop it from coming out." She turned. Her face tried to straighten. It was too late. It'd probably been too late one drink ago. "Your husband and another man come out of New York together, they wanted to open a dress company, like this one, but they didn't have enough money."

Her forehead wrinkled. "They had a shop, Santa Monica and Fairfax. They sold dresses." She looked at the whiskey in her glass. "It wasn't much, it didn't make much money, but it was a nice little shop." She smiled. "We were happy."

"We?"

"I was the salesgirl."

I didn't move. "They designed a movie, the two of 'em."

Her mouth turned up at the corners. "*The End of Pamela*. It was beautiful." She leaned back and looked past me. "They worked around the clock, Max and Joe. They had to cut corners. The producer couldn't give them much of a budget." Her mouth opened wider. "It was fun. God, we were happy."

I let her see it again, for a moment, then I said, "The film made money. They had a percentage. They got enough to open Lybart. Business was bad, very bad. I was sitting with your husband one night in a bar, he told me how he'd had to do things he didn't like, to keep the business going. He said if people had to be paid off he paid 'em off. He couldn't get money from banks, he got it other places." She nodded. "I got to know what those other places were, or you're going to have a lot of trouble here." Her hands crawled off the edge of the desk and hid in her lap. "Mrs. Isenbart—"

"The only thing they had was their earnings from *Pamela*. There was no way of telling how much that would continue to bring in. The banks wouldn't give them any credit. Max didn't have any choice about it, he had to go to a loan shark."

I let it sit. That had come awfully quickly. What if there was another source of money she *didn't* want to tell me about? "Loan sharks're expensive, but if you got no choice you got no choice. *Max* went to him? His partner wasn't much help?" She didn't answer. "Your husband told me he could never count on anyone, he had to do everything himself." Still no answer. "Your husband told me he wanted to make it in films. He said he did design another film—"

"Yes. One other film." She put the glass on the desk and filled it slowly. "One more, that was all. Max was never able to get anywhere with the movie people."

"His partner did. His partner made a couple films around the time they were just starting Lybart." She set down the bottle. "Must've been rough for the partner, trying to split time between the films and Lybart."

Her eyes floated up to me. "You know so many things. Why do you know so many things?"

This time I didn't answer. One of her hands came up to the desk and took the glass. "Joe was very unfair to Max. He started spending all his time with these people in the movies. He turned into a different man." She looked down sadly. "Joe got to be very loose. Morally,

I mean. He was always going to parties, and seeing people and doing things."

"Did Lydon want to leave the company?"

She took in a very long breath. "They had a fight about it. In the office here. They were yelling, and Joe was hitting Max, it was awful. We ran in, the receptionist and me, and we yelled at Joe to stop. He wouldn't. He kept hitting Max. We finally got Max out of there. I thought Joe was going to kill him. It scared me to death." She sat quietly looking at nothing.

"How long was it, after that, that Lydon was killed in that mugging outside that bar in West Hollywood?"

She shuddered and turned away.

110

She stood by the window and looked out. "Joe was a wonderful designer. Max almost went bankrupt after Joe died. Max couldn't've had anything to do with Joe's death. It almost ruined him, losing Joe."

"Max was going to lose him anyway."

She shook her head. "Why? Because they argued? Joe was getting a few films but he wasn't getting much money to do them. And he couldn't afford to leave the company unless he could get his money out of it." She turned and her eyes begged me to believe her. "The money wasn't there. It was tied up in the office and the factory materials. And Joe had started to spend money like it was water. Max was the one who was getting fed up with Joe, but they were both stuck together. They had too much money tied up here for either of them to get out."

"All the more reason for your husband to get rid of him."

Her eyes turned to fire. "Max wouldn't do that!" She sat. "Anyway, he couldn't. Joe was too good a designer. When Joe died it took Max a year to find a designer who was good enough to get the company going again."

"A designer? David Greene?"

"Yes."

I reached for the bottle and filled my glass.

Her breathing came heavy now. I waited till it slowed down. "It won't wash, Mrs. Isenbart. Your husband was going to loan sharks, he was paying off buyers, he was piling up debts. Lydon wanted to cut and run. He figured the sooner the better. Your husband wasn't willing to let him go." I took a long drink. "I'm afraid he did something, and I think someone knew what he did, and I think someone was blackmailing him about it." I took another drink, almost as long. "It's in the books, Mrs. Isenbart. Checks made out to cash for a hundred bucks each. They started in July 1955, two months after Lydon died."

"Blackmail." She laughed, but it was a sad laugh. "I know about those checks, they went to a man named Chellick. Chellick wasn't a blackmailer, he was the loan shark. That was all over, years ago. Max paid him everything and it stopped."

"Once you owe a loan shark you owe him forever."

"No. It stopped." She spread her hands on the desk in front of her and stared at her fingers. "Max finally got enough money to stop it. Blackmail? You seem to know so much, and you don't know anything. I don't know how Joe died, but Max. . . ." Her head dropped slowly to the desk and her breathing came heavy again in long slow waves.

Something very nasty started working its way through me. "Max needed money. For the loan shark. Over the years it'd just keep building. The vigorish on the loan. He wanted to stop it."

She nodded. "I've tried to rationalize it away, that he did it because he had to. Max didn't do very well at all till just a few years ago. We couldn't even have a house till three years ago. Max always needed money. I guess

269

he did some things he wouldn't've done if things had been different." She looked up. "He didn't pay blackmail. He collected it."

I put the glass down. I didn't want any more to drink.

"Someone who was working at the company when Joe was killed. I think she had something to do with Joe's death, and apparently later she came into some money, and Max knew about it, and where she was, and he blackmailed her."

"The receptionist who helped you get Max out of the office when they had that fight."

Her eyes showed confusion. "How did you—"

"Why do you think Max was blackmailing her?"

She shook her head sadly. "I didn't understand you at all, Mr. Thieringer. What you were after. Why you were helping me. I still don't."

I almost yelled it. "Why do you think Max was blackmailing her?"

She stared at me. "You were right about when Joe died. It was the day after they had that fight. This woman, the receptionist, she left the company a few weeks later and I never knew where she went. I didn't think Max knew, but several years ago I saw an envelope from her. The envelope was empty and Max wouldn't tell me what it was. A couple months later I was here and I saw another envelope here on the desk, and it had a money order in it for a thousand dollars. I didn't understand, she hadn't had any money, but after she left here I guess she must have come into some. And Max found out about it, and found out where she was living. . . ." She stopped there and turned away and sat like a stone woman.

Suddenly I felt very tired. It was too late in the day and it was too confusing and I felt very tired. Too tired to stop from asking one last question that just had to be asked and this was the moment for it. "Mrs. Isenbart, did you kill Joseph Lydon?"

Her face turned quickly and the reaction was honest, just the way I needed it. It was the most horrible look

I'd ever seen in my life and it just made me feel more tired and dirty. But it told me what I had to know.

I pulled myself out of the chair. "I'm sorry, Mrs. Isenbart. Somewhere deep down it takes a very special kind of hardness to kill a man. You're lucky. You haven't got it."

And something not so far in the back of my mind told me it was a hardness I *did* have.

I put on my hat and got out of there quickly.

111

I parked in front of my house. All I wanted was a long, long shower, as if it could make me feel any better, but I couldn't even settle for that. I had to check something out first so I went to the house next door and rang the bell. Dorothy opened the door. "You look terrible."

"I know. Sometimes you feel you got to ask one more question, and so you ask it, and then you spend the rest of the day hating yourself for asking it. And the worst part is you know if it happened again you'd ask the question again, just 'cause it's got to be asked."

She didn't say anything for a while. Then she said, "Your new girl came over."

I glanced quickly at my house. "What'd she want?"

"Flour. She said she was making a cake."

"She ask any questions?"

Dorothy came forward and looked at my face. "You're even worried about your girl friends? You're in bad shape, Fritz." I said nothing. Dorothy stepped back. "You're not the only one, either."

"Where is he?"

"Out back. He won't tell me what's wrong."

"I'll talk to him."

She laughed. "Great. See if you can pry the bottle out of his hand." She went into the house.

I found him on the grass in the back with his back propped against the house and a bottle by his knee and an empty glass in his hand and his eyes on the sky and his cat sprawled fifteen feet away watching him.

Joe's eyes shifted slightly. "Evening, Fritz. Want to hear a funny?"

"Love to."

"LAPD's minus two cops tonight, going to be minus a couple more."

My stomach felt like it was full of lumps. I knew what being a cop meant to him. I dropped to the grass and leaned against the house. "You?"

"Me? No, not me. I told you, it's a funny. Two guys quit, two others got suspended. They got caught screwing around with a couple Explorer Scouts. Teenagers. Going to be seven more up at a department trial and four more waiting to see if they're going to be charged, too. Sex, that's what's getting 'em kicked out. You don't get kicked out for doing what I did."

The lumps had just started to go away, but now they were back waiting to hear what he'd done. He threw a pebble toward the cat. The cat leaped at it and started batting it across the grass.

"By the way, Fritz, if you're going to come visit me the next couple days, use the back door. You're on the shit list. Hilinsky's after your ass."

"I heard something about it. You scared of Hilinsky?"

"I know plenty who are." His mouth grinned. "Don't think I'm one of 'em." The grin went away. "I told you, they put Lynch back with me."

"He get you into trouble?"

He left the glass empty and drank from the bottle. "Nope. I got him. We're on our way to a bar yesterday to break up a fight and I figured he was going to fuck it so I told him he better not or I'd kick his ass. It worked, he backed me up like he was supposed to. Today we got a buy going down in an apartment. I told him I'll go around back, he should call for backup and wait for it. Couple minutes later I'm around back, the backup shows, they want to know where my partner is. I told 'em he's out front. They say he isn't. I don't know what the fuck's going on so we go up to the apartment, it's been cleaned out, Lynch's up there already, he'd gone up himself to show he had the balls to do it. They'd busted one of his goddamn legs for him and knocked a couple teeth out. I'd been downstairs around back, I hadn't heard a thing." Joe pulled some grass out by its roots and stared at it. "Had to show me he had guts, had to get himself busted up. Just to show me he had guts." He threw the grass away. "*I* won't get kicked out for that. *He'll* get his ass chewed 'cause he went against regulations, but I pushed him into it, nothing's going to happen to me. Nothing at all. Shit."

You hear a lot of stories in my business. Nobody ever tells you what you're supposed to say after you hear them. Sometimes you're smart enough not to say anything at all.

We watched the day grow a little older and then Joe said, "Don't tell Dorothy about it. I'd rather she didn't know. You wanted something?"

"Hilinsky. It's the Griffith Park thing. A guy named Frank Jarvis, he was the explosives man, he's gone like last year's profits. Mag and me're trying to find him and Hilinsky doesn't want us to. There's an assistant D.A., Steeg, he doesn't think much of Hilinsky."

"Two cheers for Steeg."

"Steeg says the day after the explosion there was money in Jarvis's apartment and Jarvis was already gone. Steeg thinks it was payoff money and Jarvis took off so fast he left it behind. What Steeg doesn't know's that Hilinsky was already knocking on our door telling us he wanted us off the case the day after the explosion."

"You were on the case that quick?"

"We'd already been onto something else, which might tie in to the explosion and might not, and we're keeping that part of it quiet. The point is, why'd Hilinsky want us off the case, and why'd he want us off it that soon? Steeg says he doesn't know where Jarvis is but he's got a hunch it's out of the country. Hilinsky says he doesn't know where Jarvis is either, but he says it very badly. Like someone wants him not to know."

Joe flipped another pebble toward his cat. "If you're going to buy a cop, Hilinsky's as good a buy's any."

"But if Hilinsky got to us that fast someone would've had to've gotten to Hilinsky fast. Maybe you could trace whatever Hilinsky was doing from the morning before the explosion to the middle of the next afternoon."

Joe shrugged. "I can trace some of it, probably not much."

"See what you can find. I think Hilinsky's part of it. I want to know if it could've been planned that way, or maybe he just stumbled into it."

112

My barbecue grill sat on the grass next to the back steps. The charcoal in it was already white. I could see the glow from thirty feet away. When they start to move in on you, they move in fast.

I went through the back door and into the kitchen. Annie put her arms around my neck and gave me enough of a kiss to last me all week. "About time you got here. Can I put the steaks on?"

"You keep a man well fed."

"I can do more'n that." Her mouth found mine again. It was even better than the first time. Her hands started traveling. "You interested in doing something, before I put the steaks on?" Then her mouth stopped talking. It was a very talented mouth, it knew how to do lots of things besides talk.

The phone started ringing. She laughed. "Forget it, we had enough of the phone last night." I reached for it anyway but she took my hand away. "Come on, aren't you interested?" Her fingers caressed my neck. "What're you so tense for? Loosen up. I'm not going to bite." Her teeth touched the edge of my ear. "Unless you want me to."

I held her at the waist and put my mouth on hers and got a hand free and my hand found the phone. "Hello?"

"I'm calling for someone named Fritz."

Annie tried to take the phone away. I took her arm and pushed her away. "Hold it!" She looked at me. I looked back and spoke into the phone. "This's Fritz. Who're you?" Annie straightened her face and gave me a hard stare.

"Look, man, this's the bartender, out here at the Holiday Inn in Encino. I got this woman here, she looks like hell, man. I mean she's really beat up. I asked her if I should call a doctor or something, she gave me your number and told me to call you. You better get out here right away, man."

113

It took forty-five desperate minutes to get me to Encino. I parked in the lot and looked for a red Volvo. It wasn't there. I went into the bar and at first I didn't see her but then I did. She was sitting in the last booth on the right. From across the length of the bar she looked bad. Every step closer, she looked worse. Her blouse was torn at its collar and sleeve and the bruises were already showing along the side of her jaw. She had a full glass in front of her and she was just staring at it.

I sat down across from her and said nothing. After a moment she took off her dark glasses and let me see her eyes. Then she put the glasses back on. I controlled myself and said nothing.

"This place serves very small drinks, Fritz. Order me a double, will you?"

"You already got a double in front of you."

She looked at the glass again. She raised it to her mouth and her hand shook and a third of it spilled down her blouse. She put the glass on the table. "Ask the barkeep if I've paid my bill. I don't recall if I did or not." I nodded. And waited. "Well, how about some money?"

"No, Fritz. Show me some sympathy. Pay the bill with your own money, I want to see if you know how to do it."

I went to the bartender. "I'm Fritz. You called me."

He shook his head. "Glad you got here, man I was getting ready to call the cops."

"She come in here alone?"

"Yeah. I had to help her over to the booth down there. She wouldn't let me do anything else for her." He looked over my shoulder at her, then quickly looked down and started mopping the bar. "Christ, man. Sometimes I get a hooker in here, they been down in one of the rooms, they get beat up real bad, but I never seen any of 'em look that bad."

"She's looked worse on occasion. She owes you for some drinks?"

"Twelve bucks even."

I looked at him. "Expensive drinks."

"She drank a lot of 'em, man."

I took out my wallet and gave him the twelve and put a five on top of it. "Thanks for calling me." He nodded and I turned and saw her again and I turned back. "Give me a shot of vodka, quick."

His hands were already on the bottle. He poured two shots and we both drank.

"How much I owe you for that one?"

"Nothing, man, nothing." He shook his head and went down the bar.

I went to the booth. "Ready to move?"

"Are you kidding?" She worked at what was left in her glass. I sat across from her. She leaned across the table at me, then leaned bark and laughed sadly. "This has really been my day." Her eyes wandered across the room. "Sorry if I dragged you away from something exciting."

"What?"

She closed her eyes for a moment, then opened them and spoke quickly. "You smell of perfume. It's not mine. It's not Elizabeth Isenbart's, she wears Chanel. This's something with a little less money in it, and a hell of a lot more earthy."

I folded my arms across my chest. "Deveraux."

"Deveraux?" Her eyes closed again. "You never told me Deveraux was a woman.'"

"I didn't know."

"Does she have anything to back up the perfume with?" I said nothing. Maggie laughed weakly. "Deveraux. *C'est la vie.*" She pushed at her glass with a thumb. "Anything to do with current business?"

I sat still. It was a thought I didn't like, but it was there just the same, no use pretending it wasn't. "I don't know yet. She might." I looked across the bar as if there was something there to look at. "If she's part of it, we won't have to go looking for her. She's staying at my place."

"Your place?" Maggie picked up the glass and drained it. "Sounds like you're on dangerous ground, Fritz." She put the glass down and shoved it aside. "Sorry. Forget I said it." She laughed. "Think you can get me out of here before I fall apart?"

I got her standing with my left arm around her waist and her right arm over my shoulder and we started walking. It only took us three minutes to get to the door.

114

The phone woke me up and it wasn't even my phone.
I grabbed it before it could ring a second time. "Hello?"

"Fritz? That you?"

I grunted.

"What're you doing there? Maggie there?"

"She's sleeping. So was I. What's up?"

"I just got to the office. I saw Maggie's car downstairs, but she wasn't here. I looked in your office, her
pocketbook's on the floor and all the stuff that was in
it's all over her desk."

I rolled over on my back. "I don't know what happened yet. I had to go get her out of a Holiday Inn in
Encino last night. Time I got her home she was out. I put
her to bed. Whatever they did to her doesn't look pleasant."

The line went silent. Then, "What do you mean?"

"She's been beat up. Severely. She'll be all right
but she's not much to look at right now."

The line went silent again. "The guys from Vegas?"

"I don't know who it—"

"We got to do something!"

"Okay, we'll do something. But we'll try to wait
till we know what we're doing, okay?" I looked at my
watch. Not even nine yet. "I got to meet a guy at noon.
I'll be down at the office around one. Keep the door locked
till I get there."

115

"What are you doing here?"

I opened my eyes and squinted at her. "Trying to sleep. You looked in the mirror yet?"

Her mouth tightened. "Yes." She walked across the living room. "I'm making breakfast. Want some?"

"If it's edible. Sure you can make it all the way to the kitchen?"

"I'm all right."

It sounded a little mean the way she said it. Maybe she was all right.

I did some exercises and went into the bathroom and took a shower. I got out and dried off and got dressed and went into the kitchen. She was lying on the floor with her eyes closed.

116

"I don't want soup. I want something solid."

I pushed the spoon at her. "Open your mouth. It's solid. I put some rice in it." I forced the spoon into her mouth. "Hold still, you're making it dribble down your chin."

She pulled back. "I do eat better when I feed myself."

"When you're strong enough to hold the spoon without dropping it I'll let you eat by yourself."

She grabbed my hand and stopped the spoon. "How about pancakes? Pancakes are soft. Smothered in syrup?" I got my hand free and poked the spoon at her but her mouth closed. Words came out of it through clenched teeth. "I want pancakes!"

I got off the bed and went to the door. "You're a pain in the ass when you're sick."

I went to the kitchen and got out what I needed and mixed some batter. I heated up the skillet and started pouring pancakes and stacked them on two plates and put the plates on a tray and got out silverware and syrup and went back to the bedroom. Too late, she was out again. At least this time she hadn't fallen on the floor.

117

"Paul had gone home," she said. She stared at the far wall. "I was typing up some stuff when two goons came in. One of them had a bandage across the side of his head. They looked around and one of them asked me where the people I worked for were. I told him they'd gone home for the day and I reached for my pocketbook but then I remembered I didn't have a gun there, all the guns were in the safe. One of them looked at his watch and said maybe they'll come back and he sat on the sofa. The other one sat at your desk. The one on the sofa took out a gun and put it next to his leg and looked at me. I started typing again. After a while the one on the sofa looked at his watch again and said, 'It's almost five-thirty.' The one at your desk took out a deck of cards and started playing solitaire.

"I put the cover on the typewriter and got my stuff together and the one on the sofa asked me what I was doing. I told him I go home at five-thirty. He told me I go home when they tell me to go home. I took off the cover and did some more typing and after a few more minutes I went over to the safe like I needed something. I ran through the combination and the last number clicked and I started to turn the handle. The one on the sofa told me to stop what I was doing. I had my hand on the handle and I figured if I turned the handle quickly I could get the safe open and grab one of the Smith and Wessons, and I also figured with my luck I'd probably grab one that wasn't loaded, so I turned around and looked at him and he had his gun leveled at me.

"He asked me how come I hadn't been working at the desk in the front office. I told him there's no typewriter out there. He thought it over and the one at the desk said, 'What's the matter, Al?' Al told him he was a schmuck and not to call him by name and to look in my pocketbook. The schmuck looked in my pocketbook and then he asked what it was he was looking for and Al told him to get out my wallet. The schmuck emptied my pocketbook on my desk and looked in my wallet and said there was fifty bucks in my wallet. Al yelled at him and told him he didn't give a fuck how much money there was, he wanted him to look at my identification. The schmuck took out my identification and laughed and said, 'Guess what, she's McGuane.' I was hoping he'd laugh a little more 'cause I think if he had, Al would've shot him.

"They shoved me in their car and drove out to Encino. I didn't get a chance to see the license plate. We got to the Holiday Inn and they each took an arm and dragged me into Room Twenty-five. Al threw me into a chair and told me to stay there and he sat at a table and slapped the gun down hard so I'd be impressed. The schmuck took his cards out and they played cards.

"I couldn't see outside. The curtains were drawn. I could hear voices out at the pool but that's about all. We sat there for an hour and then I heard a car pull up right out front. I stood up and stretched and I got a little closer to the window but then Al started yelling at me and he was holding the gun so I sat down. A man came in and he was pretty big but I've seen bigger. He looked at me and then he asked Al what the hell was going on. The schmuck laughed and told him I was McGuane. The man looked at me and then he sat on the bed and Al told him I was the only one at the office. The man looked at me again for a while and then he asked me what I knew about the Griffith Park thing. I told him I didn't know anything about it and he told me not to give him any shit.

"He started to get up and then he sat down again and he said, 'Look, I had a guy working for me and he got killed in that explosion and I want to know what happened. I think maybe you know something about what happened.' I pretended to think it over but I couldn't come up with anything so I just told him I didn't know what he was talking about.

"He looked at me some more and then he got up and came over and grabbed me by the arms and pulled me out of the chair and started swearing at me. He pushed me against the wall and I didn't say anything so he started slapping me and then I must've blacked out because the next thing I knew I was lying on the floor. He was kneeling down next to me and he told me I better get something straight, he was looking into what happened at Griffith Park and if he found out it wasn't an accident, if there was something behind it, whoever was behind it was going to pay. He told me I better not be behind it and then he hit me again and I blacked out again.

"When I woke up he was gone. Al and the schmuck were playing cards. I tried to get up and Al pointed the gun at me and told me to stay where I was. After about fifteen minutes the schmuck put away the cards and Al shoved the gun in his belt and they left, just like that. I tried to get over to the window to see the license plate on their car but I couldn't get to the window quick enough.

"I got to the bathroom and tried to clean myself up a little. I got most of the blood off my face and I sat on the bed for a while and then I felt a little better so I went down to the office. I told the man I wanted to see the registration book. One good thing about getting beat up is that when people see the way you look they get scared. You tell them to do something and if you say it like they better do it they do it. You think they'd be scared of whatever it was that made you look that way but instead they get scared of you. Anyway, there was nothing in the book. Room Twenty-five had just been occupied by someone named Joseph Smith and he'd paid in cash. I gave the book back to the guy and went into the bar."

Her eyes moved across the floor and the fingers of her right hand rubbed her left arm methodically just above the elbow. I adjusted the pillow for her and she leaned her head back.

"Any of these guys look like either of the two guys you saw up in Vegas?"

She shook her head. "Same personalities. Different faces."

"You said one of 'em had a bandage on his head. That night Paul got caught behind the restaurant there were two guys. I sapped 'em both. One of 'em could still be wearing a bandage."

Her mouth grinned. "I'll ask him next time I see him."

I looked at my watch—11:30. "I got to meet a guy at noon, Mag. Can you come to the door with me and double lock it and put the chain on?"

"Give me a hammer and nails and I'll nail it shut so tight a tank won't get through it."

118

A yellow Datsun. It didn't seem to be paying all that much attention to me but it might've been paying some. Some was more than I was in the mood for. When I got to Fairfax I swung right and drove up to Farmer's

Market. Then I circled down and drove across Metropolitan Plaza to the La Brea Tar Pits. Then back to Farmer's Market, then back to the Tar Pits. I spent ten minutes at it and no more yellow Datsun. I drove up Highland and parked in front of Tulley's Bar.

Tulley's eyes sparkled. "Fritz! What're you eating today?"

"Already had two helpings of pancakes this morning. They'll hold me to dinner."

He filled a large glass with Coke and ice and slid it to me. "Enjoy yourself."

I nodded and carried the Coke down to the last booth. Joe was sitting there smiling and spooning up chili. "You're late."

"A yellow Datsun might've been playing tag with me."

His eyes twinkled. "Might've been?"

"I'm not sure. I'm not taking chances today. Got anything?"

He wiped chili off his mouth. "Hilinsky and a guy named Blocker got assigned to the Griffith Park thing the day after it happened. They went over to Jarvis's apartment and found the money and didn't find Jarvis. I talked to Blocker about it. I know Blocker, he's straighter'n I am."

"Is that saying much?"

He smiled and waved his hand at me. "Blocker's okay."

"How come you're so happy?"

"I went to see Lynch at the hospital. He's okay, he says another two weeks, he'll be back."

"You *want* him back?"

He filled a spoon with chili. "Aww, hell, Fritz, he's okay."

"He's okay. Blocker's okay. Why weren't Hilinsky and Blocker assigned to the case soon's it happened? Sounds screwy. Why the wait?"

"I don't know. I'm a cop. Nothing sounds screwy to a cop. You get used to it. What're you so excited about?" I leaned against the back of my seat and stared at the table edge. He chuckled. "Don't look so glum,

284

Fritz. Maybe I got more." I sat up. "I'm going to tell you some stuff I don't know, and just to keep it clean you don't know it either. If by chance you ever do know it, you don't know it from me. The night of the explosion Hilinsky was assigned to another case, a suicide. Some guy took too long a walk off too high a roof. Out in Hollywood." Joe paused to scrape the remains of the chili from the sides of the bowl. There was nothing there to scrape but he scraped anyway. "This leaper, he's still in the morgue. The body remained unclaimed, unidentified, John Doe." He looked at his chili bowl one final time, gave up on it and pushed it aside.

"Could it be Jarvis?"

"Could be anyone." He took my Coke and sipped it. "You're anxious's hell on this thing, Fritz. Too anxious."

"I know. I got reasons. But if it's Jarvis, and someone killed him to keep him quiet, maybe Hilinsky walked in on it and someone paid him to keep it quiet." I tapped the table three times. "But if it's Jarvis, how's Hilinsky going to cover himelf when it comes out? Steeg's going to be pissed, he's got men looking in Mexico."

Joe shrugged. "I'm not saying it's Jarvis." He leaned forward. "But whoever it is, his face's all smashed up, there's no ID, his prints aren't on file, he's set up nice so he *can't* be identified."

I sat quiet a moment. "Hilinsky'd have to get some big money to run that kind of risk. More'n money. Someone'd have to be able to arrange protection all the way up and down the line. Someone'd have to have connections."

Joe grinned. "If someone's got money, connections're where you buy 'em." He shook the grin away. "But I wouldn't know about that. I'm just a poor struggling cop." He slid a piece of paper at me. "And I don't charge for information, but you got to pay for my lunch." He pulled himself up and away from the table and sighed and loosened his belt a notch. "Just don't get complacent about your conclusions, Fritz. There's always a chance it ain't Jarvis." He sighed again and went away.

I sat for a few minutes and thought about things

285

and finished my Coke. Then I went to the bar and took out my wallet. Tulley's mouth dropped open. "You're paying the bill?"

"Once in a while even I pay, Tulley."

He took my money and held one of the bills in his fingers and stared at it in disbelief. "I'm going to frame it and put it on the wall, Fritz."

"Go ahead. Second time I got stuck with a bill in less'n twenty-four hours."

"You changing? Or you sick?"

I shrugged and went out. I walked to my car and stood by the door and started thinking about things again and then I noticed the yellow Datsun parked down the block.

119

I considered trying to lose him again but last time I'd spent ten minutes at it and it hadn't worked so it probably wouldn't work this time. I drove along Wilshire and gave him no problems. I drove into Westwood and into the basement garage but he didn't come after me. I waited for him and he still didn't come. I walked across the garage and sneaked a look at the street and I spotted the yellow Datsun parked near the corner. Nobody was in it.

I searched through my pockets and found two loose cigarettes but no matches. I went back to my car and opened the glove compartment and found a matchbook. I put it in my pocket and walked to the elevator.

When the elevator arrived it was empty. I got in and pushed the button for three and took out a cigarette and played with it. The elevator stopped at the lobby. A man smiled at me and got in and didn't bother with the buttons. The elevator continued up.

I smiled. "I been thinking about getting a new car. You satisfied with your Datsun?"

He smiled back. "Good car for the money."

I put the cigarette in my mouth. "Didn't think cops were driving Datsuns these days."

"They're not."

I smiled again and took the matchbook out of my pocket and cupped my hands around it so he couldn't see what I was doing. I bent several matches double and struck them against the cover and as the thing lit up like the burning bush I threw it at him. He tried to get away from it and I pushed him hard against the wall. My hands went inside his coat and found a shoulder holster and came out with his gun. The elevator door opened at the third floor. "All right, friend. Out."

The smiler nodded once and walked. I pointed him toward the office and he went where I pointed. We stopped at the door. "Paul, it's me. Unlock the door."

At first there was no answer, then, "The door's unlocked."

I didn't like the sound of that. I kept the gun and my eyes on the smiler and twisted the doorknob and kicked the door open. Paul was sitting behind the front desk and he had the face of someone who's been hit recently and hard. There were two men sitting on the sofa and another in the chair by the door to the inner office. A fourth stood with his back against the far wall. They were all big and they were all looking at me. Three more came out of the inner office. I recognized the first, I'd seen him that day in Griffith Park, the Los Angeles Ram who handed out the warning to stay at the top of the hill. I didn't recognize the second. I recognized the third, his name was Bellino and I'd helped him make a hotel reservation once upon a time. He liked the accommodations so much he'd stayed almost six years. Then he'd gotten lucky and the parole board had let him out. Bellino's right hand was in a cast all the way to the elbow and the cast was in a sling. "Hello, Fritz. Long time no see. Still wearing hats, huh?"

The smiler looked at me, and my gun, and walked away like I was no longer there and the gun was no longer there either. He went across the office and sat with the two on the sofa.

Bellino laughed acidly. "Last time I saw you you had a gun in your hand. 'Course that time there weren't so many of us. And so few of you." I didn't move. "You wanna give us trouble? Your boy wanted to give us trouble."

I looked at the whole group of them again but there was no need to look, once was enough. I put the gun on Paul's desk. "Leave the gun where it is, Paul. Keep it cool."

Bellino looked surprised. "Whatsa matter, Fritz? You didn't used to give up this easy, the old days."

"I'm a little older'n I was in the old days."

Bellino laughed and nodded at a man and the man came over and gave me a frisk. He found nothing so he went away. Then Bellino came over. "Not carrying your own gun, either. You *have* changed. But you're still wearing hats." He lifted my hat off my head and stuffed it in the wastebasket and ground it down with his foot. His eyes sneaked up toward me. "Nice seeing you again, Fritz."

"Anything here's between you and me, Bellino. Nothing to do with him."

Bellino bent down and squinted at Paul. "I got no interest in him, long's he stays quiet."

I turned to Paul. "Anything happens, you let it go."

Bellino smiled and swung his cast so it tapped my elbow. "The other room, Fritz."

120

Bellino made himself comfortable behind my desk. Three others sat on the sofa. I stood in the middle of the floor. The filing cabinets were open and so was the safe. "Who did the job on the safe?"

One of the thugs on the sofa said, "Wasn't tough to open."

"Thanks for leaving the door on it."

An old man, very wrinkled, very thin, sat behind Maggie's desk. His face was tanned dark enough to hide a shadow but it was all artificial to let him fool himself when he looked in the mirror each morning, because his hands told a different story. They were whiter than the bleached skull of a dead animal left to rot in the desert hundreds of years ago. And his fingers, they were as straight and thin and lifeless as sticks of chalk. One of them, the right forefinger, tried to trace a straight line across a sheet of paper to stop his eyes from losing their place as they read. The eyes squinted through glasses as thick as the bottoms of Coke bottles. The glasses were so thick and his neck so thin you'd wonder how he managed to keep his head from falling over from the weight. He didn't look at me. "Don't you keep any files? What kind of business you run here?"

"A small one, but we struggle."

"This's disgraceful, no files. Even I keep files." His forefinger had lost its place and was trying to find it again. "You McGuane?"

"I'm Thieringer."

"McGuane writes about movies, huh?" His head nodded up and down like maybe he *couldn't* hold up his glasses. "What do you think of head doctors, Mr. Thieringer?"

I shuffled from one foot to the other. "I don't know. That's a country I haven't visited yet."

"My son's got a permanent passport." He shook the paper at me. "My son is a movie producer. It's my fault, I got him started. I had some money I had to do something with so I put it in movies in his name. A lawyer told me it was better for taxes that way. Now my son is a movie producer. And he goes to a head doctor and the head doctor tells him he should do what he wants to do." His fingers pressed the paper flat on the desk and fluttered to another piece of paper. "I'm going to have to talk to that head doctor." He started reading again.

I looked at Bellino and Bellino looked at me. I

didn't have to ask what was on his mind. The old man shoved the paper aside. "Looks like McGuane likes comedies." He eased back in the chair and his hands fell into his lap with a light slap. "My son'd be better off working with me, least it's a guaranteed profit every year. Hollywood, they don't make money, they just live like they do. And they all go to head doctors. I don't go to head doctors. My friends don't go to head doctors." His eyes flickered at me. "Do they really make money in movies these days?"

"They can either make a hell of a lot or none at all."

"My son is raising the odds so somebody else can make a hell of a lot. He puts money into fifteen films this past year and two of them he produces himself and every one of them is a total loss. You ever hear of a man named Skurnick?"

I shook my head no. Bellino rapped my desk with his cast. "You got asked a question, Fritz. Answer it."

I spoke loudly. "I never heard of the guy."

The old man nodded. "My son told me there's this director, Skurnick, Russian I think, my son wants to use him. What do you think of that?"

I said nothing. Bellino rapped my desk with his cast. I said, "I don't know what to think of it."

"It'll be directed by a Russian, they'll make it in Mexico. Mexico, you can't even drink the water down there. My son had another film couple months ago, it was rated X. Me, I don't care he wants to make that kind of thing, but he says you get rated X you can't get the film into all the theaters so you can't make money. No film my son makes is going to make money. But my son tells me I should talk to some people and tell them to give his film a better rating so it can make money." His body strained forward in the chair. "My son makes a filthy movie! He gets rated X! I'm supposed to talk to people? What people? My son's got his brains in his pants!"

He fell back in the chair. His gasps filled the room. The thugs looked at him desperately and Bellino nodded and one of them started to get up.

"Now he wants to make a film in Mexico with a Russian." His voice sounded the same. The thugs sat down. "Those people are out to destroy us, everything we stand for. Do you consider yourself a patriot, Mr. Thieringer?"

"I don't know exactly what's passing for a patriot these days. I think this's a pretty good country if that's what you're asking. I'm glad I live here."

"This's a wonderful country! A land of freedom. Opportunity. A land where every man has a chance to make his way. This's a country with ideals. That's very important, to have ideals. Standards." His face tightened up and looked disappointed. "And rules. Rules're very important. And the people who run things, they're supposed to go by those rules, but sometimes the people who run things don't believe in the rules. They pretend they're patriots, they believe in the Constitution, the laws. They say they believe in them and maybe they think they believe in them but they only believe in themselves." He glanced at me. "What do you think, Mr. Thieringer, about people who run things and don't play by the rules?"

Bellino hadn't taken his eyes off me since I'd opened the front door to the office. Whatever was going to happen was going to happen anyway so what the hell. "I don't know what I think. Do *you* play by the rules?"

His eyes blinked at me but nobody moved. "No, Mr. Thieringer, I don't." He leaned toward the desk. "But I'm not in public office. I don't *write* the rules. I'm what you people call a crook. I don't go around saying I'm not one. But when the people who are supposed to run this country go around saying they aren't crooks and everyone knows they are, this country is in very big trouble. I don't like it."

He subsided and nothing seemed to have broken. His face showed a strange mixture of anger and sadness. "It's their duty to be honest and fair and to obey the laws. They take oaths. They're charged with it." He snorted. "And they're so self-righteous. I'm not self-righteous. I know what I am, and people know what I am, but I'm too good at it, and too smart, and they can't prove anything against me." His hand came out and faced me. "It's their job to prove it, that doesn't bother me. But if they're going to set the rules, they ought to live up to the rules. It makes me sad what's happened in this country in the past couple years." His hand dropped and pounded the desk. "I thank God this country's strong enough to get through something like that, but it's still discouraging." He laughed weakly. "They're all the same, all of them. Best thing is to pay them off before someone else pays them off."

121

The old man tooked tired now. He didn't look so good when he looked tired. He hadn't looked so good before he'd looked tired. He rubbed his hands together. "Getting cold in here. I need something. Coffee."

"We got coffee in the front," I said.

Bellino said, "Nick," and one of the thugs went out. He came back with coffee and put the cup on the desk. The old man's hands touched the sides of the cup gently but didn't try to lift it. The thug took off his jacket and draped it across the old man's shoulders.

"Mr. Thieringer, do you people know anything about this explosion in Griffith Park?"

I answered quick and loud. "What do you want us to know?"

He looked up and almost smiled. "I want you to know nothing."

"Fine. We're very good at knowing nothing. People hire us all the time to know nothing."

"But your boy out front was seen in Griffith Park the day before it happened. You were seen there the day it happened."

"There's a difference between seeing something and knowing what it is you saw."

He nodded and tried to raise the cup. He got it two

inches off the desk and then dipped his head down to meet it. The cup shook but his head shook too in approximate rhythm and it all worked out. "I got too many problems, Mr. Thieringer. I don't want you to be one of them."

"I don't want that either, but I don't see why you're worried, you're already covered."

He put down the cup and pulled the thug's jacket tighter around himself. "How am I covered?"

"You paid off a man named Hilinsky, maybe a man named Blocker, maybe even a man named Steeg."

"Steeg!" He spat it out. "He's got the face of a baby but he's like a snake. He's got all my son's books in his office. I don't like it."

"Your son got stuff to hide?"

"My son's a businessman, he's no different than anyone else." He shook his head. "None of us are different, we're all human. That's what's wrong with us." His eyes strained at me behind the glasses. "Steeg says there's fraud on one of my son's movies and that my son made money on another one and didn't pay taxes on what he made."

Nobody had hit me yet so I kept going. "Any of that true?"

His face wrinkled up and he settled back. "I don't know. My son doesn't talk to me. He talks to his head doctor." Something seemed to creak. Maybe it was just the chair. "Steeg doesn't want my son, he wants me. Parents, husbands, wives, they're all hitting my son with lawsuits. My son'll be tied up in litigation for years. That'll make Steeg happy." He went quiet, then suddenly he laughed. "Maybe it'll keep my son out of the movies for a while." He was quiet again. "I was going to ask you, Mr. Thieringer, the police traced this man Frank Jarvis to Las Vegas but they didn't find him. Did you find him?"

"No."

He nodded slowly. "You looking for him?"

"No."

"That's good." He warmed his hands on the coffee cup.

"Maybe Fritz's looking and he doesn't want us to

know he's looking," Bellino said. Bellino always had been a sweetheart.

The old man looked at me. "Is that possible?"

"I'm not looking for Jarvis." I faced Bellino and spoke loudly. "I think you already caught up with Jarvis, Bellino. When you were in Vegas."

Bellino's eyebrows went up. "What'd I be doing in Vegas?"

"Getting your arm broken when it got caught in someone's car door. Sometimes it isn't so smart to play rough with a woman, is it?"

The old man turned his head so one ear faced me. "Woman?"

"My partner, McGuane, is a woman," I said loudly and clearly.

"Really?" The old man smiled and looked at Bellino. "You didn't tell me it was a woman."

Bellino said nothing. It was going to cost me but it was worth it. The old man laughed and then waved some fingers at the thug who'd brought him the coffee. The thug helped him to his feet and the old man looked straight at me, keeping his head as still as he could. But he'd stopped smiling and laughing. "My son's got cops on him, Mr. Thieringer. Public cops. I don't like it. I don't want him to have to worry about private cops too. I haven't got much left I care about, but I care about my son. No matter what I think of him, he's still my son. Don't go looking for Jarvis, don't go looking for anybody. I'll find Jarvis." He paused. "I hope I've made myself clear."

You couldn't freeze the sound of that voice. You can't freeze things that are already frozen. I nodded my head evenly and the thug guided him toward the door.

"Mr. Capanegro," Bellino said. The old man turned slightly. "You don't mind, I got some things of my own I'd like to discuss with Mr. Thieringer. If you don't mind."

The old man looked at me, then at Bellino. "Is it necessary?"

"Yeah. It's personal."

"I see." The old man looked at me. "He's a loyal

man, Mr. Thieringer. I could stop him, but I got to consider he's loyal. Loyalty's got to be rewarded occasionally or it doesn't remain loyal very long. I'm sorry. So far, I got nothing against you myself."

He shrugged helplessly and the thug carried him out of the office.

122

Two of the thugs each took an arm and they pressed me against the wall. Bellino went from my desk to the safe and kicked the door shut so the guns were locked inside. He came to me. "What'sa matter, Fritz? You ain't putting up any fight?" He held his right arm in its cast close against his body and held his left hand up in a fist. "Six long years, Fritz."

"You were guilty."

"Doesn't make the six years any shorter."

"Everything I had on you was clean. I didn't stack anything against you except what you'd done."

"True, Fritz, very true." His left started coming into my stomach. They held me against the wall so I wouldn't fall down and his left kept coming.

Water hit my face. I opened my eyes. "Pick him up." There was no answer. "Pick him up!" They picked me up and spread me against the wall and Bellino started swinging his left fist again and I felt myself coming closer to sickness again. There was noise from the front office and Bellino stopped hitting me. The noise continued, something cracked, there was a groan, a thud. "What the hell's going on out there!" "It's okay, Augie. The kid tried to make a play for the gun on the desk. He won't try it again." Bellino started putting his left into my stomach again.

A hand slapped my face. My eyes opened. It was a blur. It was Bellino. He was kneeling in front of me. "Come on, Fritz, we're not even halfway there yet." His hand slapped my face. "We ain't even got through three years' worth yet." He got to his feet. "Pick him up." ". . . Augie—" "Pick him up!" They picked me up and he went at me again.

I came back to consciousness and tried to keep my eyes closed but I was too late. They'd opened involuntarily. "Pick him up." "Augie, it's enough." "Not yet it ain't enough!" "Augie—" "Pick the bastard up!"

Silence.

Footsteps went away from me and I opened an eye and saw two pairs of shoes going through the door. "Hey! Where the hell you going?" "It's enough, Augie. Leave him alone." "Hey!"

Silence.

A shoe kicked at my shoulder. I slowly rolled away from the shoe and turned so I was facing the floor and tried to get to my hands and knees. Bellino laughed. I grunted. I tried to stand and a shoe kicked my hand out from under me. I went down and the laugh came again.

I got back on hands and knees and started moving slowly toward the door, very slowly. He came along at my side. "That's it, Fritz, don't give up." He laughed. "Go. The door." I went toward the door. "There's a gun out there, Fritz. On the desk, remember? Maybe it's still there, wanna see if it's there?" I nodded like I wanted to see if it's there. I crawled toward the door. "Go! Get the gun! The gun!" Get the gun, the gun.

I raised up more so I was on my feet and I stumbled toward the door and it didn't make much difference, I couldn't've gotten through it if I'd wanted to. He was barely a foot away from me. I started to fall and caught onto the door for support and he didn't touch me yet. My free hand slid down the edge of the door and stopped for a moment when it reached the buttons that set the lock and as soon as it'd pushed the button my hand moved down again. I tried to face him but I stumbled and fell and as I fell my shoulder knocked the door and the door closed so it was locked but he didn't even realize. .He laughed as I slid to the floor.

I kept my eyes closed. I heard him getting down on his knees. His voice was close. Only inches away from my ear. "Come on, Fritz, we still got a ways to go."

His hand worked my shoulder but didn't wake me, so he leaned closer and his left hand slipped under my right arm and tried to get me sitting. His left hand went farther under my right arm and around toward my back. I brought down my right arm and my right armpit trapped his left arm at the elbow. Before he could move back my right hand came up and grabbed the tail of his tie as my left hand grabbed the knot. My right hand pulled down on the tail and my left pushed up on the knot. His eyes opened wide and his mouth spread in a yawn but no sound came out. He struggled to get his left arm free and he couldn't do it. He struggled against me while still on his knees and half off balance and I forced the knot tighter against his throat. We glared at each other and neither of us made a sound and I tightened the knot. His right arm moved and the cast came out of its sling and swung at me. The cast bounced off my arm and it hurt but I ignored it and tightened the knot. He tried to rip loose and swung at me again with the cast and the cast went straight for my head and connected. I saw sparks but I kept my grip and he was yelling now and I tightened the knot. I had my back against the door and they were pounding on the other side of it and yelling and trying to get in. I tightened the knot and he screamed at me and swung the cast savagely. I tried to move but the cast was going straight at my head and then I heard an awful crack.

123

I was lying on my back. There was a weight across my legs. I heard another crack. I opened my eyes. The door busted open. They came in. They pulled him away from me. He was moaning. The cast was broken. Blood dripped out of it. His moaning got louder. I got one look at his face. That's all I needed. I closed my eyes.

The moaning got louder but not loud enough to cover the sound of feet going across the floor away from me, then the sound of the front door opening and closing. I lay still a minute, then got so I was sitting. I was alone. I looked at the wall next to the door and there was a small dent in it and paint chipped off right where it'd been hit by the cast. I crawled through the door to the front office.

Paul was lying on the floor behind his desk and when he heard me coming he turned his face. "Fritz. . . ."

"You all right?"

" . . . Yeah."

I tried to move closer but couldn't make it so I stopped and rested my back against the wall and dropped my chin against my chest. After several moments Paul started moving and said, "Fritz? *You* all right?"

I laughed as much as I could. "Sure. . . . Welcome to the agency."

124

"Operator. May I help you?"

"My name's Fritz Thieringer. I want to make a collect call to Mrs. Virginia Morrison in San Francisco."

I gave her the number and she went away and the phone made those funny noises it always makes and finally a voice said, "Hungry Pirate. Good afternoon."

"I have a collect call for Mrs. Virginia Morrison from Mr. Fritz Thieringer. Will you accept the charges?"

"One moment, please."

She went away and there were no noises at all and my stomach hurt and then I heard a voice I recognized. "I'll accept the charges."

"Thank you. You may go ahead, Mr. Thieringer."

I breathed in deeply. "Mrs. Morrison, you ever hear of a man named Isenbart, Max Isenbart, down here in L.A.?"

"No. Why? Should it mean something to me?"

She came up with the answer pretty quick. Almost as if she'd been waiting for it. "We found the name Max Isenbart written in your son's handwriting on a piece of paper in your son's house."

"I see." She paused. "Well?"

"We tried to find Isenbart. He's dead. He committed suicide the same night your son died. They found him the next morning. Sounds like there might be a connection."

That got me some more silence, then, "What're you telling me, Mr. Thieringer?"

"This name Isenbart's the only lead we've come up with and Isenbart's dead. Let's say it turns out Isenbart was in some way responsible for what happened to your son. I didn't think you'd want us wasting your money trying to pin something on a dead man."

"Oh. I see." She paused. "Could you wait a minute, Mr. Thieringer?"

"I can wait all day, you're paying for the call."

She went away. Take all the time you want, lady, just tell me something when you come back. Lord, I wished someone else owned my stomach just then.

"Mr. Thieringer, considering whatever you've found out so far, do you have any evidence to make you think the police're right in what they say happened regarding the explosion?"

"That it was set up by the movie company? Or negligence on their part? I got no evidence to say it happened either of those ways, or any other way."

More silence.

"It's my money, Mr. Thieringer. Continue your work and see what you find."

It just made me feel even worse.

125

I put my key in the lock and turned. The door opened an inch and a half, then the chain stopped it. I rapped my fist on the door till steps came forward on the far side of it. An eye looked through the crack at me. She unchained the door. "Why'd you try the key, you're the one who told me to put the chain——" She saw what I looked like.

I stumbled in. "You're not the only one who gets visitors at the office." She put a hand on my shoulder but I brushed by it and headed toward the kitchen.

"Like yesterday, huh?"

"Different faces, same personalities." I dropped her pocketbook on the kitchen table and opened the refrigerator. "Part of it was a piece of my past paying me a visit."

"I don't think I want to hear about it."

"You met him in Vegas. You put his arm in a cast." I stared into the refrigerator and cold lifeless air stared back at me. I reached for a Coke bottle but my stomach got angry and I left it there. I sat at the table and watched her drink coffee. "He works for Tony Capanegro. Capanegro was there, too. The office." She poured another cup of coffee. "Want to go for a ride?"

"Just as long as we don't go anywhere near the office."

"I'm with you. Remember that blackmailer last week, the one with the pictures, you left him on the cliff?"

Her face hardened. "Oh, lord. *He's* not in this, is he?"

"Who knows?" I touched my stomach lightly with my fingertips. "You said he had a Nikon and you kept it. We might put it to some use."

She nodded and gulped more coffee and made a face and pushed the mug aside. She pulled her pocketbook closer and opened it up and her hand dug into it and came out empty. She blinked at me. "You didn't put a gun in here."

"I don't like guns."

"You look terrible, you know that?"

"Look in the mirror yourself."

"I feel like that's what I'm doing!"

She looked at me and I looked at her. Then she smiled. I smiled back.

"Well, Fritz, let's get on with it. I can't hide here all day."

126

My eyes ran across the mailboxes and stopped at F. Jarvis, Apartment 4D. I checked another row and found Manager, L. Stockhausen, Apartment 1A. I adjusted my glasses and pulled down my hat and got as solid a grip on my clipboard as I could manage and walked around the corner to 1A. I rang the bell and a woman opened up and looked at me without running away.

"Mrs. Stockhausen? I'm Mr. Fredericks from Allstate. Frank Jarvis filed a claim, repairs to his apartment. I got to look it over." She put on her glasses and took another look. I rubbed some fingers along my cheek so my hand would cover the bruise on the side of my jaw. "Jarvis had the repairs done, now he puts in a claim. You're not supposed to do it that way. Not supposed to fix anything till we've seen it. I got a half a mind to discount his claim entirely. You know Jarvis? He the kind who'd file a false claim?"

She put her glasses away. "I don't know what kind of person does that."

"Every kind of person does it. That's what makes your insurance rates go up. Everybody complains about the rates, they're just getting what they deserve." I shrugged. "Jarvis didn't contact you, huh? Fine. I'm not going to look at his apartment, I'm rejecting his claim." I drew a line through some writing on my clipboard and turned away.

She came after me. "Well, now, you better wait a minute. I don't want to make any trouble for Mr. Javis. If you're supposed to see his apartment I can show it to you."

I shook my head. "A claimant hasn't got the courtesy

to make things easy for me when he files a claim, it's just too bad for him." I crossed out more writing.

She touched my arm. "Can you just wait a minute?" She giggled. "I'm watching *The Edge of Night*. It's almost over."

I looked at my watch. "Haven't got much time. If you gave me the key—"

"I couldn't do that." She turned professional. "I have to go with you. Just wait a few minutes, I won't watch the credits today." She went back into her apartment.

I walked to the corner of the building and looked down the street to where the car was parked and nodded at Maggie and Maggie nodded back and then I leaned against the wall and waited. Mrs. Stockhausen came out with a ring of keys like a head jailer at San Quentin would carry. She turned and locked two locks on her apartment door and smiled at me and we went up in the elevator. Thank God for the elevator, the shape I was in I couldn't've made it up the stairs even if someone had carried me.

Mrs. Stockhausen giggled again. "That Noel Douglas, he's such a caution. He's always fooling around. He's going to get into trouble one of these days."

"Noel Douglas?"

Her eyes twinkled. "*The Edge of Night*. The things they do." Her tongue made sounds against the roof of her mouth.

We went into Jarvis's apartment. The paint smell was gone. I looked around carelessly and let her see my frown. "All Jarvis wrote, there's some kind of damage, like I'm supposed to know what that means. He sent us a repair bill, all it tells me's what it cost to repair things, doesn't tell me what had to be repaired. People want their money quick enough, but they never think to give you the information you need to check it out. You know why they do it that way?"

"No. Why?"

I flopped in a chair. "They're trying to pull a fast one." I glanced this way and that and then walked across the room and looked into the bedroom. I waved my hand at it. "I'm not going to bother with it. I'm going to bounce the claim right back in his face. They're all trying to get something for nothing. I see it all the time." I started for the door.

"Shouldn't we look around? I know he did have something repaired, there were workmen here. Maybe if we look together we can figure out what it was."

Whenever you run up against the kind who think they've got to keep an eye on you it's always best to give them a reason to go to work for you. Keeps them occupied and occasionally turns up something you would've missed. Mrs. Stockhausen was an eager worker. She wasn't too good, though. She'd already missed the first thing. The front door. It had a new chain. It was a different size than the one that'd been there before, they'd had to drill new holes when they put it on. She did notice that the balcony doors stuck like either they were new doors and they didn't fit right, or they'd been painted and the paint had dried in the tracks, or both. I thought it was just the paint, that the doors were the original ones, but it looked like they had a new lock.

I had all I needed but I'd done too good a job on Mrs. Stockhausen. She was so anxious to make sure Jarvis wouldn't lose out on his insurance claim she was turning the apartment upside down and inside out and whatever else she could think of. I decided I better help her 'cause I wanted to get out of there, I had places to go.

127

Maggie opened the car door from the inside. "Find anything up there?"

"Enough, I think. Mrs. Stockhausen's a born snoop, I didn't think I was going to get out."

"Take a look at what drove up and parked down the street five minutes ago. The blue Volkswagen."

I turned and looked and I didn't like what I was looking at. "We got the whole world watching us." I pushed the car door shut and stayed outside.

"Easy, Fritz. Don't make enemies you don't have to make. We already have our share coming out of the woodwork."

"I'll put on my best behavior, Mag."

"I mean it, damn it."

I went down the street trying to walk naturally but my stomach wouldn't let me. Steeg got out of the Volkswagen with a half-eaten tuna fish sandwich in one hand and a pint container of milk in the other. Make small talk, Fritz. Act friendly. "Glad to see I'm not the only one in the world with a job built to give me instant indigestion."

His eyes stared at the sandwich. "First chance I've had to eat since breakfast. Look what I'm eating." He looked at the side of my jaw. "You been meeting the wrong kind of people?"

"I usually do." I leaned against the side of his car. "You ought to put Mrs. Stockhausen on your payroll full time. Someone comes to look at Jarvis's apartment, she goes inside to catch the rest of her soap and gives you a call, then she keeps 'em around till you get a chance to come over. I hope the guys you got looking for Jarvis're as good's she is."

He leaned on the car, next to me. "They haven't turned up a damn thing. What about you?"

"Still looking. Thought you didn't mind."

He studied my face. "I don't think Jarvis's out of the country after all." He picked up his sandwich and then put it down. "You ought to see a doctor about that bruise."

"I did. He charged me an arm and a leg and all he gave me was a bottle of yeast pills."

He put the sandwich on the hood of the car and frowned. "Yeast? Doesn't sound like much of a doctor." He picked up the sandwich and almost took a bite but didn't and instead looked at the apartment house.

He looked so interested in the apartment house I decided to give it a look myself. "Don't suppose you'd want to tell me if there's been anyone else coming to see Jarvis's apartment?"

"If there had been, I wouldn't tell you. Since there hasn't been, I'll tell you. Nobody." He gave me a moment to absorb that. "Except for your partner, couple days ago."

"She'll be glad to know she was watched."

He took a few steps toward the apartment house, then shook his head and got in his car. He put the sandwich into some waxed paper and then turned and gave a look that was meant to impress me. "You get anything, you let me know. When this thing's settled, you and me better be on the same—" He stopped and grinned sadly. "What the hell'm I wasting time on you for? The way you look, you're not going to be any help."

I moved off his car. "I'm afraid you're probably right."

I stepped away and watched him drive off and then I walked back to the car. Maggie opened the door for me. "I hope you were nice to him."

"I was gorgeous to him. He asked me to marry him. I told him I needed a couple days to think about it."

We drove away.

128

We sat parked on the street for almost an hour before anything happened. When it did and Maggie didn't react I poked her to wake her up. "Across the street, Mag. He's wearing a gray suit and a blue-and-red-striped tie."

"I see him. Nice-looking man."

"The famous dress manufacturer. David Greene."

"He looks nicer, now that I know he's got money."

"Want to follow him?"

"This's your game, not mine."

"Okay, then we won't." I started the engine. "Let's go get something to eat."

Maggie looked out the side window at Greene. "I've got the camera. Want me to take a picture of him?"

"Good idea. Go ahead."

She reached behind her. I stepped on the gas and we were halfway down the block before she could get her camera out. Her head snapped around at me. "What's going on with you today? You crazy?"

I drove all the way to Westwood to a French place she likes. She ate like a horse. I could hardly handle a bowl of soup. Then we went over to the office and exchanged my car for hers and drove out to West Hollywood and parked in the middle of a big shadow and waited.

An hour and a half later a car pulled up and Carl got out. He went into his house and the lights went on. Thirty minutes later Carl came out with the German shepherd. No leash. He and the dog walked toward Sunset and then turned and came back and kept coming toward us. We squeezed down behind the dashboard and let them go by. I sneaked my head up and saw them down at the other end of the block and the dog was sniffing a tree and then raising a leg. When they turned and started back I hid again.

They reached the yard in front of the house and Carl picked up a stick and threw it. The dog leaped after it and took it in his teeth without snapping it in two and paraded triumphantly around the edges of the yard. He went to Carl and dropped the stick at Carl's feet and Carl threw the stick and the stick sailed far up the street. Carl threw it high and while it was still up there the dog got under it and when it came down he leaped into the air and closed his jaws on it. Fast dog. Damn fast dog. He pranced along the street and delivered the stick back to Carl.

This went on for another five minutes and then a car pulled into the street and came down toward us but turned and parked in front of the house. The car door opened and a man got out and the shepherd ran to him and jumped up and down. The man took the stick and threw it hard and long and this time the dog wasn't fast enough to get under it but he caught it on the bounce and ran with it. While he was still running the man walked across the yard to Carl and embraced him and kissed him.

I turned to Maggie. "Well?"

"It's him."

"Mr. Joseph Smith at the Holiday Inn in Encino?"

Her shoulders shuddered briefly before she could control them. "What do you want to do?"

"Go home and feed some Pepto-Bismol to my stomach. Before we go you better take a couple pictures of 'em. It'll give us something to put in our files."

PART FOUR

129

The next day we did nothing. We stayed home and recuperated. We left the office locked and empty. There was always the chance someone might want to see us, and we didn't want to see them. Around four o'clock Maggie came by. She drove me to the airport and I caught the 4:45 for San Francisco. When I got there I rented a car and it was still early so I drove down to Fisherman's Wharf and parked the car and went for a walk. There were lots of things to look at and after a half-hour I found myself facing a restaurant—The Hungry Pirate. I kept walking. I had no business there, at least not then. I walked all the way to Ghirardelli Square and bought six large bars of semisweet chocolate. Maggie goes bananas over the stuff. For myself I bought three loaves of sourdough bread. They've got sourdough bread in L.A. but it's never as good. I walked back to my car and drove across the Golden Gate into Sausalito and found a decent looking motel and checked into it and ate a light enough dinner so my stomach wouldn't get too mad at me. I went back to my room and read an entire play, *Major Barbara*, and got to sleep by eleven.

130

At seven the next morning I was showered and shaved, dressed and alert, bright and sassy, drinking a Coke, munching sourdough bread, wearing an Irish walking hat, listening to a Charles Aznavour tape, sitting in my rented car, watching the front door of Virginia Morrison's house.

It was a nice-looking neighborhood. No overdoses of money showed in the houses or the yards or the cars parked in the driveways. The kind of place where people weren't out to prove anything. You don't find those places as often as you'd like to.

At five minutes after eight Virginia Morrison came out of her house and got into her car and drove off. I stayed where I was. It was too early for me to do anything. I didn't want to wake anyone up, so I waited till nine and then started making rounds.

The story I told was this. I worked for an insurance company, an old man had died, I couldn't give out his name, he'd left lots of money to a woman named Virginia Morrison but it'd only go to her if we could locate her in time. We didn't know who she was or where she lived, we'd been searching for six months. This Virginia Morrison was the seventeenth we'd located. I'd knocked on her door and she wasn't there, so I'd thought I'd check with her neighbors till she got back. Did they know anything about her, where she'd come from, did she have a husband, or children, or relatives?

One neighbor told me she had a son but no husband. They didn't know her very well and didn't know if she'd been divorced or her husband had died or what.

The next one knew her a little better. Mrs. Morrison's son had just died in some kind of accident out of town somewhere. What about her husband? They didn't know.

I reached the end of the block and my fifth try was an old lady who was planting petunias in a back-yard garden and was glad for the company. She offered iced tea. I got her to offer a Coke instead and we sat on the grass. She dug into soil with gloved hands and I gave her a petunia. She looked like a talker.

"Virginia's lived here—must be fifteen, sixteen years now." She patted down the soil around the petunia and started digging another hole. "Gene, that's her son, he was only about three or four years old when they moved in. That'd make it about fifteen years ago."

I sipped Coke. "Where'd they live before they moved here?"

"Oakland."

"It's too bad about the son. One of your neighbors told me."

She seemed to react. She had a plant in her cupped hands and brushed bits of dirt off one of its leaves. "They're each all a little bit different, aren't they?" She held the plant up to the light. "Lots of them look like they're the same, but they're not. There's something in the coloring, or the shape. A little bit different. It makes you wonder. It's quite a world. It's full of wonderful things, if you take time to look at it. You just have to look and let yourself take things as they come." She turned the flower some more, then carefully planted it in the ground. "Well, it's finished. Everything's got to be finished sometime."

I moved closer and dug out a hole for the next petunia with my fingers. "You mean the son?"

She ran the edge of her trowel across the dirt, spreading it evenly. "Gene was living down in Los Angeles. He was working in movies. Can you imagine that? He hadn't even told me he was working in movies."

I tried not to look at her. "Hadn't told you? You talked to him recently?"

"He was up here just a month ago." She picked up a pair of shears and trimmed excess foliage from a patch of ivy. Her eyes glistened.

I changed the subject. "They told me Mrs. Morrison

313

owns these restaurants, the Hungry Pirates. How many of 'em are there?"

"Five. The one out here, it's right on the water. The food is excellent. You ought to go down there for lunch. The prices are very reasonable."

"Mrs. Morrison decided to open up one out here where she lives, huh?"

"No, this one was the first. Been here longer'n I have. Used to be called Pirate's Cove."

I took two more plants, handed one to her and started putting in the other myself. "What'd she do, move here from Oakland and buy into it?"

"Lord, no, she was just a waitress there when she started. It's really something, the way she's built herself up. The restaurant too. It used to be just a small little thing." She put down her trowel and turned to me and smiled. There are two kinds of friends in this world. One kind hates you for anything you accomplish. The other kind is more secure and loves to share in it. "The people who owned Pirate's Cove, they wanted to retire. Virginia got some money, a bank loan I think, and she bought into it. She modernized it and expanded it. She changed the name, she used all these wonderful advertising ideas, she really made a go of it. About ten years ago she opened another one, down on Fisherman's Wharf. She's got five now. She told me she's thinking about opening two more, one in Los Angeles and the other in San Diego. She's a very shrewd woman when it comes to business. It hasn't changed her one bit. I mean, look at her, she still lives right here, in the same house. She's not stuck up at all. There's not many like her, I can tell you that."

It didn't sound much like the Virginia Morrison I'd seen, but the old lady wouldn't see the Virginia Morrison I'd seen. "I can see you know her pretty well, Mrs. Grant."

"We've been friends right from when she first moved here. Gene was just a child. I always looked after him so she could work." She moved a few feet farther down the grass and got herself settled. "It was nice having a child around the house again. My children were both grown and moved away already. They always move away these days, don't they. I guess there's nothing wrong with it. It's just, things are different now. Different world."

"Did you know Mrs. Morrison's husband?"

She answered quickly. "No, I didn't."

"Not at all?"

"No. Her husband died, before she moved here."

"When she was still living in Oakland?"

She turned to the crate of petunias so I couldn't see her face. "Yes, I think so."

I wondered just how close she was to Virginia Morrison, and how much she knew of whatever there was to know. "Mrs. Grant, about this inheritance, if I told you what I'm looking for, there's always a chance it might influence what you tell me, or the way you tell me. Not that I don't think you're an honest woman, I'm sure you are. It's company policy. When you're working on a trace that involves a lot of money, the company tells you to hold certain things back. For instance, I told you a man died and left some money to a woman named Virginia Morrison. I didn't tell you if Morrison was her married name or her maiden name. The company likes us to do it that way so the people we interview can't be sure what it is we want to hear. It's a precaution. In the end, there's anything a little bit off, we'll catch it anyway, but sometimes it saves us time this way."

She looked up. "I'm not sure I understand. It makes a difference if Morrison is her married name?"

I nodded. "You said her husband died years ago. If I knew if his name was Morrison or not, it might tell me if this could be the Virginia Morrison I'm looking for."

She rubbed soil off her gloves. "Well, she's probably at her office on Geary Street. Why don't you go see her?"

She knew something all right. "I called out here this morning around nine and there was no answer so I tried her office. They told me she'd already been in and there was some kind of trouble in Los Angeles, about the restaurant she's trying to open. She had to fly down and she might not be back for a couple days. The problem is, either they can't or they won't give me a number where I can reach her. If I have to fly down there it's going to

315

cost me some time, so I thought since I'm here if I could find out a few things it might save me that time. See, I been working on this trace six months, I don't locate the right woman by the end of the month, the will stipulates the money goes to charity, all of it. I'd hate to see the woman lose out just 'cause I couldn't find her in time. It's a lot of money."

The old lady's face looked bothered. Her eyes were sympathetic. "I can tell you this much, if it helps. I'm quite sure Morrison isn't her married name."

I rubbed my chin and thought it over. I was almost there but I couldn't push too hard. "That's helpful, Mrs. Grant, but I'm afraid it isn't helpful enough. If you were absolutely sure, I'd know how to handle it. If you're only *quite* sure. . . ." I put on my hat and got to my feet. "I'll have to take the time and see if I can find her in L.A. I hope it's not another dead end."

Her hand flew up. "Wait a minute." We waited. "If I can be sure you won't tell anyone. . . ."

I kept my face impassive. But she was still having trouble deciding and I had to take a chance. "If it's something Mrs. Morrison might not want people to know about, that's no concern of mine. I just have to know if she could possibly be related to the man who died."

"Morrison is her maiden name. I'm sure."

I sat on the grass and looked into her eyes. "I understand what you're saying. You're in this business awhile, you learn to read between the lines. I won't say anything." Her eyes darted away. "She had a son. I suppose she always pretended she'd been married and her husband's died, so the son wouldn't know. You don't want to be responsible for it getting out now, that she really wasn't ever married."

Her face turned red. "I didn't say that. All I said was. . . ."

I had to calm her down. "The woman I want *was* married. To a man named Morrison. He left her a long time ago and about three years ago he died. She probably wouldn't even know he's dead. His death made her the only person in the world related to the man who just died now. The link was through the marriage. Going by what you've told me, this Virginia Morrison can't be the one I'm looking for."

She was quiet. "No. No, it couldn't be her."

I sat for a moment, then got up again. "It must've been hard on the son, growing up without a father."

She looked at her garden. "It really doesn't matter any more, does it? It's over. Finished. Things don't last." She stood up suddenly and walked to where a tall rosebush displayed its proud flowers to the sun. Her gloved hand took a rose and she snipped it off with her shears. "Things aren't meant to last, not forever. The important thing, while they're here they're wonderful. You just have to appreciate them while you can. You have to do that."

She held the rose and admired it another moment, then came across the grass and gave it to me.

131

Before I reached my car someone came out of the house across the street. He fixed a red scarf around his neck, he carried a white cashmere jacket slung over one shoulder. I didn't have time to avoid him so I didn't try. He stopped when he saw me. I leaned against the side of my car and waited for him.

He came halfway into the street. "What're you doing here? Why aren't you in Los Angeles?"

I smiled. "I thought you were just the flunky. I didn't know you were the houseguest too." His eyebrows squeezed together across his forehead. "When Gene came up to Sausalito last month, maybe he knew his mother was living with a man ten years younger'n her. Maybe he didn't want to stay in the same house. Or maybe Gene and his mother didn't get along anyway. Maybe they never did."

One hand closed in a fist. "It's none of your business how they got along! Just 'cause I—"

"I don't care if you live with her, Parking. I don't care what you do with her. That's not what I was hired to find out."

He started forward. I didn't move a muscle. "Please don't try anything, Parking. I'm not in the mood."

His feet stopped, then shuffled tentatively in a different direction. His eyes stayed on me. "What're you doing up here?" He looked confused. Maybe he was.

"Maybe you really don't know, Parking. Maybe she keeps you on a leash and she only lets you know what she wants you to know. I don't care. Tell her I'm up here. Tell her I'm close. Tell her I want to put some things together, then I'll come and see her."

His feet wanted to move forward but something held them back. "What're you—"

"Stop asking questions. If you don't know, I'm not going to tell you."

I turned my back on him and got in my car and drove away.

132

I drove to Oakland. Oakland because there was no reason for Virginia Morrison to lie to Mrs. Grant about where she'd lived before she'd come to Sausalito. And because something had to be somewhere for someone else to find, and if someone else'd found it I could find it. It didn't have to be in Oakland, of course. It could've been anywhere, but my feelings told me Oakland.

I went to the registrar of vital statistics and started flipping through books. I knew Joseph Lydon had been killed in May 1955 and Virginia Morrison's last paycheck from Lybart had been that June. I started looking in June even though I knew if what I was looking for was listed there, it probably wouldn't be listed till several months later.

133

"My name's Fritz Thieringer. I want to see Virginia Morrison."

The girl looked at a sheet of paper. "Do you have an appointment?"

"No, but she'll see me."

The girl gave me a look and left her desk and went through a door. A moment later the door slammed open and Ross Parking came out. He looked angry and scared and came right up next to me. "What's going on here! Tell me what's going on here!"

I spoke softly. "It's between Mrs. Morrison and me. If she—"

"What're you doing to her?" His hands grabbed my lapels. He began to shake me.

I tried to get his hands off and he pushed me against the desk. I reached back to catch my balance and he struggled for my neck and we both went over to the floor. His fingers dug at my throat. I heard a door open behind us and the girl shrieked. I tried to get loose but he was on top, sitting across me. I got my head turned and saw the girl. She was near the desk. Her hand was reaching slowly for the phone.

I put my hand under Parking's chin and pushed. I had to be careful, if I did it too quickly I could've killed him. I could just make out the girl putting the phone to her ear.

I forced Parking toward the wall and punched him hard enough to keep him there. I lunged for the desk and took the phone away from the girl. I turned quickly, Parking was crawling toward me.

"For Christ's sake, Parking, use your head! Tell the girl it's okay or she'll call someone!"

Parking's eyes blinked at me, then he saw the girl. "God! Ellen! No! Don't call anyone! It's all right!"

The girl spread her back against the wall. Parking realized what'd almost happened. He tried to get up. I put him in a chair. I sat next to him. The girl didn't move.

"You all right, Parking?" His head nodded at me. "I'm not going to do anything to her. She's done it to herself. If she's hurt, it's already happened. I can't hurt her. You understand?"

His slack face pleaded with me. "You won't do anything to her? You won't say anything to her? You won't—"

"I'll say what I have to say. She already knows it, it won't make a difference."

He didn't understand. "She's scared! What's she scared of?"

I didn't answer. He tried to speak again but couldn't. Tears came down his face. All I could do was watch him. I sat there and waited for him to quiet down.

"I had you wrong, Parking. I thought you were just the kind who goes along for the money. I didn't know you cared about her. You better calm down. If she needs you, she's going to need you in better shape'n you're in right now."

I went down the corridor to the last office. Virginia Morrison stood by the window, looking out. Finally she turned and her face was white. There was a thin smile but it meant nothing. Her fingers held a cigarette. No holder this time. The cigarette was shaking.

She sat at her desk and filled a glass with whiskey. "Would you like something to drink, Mr. Thieringer?"

I said I didn't.

She filled her glass but left it in the middle of the desk and stared at it.

"Are you ready, Mrs. Morrison?"

She nodded slowly and looked at the glass.

134

Except I didn't know if I was ready. I took a long time to get settled in a chair. I took off my hat and set it on the floor. I still wasn't ready.

Mrs. Morrison leaned forward. "Do you know what happened or don't you?"

I breathed in and out sharply. "I think I do. It started out as a simple matter. He was an open shadow."

She put her glass down and gasped. "Yes. A shadow. That's a good word for it."

"No, Mrs. Morrison. I'm not talking about Joseph Lydon. Not yet. I'm talking about Gene." I rubbed the back of my neck. "An open shadow's a guy who follows someone else but does it in such a way that the guy knows he's being followed. The whole point of it's for the guy to know he's being followed. Gene was doing it to Max Isenbart. Mrs. Isenbart got her husband to hire us to keep Gene away. Max Isenbart didn't know it was your son, he just thought Gene was some boy who'd been hired to scare him.

"Before we could find out who Gene was and why he was doing what he was doing he died in that explosion. Then Max Isenbart was dead. You came down to L.A. and hired us to find out if the explosion was accidental or not. You hired us because Gene had our card and you weren't sure what that meant. It might've meant Gene'd hired us to find out how Joseph Lydon had died. Or to track down Max Isenbart. Or maybe someone'd hired us to get rid of your son. If that was it, you thought your only way to know would be to hire us yourself and see what we did. You didn't trust us, so you thought you better try to buy us.

"Gene grew up without a father. I suppose you told him his father had died before he was born, or maybe that his father'd run off, something like that. You give his father a name?"

She nodded quickly. "Joe Morrison. I told Gene he died."

"Your real name was Moore. You changed it to Morrison so nobody in L.A. would be able to trace where you'd gone to and nobody here'd be able to trace where you came from or if you'd really been married or not. It must've been hard on Gene, no father, a mother who was always working."

"Gene hated his father. For not being there. For being dead." She tapped a fresh cigarette out of a pack. "I didn't know what to do about it."

"Maybe he hated his father because he saw you hated him." She didn't react. "You may've had reason to hate him. I think he got you pregnant and he wasn't going to marry you. He was rubbing shoulders with the Hollywood crowd and was changing into a different man. Maybe he wouldn't even admit the baby could be his."

"He admitted it. He didn't care." She lit the cigarette. Her eyes watched the flame with little interest. "He was going to have a new life, in films. He wasn't going to let himself get tied down to anything." She started to get out of her chair, but halfway up, all the strength left her. She sat. Then her fist banged the desk. "Yes! I hated him! I had a right to hate him!"

"The hate spread, from you to your son." But what good would it've been to make her feel worse? There was no point. I continued quietly. "You needed something. You took over the restaurant, Pirate's Cove. Gene needed something, too, a family. A nice old lady who lived down the street must've been the only family he could find. When they broke his foot for him down in L.A. and he had to get away, he came up here and stayed with her."

Her head snapped up. "Who broke his foot?"

"I'll get around to it. Gene must've seen letters from L.A. while he was growing up, but they weren't letters, they were checks. Maybe he noticed that. Maybe he saw the name Max Isenbart, but eventually the checks stopped and maybe they stopped before Gene realized they were blackmail."

Her finger rubbed the edge of her glass. "They weren't blackmail. Not at first."

I gave it to her hard. "Then what the hell were they?"

Her face turned away. "I didn't know what to do. I wanted to leave Los Angeles, and Max was a good man, he gave me three thousand dollars. When I needed more I wrote him and he sent me more."

"He sent you one hundred dollars every two weeks."

"Yes. For a while. Then he wrote that he was having trouble with the business and he couldn't afford to send me any more."

"So you wrote back and told him he better send you more. The payments jumped to every week. *Then* it was blackmail."

She breathed in heavily. "I was alone. I didn't have any money. I had a baby I had to support, I'd lost the man I loved. Someone owed me something."

"And then it was blackmail."

She started to fix me with a look but realized there was no point to it. She poured herself another glass of whiskey and drank it.

"You got enough money to get yourself the house in Sausalito. Probably rented it at first, and worked at the restaurant, and after a few years you had enough to buy your way in. You were very successful. So successful maybe you told Max Isenbart he could stop the payments."

She nodded her head quickly. "I stopped it. I always planned to pay him back and I did, all of it."

"You sent money orders to him. Elizabeth Isenbart saw one of them. You used your real name, Virginia Moore."

"I always used the name Moore. I worked through a

323

post office box in Santa Cruz so Max wouldn't know where I really was."

"When Mrs. Isenbart found your money order she thought it meant you had something to do with Lydon's death and Max was blackmailing you about it."

She stiffened. "Betty thought that?"

"Why wouldn't she think it?"

Mrs. Morrison sighed. "Yes. She would think it."

Then I felt really awful. "I don't know if I want to tell her different. I'm worried about telling her the truth. If I know the truth, and I'm afraid I'm pretty close to it. Anyway, somewhere along the line Gene must've started believing, wanting to believe, that his father could still be alive somewhere. You weren't telling him much of the truth but you'd given him the name Joe Morrison. He'd try to find either an address on him or a death listing. There was nothing in Sausalito so he tried Oakland."

"Oakland!" Her eyes shifted back and forth. "I never told him anything about Oakland!"

"You told Mrs. Grant down the street that you'd come from there. She told me, she probably told Gene. He'd check the vital statistics in Oakland and there'd be no Joe Morrison but there would be a listing of his own birth." She put her head in her hands. "Gene would've found what I found today. The mistake you made. The one that made you leave Oakland in the first place. You were a frightened young girl and you were about to have a baby and when they asked you questions you didn't know what you were saying. They asked you for the father's name and you gave it to them. Joseph Lydon. Gene tried to find Joseph Lydon and he couldn't and he wouldn't ask you about him because he didn't think you'd tell him. He knew you lied about it and he thought you must have something to hide and then he must've remembered that money you used to get from L.A.

"He went down there and couldn't find Lydon, so he checked the vital statistics, probably started at his own birth date and worked forward and backward and pretty soon he found it. Lydon's death. He went to the libraries and got microfilms of the L.A. papers about it

324

and found out Lydon died in a shotgun mugging and that he'd never been married and that he'd been a partner in a dress company and his partner'd been a man named Max Isenbart. Gene remembered the name Max Isenbart from the checks. That's when he would've started thinking about blackmail and why there could've been blackmail.

"Gene wanted something, but he didn't know what. He thought he knew something, but he didn't know what he knew or how to prove it. He'd hooked into some kids by then and either they got him on pills or he got them and pretty soon he was high most of the time. He was very bitter. First he'd blamed his father for dying on him, then you for lying about it, now he blamed Isenbart. He couldn't go to the cops, you were the only one who might know anything and he didn't trust you. He wanted some kind of revenge against someone and maybe he figured driving Isenbart nuts was the best revenge he could get."

I got out of my chair and went to the window. It's a beautiful city, San Francisco. But right then nothing looked beautiful. "I think that's pretty close to what happened. We'll never know for sure. Only Gene knew, and he never told anyone. He didn't know anyone he could trust to tell it to."

It was silent for a moment and then the words came softly from behind my back. "Tell me about the explosion."

135

I took a glass from the bar at the side and filled it half-way to the top with vodka and drank some of it and went back to my chair.

"Like I said, Mrs. Isenbart thought Max Isenbart was blackmailing you 'cause you had something to do with Lydon's death. I didn't believe it. You'd been pushing us too hard to get on with our investigation. I also wondered why you were so suspicious about the explosion, so I checked you out and found you worked for Lybart Pe-tites, which made you the connection between Gene and Isenbart. I found out about Lydon's death and the money going back and forth, first from Isenbart to you, then from you to Isenbart. I called you yesterday and told you Isenbart killed himself the day after the explosion. Maybe you already knew that, you probably did, but I had to make sure you did. When you told me to keep on with the case that meant there still must be someone else around who you thought could be responsible for the explosion. If there *was* someone, it could also mean you'd never thought it was Isenbart. You never did, did you?"

She shook her head.

"You didn't think it was Isenbart 'cause you knew he wasn't a killer. And if he wasn't, someone else must've killed Lydon." I stared at the floor. "And it had to be someone Isenbart would protect, or he never would've sent you any money." I drained the rest of the vodka and gave it a good long chance to circulate inside me. Then I went on. "All right, he was protecting his wife. She says she thinks you killed Lydon and you say it's possible she thinks that. Tell me how it happened."

Virginia Morrison kept her eyes on her desk. She

started speaking steadily like you do when you've had plenty of time to think about something. "I waited till everyone else had gone to lunch, then I went into Joe's office and told him I was pregnant. I asked him to marry me, I begged him. It didn't mean a thing to him. He just didn't care. I went out front and sat at the desk, he didn't even come out to see if I was all right. When Max and Betty came back they saw how I looked. I wouldn't tell them what happened but I think Max knew. He went in to see Joe.

"We could hear them in there, just yelling at each other. Joe started threatening Max, saying he knew how much money they owed, that he'd found out Max had gone to a loan shark to get money, that Max was paying kickbacks to buyers, things like that. Joe told Max he'd had enough of the business, he wanted to get out. Max told him he didn't have the money to buy him out and Joe said if he didn't buy him out he'd sue Max for everything Max had. Max told him to go ahead and sue, he didn't care. Then we heard a lot of noise and we ran down the hall. They were fighting and Max was on the floor. Joe was kicking him and hitting him. We tried to get them apart, I grabbed Joe's arm and he hit me and then I heard something crack and Joe fell on the sofa.

"Betty and I got Max out to the front. He had a cut on his face, we cleaned it up and got it bandaged. After a while I went back to the office and Joe was still on the sofa. He wasn't moving. Then I saw what it was, the back of his head was bleeding and there was a lamp on the floor. It was broken in pieces.

"I went out front. Betty had gone to get some more bandages so I told Max what'd happened. We didn't know what to do. We knew if Betty found out what she'd done, even though it was an accident, she'd never be able to live with it. She was like that. She couldn't bear to see people hurt. When she came back Max told her Joe had already left and we were going to close the office for the rest of the day. He told her to go home and he'd meet her there in a little while."

Virginia Morrison got up from her desk and walked slowly across the room, like she was looking for some-

327

thing. Whatever it was, she didn't find it. She came over and sat in the chair next to me. "He wrote me after I left L.A. Max. He told me he'd married her and he wasn't going to let her work any more, and he was going to protect her so she'd never know."

The words just came out, almost a reflex. "And when he wrote you that, you knew you had him."

She nodded. "It was an awful thing to do. Max was one of the nicest, kindest men I've ever known. He loved her very much. I should never've used it against him. But I did. I knew I could, so I did. Years later I thought paying him back might make up for it but I knew it wouldn't."

"It never does. Tell me how Max got rid of the body."

She looked at me. I gave it to her again. "If you want to know about the explosion, tell me."

She held her hands together. "Max told me to go home, but before I'd gone I heard him in the office, calling someone to come over. I should've gone home then, but I didn't. I went into the back."

"Did you recognize the man, when he came?"

"I'd seen him around a few times. He was the loan shark Max'd gone to."

"A man named Chellick. Elizabeth Isenbart told me about him."

"Max told Chellick he'd killed Joe, and if anybody found out about it he'd go to jail and Chellick'd never get his money back. So Chellick took the body away, and the next day the police came and said Joe was dead, that he'd been killed in a robbery."

"And Max didn't say anything, and you didn't say anything, and maybe Elizabeth Isenbart suspected something but if she did she was too scared to say anything. So the police went away. And then Max gave you some money and you went away. And then you blackmailed him and years later you felt bad about it and you paid him back." She nodded silently. "But you never paid Chellick back, did you?"

136

She said nothing. She got quickly out of her chair and went to her desk. She stood there, her back to me, and I gave it to her quick and it started coming out harder than I wanted it to but I couldn't stop it. "You knew what you were doing when you didn't leave that office, you wanted money. More money than Isenbart would be able to give you. You heard who he was calling and you knew who he was and you figured a loan shark was vulnerable. If he disposed of the body he'd be an accomplice to murder after the fact. That's why you had to leave Los Angeles and change your name to Morrison and postmark everything through Santa Cruz. You knew the kind of man Chellick was and you knew before you'd be able to tap him you'd have to make sure he'd never be able to find you."

She still said nothing. I got out of my chair and went to her and took a picture from my pocket and slid it onto her desk. "Put twenty years on him. Is it Chellick?"

She stared at the picture and her upper lip tightened and pressed against her teeth. "Where'd you get this picture?"

"Is it Chellick?"

"Yes. Damn it, yes!" She started to shake. "The explosion—"

"I think so. I don't know for sure but I think so." I took the picture and put it back in my pocket.

Her hands closed up into tight little balls of anger. "But I stopped blackmailing Chellick years ago! I stopped it the same time I stopped it with Max! I didn't need it any more! It was over! It's been over for ten years!"

"What you knew wasn't over. It never could be.

Once something's known it's always known. That's what Chellick was afraid of."

She brought her fists up to her face and started to yell.

Then she stopped. It was sudden, and cold. She turned away and went around her desk and sat. It was like a switch had turned off, there was no emotion at all.

I gave her this much. Maybe she didn't know how to handle it and this was the best way she had. But I didn't know.

And then she spoke and I began to know more than I wanted. "Can you prove anything, Mr. Thieringer?" And her words were like pieces of ice and they scared the hell out of me.

"I don't know."

"If he killed my son—"

"If he killed your son he killed lots of people. He was in a hurry and he got messy about it. That doesn't mean I can prove it."

Her face didn't change. She opened a drawer and took out a checkbook and put it on her desk. "How much will it cost?"

I didn't even answer.

"I want you to take care of this. How much will it cost?"

I went to the chair and picked my hat off the floor. I'd thought I'd felt bad before, but I hadn't known this was coming. "I'm sorry, Mrs. Morrison. You haven't learned a damn thing. There's some things you can't buy."

"I have the money now. I can buy whatever I want."

I wanted to scream it at her. "No. You can't. For God's sake, don't you understand? You can't."

What was the use? What the hell was the use? I didn't know what I wanted to do most. Sit down, walk away, run away, I didn't know.

I sat down and stayed quiet a moment. I talked as evenly as I could. "We'll send you a bill for what you owe us, Mrs. Morrison. It'll cover from the day you hired us through my return trip to L.A." It even sounded like nonsense to me. "What you already paid us, we'll deduct it from—"

"Something's got to be done." She came out of her chair and leaned across the desk. "I don't care what it costs, something's got to be done."

I started up again. "We'll send you a bill, it'll cover . . ." But then I couldn't go on. I pulled myself out of the chair and started for the door.

"No! Please! Don't leave me alone!"

It was a different voice. Not commanding any more. Not cold. A tired voice. Scared and desperate.

I took my hand off the doorknob and turned slowly and looked at her. She was down in her chair again and her eyes were like dead things.

I went back to the chair and sat. She turned in her chair and faced the wall, looking something like the only survivor of a plane crash. And she knew she was the only survivor and she couldn't figure out why she was. And worse, she didn't know if she'd be able to live with it. She was struggling hard to find a way.

.   Finally she said, "It doesn't even matter. About Chellick. It's my fault. If I hadn't taken the money, Gene never would've known. I'm the reason he's dead." She put her hands on the arms of her chair and swiveled to face me. "Did I need it that much? The money? We were poor, but we weren't starving. Did I need it that much?"

That's all she said. I said nothing. I didn't have an answer for her.

I went out of the office finally and down the hall and found Ross Parking waiting for me.

"Is she all right?"

"She's quiet now."

"If you did anything to her—"

I just looked at him and he stopped. "I didn't do anything. She did it herself, years ago. She's known she did it ever since before she hired us. She hired us 'cause she needed someone to tell her she was right. Maybe part of her was hoping we'd tell her she was wrong, but she knew we wouldn't."

We stood there. The room seemed to be getting emptier. Maybe it was just the day turning to night.

"Don't ask her about it. If she wants to tell you, she'll tell you, but don't ask her."

I tried to go out but he stopped me. "There's got to be something I can do for her."

"The only thing that can do much for her is time. I don't know if there's enough time. I'm sorry."

I went out of the building as quickly as I could.

137

Joe Bergen came in through the back door and saw me sitting in darkness. He flipped on the kitchen light. I nodded at him. He went to the stove and touched the side of the coffeepot lightly. He took a cup from the rack and poured himself coffee and sat across from me. He looked at the vase in the middle of the table. "Nice-looking rose."

"Old lady gave it to me yesterday, up in Sausalito."

He touched a petal lightly with his finger. "Not going to last much longer."

"It's nice while it lasts." I was quiet a moment. "What've you got?"

"Not much. Chellick started out as a loan shark, he's still a loan shark, he's branched out to other things over the years. Hot cars, drugs, pretty deep into drugs, they almost caught him about two years ago but they couldn't get enough evidence."

"Hungry man for money."

"Money's something we're all hungry for."

"Till we get too much of it and it comes around and slaps us in the face a little too hard."

Joe sipped his coffee. "That supposed to mean something?"

"Probably not. So you want him and you can't get him."

"Keeps himself pretty well insulated. Works through lots of other people." Joe waited for me to say something but I didn't. "Anything special you were looking for?"

"No, forget it, Joe. Thanks." I ran a finger across my upper lip. "What about the guy in the morgue? Anyone identify him yet?"

"Guy's still lying there."

I thought he might be.

Joe's eyes squinted at me. "Maybe I'm wrong, Fritz, but I think you look like you're getting ready to do something." He waited for me to answer and again I didn't. "You need help? Tell me."

If I'd found a way to put it together, and it didn't stick, for me it'd be my license. For him it'd be his job and his pension.

"No, Joe, I'm stuck. There's nothing I can do."

He watched me some more. Then he drank the rest of his coffee and pushed the cup away. "All right. It changes, let me know."

He got up and went out. I took his cup to the sink and washed it and put it in the rack. I turned off the light and went into the bedroom. The only light came from the moon through the window. I opened the closet and reached into a suit pocket. I came out with a handful of pills. I went to the bureau and spread the pills across it and looked at them. I stayed in the room and pulled the phone over beside the pills and dialed.

"Hello?"

I spoke very softly. "It's me, Mag."

"Oh. I haven't come up with anything yet."

"I have." She waited for me to go on. "I think I got enough to cover ourselves if we're lucky. I'll have to pick up some stuff tomorrow. You talk to Paul and get him ready."

She asked only one question. "When do you want to move?"

"Tomorrow night. Late."

She hung up. So did I. Then the strands of blond hair that came from under the blanket started to move. The head rose and turned slowly and two sleepy eyes opened and looked at me.

She came up on an elbow. "Hi." She yawned. "Coming to bed now?"

I hesitated but then I nodded. I guess she saw it.

"Well, come on." She threw the blanket aside.

I didn't move and she said, "What're you thinking?"

"Nothing."

"Come on. Sure you are. Tell me what you're thinking."

I laughed as good as I could. "I don't know what I'm thinking."

I took off my clothes and got into bed.

I knew exactly what I was thinking. I was hoping she was for real, really for real. Maybe by the end of tomorrow I'd know for sure.

138

I walked across the damp grass without a flashlight. There was enough of a moon to show me what I had to see. The screen door was locked and I could see through it to the dim empty kitchen. I went along the side of the house to the bedroom window. I could make out the bed inside, and the two naked bodies lying across it, and the German shepherd lying on the floor, and the gun on the night table.

I pushed the window slightly. It wasn't locked. Then I tapped it and the shepherd pricked his ears up. He saw me and growled and came toward the window.

I went flat to the ground and leaned with my back against the wall of the house and there was more growling above me. Then a voice, Carl's voice, soothing the dog.

Then silence.

I crawled back to the screen door and scratched against it with the tips of my fingers and that brought the sound of heavy paws on bare floor. The shepherd came running into the kitchen and saw me on the other side of the screen door and leaped, barking his head off. I had already moved away across the yard.

I went out to the front and crossed the street quickly and got into the red Volvo. I could still hear the growling in the distance and half a minute later it got louder. He must've been outside by then, searching for me. Then the barking stopped.

Finally the dog came silently around the side of the house, sniffing the grass, searching for my scent. None of the lights in the house had gone on. I got out of the Volvo and stepped away from it and into the street. The dog saw me. He stayed where he was. His lips curled back, there was enough light for me to see his teeth and just enough silence for me to hear the slight growl.

I fought my fear and moved forward several steps. He moved forward several steps. I was scared to go farther. I could hear the growl better, or maybe it'd gotten louder. Then he set himself in a crouch, ready to leap. There was thirty feet between us. It would take him a run to get at me, a run that would last a second and a half, maybe less, when it came. But it didn't come.

I couldn't wait him out. I was already too nervous. I brought a low answering growl from the back of my throat, just loud enough for him to hear it.

He was off. Running forward. He was fifteen feet away. Ten feet. His front paws dug the ground and he leaped.

I brought my right hand forward and aimed the nozzle at his eyes and pressed down on the top of the spray can. The stuff squirted in his face and he went down to the street. He lay flat. He was still conscious. He tried to move. Moved in slow motion. I didn't know how effective the stuff had been. One paw reached toward me. There was no strength behind it.

I found myself lying across the hood of the car and I signaled with my hand. Maggie and Paul got out of the car. They brought the cage with them and tipped it on its side and I leaned toward the dog and extended my arm and sprayed more of the stuff at his face. He stopped moving. I didn't know how long it would last but it didn't have to last long. We rolled him into the cage and closed it and locked it and put it on the grass on the far side of the car.

139

I rubbed my fingertips against the screen door again. I kept it up and then a hand touched my back and I turned around and Maggie was nodding at me. I looked past her and down the wall. Paul was standing near the bedroom window and he was nodding too.

I rubbed my hand against the screen door again and kept doing it till I heard steps. Then I flattened my back against the wall of the house and waited. I kept my eyes on the door and reached behind me and heard the sound of liquid pouring. I felt the moist cotton placed into my left hand and smelled a slight sweetness in the air.

Footsteps came across the kitchen floor. "Ceasar?"

I pressed my back harder against the house. The door didn't open. Then behind me I heard something hit a tree.

"Caesar. Come on, Caesar." But the door still didn't open.

Paul threw something else against the tree and it made enough of a sound and the door started to open. "Caesar. Come on, Caesar."

A foot came onto the top step and my right hand grabbed Carl's arm and pulled him toward me and my left

336

hand pressed the cotton against his nose and mouth. A muffled cry came out but nothing loud enough to travel. Carl struggled to get out of my grip but I had his left arm and by that time Maggie had his right and all he could breathe was the chloroform.

140

I tried to control my nerves. "The bedroom window's unlocked. Don't try to get inside till you hear me talking to him. Soon's you got it, let us know. Whistle a note, just one note."

Paul reached toward me and his feelings showed all over his face. "What if he takes the gun with him?"

"Let's hope he doesn't. He's not expecting anything. He figures he's big enough to handle anything if there's anything out here." I breathed in and out a little too fast. "He takes it with him, you better give a yell so I can get out." I put my hand on the door and took a quick look at Maggie and a longer one at Paul. "Remember, he doesn't look it, but he can move damn fast."

I inched the screen door open. It squeaked a little but not much. I moved into the kitchen. There was a cast-iron skillet on the stove. I rubbed it back and forth across the burner and it made a sound like a saw rubbing metal.

"Carl?"

Even the voice did something to me but I stood still and kept rubbing the skillet in a regular rhythm.

"Carl?"

I heard movement, far away. Nothing distinct. Nothing I could identify. Then it seemed to be coming closer, down the hall. I listened for Paul's yell but it didn't come and I wondered if I'd hear it if it did come.

The first thing I saw was a large shadow coming into the living room. It looked as big as a bear. It was wearing nothing but a bathrobe. It didn't look like it had a gun.

It came across the living room, came close enough to see me. I stopped rubbing the skillet. It was very quiet. Nothing was ever quieter. There was just enough light for him to see me, to see that my hands were empty. There was just enough light for me to see him, to see that his hands were empty. I didn't think it made that much of a difference.

He came into the kitchen stepping carefully. I gently opened my jacket and showed him I had no gun. He looked at me wearily, almost as if he wasn't surprised I was there. "Where's Carl? You hurt him, I'll kill you."

"He's outside on the grass. I just gave him chloroform. He's okay."

He went toward the screen door and looked through it. "He better be okay." He turned and glared at me. He looked tired, and his voice sounded tired, but not that tired. "I knew I should've taken care of you. Shit." He stepped closer.

I stepped back. "I just want to talk. I'll tell you some things, that's all."

He went around the table toward the refrigerator and boxed me in. Then he sighed. "Go ahead. Talk."

"You had Max Isenbart two ways. He owed you money, and you knew something about the way a man named Joseph Lydon died. You helped Isenbart cover it. You demolished Lydon's head with a shotgun so nobody'd see how it'd really been cracked. You stopped bleeding Isenbart on the loan a couple years ago when he agreed to hire Carl and let Carl design. But Carl didn't like it there, he wanted to go east, to New York."

His face looked drawn and sad. He looked toward the screen door. "New York. That's all he'd talk about, making it in New York. He'd never have a chance in New York. Not by himself."

I tried to get him to look at me again. "You didn't

want to lose Carl so you tried to buy Isenbart out for peanuts and put Carl in charge of the company. Isenbart couldn't refuse to sell because of what you knew about Lydon, and he couldn't find anyone else to buy Lybart for a reasonable price, so he siphoned off money to make it look like Lybart was going to fold."

He stared at me. "That son of a bitch! He told me he was going bankrupt! He showed me his books! He told me if he folded Carl'd go to New York! He got me to put my *own* money in to keep it going!"

It almost made me laugh but I stopped in time. "You bled him, then he bled you. All the time he was telling Carl he ought to go to New York if he really wanted to make it."

He turned and drove his fist into the refrigerator door.

"One day Carl must've told you some doped-up kid was bugging Isenbart and seemed to have him scared. Isenbart thought the kid was from you, to spook him into selling, and if he was, and we found out about it, and about you, we might find out what you knew about Lydon's death.

"You didn't know who the kid was but you needed Isenbart to pay attention to business so you sent your goons to take care of it. They broke the kid's foot and found out his name was Gene Morrison. You connected the name to Virginia Moore, who'd blackmailed you years ago. You got scared the kid might bring out the only crime you'd ever been close enough to for the cops to get an indictment.

"The kid disappeared, but then he came back, so you told your men to kill him. We were in your way by then. I turned up here that night with Carl. You beat me up out of jealousy, I lost part of my beard and when you saw the beard was fake you went through my wallet and saw I was a detective. You thought you better cut off whatever was going on as fast as you could."

A soft whistled note came from the far end of the house. He turned to look. I talked quickly. "It had to be done fast, but it had to look accidental. The kid was working in a movie. The guy who handled the explosives

339

was a drunken gambler named Jarvis. Jarvis always needed money. You gave him plenty. But Jarvis did it too fast, he ended up killing a lot more'n he meant to. Isenbart found out about the explosion and by then he knew who the boy was and he realized what'd happened. He took his gun and got himself drunk enough to work up some courage. He was mad and scared. Scared the real story of Lydon's death'd finally come out. He had to shut you up. But he didn't kill you. You killed him. Carl told you how he was always going up on the roof of his building, so you took the body up there and made it look like a suicide."

He faced me again. "You do a lot of talking, but you got no proof."

"No proof at all. Mrs. Isenbart came into the office and started straightening out the company and that must've made Carl happy. But when he told you about it he must've mentioned I was there, too. He didn't know I was the one he'd picked up at the bar, but you knew. You sent your goons to my office to kill me and close everything up for good, but your goons didn't get me."

Before I could go on the screen door opened. She looked smaller than she is, but then we saw the gun in her hand and she looked bigger than she is. I said, "Put away the gun, Mag. You don't need it."

She said, "Stay where you are, Fritz."

None of us moved. I knew we were sunk.

She said, "You came into that motel room and you saw me. First you made up a story that Morrison'd been working for you, and you figured that way if we ever did find a connection to you we'd think it was all some kind of squeeze you'd been putting on Isenbart, and so you wouldn't't've had anything to do with the explosion. But you couldn't leave it there. To get me to believe it you worked me over. You liked working me over. You liked it a lot."

I watched him carefully. He stepped sideways a foot. "That's what you're here for? To pay me back?" Then he stepped toward her.

Maggie brought her hand up with the gun. "If you come near me, I'll kill you."

I'd heard her voice like that before. I knew it was bad. Chellick knew it too. He stepped back toward the living room.

"Don't try it," Maggie hissed at him. "We have a man in the bedroom, he's already got your gun. That's the whistle you heard before."

I couldn't move. Chellick's eyes stuck on her a long time. Then they moved to me, then back to her. "You got me pretty well."

"We've got you well enough." And she smiled. I think it was the smile that sealed it.

He leaned against the refrigerator and his shoulders sagged. He looked toward the screen door, toward the back yard. "New York. All he wanted to do was go to New York. He didn't care what it meant to me. Didn't care at all."

There was a kind of desperate sadness that was dangerous as hell. He looked at me and he shook his head, it was a long silent shake. There was too much finality in it. I looked around for something to grab. There was only the cast-iron skillet and he was closer to it than I was.

He looked at Maggie with empty eyes. "Guns. The hell with guns. Isenbart had a gun, it didn't help him much."

Then he laughed very sadly and turned to me and came forward.

141

His fist caught my chin and for a moment I didn't know where I was and then I was on the floor flat on my back and he was straddled on top of me, swinging at my head. Maggie was beside him with the gun. She seemed to be yelling at him. One of his hands swung at her and found her and I saw the gun flying and then I didn't see Maggie any more.

He grabbed my shirt and started pulling me toward him, then shoved me back down till the floor stopped me. He picked me up by the shirt again, then threw me down. His fist came into my face. I heard Paul yelling and saw Paul above us and Paul had a gun.

Chellick reached back and grabbed Paul by the front of his shirt and threw him forward. I saw Paul's legs flying by and then Chellick had my throat. His right leg was across my left arm pinning it to my side. I had my right hand free and I tried to pry his hands off my throat but I couldn't. I concentrated on his left index finger. I took it in my right hand and pushed it back and kept forcing it. Maggie was behind him again now. She didn't seem to have the gun. She had both her hands together in a big fist and she was swinging at his back. It seemed to make no difference.

I ignored it and concentrated on his left index finger. I kept forcing it back. It finally popped. His other hand left my throat and went into the air and came back against my face and everything was black.

I opened my eyes. He was right in front of me. He was on his knees and Maggie and Paul were both struggling with him but he was too much for them. He swung an arm and Paul went toward the screen door and I heard a crack and the screen door opened the wrong way and Paul went through it. Then Chellick had both his hands on Maggie. I was still on my back, he was still on his knees in front of me. I brought my right knee to my chest and kicked out straight. He groaned and before he could move I brought my right knee up and kicked him again. He went over on his back but he still had Maggie's wrist and she went with him.

I pulled the handcuffs off my belt and tried to get one end around his left wrist but he started rolling and for a second I saw Maggie and then him and then my face was against the wall and I knew I didn't have the handcuffs any more.

Then he was on his feet and he lifted me off the floor and held me around the waist and slammed me into the wall and I couldn't breathe. Somehow I managed to get my hands under his chin and I was pushing it back and then I saw Paul staggering beneath me. Paul was trying to grab his arm so he turned and kicked Paul and Paul went down on the floor and Maggie was down there too. Maggie looked at me and tried to get up but she couldn't get up. There was blood on her mouth.

I got a hand above my head and closed it in a fist and brought it down against his neck. His neck was vulnerable, I hit it again. He growled like an animal and threw me away. I landed on the kitchen table and the table went over and I went with it.

By the time I could see anything he had Maggie by her arms and her face looked terrified. Something got me moving and I closed my hand on the sugar bowl and came at him from behind. I smashed the sugar bowl against his head and he staggered and let Maggie go. I took the front of his bathrobe and swung him away from her and against the refrigerator. Paul was on the floor beneath us and I yelled for Paul to get away but then Chellick's fist went into my stomach and I couldn't yell. I tried to get my footing and I stepped on something which must've been Paul. Chellick hit me in the chest and then suddenly he had me bent over the sink and it felt like my back was breaking.

I saw Paul standing but instead of hitting Chellick, Paul was reaching for my arm. Chellick was hitting me and Paul was holding my arm and trying to tear me away. I didn't understand what was happening and I couldn't breathe and I took whatever I had left and threw my fist at Chellick's throat and got him hard. His eyes almost came out. He went back a step and I tried to hit him again in the same place but Paul had my arm and pulled me across the kitchen toward the screen door. Maggie was lying in the corner. I knew we wouldn't be able to get outside, not the three of us, and I stepped back toward Chellick and cocked my fist. He was already coming. He leaped straight at us and suddenly his foot went out from under him and he was down on the floor. He turned like an animal and reached out for me but couldn't get close enough. One end of the handcuffs was around his right ankle and the other end was around a pipe under the sink.

142

I had my shoulder against the wall and Paul was holding on to the shattered screen door and Maggie got up and stood between us. Chellick had his back to us now. He was trying to pull the handcuffs off the pipe. Finally he gave up and lay there, breathing heavily. He turned his head and his eyes flashed at us and there were tears in them. He turned away and reached above him and his hand closed on the edge of the sink. He pulled himself to his feet with that hand, his other hand with its broken index finger stayed limp. He looked at us again and the tears were streaming down his face and he moaned and he turned and I heard a drawer open.

I rushed straight at him and put my shoulder into his back and he went forward and the drawer slammed shut. I jumped away before he could get me and when he saw he couldn't reach me he tried to pull the drawer open again. It opened and his hand went into it and came out with a kitchen knife. I took the cast-iron skillet from the stove and swung it at him and the knife flew away. He cried but it still didn't stop him. His hand went back into the drawer. I lifted the skillet over my head and I think I was crying myself when I brought it down across his hand and into the open drawer. He yelled again and the drawer splintered and utensils fell out and covered the floor. His hand was full of blood and it still didn't stop him. He went down on his knees and reached for a knife. I didn't know if I had it in me to hit him again with the skillet but I didn't have to. Maggie put a bullet into the floor in front of his knees.

143

Chellick sat on the floor, still handcuffed to the pipe. We'd swept all the knives out of his reach. His hands were in his lap, wrapped in a towel. The bleeding had stopped. He wasn't moving. That part of it was over.

I sat at the kitchen table watching him. Paul came in, he'd washed his face off, and he looked at Chellick. Paul pulled a chair away from the table and sat by the far wall.

Maggie came in from outside and leaned against the open door like she'd never moved away from it. "We're okay, so far. No cops." She laughed. "When people hear something that might be a gun in the middle of the night, they turn over and go back to sleep. If it's serious, someone else'll probably call the cops. That's the way it goes these days—everyone figures the hell with it." She laughed again. Then she put her hands to her face. "He was coming to. I had to give him some more chloroform."

"Don't give him any more of that stuff!" Chellick snarled at her. "You hurt him, I'll kill you!"

"We aren't going to hurt him." There was a gun next to my hand. I picked it up by the butt but didn't put my finger against the trigger. I let him see I had it. "And you aren't going to do a damn thing."

Maggie rubbed her forehead and went out of the kitchen. I heard her moving through the house and after a while she came back and her face looked cleaner. She opened the refrigerator and took out ice and wrapped it in a towel and held it against the side of her face.

I turned to Chellick. "Gene Morrison's dead. Max Isenbart's dead. The only one left is Jarvis, but sooner or later the cops'll pick him up and when they do he's going to identify you as the guy who paid him to set the explosion."

Chellick didn't have many cards to play but he played what he had. He laughed dully. "Still looking for proof. No, Jarvis never saw me, he saw someone else. Someone he'll never see again."

That told me what I wanted to know. I went across the room and gave the gun to Maggie and tapped Paul on the shoulder and took him outside with me.

Paul shook his head. He looked dead tired. "You were wrong about Jarvis being the guy in the morgue."

"I still think it's Jarvis."

He looked at me. "But Chellick doesn't even know he's dead."

"I didn't think he did. I had to know for sure."

Paul tried to put it together. "But if Jarvis's dead, Chellick's right, we got no proof." Then he hit something. His face lit up. "Lydon. We can tie him into Lydon's death. Virginia Morrison can tie him in to Lydon's death."

He was excited. I waited for him to come down. "If she testifies to that, she'll be laying herself open to charges of blackmail and complicity."

"She'll testify! She wants to get him! He killed her son!"

I waited again. "Okay, let's say she testifies. What if the whole story comes out about Lydon? About Elizabeth Isenbart? That what you want?"

He started to say something but didn't. He rubbed his shoulder. I turned away. "Stay out here and watch Carl. Tell us if he starts to come to again."

I left Paul outside and went into the kitchen and sat at the table.

Maggie looked at me. "What was that all about?"

I spoke quietly. "I didn't want Paul hearing this." I leaned toward Chellick. "Jarvis's been dead since the night of the explosion." Chellick looked up. "You know how Tony Capanegro fits into this? The cops're trying to pin the explosion on his son."

Chellick rubbed the side of his mouth with his shoulder. "I didn't have time. If I'd known Capanegro's son was in it, I would've done it some other way. I had to do something fast. I didn't have time."

"The night of the explosion Capanegro sent some men to bring Jarvis in for a talk. They found him in his apartment with money. Your money. They tried to make him talk and, like you said, he didn't know who'd paid him and he couldn't talk. They got impatient and too rough and Jarvis ended up going off his balcony. Capanegro paid a cop to keep it quiet. The cop put Jarvis in the morgue as a John Doe and Jarvis'll stay that way till the investigation into the explosion's quieted down and the payoffs've been taken care of up and down the line. You'll know I'm telling the truth 'cause as soon as Capanegro thinks he's covered, Jarvis'll be identified, but nobody'll try to prove he was murdered or that Capanegro could've had anything to do with it." I gave him a moment. "But Capanegro'll still have one problem. There's an assistant D.A., Steeg, who's trying to prove the son set up the explosion. Capanegro hasn't figured a way out of that yet." I leaned farther across the table and spoke bitterly. "We'll have to give him a way."

Chellick didn't move. He stared straight back at me.

"We'll have to go to Capanegro and give him our story. Maybe he'll believe us, maybe he won't, but that won't matter. He'll see you're the one guy available to take the heat off his son. He'll make you talk, and if he can't, he'll kill you."

His eyes narrowed in hatred. He didn't look away. "It's no good. You think I never been up against that kind of shit before? There's still no proof, so I'm no good to Capanegro unless I'm alive, and long's I know that and he knows it, he won't kill me. I can take whatever else he tries. I been through it."

I stayed quiet a long time. I had to make it look good. I got out of my chair and walked across the room and stood at the screen door and let another minute pass. Then I did it. "Capanegro won't waste time on you. He'll go after whoever or whatever he thinks means something to you. He'll do whatever he's got to do to protect his son."

I looked outside. I couldn't look at Chellick. I heard

him moving, straining at the handcuffs, crying. "Carl's not part of this! Carl didn't know anything about it! You can't tell him about Carl!"

I kept looking toward the back yard and spoke quietly. "What I can't do is forget what you did to Gene Morrison and five other kids. Kids who didn't have a damn thing to do with you, and they're dead just the same. And Max Isenbart, he's dead. You got to pay for that. If the only way I got is the gamble that you'll crack before Capanegro kills Carl, I'll take that gamble. I won't like it, but I won't give a damn if I like it or not. It's got to be done. I'll do it."

I pulled myself together and turned around and walked to the table and sat down stiffly and looked at him. His eyes had turned dull and his lips were tightened against his teeth. "You're going to go down on this one, one way or the other. You can choose which way you want it."

That was it. His face collapsed and he slumped against the wall. I don't know if I could've kept it up much longer. I spoke quickly. "I want a confession. A certain kind of confession."

But I don't think he even heard me just then. He looked toward the broken screen door and his face filled with tears again. "Carl. Who'll look after him? How'll he take care of himself?"

144

It was too long a wait in too dark a hall. It felt like a snake pit. Paul couldn't sit still, he kept pacing back and forth. I couldn't take that. "Stop pacing."

"What?"

"Stop pacing and sit down!" I tried to control it. I

think I tried to smile. "You obviously never been in a police station in unfriendly circumstances. Sit down and play it easy."

He looked at me, then walked across the corridor and sat next to Maggie. He didn't speak soft enough. "What's the matter with him?"

"Leave him alone."

"What's he nervous about?"

Maggie tried to whisper. "He's got a lot of things on his mind. He had to do something and he's not too happy with the way he had to do it. Be quiet and—"

A door opened far away. A man came into the hall and walked toward us and stopped in front of me.

"Hello, Freddie."

I smiled at him. "Morning, Hilinsky."

"Ain't quite morning yet." He put his foot on the bench and leaned his face close to mine. "You comfortable sitting there?"

"Reasonably. They got you up pretty early."

"They always do."

"Good for them."

He shook his head in my face and chuckled. "Always the same, huh, Freddie?"

He turned and went down the hall, into a room. Maggie came over and sat beside me. "Are you going to be able to get all the way through this?"

"Thanks for the vote of confidence."

She put her hand on my shoulder. We stared at the floor. She said, "Mrs. Isenbart. She's going to have to know her husband didn't kill himself."

"I know, Mag. I'm trying to work it out. Let's say some man was pressuring Isenbart to sell Lybart, that's why Isenbart tried to make it look like he was going bankrupt, but Isenbart was doing nothing illegal. The man found out about it and killed him. We couldn't prove it, but the cops've got the man on another murder charge and he can't get out of that one."

Maggie thought it over. "Where does the boy fit in?"

I nodded. "That's what I can't figure. Not so it sounds clean."

A door opened down the hall, the door Hilinsky had

gone through. Steeg came out. He walked toward us, looked at us briefly, rubbed his hands together and kept on going around a corner.

We sat quietly. The door opened again and cops came out. Chellick was in the middle of them. He looked better, we'd cleaned him up as much as possible before we'd brought him down there. His eyes turned and saw us for a very long moment, but then the cops took his arm and led him away.

It was quiet again. The door opened and Hilinsky came out. He came down the hall to us, his face showed us nothing. One thing about Hilinsky, he knew his business in the clinches.

"Steeg wants to see you, in his office."

"How many of us he want? Just Maggie and me all right?"

He looked over his shoulder at Paul. "Sure, just the two of you ought to do it." He hummed his usual song and started walking.

We followed him down the hall and around the corner.

Maggie said, "Easy."

I said. "Sure."

Hilinsky opened the door and we went inside. Hilinsky closed the door and stayed outside.

145

Steeg reached across his desk and picked up a paper cup. He brought it to his mouth but found it was empty so he put it back down. He set it just at the edge of his desk and tapped it with one finger. It fell over, into the wastebasket. He watched it fall, then watched where it lay in the wastebasket.

Maggie said, "Mrs. Morrison's son had our card on him when he died, so we figured he must've wanted to see us about something. We checked the place where he lived. They had a big bottle of pills up there—you could open your own drugstore." I reached into my pocket and took out a handful of pills and spilled them across Steeg's desk. "We traced the source, it was this guy Chellick. Apparently Gene Morrison was always stoned and always needed money and he knew about other stuff Chellick was dealing. He tried a shakedown. Chellick was worried that if Morrison ever got picked up for taking drugs, which he probably would sooner or later, Morrison might try to get out of it by telling what he knew about Chellick. Chellick was scared of the cops so he paid Frank Jarvis to set the explosion and get rid of the kid. He didn't know Jarvis was going to get so careless."

Steeg took the paper cup out of the wastebasket and set it on the desk. He tapped it again, it fell. Then he looked at us. "Yeah, that's how Chellick tells it, too. Chellick got bruised up. So'd the two of you. Should've called us for help."

"We didn't have time," Maggie said. "We had to move fast."

Steeg nodded. He took a pencil and paper and started to write something. He stopped and picked up the pencil and looked at it. "What've you got on Chellick to make him talk?"

We said nothing.

"Maybe you think we get people in here every day confessing to murder. Matter of fact, we do. But they're never the ones who did it."

"Chellick's the one who did this one," Maggie said.

Steeg looked up with a face of ice. "You don't seem to understand. I want to know what you got on him to make him give me that confession."

I didn't like the way he said it but I was too tired to think about it. He was going to have to have an answer of some kind so I gave him the best answer I had. "I told Chellick, if he didn't come in here and confess, I'd go to Tony Capanegro and tell everything I knew. Chellick didn't want me to do that."

Steeg stared at me awhile. Then he settled back in his chair and rubbed a thumbnail against the point of his chin. "You're a goddamn bastard, aren't you?"

"I suppose I am."

We stared at each other some more and then he leaned forward. "I don't believe it." He waited for a reaction. "Pills, drugs, shakedown. No, I don't believe it. You're hiding something." He came from behind his desk, leaned against the front and looked at me. "What's this about Jarvis being dead in the morgue?"

"He's down there," I said. "Check it."

His words came quickly and harshly. "I already checked it. I want to know how long you've known he was down there."

I nodded. "I had an idea, but I guess I knew for sure when I went to his apartment and saw the way it'd been repaired."

His eyes opened a little wider. "When you went to his apartment? I talked to you there. You told me you didn't know where Jarvis was."

I was too exhausted to pay much attention. "Yeah, I said something like that. You got a good memory."

His fist came out of nowhere. I went backwards in my chair and onto the floor. Something very hard pounding my chest. I heard yelling but I couldn't hear it clearly and I couldn't move.

But just as suddenly the pounding went away. When it did I tried to get up and I heard a door swing open and I turned on my side and saw Hilinsky in the doorway, his mouth open, one hand still on the doorknob. I ignored him and turned to see what had happened to Steeg. He was on his back and Maggie was on top of him, pressing her gun against his throat. I said, "He didn't hurt me, Mag! I'm okay!" She didn't move. "Mag! Please! Don't do anything!"

She bent her head closer to his. "It's not so nice when you get hit back, is it?"

He didn't answer. He couldn't. Maggie slowly drew the gun away from Steeg's throat and got off the floor but kept her eyes and the gun on Steeg's face.

I turned to Hilinsky, he was still in the doorway. "Close the door."

Hilinsky breathed heavily. Then he stepped in and closed the door behind him.

"Mag—"

"I'm okay, Fritz. I know what I'm doing this time." She cocked her thumb toward the desk. "Over there, Mr. Steeg. Move, but don't say anything. It's been a long night and I'm tired and I might do something I know I shouldn't do."

Steeg rose slowly with blank eyes. He moved like a drunken man across the office to his desk. She motioned him to sit and he sat. She kept her gun on him.

She looked at Hilinsky. "Hello, Pete. What're you doing?"

"Nothing."

"Sit down."

Hilinsky laughed. "All right. Maggie. Whatever you want." He pulled a chair till it was in front of the closed door and sat.

146

Maggie sat on the edge of the desk with the gun across her leg and her eyes stayed on Steeg. "If Jarvis was dead in the morgue it'd take one of two things to keep it secret. One was money, lots of money, from someone like Chellick, or Capanegro, but Capanegro was trying to find Jarvis and Chellick didn't know Jarvis was dead. That left the other thing it'd take. Authority." She looked across her shoulder at Hilinsky but didn't look at him long. "A lot more authority'n Hilinsky's got."

Steeg's mouth dropped open a quarter of an inch.

"Pete got put on the Griffith Park case right after it

happened. He went up to Jarvis's apartment and Jarvis was there, he'd gone back to get his money. Pete knocked on the door. Jarvis was too scared to open it, Pete had to burst in. That's why the door's got a new chain.

"I don't think Pete killed Jarvis. I think Jarvis panicked and tried to get away, and the only way was the balcony. Maybe Jarvis broke open the balcony doors, maybe Pete broke them going after him, maybe they fought, maybe they didn't fight, maybe Pete didn't even reach Jarvis that quickly, but whichever way it was, Jarvis went off the balcony.

"Then you got over there pretty quickly, Mr. Steeg. You had the payoff money but with Jarvis dead you had no lead, the case was dead. You wanted the case alive, so you had to have Jarvis alive. You got the apartment cleaned up and set up a false trail to Las Vegas. You never gave a damn whether Capanegro's son was behind that explosion or not. You thought he had to be involved somehow, and that there would be something illegal in the books. You needed time to find it.

"The problem was us. Did we know something or didn't we? Pete tried to get us off the case and couldn't, so you had him call us in here to give us the rough treatment so you could get us away from him and show us what a nice cooperative man you were. You gave us information that didn't mean a thing, to see if we'd let anything slip about what we had. You wanted to know if we came up with anything because if we did you'd probably need time to cover what'd happened with Jarvis and how you were trying to get Capanegro's son."

She got off the desk and sat in the chair next to me. She put the gun in her pocketbook.

Steeg's hands came out of his lap and rubbed along the edge of his desk. He didn't look up. "You're sure it's Chellick? You're sure he was the one behind it? The only one?"

"The only one."

He kept rubbing his desk like he was trying to smooth it out. "I thought Capanegro and his kid were behind it. I swear, that's what I thought." His head dipped down. Then it came up and his hands turned to fists and they

354

banged at his desk. "It had to be Capanegro! Damn it, it had to be!"

He looked frightening. He jumped up and went to a file cabinet and ripped open the top drawer and reached in with both hands. He came out with an armful of folders and came around the front of the desk. He looked at Maggie but then stepped back and looked at me and dumped the folders in my lap. "Read these things! Read 'em! Look at how many times we almost had him and we couldn't get him! He's a killer! I got seven things I could tie him to but I can't prove any of 'em! There's hundreds of things I could tie him to! He's got connections! He's got money! He's got more lawyers'n we got! Don't you understand?" He kept sputtering. "Don't you understand what he's getting away with?"

I left the folders closed in my lap.

His voice screamed at me. "Come on! Open 'em up! Read 'em! Read what's there!"

I didn't move. He turned suddenly and went to his desk. He picked up another folder, a single folder, and waved it at me. "You know anything about Chellick? I know *everything* about Chellick! This's his file! Just *this!* This's all there *is!* He's nothing! *Nothing!*"

He finally looked at Maggie, then quickly looked away. He threw the single file at his desk. His hands went high into the air but they came down again and made no sound. After a moment he sat. He was very quiet. Then he mumbled, "You're hiding something. Pills. Shakedown. No. You're hiding something."

"Don't ask any questions about whether we're hiding anything or not," Maggie said. "You don't mind hiding something. You just mind it when we do it. You've got your killer. Prosecute him."

He didn't answer.

I took Capanegro's files and stacked them on his desk. "You want anything else from us?"

He hesitated, then shook his head. He swiveled his chair so he was facing the window. I heard a sound behind me, it was Hilinsky moving his chair and opening the door. Maggie went to him and they looked at each other. I looked back at Steeg, he was still facing the windows. I looked at the desk. The folder I'd noticed sitting under the phone was still there. I took it to see if it was what I'd thought it was. It was. It was my folder. I put it under my arm and walked to the door. Maggie and I went out of the office together.

147

Paul was sitting on the bench and looked asleep but he turned when we came closer. Maggie took her keys from her pocketbook and gave them to him. "Do me a favor, Paul. Get my car and bring it around front. We'll be right out."

"We're finished?"

Maggie didn't answer. I said, "We just got a couple forms to fill out. Time you get the car around front, we'll probably be there."

Paul took the keys and went down the hall. As soon as he'd gone around the corner and the hall was empty Maggie dropped to the bench and leaned against its back and rested her head against it. I sat next to her. "Don't want to drive, huh?"

She looked at me. "I had it under control, Fritz. It was close for a second, right after he hit you, but I caught it."

I put my hand over hers.

We sat staring at the opposite wall and she said, "Think it came out even?"

"Probably not, Mag. It usually doesn't."

We heard steps. We sat up. Hilinsky came down the hall to us. "Maggie? You all right?"

She smiled at him. "Sure, Pete, I'm fine."

He looked at her with a doubtful face, then nodded. "Just wanted to make sure." He started away but came back. "Freddie." The toe of his shoe played with a cigarette butt on the floor. "I don't like you, Freddie. You don't like me. The world's big enough for a couple people who don't like each other. Even L.A.'s big enough." He nudged the cigarette butt toward the bench. "But you see how things were, this thing. I didn't have any choice about it. I was just following orders."

"Sometimes you're a little too good at following orders. Sometimes you're no good at all. That's the trouble."

He kicked the cigarette butt under the bench where nobody'd see it. "All right, take it however the hell you want to take it. Makes no difference to me." He put a and on Maggie's shoulder. "Take it easy, Maggie. I'd ate to see you get into trouble. I wouldn't mind losing eddie, but I'd sure hate to lose you."

Steps came around the corner. It was Steeg. He saw s and stopped, then turned quickly and went back in the direction he'd come from.

"He's awfully young," I said. "He's going to be around a long time."

Hilinsky grunted. He leaned over and spoke softly. "If I was you two, I wouldn't sit around here too long, you know what I mean."

Maggie and I got up and started to walk away.

"Hey, Freddie. We'll see each other around, huh?"

I smiled at him. "Yeah, I guess we will."

He shook his head and laughed. Never try to figure out why a cop's laughing. Whatever reason you come up with, it probably won't be the right one. If it was the right one, you probably wouldn't want to know it.

148

We went down a flight of steps and passed lots of sleepy faces. Cops. Some of them clean, some of them not. It was becoming harder and harder to tell one from the other.

We went across the lobby and through a set of door that always let you come in a hell of a lot more easi than they ever let you go out.

Paul was already below us with the red Volvo.

"He handled himself pretty well tonight, Fritz. Wit the handcuffs." She paused. "Still think we ought to check him out at Carne?"

She thought she had me. What the hell, I let her think it. "No, Mag, the hell with it. We'll give him a try." I stepped out into the sunshine. "You had a wish right now, what'd you wish for?"

"Breakfast."

"You're not much of a wisher."

"It's been too long a night for wishes. What about you?"

"I'd wish for a new jaw. Something made of concrete. And a year's supply of Coke. And somewhere where it's safe enough to sleep for about twelve hours. And maybe someone to sleep there with me. A full checkup by a competent doctor. Maybe something back on my tax returns. A week's free vacation in a tropical paradise."

"You want too much." She walked down the steps and got halfway to the street before she realized I was still at the top. "Fritz? What's the matter? Run out of wishes already?"

I started down slowly. "I had all of 'em, right now I'd trade the whole goddamn lot for a story that'll be good enough to fool Elizabeth Isenbart and keep her fooled." I shook my head. I was damn tired and worn out. "Damn it, Mag. I just don't know what the hell I'm going to tell her."

Maggie came back up the steps and stood in front of me. "I don't know either, Fritz, but it's okay. We'll go get something to eat and then we'll think of something, won't we."

The sun hit her from behind and combed it's rays through her hair. Whenever it does it that way there's nothing quite like it in the world. There are plenty of things more perfect, even more beautiful, but nothing quite like it. It's a good face, too. Strong. Healthy. Sometimes it gets bruised up, but somehow the bruises always go away. She's good at that.

CHINAMAN'S CHANCE

by ROSS THOMAS

The search for Silk Armitage, a beautiful blonde rock star with some secrets to spill about the CIA and the Mafia, embroils two colorful rogues in a worldwide intrigue from Saigon to Scotland to a sunbleached crime haven near Venice Beach, California, where a deluxe cast of henchmen, musclemen, and maniacs—both nympho and psycho—struggle to find her . . . and kill her . . . and love her.

MAIN SELECTION OF THE MYSTERY GUILD

Avon ◭ 41517 $2.25

CHINA 3-79